PREDATOR

Also by Wilbur Smith

The Egyptian Series

River God
The Seventh Scroll
Warlock
The Quest
Desert God

The Ballantyne Series

A Falcon Flies
Men of Men
The Angels Weep
The Leopard Hunts in Darkness

The Courtney Series

When the Lion Feeds
The Sound of Thunder
A Sparrow Falls
The Burning Shore
Power of the Sword
Rage
A Time to Die
Golden Fox
Birds of Prey
Monsoon
Blue Horizon
The Triumph of the Sun
Assegai
Golden Lion

Thrillers

The Dark of the Sun
Shout at the Devil
Gold Mine
The Diamond Hunters
The Sunbird
Eagle in the Sky
The Eye of the Tiger
Cry Wolf
Hungry as the Sea
Wild Justice (U.K.); The Delta Decision (U.S.)
The Elephant Song
Those in Peril
Vicious Circle

PREDATOR

A CROSSBOW ADVENTURE

WILBUR SMITH

AND TOM CAIN

wm
WILLIAM MORROW
An Imprint of HarperCollins*Publishers*

PREDATOR. Copyright © 2016 by Wilbur Smith. All rights reserved. Printed in the United States of America. No part of this book may be used or reproduced in any manner whatsoever without written permission except in the case of brief quotations embodied in critical articles and reviews. For information address HarperCollins Publishers, 195 Broadway, New York, NY 10007.

HarperCollins books may be purchased for educational, business, or sales promotional use. For information please e-mail the Special Markets Department at SPsales@harpercollins.com.

FIRST U.S. EDITION

Library of Congress Cataloging-in-Publication Data has been applied for.

ISBN 978-0-06-227647-6 (hardcover)
ISBN 978-0-06-245402-1 (international edition)

16 17 18 19 20   DIX/RRD   10 9 8 7 6 5 4 3 2 1

I dedicate this book to Niso, who is the Sun that lights my days,
and the Moon that glorifies my nights.
Thank you for those countless delights, my darling girl.

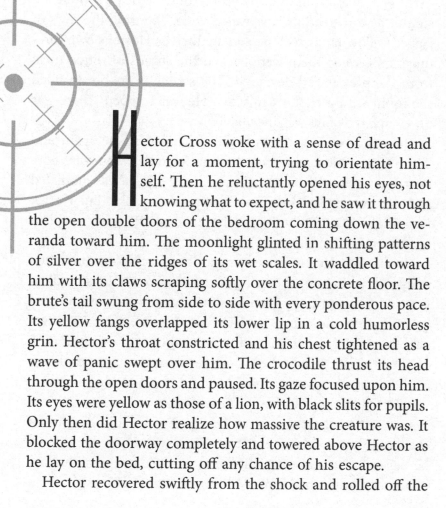

Hector Cross woke with a sense of dread and lay for a moment, trying to orientate himself. Then he reluctantly opened his eyes, not knowing what to expect, and he saw it through the open double doors of the bedroom coming down the veranda toward him. The moonlight glinted in shifting patterns of silver over the ridges of its wet scales. It waddled toward him with its claws scraping softly over the concrete floor. The brute's tail swung from side to side with every ponderous pace. Its yellow fangs overlapped its lower lip in a cold humorless grin. Hector's throat constricted and his chest tightened as a wave of panic swept over him. The crocodile thrust its head through the open doors and paused. Its gaze focused upon him. Its eyes were yellow as those of a lion, with black slits for pupils. Only then did Hector realize how massive the creature was. It blocked the doorway completely and towered above Hector as he lay on the bed, cutting off any chance of his escape.

Hector recovered swiftly from the shock and rolled off the

1

mattress. He seized the handle of the drawer of the bedside table in which he kept his 9-mm Heckler & Koch pistol and yanked it open. His fingernails scrabbled frantically over the woodwork as he groped for the weapon, but it was gone. The drawer was empty. He was defenseless.

He rolled back to face the gigantic reptile, coming up into a sitting position with his legs folded under him and his back pressed to the headboard of the bed. His hands were crossed at the wrists in front of his face in a defensive karate posture. "Yah! Get away from me!" he yelled, but the beast showed no sign of fear. Instead its jaws gaped wide, exposing the rows of jagged yellow fangs, as long and as thick as Hector's own fore-fingers. Between them were packed the shreds of rotten meat from the prey it had devoured. The stench of its breath filled the room with a choking miasma. He was trapped. There was no escape. His fate was inevitable.

Then the head of the crocodile changed shape again and began to assume a monstrous human form that was even more horrifying than the reptilian image had been. It was mutilated and decomposing. Its eyes were blind and milky. But Hector recognized it instantly. It was the head of the man who had murdered his wife.

"Bannock!" Hector hissed as he drew back from the hated image. "Carl Bannock! No, it can't be you! You're dead. I killed you and fed your filthy corpse to the crocodiles. Leave me and go back into the depths of Hell where you belong." He was gabbling hysterical nonsense but he could not prevent himself.

Then he felt disembodied hands reach out from the darkness of the room to seize his shoulders and begin to shake him.

"Hector, darling! Wake up! Please wake up."

He tried to resist the sweet, feminine voice and the pull of the hands but they were insistent. Then with burgeoning relief he began to untangle himself from the coils of the nightmare which had enmeshed him. At last he came fully awake.

2

"Is it you, Jo? Tell me it's you." Desperately Hector groped for her in the darkness of the bedroom.

"Yes, my darling. It's me. Hush now. It's all right now. I am here."

"The lights," he blurted. "Switch on the lights!"

She wriggled out of his arms and reached for the light switch above the headboard. The room was flooded with light, and he recognized it and remembered where they were and why.

They were guests in a medieval castle in Scotland on the banks of the River Tay on a chilly night in autumn.

Hector picked up his wristwatch from the table on his side of the bed and glanced at the dial. His hands were still shaking. "My God, it's almost three in the morning!" He reached for Jo Stanley and held her to his naked chest. After a while his breathing settled. With the reflexes of a trained warrior he had shaken off the debilitating effects of the nightmare, and he whispered to her, "I do apologize for the alarums and excursions, my love. However, the damage is done. We are both awake, so we might as well take full advantage of the moment."

"You are incorrigible and indefatigable, Hector Cross," she told him primly, but made no effort to resist his hands; rather she clung to him and sought out his lips with hers.

"You know that I don't understand big words," he told her and they were silent again. But after a moment she mumbled into his mouth without pulling away from him.

"You frightened me, darling."

He kissed her harder, as if to silence her, and she acquiesced as she felt his manhood stiffening and swelling against her belly. She was still lubricious with their earlier lovemaking and almost at once she wanted him as much as he did her. She rolled on to her back with her arms locked about his neck and as she pulled him over on top of her she let her thighs fall apart and reached up for him with her hips, gasping as she felt him slide deeply into her.

3

It was far too intense to last long. They mounted together swiftly and irresistibly to the giddy summit of their arousal; then, still joined, they plunged over it into the abyss. They returned slowly from the far-off places where passion had carried them and neither of them could speak until their breathing had calmed. At last she thought that he had fallen asleep in her arms until he spoke softly, in almost a whisper: "I didn't say anything, did I?"

She was ready with the lie. "Nothing coherent. Only some wild gibberish that didn't make any sense." She felt him relax against her and she carried on with the charade: "What were you dreaming about, anyway?"

"It was terrifying," he replied solemnly, his laughter almost hidden beneath his serious tone. "I dreamed that I pulled the hook out of the mouth of a fifty-pound salmon."

It was an unspoken understanding between them. They had come to it as the only way they could keep the fragile light of their love for one another burning. Jo Stanley had been with Hector during the hunt for the two men who had murdered his wife. When at last they had succeeded in capturing them in the Arabian castle they had built for themselves in the depths of the jungles of central Africa, Jo had expected that Hector would hand the two killers over to the United States authorities for trial and punishment.

Jo was a lawyer and she believed implicitly in the rule of law. On the other hand Hector made his own rules. He lived in a world of violence wherein wrongs were avenged with biblical ruthlessness: an eye for an eye and a life for a life.

Hector had executed the first of the two murderers of his wife without recourse to the law. This was a man named Carl Bannock. Hector had fed him to his own pet crocodiles in the grounds of the Arabian castle where Hector had apprehended him. The great reptiles had torn Bannock's living body to shreds and devoured it. Fortuitously Jo had not been present to witness the capture and execution of Carl Bannock. So afterward she had been able to feign ignorance of the deed.

However, she had been with Hector when he had captured the second killer. This was a thug who used the alias Johnny Congo. He was already under sentence of death by the Texas court, but he had escaped. Jo had intervened fiercely to prevent Hector Cross taking the law into his own hands for a second time. Ultimately she had threatened to end their own relationship if Hector refused to hand Congo over to the law enforcement agencies of the state of Texas.

Reluctantly Hector had complied with her demands. It had taken several months but in the end the Texan court had confirmed the original sentence of death on Johnny Congo and had also found him guilty of further multiple murders committed since his escape from detention. They had set the date for his execution for 15 November, which was only two weeks ahead.

J esus Christ, Johnny, what happened to your face?"
Shelby Weiss, senior partner of the Houston law firm of Weiss, Mendoza and Burnett—or Hebrew, Wetback and WASP as their less successful rivals liked to call them—was sitting in a small cubicle in Building 12 of the Allen B. Polunsky Unit in West Livingston, Texas, otherwise known as Death Row. The walls to either side of him were painted a faded, tatty lime green, and he was speaking into an old-fashioned black telephone handset, held in his left hand. In front of him he had a yellow legal pad and a line of sharpened pencils. On the other side of the glass in front of Weiss, in a cubicle of exactly similar dimensions but painted white, stood Johnny Congo, his client.

Congo had just been repatriated to the United States, having been rearrested in the Gulf State of Abu Zara several years after breaking out of the Walls Unit, as the Texas State Penitentiary, Huntsville, was known. He had spent most of that time when

5

he was on the run in Africa, carving out a personal kingdom in the tiny nation of Kazundu on the shores of Lake Tanganyika with his former prison-bitch, turned business associate and life partner, Carl Bannock. That was Weiss's connection. His firm had represented Bannock in his dealings with the family trust set up by his late adoptive father, Henry Bannock. The work had been entirely legitimate and extremely lucrative, for Carl Bannock and Shelby Weiss alike. Weiss, Mendoza and Burnett also represented Bannock in his role as an exporter of coltan, the ore from which tantalum, a metal more valuable than gold that is an essential element in a huge array of electrical products, was refined. Since the ore originated in the eastern Congo and could thus be considered a conflict mineral, no different from blood diamonds, this aspect of Carl Bannock's affairs was more morally debatable. But even so, he was still entitled to the best representation money could buy. If Shelby Weiss had reason to suspect that Bannock was living with an escaped felon with whom he engaged in a variety of distasteful and even illegal activities, from drug-taking to sex-trafficking, he had no actual proof of any wrongdoing. Besides, Kazundu had no extradition treaty with the U.S., so the point was moot.

But then Johnny Congo had turned up in the Middle East, captured by an ex-British Special Forces officer called Hector Cross, who had been married to Henry Bannock's widow, Hazel. So that, Weiss figured, made him Carl Bannock's brother-in law, except that there didn't seem to be much brotherly love in this family. Hazel had been murdered. Cross had blamed Carl Bannock and had set out to get his revenge. Now Bannock had vanished from the face of the earth.

However, Hector Cross had seized Johnny Congo and handed him over to U.S. Marshals in Abu Zara, which did have an ex-tradition treaty with the United States. So here he was, back on Death Row, and Congo wasn't a pretty sight. He had obviously been badly beaten.

Johnny Congo was crammed into his cubicle like a cannonball in a matchbox. He was a huge man, six foot six tall, and built to match. He was wearing a prisoner's uniform of a white, short-sleeved cotton polo shirt, tucked into elasticized, pyjama-style pants, also white. There were two large black capital letters on his back—"DR"—signifying that he was a Death Row inmate. The uniform was designed to be loose, but on Johnny Congo it was as tight as a sausage skin and the buttons strained to contain the knotted muscles of his chest, shoulders and upper arms, which gave him the look of a Minotaur: the half-man, half-bull monster of Greek mythology. Years of decadence and self-indulgence had made Congo run to fat, but he wore his gut like a weapon, just one more way to barge and bully his way through life. His wrists and ankles were manacled and chained. But the aspects of his appearance that had caught his attorney's attention were the white splint crudely placed over his splayed and mangled nose; the distended flesh and swollen skin around his battered mouth; and the way his rich, dark West African skin had been given the red and purple sheen of over-ripe plums.

"Guess I must have walked into a door, or had some kind of accident," Congo mumbled into his handset.

"Did the Marshals do this to you?" asked Weiss, trying to sound concerned but barely able to conceal the excitement in his voice. "If they did, I can use it in court. I mean, I read the report and it clearly states that you were already in restraints when they took you into custody in Abu Zara. Point is, if you posed no threat to them and couldn't defend yourself, they had no grounds to use physical force against you. It's not much, but it's something. And we need all the help we can get. The execution's set for November the fifteenth. That's less than three weeks away."

Congo shook his massive, shaven head. "Weren't no Marshal did this to me. It was that white sonofabitch Hector Cross. I said something to him. Guess he took exception to it."

"What did you say?"

Congo's shoulders quivered as he gave a low, rumbling laugh, as menacing as the sound of distant thunder. "I told him it was me gave the order to kill, and I quote, 'your fucking whore wife.'"

"Oh man . . ." Weiss ran the back of his right hand across his forehead, then put the handset back to his mouth. "Did anyone else hear you?"

"Oh yeah, everyone else heard me. I shouted it real loud."

"Dammit, Johnny, you're not making it any easier for yourself."

Congo stepped forward and leaned down, placing his elbows on the shelf in front of him. He stared through the glass with eyes that held such fury in them that Weiss flinched. "I had grounds, man, I had grounds," Congo growled. "That sonofabitch Cross took the only person I ever cared about in my whole fricking life and fed him to the goddamn crocodiles. They ate him alive. Did you hear me? Those scaly-assed mothers ate Carl alive! But Cross was dumb. He made two mistakes."

"Yeah, what kind of mistakes?"

"First, he didn't feed me to the crocodiles also. I wouldn't have known anything about it if he had. I was out, man, pumped full of some kind of sedative, wouldn't have felt a thing."

Weiss lifted his right hand, still holding the pencil, with his palm toward the glass. "Whoa! Hold up. How do you know about these crocodiles if you were unconscious at the time they were eating your buddy?"

"Heard Cross's men mouthing off about it on the plane, laughing their asses off about the jaws crunching, Carl screaming for mercy. Lucky for them I was all tied up to a chair, wrapped in a cargo net. If I could have moved I'd have ripped their heads off and shoved them up their butts."

"But you don't have any proof that Carl is dead, right? I mean, you didn't see a body?"

"How could I see a body?" Congo cried, his voice rising

indignantly. "I was out cold; Carl was in the crocodile's guts! Why do you wanna ask me a stupid question like that?"

"Because of the Bannock Trust," said Weiss quietly. "As long as there is no proof that Carl Bannock is dead, and Hector Cross sure won't produce any proof, because that would make him a murderer, then the trust will be obliged to keep paying Carl his share of company profits. And anyone who, hypothetically, had access to Carl's bank accounts would therefore benefit from that money. So, let me ask you again, for the record: do you have any direct, personal proof that Carl Bannock is dead?"

"No, sir," said Johnny emphatically. "All I heard was people talking, never saw nothing, 'cause of being sedated at the time. And, come to think of it, I was still kinda spacey from the drugs when I was in the airplane. Could have been imagining what I heard, maybe dreaming, something like that."

"I agree. Sedative drugs can certainly create an effect akin to intoxication. It's entirely possible that you never actually heard any conversation like the one you initially reported. Now, you said Cross made two mistakes. What was the second one?"

"He didn't dump me out the back of the plane. All he had to do was open the ramp at the back of the plane, slide me down it and just watch me fall . . ." Johnny Congo whistled like the sound of a dropping weight. ". . . all the way down, twenty-five thousand feet till—bam!" He slammed a sledgehammer fist into his palm.

"You would've made a helluva crater," Weiss observed drily.

"Yeah, I would that." Congo laughed and nodded his great bald head. "And if it'd been Cross in that chair and me lookin' at him, I've have tossed him outta there like a human Frisbee. Wouldn't think twice about it. He wanted to do it, too. Woulda done, weren't for that dumbass bitch of his shooting her mouth off."

Weiss looked back down at his notepad, frowning as he leafed back to what he'd written on an earlier page. "I'm sorry, I thought you said she was deceased."

9

"I said I had his wife killed, don't be shy about it. But this was a different bitch, the one he started up with after the wife was dead. She's an attorney, jus' like you. Anyway, Cross called her Jo. This bitch started up whining at Cross about how he shouldn't have killed Carl. How he'd gone far beyond the law of America . . . yeah, 'the law that I practice and hold dear,' that's what she called it. And what it came right down to was if Cross offed me too, same as he'd done Carl, he wasn't getting no more of her sweet pussy ever again." Congo shrugged his shoulders. "Dunno why Cross let her whip him like that. I wouldna took it, some stupid slut running off her mouth, lecturing me about right and wrong. I'd have told her, 'Your pussy belongs to me, bitch.' Teach her a lesson so she don't make the same mistake twice, you know what I'm saying?"

"I get the picture, yeah," said Weiss. "But do you? Let me paint it for you, just in case. When you broke out of the Walls Unit—"

Congo nodded. "Long time ago, now."

"Yes it was, but the law doesn't care about that, because when you broke out, you were two weeks away from your execution date. You'd been found guilty of multiple homicides, not to mention all the ones carried out at your command during the period of your incarceration. You'd exhausted every possible avenue of appeal. They were going to strap you to a gurney, stick a needle in your arm and just watch until you died. And here's your problem, Johnny. That's what's going to happen now. You were a fugitive. You were reapprehended. Now you're right back where you were, the day you climbed into a laundry sack, got thrown in the back of a truck and drove right out through the main gates and on to the Interstate."

If Weiss had been trying to impress Congo with the gravity of his situation, he failed. The big man's face twisted into a ghastly, wounded parody of a smile. "Man, that was a sweet operation, though, wasn't it?" he said.

Weiss kept his expression impassive. "I'm an officer of the law, Johnny, I can't congratulate you on what was obviously a criminal activity. But, yes, speaking objectively I can see that both the planning and the execution of the escape were carried out to a high standard of efficiency."

"Right. So how efficient you gonna be for me now?"

Shelby Weiss was wearing a $5,000 pair of hand-tooled Black Cabaret Deluxe boots from Tres Outlaws in El Paso. His suit came from Gieves and Hawkes at No. 1 Savile Row, London. His shirts were made for him in Rome. He ran his hand down the lapel of his jacket and said quietly, "I didn't get to be dressed this way by being bad at my job. I'll tell you what I'm going to attempt—the impossible. I'll call in every favor I'm owed, use every connection I possess, have my smartest associates go through every case they can think of with a fine-toothed comb, see if I can find some grounds for an appeal. I'll work my ass off, right up to the very last second. But I like to be totally honest with my clients, which is why I've got to tell you, I don't hold out much hope."

"Huh," Congo grunted. "All right, I'm on your wavelength . . ." He stood up straight, sighed and lifted his chained wrists so he could scratch the back of his neck. Then he spoke calmly, dropping the tough-guy, gangster attitude, almost as if he was talking to himself as much as Weiss. "All my life I've had people look at me and I know they're thinking: *He's just a big, dumb nigger.* The amount of times I've been called a gorilla—sometimes, they even think it's a compliment. Like in High School, playing left tackle for the Nacogdoches Golden Dragons, Coach Freeney, he would say, 'You played like a rampaging gorilla today, Congo,' meaning I'd busted up the sons of bitches in the other team's defense, so some pretty-boy cracker quarterback could make his fancy throws and get all the cheerleaders wet. And I'd say, 'Thank you, Coach,' practically calling him 'Massa.'"

Now Congo's intensity started building up again. "But inside,

I knew I wasn't dumb. Inside I knew I was better than them. And inside, right now, I understand exactly where I stand. So here's what I want you to do. I want you to contact a kid I used to know, D'Shonn Brown."

Weiss looked surprised: "What, *the* D'Shonn Brown?"

"What you mean? Only one guy I've ever heard of by that name."

"Just that D'Shonn Brown is kind of a prodigy. A kid from the projects, not even thirty yet and he's already on his way to his first billion. Good-looking as hell, got a great story, all the pretty ladies lining up outside his bedroom. That's some friend you got there."

"Well, tell the truth, it's been a while since I saw him, so I ain't fully up to date with his situation, but he'll know exactly who I am. Tell him the date they're taking me up to Huntsville for the execution. Then say I'd really like to see him, you know, maybe for a visit or something, before they put me on that gurney and give me the needle. Me and his brother Aleutian were real tight. Loot got killed in London, England, and it was Cross that done it. So we got that personal issue in common, losing a loved one to the same killer. I'd like to express my sympathies to D'Shonn, shake his hand, maybe give him a bear hug so he knows we're tight too."

"You know that won't be possible," Weiss pointed out. "The state of Texas no longer allows Death Row prisoners to have any form of physical contact with anyone. The best he can do is pay his respects to your body, when you are gone."

"Well, tell him anyhow. Let him know what I'd like. Now, I can give you a power of attorney over a bank account, right, to pay for legal expenses and suchlike?"

"Yes, that's possible."

"OK, so I have an account at a private bank, Wertmuller-Maier in Geneva. I'm gonna give you the account number and all the codes you'll need. First thing I want you to do is get someone to empty my safe-deposit box there and send it back to you, express delivery. I want the box unlocked and then sealed, with wax or some shit like that, so it can't be tampered with. Then withdraw three million dollars from my account. Two mill's for you, like a down payment on account. The other mill's for D'Shonn. Give him the deposit box too; he can open it. Tell him it's personal memorabilia, shit that means a lot to me, and I want it buried with me in my coffin. I'm talking about my coffin, 'cause I want D'Shonn to organize my funeral service and the wake afterward, make it a real event folks ain't ever gonna forget. Ask him from me to get all the folks from back in the day, when we was all boys in the hood, to come along and see me off, pay their respects. Tell him I'd really appreciate it. Can you do that?"

"A million dollars, just for a funeral and a wake?" Weiss asked.

"Hell, yeah, I want a procession of hearses and limos, a service in, like, a cathedral or something, and a slap-up party, celebrate my time here on earth: caviar and prime ribs to eat, Cristal and Grey Goose at the bar, all that good shit. Listen, a million's nothing. I read that geeky little mother started up Facebook spent ten mill on his wedding. Come to think of it, Shelby, make it two mill for D'Shonn. Tell him to lay it on real thick."

"If that's what you want, sure, I can do that."

"Yeah, that's what I want, and impress upon him that this is the wish of a dying man. That's some serious shit, right?"

"Yes it is."

"Well, you make sure he understands that."

"Absolutely."

"OK, so here's what you'll need to get into that account." Congo recited an account number, a name and then a long series of apparently random letters and numbers. Shelby Weiss wrote it down meticulously in his notebook, and then looked up.

"OK, I have got all that down. Is there anything else you want to tell me?" he asked.

"Nothing else." Johnny shook his head. "Just come back when you have done everything I told you."

Aleutian Brown had been a gangbanger. He ran with the Maalik Angels, who liked to present themselves as warriors of Allah, though most of them would have struggled to read a comic book, let alone the Koran. But Aleutian's kid brother D'Shonn was a very different proposition. He'd had it just as tough as Aleutian growing up, he was just as angry at the world, and was just as mean an individual. The difference was, he hid it a whole lot better and was smart enough to learn from what happened to his brother and all the homies he'd hung out with. Most of them were in jail or in the ground.

So D'Shonn worked hard, stayed out of trouble and made it into Baylor on an academic scholarship. On graduating, he won another full scholarship to Stanford Law School, where he took a particular interest in criminal law. Having graduated with honors, and breezed through the California state bar exam, D'Shonn Brown was perfectly placed to choose a stellar career path, either as a defense attorney, or a hotshot young prosecutor in a DA's office. But his purpose in studying the law had always been to better equip himself to break it. He saw himself as a twenty-first-century Godfather. So in public he presented himself as a rising star in the business community, with a strong interest in charitable activities: "I just want to give back," as he used to say to admiring reporters. And in private, he pursued his interests in drug-dealing, extortion, human-trafficking and prostitution.

D'Shonn understood at once that there was a clear subtext to Johnny Congo's message. He was certain Shelby Weiss could see it too, but there was a game to be played so that both men could deny, on oath, that their conversation had been about anything other than a condemned man's desire for a fancy funeral. But just the way Johnny had emphasized that he wanted D'Shonn to see him and to hug him before he died, the way he'd talked about all the vehicles he wanted to be in the procession—well, you didn't need to be an A-grade student to see what that was all about.

Still, if Johnny Congo wanted the world to think D'Shonn'd been asked to organize a funeral and wake, well, that's what he was going to do. Having accessed the full $2 million allocated to him from Johnny Congo's Geneva account he decided that an event on the scale Johnny had in mind couldn't be held in his home town of Nacogdoches. So he made inquiries at a number of Houston's most prestigious cemeteries before securing a lakeside plot at a place called Sunset Oaks, where the grass was as immaculate as a fairway at Augusta and gently rippling waters sparkled in the sun. A fine marble headstone was ordered. Several of the city's most prestigious and expensive florists, caterers and party venues, including a number of five-star hotels, were then presented with lavish specifications and invited to tender for contracts.

All these inquiries were accompanied by supporting emails and phone calls. When deals were agreed, printed contracts were hand-delivered by messengers so that there could be no doubt that they reached their destinations and were received. Deposits were paid and properly accounted for. More than 200 invitations were sent. Anyone who wanted to see evidence of a genuine intention to fulfil the stated wishes of Johnny Congo would be presented with more than they could handle.

But while all this was going on, D'Shonn was also having private, unrecorded conversations about very different matters connected to Jonnny Congo as he played around at the Golf Club of Houston, where he had a Junior Executive membership; lunched on flounder sashimi and jar-jar duck at Uchi; or dined on filet mignon Brazilian-style at Chama Gaúcha. Leaving no written record whatever, he handed over large amounts of cash to intermediaries who passed the thick wads of dead presidents on to the kind of men whose only interest in funerals lies in supplying the dead bodies. These individuals were then told to coordinate their activities via Rashad Trevain, a club-owner whose House of Rashad holding company was 30 percent owned by the DSB Investment Trust, registered in the Cayman Islands.

D'Shonn Brown was known to take no active part in the running of Rashad's business. When he was photographed at the opening of yet another new joint, he'd tell reporters, "I've been tight with Rashad since we were skinny-ass little kids in first grade. When he came to me with his concepts for a new approach to upscale entertainment it was my pleasure to invest. It's always good to help a friend, right? Turned out my man is about as good at his job as I am at mine. He's doing great, all his customers are guaranteed a good time, and I'm getting a great return on my money. Everyone's happy."

Except for anyone who crossed D'Shonn or Rashad, of course. They weren't happy at all.

Engines to neutral. Anchors away!" In the Atlantic Ocean, 100 miles off the northern coast of Angola, Captain Cy Stamford brought the FPSO *Bannock A* to rest in 4,000 feet of water. Of all the vessels in the Bannock Oil fleet, this one had the least imaginative or evocative name, and she didn't look any better than she sounded. A mighty supertanker may not possess the elegance of an America's Cup racing yacht, but there is something undeniably magnificent about its awesome size and presence, something majestic about its progress across the world's mightiest oceans. *Bannock A* was certainly built to supertanker scale. Her hull was long and wide enough to accommodate three stadium-sized professional soccer pitches laid end-to-end. Her tanks could hold around 100 million gallons of oil, weighing in at over 300,000 imperial tons. But she was as graceless as a hippo in a tutu.

The day he took command, Stamford had Skyped his wife,

back home in Norfolk, Virginia. "How long've I been doing this, Mary?" he asked.

"Longer than either of us care to think about, dear," she replied.

"Exactly. And in all that time I don't think I ever set to sea in an uglier tub than this one. Even her mother couldn't love her."

The veteran skipper, who had spent more than forty years in the U.S. Navy and the Merchant Marine, was speaking no more than the truth. With her blunt, shorn-off bows and box-like hull *Bannock A* resembled nothing more than a cross between a gigantic barge and a grossly oversized container. To make matters worse, her decks were covered from end to end with a massive superstructure of steel pipes, tanks, columns, boilers, cranes and cracking units, with what looked like a chimney, well over 100 feet tall and surrounded by a web of supporting girders, painted red and white, rising from the stern.

Yet there was a reason that the board of Bannock Oil had sanctioned the expenditure of more than $1 billion to have this huge floating eyesore constructed at the Hyundai shipyards in Ulsan, South Korea, and then appointed their most experienced captain to command her on a maiden voyage of more than 12,000 miles. As FPSO *Bannock A* made her slow, cumbersome way through the Korean Straits and into the Yellow Sea, then on across the South China Sea; past Singapore and through the Malacca Straits to the Indian Ocean; all the way to the Cape of Good Hope and then around into the Atlantic and up the west coast of Africa, the moneymen in Houston had been counting down the days to payback time. For the initials FPSO stood for "floating production, storage and offloading" and they described a kind of alchemy. Very soon *Bannock A* would start taking up the oil produced by the rig that stood about three miles north of where she now lay at anchor; the first to come into operation on the Magna Grande oilfield that Bannock Oil had discovered more than two years earlier. Up to 80,000 barrels a day would be piped to *Bannock A*'s onboard refinery, which would distil the thick, black crude into a variety of highly saleable substances from lubricating oil to gasoline. Then she would store the various products in her tanks ready for Bannock Oil tankers to take them on to the final destinations. The total anticipated production of the Magna Grande field was in excess of 200 million barrels. Unless the world suddenly lost its taste for petrochemicals, Bannock Oil could expect a total return in excess of $20 billion.

So *Bannock A* was going to earn her keep many, many times over. And it wouldn't be long now before she got right down to work.

Hector Cross unclipped the leather top of the Thermos hip flask, removed the stainless steel stirrup cup contained within it, unscrewed the stopper, poured the steaming hot Bullshot into the cup, and drank. He gave a deep sigh of pleasure. The rain had stayed away, which always had to be considered a mercy in Scotland, and there had even been a few glorious shafts of sunlight, slicing through the clouds and illuminating the trees that clustered along the riverbank, creating a glorious mosaic of leaves, some still holding on to the greens of summer, while others were already glowing with the reds, oranges and yellow of autumn.

It had been a good morning. Cross had only caught a couple of the Atlantic salmon that accumulated in the Tay's lower reaches during the late summer and early autumn, one of them a respectable but by no means spectacular thirteen-pounder, but that hardly mattered. He had been out in the open, out on the water, surrounded by the glorious Perthshire landscape, with nothing to trouble his mind but the business of finding the spots where the salmon were resting, and the looping rhythm of the Spey casts that sent his fly out to the precise point where he thought the fish might best be lured into a bite. All morning he'd been filled with the sheer joy of life, chasing the dark demons of the night away, but now, as he took a bite from the sandwich the castle cook had provided for him, Cross found his mind drifting back to his nightmare.

It was the fear he had felt that astonished him: the kind of terror that liquefies a man's limbs and tightens his throat so that he can barely move or even breathe. Only once in his life had he known anything like it: the day when, as a lad of sixteen, he had joined the hunting party of young Maasai boys, sent out to prove their manhood by hunting down an old lion that had been driven out of his pride by a younger, stronger male. Naked but for a black goatskin cloak and armed with nothing more than a rawhide shield and a short stabbing spear, Cross had stood in the center of the line of boys as they confronted the great beast, whose huge, erect mane burned gold in the light of the African sun. Perhaps because of his position, or because his pale skin caught the lion's eye more easily than the black limbs to either side, Cross had been the one whom the lion charged. Though dread had almost overwhelmed him, Cross had not just stood his ground, but stepped forward to meet the lion's final, roaring leap with the razor point of his spear.

Though he had been given his first gun when he was still a small boy and hunted from that moment on, the lion had been Cross's first true kill. He could still feel and smell the heart blood that had gushed on to his body from the mortally wounded lion's mouth, could still remember the elation that came from confronting death and overcoming it. That moment had made him the warrior he had always dreamed of being, and he had pursued the calling ever since, first as an officer in the SAS and then as the boss of Cross Bow Security.

There had been times when his actions had been called into question. His military career had come to an abrupt halt after he had shot three Iraqi insurgents who had just detonated a roadside bomb that had killed half a dozen of Cross's troopers. He and his surviving men had tracked the bombers down, captured them and forced them to surrender. The motley trio were just emerging from their hideout with their hands in the air when one of them reached inside his robe. Cross had no idea what the insurgent might have in there: a knife, a gun, or even a suicide vest whose detonation would blow them all to kingdom come. He had a fraction of a second in which to make a decision. His first thought was for the safety of his own men, so he fired his Heckler & Koch MP5 submachine gun, and blew all three Iraqis away. When he examined their still-warm bodies, all of them were unarmed.

At the subsequent court martial, the court had accepted that Cross had acted in his own defense and that of his men. He was found not guilty. But the experience had not been a pleasant one and though he had no trouble ignoring the taunts and smears of reporters, politicians and activists who had never in their lives faced a decision more brutal than whether to have full or semi-skimmed milk in their morning cappuccinos, still he couldn't abide the thought that the reputation of the regiment he loved might have suffered because of his actions.

So Cross requested and was given an honorable discharge. Since then, the fighting had continued, albeit no longer in Her Majesty's service. Working almost exclusively for Bannock Oil, Cross had defended the company's installations in the Middle East against terrorist attempts at sabotage. That was where he met Hazel Bannock, widow of the company's founder Henry Bannock, who had taken over the business and, through sheer determination and force of will, made it bigger and more profitable than ever before. She and Cross were equally headstrong, equally proud, equally egotistic. Neither had been willing to give an inch to the other, but the combative antagonism with which their relationship began was, perhaps, the source of its strength. Each had tested the other and found that they were not wanting; from that mutual respect, not to mention a burning mutual lust, had come a deep and passionate love.

Marriage to Hazel Bannock had introduced Cross to a world unlike any he had ever known, in which millions were counted by the hundred, and the numbers in an address book belonged to presidents, monarchs and billionaires. But no amount of money or power altered the fundamentals of human life: you were no more immune to disease, no less vulnerable to a bullet or bomb, and your heart could still be torn in two by loss. And just as money could buy new friends, so it also brought new enemies with it.

Hazel was an African, like Cross, and like him she understood and accepted the law of the jungle. When Cross had captured Adam Tippoo Tip, the man who had kidnapped and later murdered Hazel's daughter Cayla and her mother Grace, Hazel had executed him herself. "It is my duty to God, my mother and my daughter," she had said before she dried her tears, lifted a pistol to the back of Adam's neck and, with a rock-steady grip on the gun, put a bullet through his brain.

But death had begotten death. Hazel had been killed. Cross had killed Carl Bannock, one of the two men responsible for her murder. Now the other, Johnny Congo, was awaiting execution in an American jail. He would die, just as the others had done, but in the way Jo Stanley preferred: from a lethal injection, in an execution chamber, on the order of a court. Maybe that would end all the dying. For the first time in his life, Cross was prepared to consider the possibility that the time had come to walk away from the battlefield before he was carried away in a body bag. His life was different now. He had a daughter who had already lost a mother. He couldn't let her lose her father too. And he had Jo. She brought peace to his life and the promise of another, better, happier way of living.

"You're not as young as you used to be, Heck," Cross told himself as he got up from the folding canvas stool on which he'd sat to eat his lunch with a crack of his knee joints. Though his muscles were still as strong as ever, they seemed to ache just

21

a little more than they used to. Perhaps it was time to let his right-hand men, Dave Imbiss and Paddy O'Quinn, take charge of Cross Bow's active operations. God only knew they were up to the task. So was Paddy's blonde Russian wife Nastiya, who was as ruthlessly dangerous as she was magnificently beautiful.

Hector picked up his rod and waded back into the waters of the Tay for his afternoon's fishing. But before he settled to the task a thought flashed into his mind: that he was almost ready to give Jo the news that she longed to hear; that he was ready to settle down. For once Johnny Congo was dead, that would be the last of his enemies gone. Maybe that would allow him to enjoy a quiet, peaceful life at last.

Just maybe, he thought as he prepared to cast his fly across the river, and just maybe salmon will learn to take a fly.

As befitted his status as one of the young pillars of Houston society, D'Shonn Brown had a luxury suite at Reliant Stadium, home of the city's NFL franchise, the Houston Texans. He had invited his corporate security consultant Clint Harding, a former field lieutenant in the Texas Rangers, the state's elite law enforcement agency, to join him as the Texans took on their divisional rivals the Indianapolis Colts. Harding's wife Maggie and their three teenage kids came along, too, as did D'Shonn's current girlfriend, a ravishing blonde real-estate heiress called Kimberley Mattson, who looked kooky but hot in an insanely expensive pair of old-fashioned five-pocket jeans by Brunello Cucinelli, rolled up at the ankle to show off her new rose-garland tattoo. The party was completed by Rashad Trevain, his wife Shonelle and their 9-year-old son Ahmad. In total, then, there were ten affluent, respectable Houstonians: young and old, male and female, black and white, all cheerfully socializing at a football game. An attendant was on hand to serve them from a private buffet of hot and cold gourmet foods. Ice buckets held bottles of Budweiser, white wine and soft drinks for the kids. A bank of TV screens showed live every other game being played that Sunday. A cheerleader dressed in shiny red boots, microscopic blue hotpants and a low-cut stretchy crop-top popped in for the personal visit granted to every luxury suite. All in all, what better image could there be of twenty-first-century America?

Midway through the second quarter, the Texans scored a touchdown. As the stadium rocked to the roar of the crowd, D'Shonn leaned over, gently pushed Kimberley's hair away from her ear, which he then kissed and, while she was still smiling, said, "Excuse me, baby. Got to talk some business and nothing is gonna happen in the game for a while."

"Anything I should know about?" asked Kimberley, who had powerful entrepreneurial instincts herself.

"Nah, Rashad's got a problem at one of his joints. He thinks some of the bar staff are ripping him off. He can turn a blind eye to a free drink from time to time, but he draws the line at cases of champagne."

D'Shonn got up from his seat and made his way to the back of the box, where Harding and Rashad were already waiting for him. "Got a solution for that pilfering issue?" he asked.

"Yeah," Harding said. "I'll put one of my boys in there undercover, have him work as a waiter. Anything's going on, he'll find out what it is and who's doing it."

"Glad you got that sorted. Now, tell me about what's going to happen to Johnny Congo. It's a funny thing. I could write you a dissertation about capital punishment from a legal standpoint, but I know a lot less about the specific practicalities. For example: how do they get a guy like Johnny from Polunsky to the Death House?"

"Real carefully," said Harding, drily. He was a tall, lean man, as tanned and tough as pemmican, and he'd been a damn good cop, proud of it, too, before he came to work for D'Shonn Brown. The security job for which he'd been hired was a genuine one,

23

but as time had gone by he'd become progressively more aware of the dirty truths that lay hidden behind D'Shonn Brown's shiny, corporate façade. He'd not witnessed any actual crimes, but he could smell the lingering stench of criminality. His problem, however, lay in a second discovery: just how much he, and more importantly his family, enjoyed the extra money he was making since he'd quit the Rangers. There was no way he could go back to a government pay check, so Harding appeased his conscience the same way Shelby Weiss did, by never doing anything overtly illegal, or knowingly aiding in the commission of such activity.

Right now, for example, his old cop instincts were telling him that Brown and Rashad were up to something, but as long as nothing specific was said, and all the information he provided was in the public domain, he could honestly say that he had no knowledge of any actual felony being planned or committed.

On that basis he continued, "So, Polunsky's about a mile east of Lake Livingston, and there's nothing around it but grass and a few trees. Anyone gets out of that place, which is an impossible dream, there's nowhere for them to hide. Now, the Walls Unit is different. It's pretty much right in the middle of Huntsville."

"What happens in between?" D'Shonn asked.

"Well, it's about forty miles, I guess, as the crow flies between the two units. And the lake is right between 'em, so you got three basic routes you can take: go around the south of the lake, or around the north, or ride right across the middle on the Trinity Bridge. Now the Offender Transportation Office has a standard protocol for the operation. The prisoner always travels in the middle vehicle of a three-vehicle convoy, with state trooper patrol cars back and front. The only people who know the precise time of the departure from Polunsky are the prison warders, police and Offender Transportation staff involved in the transfer, and the route to be taken is not made public."

"But it's one of three, right? North, south or middle?" Rashad Trevain chipped in.

"Yessir, those are the basic routes. But, see, they got ways to vary them all. I mean you got two roads out of the Polunsky Unit, just to start with. Then there's a road along the west shore of the lake, from Cold Spring up to Point Blank, and that kind of links up the south route and the middle route, so you can move from one to the other."

"Multiple variables," said D'Shonn.

"Right, which is the whole idea, makes it impossible for anyone to try and guess the route in advance. Plus, when you've got three vehicles, all carrying armed officers, that's a lot of firepower. Listen, Mr. Brown, I don't know if this is good news for you or not, but your buddy Johnny Congo is going to make it safe and sound to his appointment."

"Certainly sounds like it," said D'Shonn. There was a roar from the stadium and a shout of "Turnover!" from J. J. Harding. "Time we got back to the game," D'Shonn added, but as they were heading back to their seats, he tapped Rashad on the shoulder and said, "You and me need to talk."

Modern technology abounds with unintended consequences. The pin-sharp satellite imagery of Google Earth gives anyone with a Wi-Fi connection a capacity for intelligence-gathering once reserved for global superpowers. Likewise, anyone who opens a Snapchat message immediately starts a ten-second clock ticking down to its destruction. And the moment it's gone, it's totally untraceable. That works perfectly for teens who want to swap selfies and sex-talk without their parents having a clue, and equally well for someone planning a criminal operation who doesn't want to leave a trail of his communications.

D'Shonn Brown had connections. One of them was to a specialist arms dealer, who liked to boast of his ability to source anything from a regular handgun to military-grade ordnance. He and D'Shonn exchanged Snapchat messages. A problem was defined. A series of possible solutions was proposed. In

25

the end, the whole thing came down to three words: Krakatoa, Atchissons, FIM-92.

While that debate was proceeding, a handful of high-end SUVs were stolen from shopping mall parking lots, city streets and upscale suburban neighborhoods. They were all luxury imported models, and all were built for speed: a couple of Range Rover Sports with five-litre supercharged engines, a Porsche Cayenne, an Audi Q7 and a tuned-up Mercedes ML63 AMG that could do nought to sixty in a shade over four seconds. Within hours of being taken, the cars had all had any tracking devices removed, before being driven to different workshops to be resprayed and given new license plates. Meanwhile, police officers were telling the cars' owners that they'd do their best to find their precious vehicles, but the chances weren't good.

"I hate to say it, but models like that get stolen to order," one very upset oil executive's wife was told. "Chances are, that Porsche of yours is already over the border, making someone in Reynosa or Monterrey feel real good about life."

Rashad Trevain, meanwhile, had one of his people spend a few hours online, scouring every truck dealership from the Louisiana state line clear across to Montgomery, Alabama, looking for four-axle dumper trucks, built after 2005, with less than 300,000 miles on the clock, available for under $80,000. By the end of the morning they'd located a couple of Kenworth T800s and a 2008 Peterbilt 357, with an extra-long trailer that fitted those specifications. The trucks were bought for their full asking price from an underworld dealer who sold only for cash, didn't bother with paperwork and suffered instant amnesia about his customers' names and faces, then driven west to a repair yard in Port Arthur, Texas. There they were given the best service they'd ever had. The mechanics fitted bigger carburettors and new cylinder heads, pistons and tires. Every single component was checked, cleaned, replaced, or whatever it took to make these well-used machines move like spring chickens on speed. The day before Johnny Congo was due to go to the Death House, the trucks headed over to Galveston and picked up forty tons apiece of hardcore rubble—smashed up concrete, bricks, paving and large stones—in each of the Kenworths and fifty tons in the Peterbilt. Now they were loaded, locked and ready to go. One final touch: a plastic five-gallon jerrycan was tucked behind the driver's seat in every cab, with a timer fuse attached.

Cross was half an hour into his final afternoon's fishing when the iPhone in the top pocket of his Rivermaster vest started ringing, ruining the peace of a world in which the loudest sounds had been the burbling of the waters of the Tay and the rustle of the wind in the trees.

"Dammit!" he muttered. The ringtone was one he reserved for calls from Bannock Oil head office in Houston. Since his marriage to Hazel Bannock, Hector Cross had been a director of the company that bore her first husband's name. He was thus powerful enough to have left instructions that he was not to be disturbed unless it was absolutely essential, but with that power came the responsibility to be on call at any time, anywhere, if need arose. Cross took out the phone, looked at the screen and saw the word "Bigelow."

"Hi, John," he said. "What can I do for you?"

John Bigelow was a former U.S. Senator who had taken over the role of President and CEO of Bannock Oil after Hazel's death. "Hope I haven't caught you at a bad time, Heck," he said with all the affability of a born politician.

"You caught me in the middle of a river in Scotland, where I was trying to catch salmon."

"Well, I sure hate to disturb a man when he's fishing, so I'll keep it brief. I just had a call from a State Department official I regard very highly . . ." There was a burst of static on the line, Cross missed the next few words and then Bigelow's voice could be heard saying, ". . . called Bobby Franklin. Evidently Washing-

27

ton's getting a lot of intel about possible terrorist activity aimed at oil installations in West Africa and off the African coast."

"I'm familiar with the problems they've had in Nigeria," Cross replied, forgetting all thought of Atlantic salmon as his mind snapped back to business. "There have been lots of threats against onshore installations and a couple of years ago pirates stormed a supply vessel called *C-Retriever* that was servicing some offshore rigs—took a couple of hostages as I recall. But no one's ever gone after anything as far out to sea as we're going to be at Magna Grande. Was your State Department friend saying that's about to change?"

"Not exactly. It was more a case of giving us a heads-up and making sure we were well prepared for any eventuality. Look, Heck, we all know you've had to go through a helluva lot in the past few months, but if you could talk to Franklin and then figure out how we should respond, security-wise, I'd be very grateful."

"Do I have time to finish my fishing?"

Bigelow laughed. "Yeah, I can just about let you have that! Some time in the next few days would be fine. And one more thing . . . We all heard how you handed that bastard Congo over to the U.S. Marshals and, speaking as a former legislator, I just want you to know how much I respect you for that. No one would've blamed you for taking the law into your hands, knowing that he was responsible for your tragic loss, and our tragic loss, too. You know how much all of us here loved and respected Hazel. But you did the right thing and now, I promise you, we in Texas are going to do the right thing. You can count on that."

"Thanks, John, I appreciate it," Cross said. "Have your secretary send me the contact details and I'll set up a Skype call as soon as I'm back in London. Now, if you don't mind, I've just spotted what looks like twenty pounds of prime salmon and I want to put a fly in its mouth before it disappears."

Cross dropped his fly on to the water downstream of where he was standing; then he lifted his rod up and back and into a perfect single Spey cast that sent his line and lure out to a point on the water where it was perfectly positioned to tempt and tantalize his prey. But though his concentration on the fish was absolute, still there was a part of his subconscious that was already looking forward to the task that Bigelow had set him.

It seemed to Cross like the perfect assignment to get him back into the swing of working life. His military expertise, and his ability to plan, supply, train for and execute an interesting, important task would all be utilized to the full. But the work, though challenging, would essentially be precautionary. Just like all the soldiers, sailors and airmen who had spent the Cold War decades training for a Third World War that had thankfully never come, so he would be preparing for a terrorist threat that might be very real in theory but was surely unlikely in practice. If he was really going to lead a less blood-soaked life, but didn't want to die of boredom, this seemed a pretty good way to start.

It was half past eight in the morning of 15 November and all the morning news shows in Houston were leading with stories about the upcoming execution of the notorious killer and prison-breaker Johnny Congo. But if that was the greatest drama of the day, other tragedies, no less powerful to those caught up in them, were still playing themselves out. And one of them was unfolding in a doctor's consulting room in River Oaks, one of the richest residential communities in the entire United States, where Dr. Frank Wilkinson was casting a shrewd but kindly eye over the three people lined up in chairs opposite his desk.

To Wilkinson's right was his long-time patient and friend Ronald Bunter, senior partner of the law firm of Bunter and Theobald. He was a small, neat, silver-haired man, whose normally impeccable, even fussy appearance was marred by the deep shadows under his eyes, the gray tinge to his skin and—something Wilkinson had never seen on him before—the heavy creases in his dark gray suit. When Bunter said "Good morning" there was a quaver in his thin, precise voice. He was obviously exhausted and under enormous strain. But he was not the patient Wilkinson was due to be seeing today.

On the left of the line sat a tall, strongly built, altogether more forceful-looking man in his early forties: Ronald Bunter's son Bradley. He had thick black hair, swept back from his temples and gelled into a layered, picture-ready perfection that made him look like someone running for office. His eyes were a clear blue and they looked at Dr. Wilkinson with a challenging directness, as if Brad Bunter were forever spoiling for a fight. Even so, the doctor could see that he, too, was suffering considerable fatigue, even if he was more able to hide it than his father. There was, however, nothing wrong with Brad Bunter that a good night's sleep wouldn't cure.

The patient whose condition was the reason for the Bunters' visit to Frank Wilkinson's office sat between the two men: Ronald's wife and Bradley's mother Elizabeth, who was known to everyone as Betty. As a young woman Betty had been an exceptionally beautiful, Grace Kelly blonde, with brains to match. She'd met Ronnie when they were both freshmen at the University of Texas; they had married in their junior year and they'd been together ever since.

"I don't know what I did to deserve her," Ronnie used to say. "Not only is she far too pretty for a guy like me, but she's far too smart as well. Her grades were way better than mine all the way through U. T. Law. If she hadn't given it up to marry me, she'd have been the one running the firm."

Now, though, she was a shrunken, hunched-up figure. Her hair was disheveled and her immaculate everyday uniform of slim-cut, ankle-length chinos, white blouse, pearls and pastel cashmere cardigans had been replaced by an old purple polo shirt, tucked into baggy gray elasticated slacks over a pair of cheap sneakers. She was holding her purse on her lap and she

30

kept opening it, taking out a tightly folded piece of paper, unfolding it, staring blankly at the handwritten words scrawled across it, folding it up again and putting it back in the bag.

Dr. Wilkinson watched her go through one complete cycle of the ritual before very gently inquiring, "Do you know why you're here, Betty?"

She looked up at him suspiciously. "No, no I don't," she said. "I haven't done anything wrong."

"No, you haven't done anything wrong, Betty."

She looked at him with a desperate expression of anguish and bafflement in her eyes. "I just . . . I . . . I . . . I can't sort it all out . . . all these things. I don't know . . ." Her voice tailed away as she opened her purse and pulled out the paper again.

"You are merely suffering from a period of confusion." Dr. Wilkinson said kindly, trying to cloak the awful truth with the gentlest possible tone of voice. "Do you remember we talked about your diagnosis?"

"We did no such thing! I don't remember that at all. And I'm a grown woman in her fifties." Betty was in fact three weeks shy of her seventy-third birthday. She continued forcefully, "I know what's what and I remember all the things I need to know, I can assure you of that!"

"And I believe you," Dr. Wilkinson said, knowing that it was pointless arguing with an Alzheimer's patient, or attempting to drag them from their personal reality back into the real world. He looked at her husband: "Now, perhaps you can tell me what happened, Ronnie."

"Yes, well, Betty's been having a lot of trouble sleeping," Bunter started. He looked at his wife, whose full attention had now reverted to the piece of paper, and went on, his voice tentative and his words very obviously skirting around the full truth: "She became a little confused last night, you know, and she was . . . overwrought, I guess you might say."

31

"Oh, for God's sake, Dad!" Brad Bunter exclaimed with an anger born of frustration. "Why don't you tell Dr. Wilkinson what really happened?"

His father said nothing.

"So what do you think happened, Brad?" Dr. Wilkinson asked.

"OK." Brad gave a heavy sigh, collected his thoughts and then began, "Seven o'clock yesterday evening, I'm still at the office and I get a call from Dad. He's at home—these days he likes to be home by five, to look after Mom—and he needs help because Mom's packed a case and she's trying to get out of the house. See, she doesn't believe it actually is her house any more. And Dad's on the ragged edge because she's been shouting at him, and kicking and punching him . . ."

Ronald Bunter winced as if the words had hurt him more than his wife's fists or feet ever could. Betty still seemed oblivious to what was being said.

Brad kept going. "And she's having crying jags. I mean, I can hear her sobbing in the background as I'm talking to him. So I go over and I try to get her calm enough to at least eat something, right? Because she doesn't eat any more, doctor, not unless you make her. Then I get home about quarter of nine, to see my own wife and kids, except Brianne's already put the kids to bed, so we watch some TV, go to bed."

"Uh-huh," Wilkinson murmured. He wrote a couple of words on his notes. "Was that the final disturbance last night?"

"Hell no. Two o'clock in the morning the phone goes again. It's Dad. Same thing. Can I come over? Mom's out of control. I'll be honest, I felt like saying, you want help in the middle of the night, call an ambulance. But, you know, she is my mom, so I go over again, same story, except this time—and I'm sorry, Dad, but Dr. Wilkinson needs to know this, she's walking around stark naked, babbling God knows what nonsense . . . and she's got no modesty or embarrassment at all about it."

"There's nothing embarrassing about the human body, Brad," Wilkinson said.

"Well, just you remember that the next time one of your parents turns your home into a nudist colony."

"Excuse Brad please, Dr. Wilkinson. You know that he can be a little abrupt sometimes," said Ronald with exaggerated politeness that failed to hide his anger.

"No, Dad, I just tell it like it is. This can't go on, doctor. My parents need help. Even if they say they don't want it, they need it."

"Hmm . . ." Wilkinson nodded thoughtfully. "From what you say, it certainly sounds like we're reaching a crisis point. But I don't want to rush to any conclusions. Sometimes there's a physiological cause for a series of episodes like the one you describe. I have to say, I doubt that in this case, but it pays to make sure, just in case there's a little infection or something going on. So, Betty, if you don't mind I'm going to do a few tests."

Now she perked up again. "I'm certainly not sick. I know I'm not sick. Never felt better in my life."

"Well, that's great to hear, Betty. And don't you worry, I won't be doing anything too serious at all, just checking your blood pressure, listening to your chest, simple stuff like that. Are you happy for me to do that, Betty?"

"I suppose so."

Ronald patted her arm. "You'll be fine, Betsy-Boo. I'll be right here watching over you."

From nowhere, like a sudden ray of sunshine on a cloudy day, Betty Bunter produced a dazzling smile that just for a moment brought all the life and beauty back to her face. "Thank you, sweetheart," she said.

It took Wilkinson less than five minutes to go through his tests. When he'd finished he sat back in his chair and said, "OK, well, as I suspected, there are no physiological problems to report. So what I'm going to do is prescribe something for

Betty to help calm her at moments of particularly acute anxiety. Ron, if you or Brad can make sure Betty takes half of one of these pills whenever you feel things are taking a turn for the worse that should help a lot, but no more than two of those halves in any one day."

He looked around to make sure that the two Bunter men had taken in what he'd just said, then he continued, "We have an established crisis-management procedure for cases like this, to make sure we can get our patients effective care. I'm going to make a few calls this morning and try to work out something for you guys by the end of the day. Brad, I wonder if you could take Betty out to the waiting room for a moment. I just want a quick word with your dad . . . because he's my patient too, after all."

"That sounds alarming. Should I be worried?" Ronnie asked.

Wilkinson gave the kind of chuckle that's intended to reassure, though seldom does. "No, I simply want a chance to talk, on a doctor–patient basis."

No more words were exchanged until Brad had led his mother out of the room; then Ronnie Bunter asked, "So, what's this all about, Frank?"

"It's about the fact that Betty isn't the only one I'm worried about," Wilkinson replied. "You're exhausted, Ron. You've got to get more help. At this stage, Betty really needs around-the-clock care."

"And I'm doing my damnedest to give it to her. I swore an oath, Frank: 'in sickness and in health.' And in my business, oaths matter. You don't break 'em."

"Nor in my business, either, but you're not being a smart husband to Betty if you make yourself sick trying to look after her. Caring for someone with a severe psychological and neurological condition like Alzheimer's is a tough, tough job. It's non-stop. You look exhausted, Ron, and you've lost weight, too. Are you eating properly?"

"When I can," Bunter said. "It's not like we're sitting down at the dinner table for a three-course meal. That's for sure."

"How about work?"

"Well, I try to go into the office most days, and my staff all know I'm always on call, my clients too."

Wilkinson laid down his pen, leaned back in his chair with his arms folded and looked his old friend straight in the eye. "So you're trying to look after Betty, day and night, and the phone keeps ringing with people asking for legal advice. Tell me, do you think you're giving your clients the best counsel they could get for their money? Because I know for sure I couldn't treat my patients properly if I were going through the same things as you are now."

Bunter's shoulders sagged a little. "It's hard, I'll give you that. And yeah, there are times I put the phone down and think, *Shoot! I just forgot something*, or I realize I got a point of law wrong. And it's not because I don't know the right answer, I'm just so darn tired."

"Right, so now I'm going to give you a prescription, and you're not going to like it."

"Do I have to take it?"

"If you've got any sense left in you at all, buddy, yeah, you do."

"OK then, doc, tell it to me straight," Bunter said, making Wilkinson smile with his attempt at portraying a character in an old cowboy movie.

"Right, first thing I'm telling you is that you have to get Betty the best around-the-clock care that you and your insurance plan can afford."

"I'll think about it."

"Ron . . ." Wilkinson insisted.

"OK, OK, I'll do it. Anything else?"

"Yes. I want you to cut right back on your work. You've got good people at your firm, right?"

"The best."

"Then they can take over your clients. And Brad can run the business day-to-day. If you want to call yourself by some fancy title that means you're still the top dog, even though you don't bark any more, that's fine by me. But I don't want you setting foot in the office more than once a week, preferably once a month. Let Brad do all the heavy lifting."

"I'm just not sure he's ready for it."

"Bet that's what your old man said about you, too, but you showed him."

"And there's . . ." Bunter grimaced. "Well, I hate to say this about my own son, but there are character issues. You heard Brad today. He can be abrasive sometimes, confrontational."

"So are many of the world's greatest litigators."

"But it's not the style I like to encourage at Bunter and Theobald. The best deals, the ones that last and don't end in bitterness and acrimony, are the ones where both sides feel like they did OK. That means we get what our client wants, or at least what he needs, while still respecting the other side and acknowledging the merits of their position, not beating them into the ground."

"Well, Ronnie, I'm not going to tell you how to run your firm, but I didn't hear a son who was abrasive or confrontational today. I heard a son who's very aware of how bad things have gotten, who's worried, just like I am, about the both of you, and who wants to get the situation, if not fixed—because there is no fix for Alzheimer's—then at least made as tolerable as it can possibly be."

Bunter frowned anxiously. "You really think I need to get help, leave work, huh?"

"Yes, I do."

"So then what am I going to do?"

"Take it easy. Spend quality time with Betty while you still can. Listen, Ronnie, it won't be long—less than a year, maybe less than six months—before Betty's reached the point where

36

she doesn't recognize you, can't hold any kind of a conversation, not even a rambling one, and there's no trace left of the woman you fell in love with."

Bunter's face crumpled: "Don't . . . that's awful . . ."

"But it's true. So make the best of the time you have. Look after yourself so you can still look after her. Promise me you'll think about that, at least."

"Yeah, OK, I'll promise you that."

"You're a good man, Ron, one of the very best. Betty's lucky to have you."

"Not half as lucky as I've been to have her. And now I'm losing her . . ."

"I know . . ." Dr. Wilkinson said. "I know."

For decades the state of Texas has carried out its executions in the Texas Death House at the Walls Unit, Huntsville. Right up to 1998, that's where Death Row was located, too. But then condemned men, Johnny Congo included, started finding ways to escape and the Texas Department of Criminal Justice determined that a more secure unit was required. Death Row was moved across to the Polunsky Unit in West Livingston, a supermax, ultra-high-security facility. No one escaped from there. The nigh-on 300 prisoners were held in solitary confinement and ate in their cells from a plate shoved through a "bean slot" in the door. They exercised alone in a caged recreation area. The only physical contact they received was the strip searches they underwent whenever they left their cells. The regime was enough to drive a man crazy and there were some who chose to waive appeal opportunities and face execution early, just to escape from it.

Johnny Congo's execution process began at three in the afternoon of 15 November. He was not offered the choice of a condemned man's final meal, nor would he be at Huntsville: that luxury had long since been abandoned. There was just a hammering on his cell door and a warder shouting, "Time to go, Johnny! Hands through the bean slot."

Every aspect of life at the Polunsky Unit was calculated to degrade and dehumanize the inmates. The procedure for leaving a cell was no exception. Johnny walked to the door. He got down on his knees. Then he shuffled around so that he had his back to the door and stretched his arms backward till his hands pushed through the bean slot and emerged into the corridor outside. A pair of handcuffs was slapped around his wrists; then he pulled his arms back through the slot and got to his feet.

"Step away from the door!" the voice commanded.

Obediently, Johnny walked back into the middle of the room with his hands now cuffed behind his back. Then he turned around again to face the door as it opened.

Two warders came into the sixty-square-foot cell. One of them was white and almost as big as Johnny, with crew-cut ginger hair and sunburned skin on his face and forearms. He was carrying a Mossburger shotgun and there was a tense, jumpy look on his face that suggested he was just looking for a chance to use it.

Johnny smiled at him. "What's the point of pointing a gun at me today, ya dumb cracker? I'm already a dead man walking. Blow me away now, you'll be doing me a favor."

Johnny turned his face toward the second warden, a portly, middle-aged African-American, his hair dusted with silver. "Afternoon, Uncle," he said.

"Good afternoon to you, too, Johnny," Uncle said. "This is a hard time for you, I know that. But the calmer we can make it, the easier it will go, y'hear?"

"Yeah, I hear you."

"OK then, what I'm going to do is prepare you for transit to Huntsville. So first I want you to stand with your feet about eighteen inches apart. You were in the service, right?"

"Damn right, was a gunny sergeant in the Corps."

38

"A Marine, huh? Well, then I guess you know how to stand at ease."

Johnny obediently snapped into the position.

"Thanks, man," Uncle said. "Now just stand still a minute while I fix these around your ankles."

Johnny did as he was told and was equally compliant as a belly chain was secured around his waist. Then his hands were released from their original cuffs and resecured in cuffs that hung from the chain. He was now restricted to the short, shuffling steps that the leg irons allowed and the minimal hand movements afforded him by the links between the handcuffs and the belly chain. As massive, as powerful and as intimidating as he was, Johnny Congo was now entirely helpless. The two warders who had come to his cell were now joined by more of their colleagues as they led him through the Polunsky Unit to the loading bay where his transport awaited him.

All those years previously when Johnny had escaped from Huntsville, his associate Aleutian Brown had shot a warder called Lucas Heller in cold blood, with a bullet through the back of his skull. Johnny assumed that the warders around him now knew that. He waited for the first punch, or billy-club blow to hit him, knowing that they could do exactly what they wanted with him and he'd be completely unable to resist. But Uncle's peaceful, civilizing presence must have been enough to inhibit any desire for violent retribution because they got to the loading bay without any disturbance. There wasn't even any outcry from the other prisoners, giving a final send-off to a fellow inmate who was heading for the Death House. They were all alone in their silent cells, shut away behind the blank steel doors that lined the corridors. They had no idea that Johnny had ever even been in the unit, let alone that he was being taken away to die.

Johnny Congo was placed in the back of an unmarked, white minivan belonging to the Offender Transportation Office and ordered to sit on one of the two gray, upholstered benches that ran along either side of what would normally be the passenger compartment. Then his ankles were chained to the floor.

There were steel grilles on the windows and a more substantial one separating the passenger compartment from the driver's seat. An armed guard sat opposite Johnny, dressed in tan slacks, a white shirt and a black protective vest. The guard didn't say anything. He looked alert but at the same time relaxed, like a man who was good at his job, and trusted the other warders around him to do theirs, even in the presence of a known multiple killer. Johnny Congo didn't say anything either, just looked at the guard, staring him down, determined to establish himself as the alpha male, even on the day he was to die.

The details of Johnny Congo's execution had been discussed all the way to the top of the Texas Department of Criminal Justice. They fully realized that he was an extremely dangerous criminal who had already proved that he could escape from a maximum-security unit. His case had received a lot of media coverage and the closer the time came to his execution, the larger that would grow. Even as he left the Polunsky Unit there were a couple of TV news crews by each gate and a chopper was buzzing overhead. Another, much bigger media pack was clustered around the back gate of the Walls Unit, through which execution convoys were always admitted.

The one thing they all wanted was a picture—any picture at all, no matter how blurred or grainy—of Congo as he looked now. The only portraits anyone had of him were the official mug shots taken when he'd got off the plane from Abu Zara, looking like someone had run a truck over his face, or old archive photographs from his first burst of notoriety, way back when. The great American public wanted and needed to see the man their legal system was killing on their behalf on his very last day on earth. But the authorities weren't making it easy for anyone, including the media, to get anywhere near the condemned man.

Bearing in mind both the wickedness of Johnny Congo and the very public embarrassment that the entire Texas criminal justice establishment would suffer if he should get away from them a second time, there had been a change in the standard convoy format. There were, as always, three vehicles. But on this occasion the third in line was not another patrol car, as it would normally be, but a Lenco BearCat armored personnel carrier, loaded with a heavily armed, ten-man SWAT team. The BearCat was a big, black, menacing war-machine and the men inside it were the police equivalent of Special Forces. Against their firepower nothing short of a full-scale military assault would stand a chance of succeeding.

On the day of Johnny Congo's execution, everyone who saw D'Shonn Brown reported that he seemed withdrawn, subdued and, in a quiet, understated way, very obviously distressed. The execution was set for six o'clock in the evening. Huntsville is only about seventy miles north of Houston, right up Highway 45, and doesn't take much above an hour if the traffic is light. But D'Shonn wanted to be sure of missing the rush hour, and so, at the same time as the convoy taking Johnny Congo to his execution left the Polunsky Unit, D'Shonn's chauffeur-driven Rolls-Royce Phantom purred out of the underground garage beneath his downtown Houston HQ. D'Shonn was sitting in the back. Clint Harding was up front next to the driver. A black Suburban followed the Rolls out of the garage. In it were another four of Harding's men, whose job would be to get D'Shonn through the mob outside the prison gates on his way to the viewing room that looked on to the execution chamber.

D'Shonn was watching the TV on his iPad. "They got Johnny live on TV, following him from the sky like he's another OJ."

"I hate the way they are making this into a circus," said

Harding, tilting his head back toward D'Shonn. "Look, I know he was your brother's buddy, or whatever, but Johnny Congo was a dangerous man. Now he's getting the most dire punishment our society can deliver. It shouldn't be turned into a TV reality show."

D'Shonn's phone rang. He took the call, listened for a moment and then said, "Yo, Rashad, my man . . . Yeah, I'm watching it too. I guess I knew this might happen, but still . . . Crazy to think, the next time I'm due to see Johnny is when they wheel him into the chamber. I'm not looking forward to that, don't mind admitting."

Harding had turned his head back to the front and was staring right out the windscreen, down Interstate 45, so as to respect his boss's privacy. He didn't see D'Shonn pick up a second phone and flash a Snapchat message: "Perfect. Go ahead. Get the chopper and the jet ready to roll."

Ten seconds after it was received, the message vanished into thin air, leaving no trace that it had ever existed.

For two weeks Rashad Trevain had been trying to figure out ways of tracking Johnny Congo's prison convoy without attracting any attention from the cops. The obvious answer was just to tail it on the road, but if one car stayed right behind the convoy all the way, it was bound to be spotted and forced to stop. They could have a relay system, handing over from one car to another, but with three routes of up to fifty-five miles to cover, that would mean three long chains of drivers, waiting to take up the surveillance if the convoy happened to come their way, which was more manpower than he wanted to use. The more guys there were on the job, the less likely he was to know them all well and, it followed, the less he could trust them to keep their mouths shut.

Rashad's next idea was to buy a spotter drone of the kind police forces use for crowd control: a couple of feet across, with three miniature helicopter-style horizontal rotors and a camera that can send back images in real time to a base-station. But that would require skilled technicians to operate, plus there were range limitations for both the drone itself and the signal it was sending. So then Rashad went back to basics. He decided to scatter half-a-dozen spotters at key turning points along the first few miles of road: places where the convoy would be forced to make a choice that would determine its route.

But when he put the problem to D'Shonn Brown as they were looking across the water to the eighth green at the Golf Club of Houston's Member Course, D'Shonn Brown had straightened up from the chip he was about to play, looked at Rashad and asked, "You reckon they'll have a helicopter following that convoy?"

"You mean a police chopper, like an eye in the sky?" Rashad replied.

"That or a TV station, taking a break from following traffic to check out the badass nigger murderer taking his final ride. Give it the OJ treatment."

"Guess so. It's possible. Why?"

"Well, if someone was tracking the motorcade that would sure make our lives easier . . ."

D'Shonn interrupted himself for a few seconds to hit the ball about ten yards beyond the hole, only for it to halve the distance as the backspin kicked in and rolled it back toward the pin.

"Whoa, lucky bounce, bro!" Rashad laughed.

"Luck didn't come into it, I played for the spin," said D'Shonn coldly. He turned to replace his club in his bag, which was mounted on a trolley since they'd decided to play without caddies: no need for anyone else to hear what they were discussing. "But anyway, about that chopper, it would sure be handy if there was one up there," he went on. "Only problem is, we'd have to get rid of it afterward. Some things we don't want getting caught on camera."

"Yeah, I follow you, man."

"So you'd better see to that. If we want to get this job done, we'd best think of every eventuality."

All Johnny Congo's roads led to Huntsville. So that was where the ambush crew were waiting. The three heavily laden dumper trucks and the five stolen SUVs were all parked up on the cracked and dusty ribbon of road that led from Martin Luther King Drive up to the Northside Cemetery. There were no funerals planned for that day, no passers-by to look at the line of vehicles. The Maalik Angel in charge of the crew was a scrawny, light-skinned brother with a goatee beard called Janoris Hall. Like all the men who would be working under him today, Janoris was wearing a hooded white Tyvek disposable boiler suit, with fine latex gloves and flimsy polypropylene overshoes covering his Nike sneakers. Plenty of crime scene investigators dress in virtually identical work-gear. They don't want to contaminate a crime scene they're investigating. The Angels didn't want to contaminate a crime scene they were about to create. They also didn't want to be identified, which was why each of the Angels had already been issued with a hockey goalkeeper's face mask.

Janoris didn't have his mask on right now. He was watching the TV news on his iPad and the moment the prison convoy turned left off Farm to Market Road 350, on to Route 190, he turned to his second-in-command Donny Razak and said, "They headed north."

Razak had a shaven head, a thick, bushy beard and deep, gravelly voice that came from somewhere down in his barrel chest. "You want us to get going, meet 'em on the one-ninety?"

Janoris thought for a moment. It was tempting to head right out there now and get in position early. The less they were rushed, the smaller the chance of making a dumbass mistake somewhere along the line. But what if the convoy took the scenic route, up around the top of the lake and on into Huntsville on Texas 19? He didn't want to be waiting in the wrong place with his dick in his hand while Johnny Congo was being taken to the Death House on another route.

"No, man, we are going to wait a while. See what happens when they get to the bridge. Soon as we know if they's gonna cross it or not, that's when we make our move."

At the Walls Unit, one of the administrative offices had been taken over for use as a command post for the Congo operation. Now the only question was, who was in command? There were three possible candidates for the job: Hiram B. Johnson III, the prison governor, who was responsible for everything that would happen from the moment Johnny Congo entered the Walls Unit alive, to the time his body was taken from it, stone dead; Tad Bridgeman, the head of the Offender Transportation Office, whose own HQ was at the James "Jay" H. Byrd Jr Unit, a mile north of Downtown Huntsville and who was himself responsible for getting Johnny Congo from one prison unit to the other; and finally, this being Texas, there was a man in a white Stetson hat.

This last man also wore a pair of plain tan cowboy boots, stone-colored denim jeans, a crisply laundered white shirt and a dark tie. His gun was holstered high on his hip, making it easy to draw if he were on horseback, and there was a Star of Texas badge on his chest, stamped from fifty-peso Mexican coins. Officially, in recognition of their roughneck, cowboy origins, the officers of the Texas Rangers Division have no uniform other than their badge and their hat. Unofficially, however, jeans and a white shirt are expected, and the man wearing these was Major Robert "Bobby" Malinga, commander of the Rangers' Company A.

He was the one who had co-ordinated the security precautions for the transport with the other two officials and would be responsible for reapprehending Johnny Congo if, by some

45

terrible misfortune, he happened to escape captivity somewhere between West Livingston and Huntsville. The situation was further complicated by the addition of a fourth person, Chantelle Dixon Pomeroy. An immaculately groomed, impeccably mannered but laser-eyed redhead, Chantelle was Deputy Chief of Staff to the Governor of Texas. Her role was to observe and advise on the various political and public relations aspects of the execution and all the events and tasks surrounding it. She had no right to give direct orders to any of the various representatives of the state's criminal justice system. But she was the eyes, ears and voice of the Governor. And he certainly could give orders.

Right now, as the Congo convoy headed north up the 190 toward the lakeside developments at Cedar Point, the four key players in the command post were all doing the same as everyone else . . . watching the convoy's progress on TV.

"I don't like those pictures," Bobby Malinga growled. "If we can see 'em so can every gangbanger in Texas. I don't want anyone thinking they can pull some crazy stunt, make a name for themselves as the guy who freed Johnny Congo. Or the guy who killed Johnny Congo before the state could do the job. It's just as bad either way. I want that bird grounded."

"That's not going to happen, Major," Chantelle Dixon Pomeroy said softly. "This isn't Russia. We have a First Amendment here. We can't just go around telling TV stations they can't film an event of genuine significance to the people of Texas."

"You ever heard of homeland security? Johnny Congo is a notorious killer. He spent years as a fugitive in Africa, led a personal militia there from what I understand, may still do for all I know. He represents a clear and present danger to national security. You want to help our enemies, Ms. Pomeroy?"

"No, I don't, Major," the Deputy Chief of Staff said, sliding a spike of iced steel into her honeyed voice. "And if he was an Islamic terrorist, I'm sure the Governor would be as concerned as you are. But what we have here, when you get right down to it, is a garden-variety killer. Justice will be done and the Governor wants the people of Texas to see, with their own eyes, that we have the finest police officers and prison staff in the nation."

"Can you at least call the Governor's office to ask if he'll approve a no-fly order?" Malinga wheedled.

"Sure I can, but I don't need to. I have absolutely no doubt about the Governor's wishes. Sorry, Major, but the helicopter stays."

The Trinity River flows into the northern end of Lake Livingston by the small waterside community of Onalaska. The mouth of the river is almost three miles wide and it's spanned by the Trinity Bridge. As the minivan containing Johnny Congo drove along Route 190, through what passed for the center of Onalaska, Congo turned his head to look out of the window behind him. He saw a low-slung shed that contained a barbershop, an insurance office and a store that sold carpets and floor tiles. Just beyond it there was a Subway.

"Man, what I'd give right now for a foot-long Italian B.M.T.," the guard sitting opposite him said. "Italian herb'n'cheese bread, extra provolone, plenty of mayo, mmm . . . What's your favorite sub?"

"Huh?" Johnny Congo stared at him, uncomprehending.

"Subway, man, what kinda sandwich do you like?"

"Dunno. Never been."

"You're kidding me! You never once ate at Subway?"

"Nope, never heard of the place." Johnny Congo looked blankly at the guard, then sighed, as if abandoning the policy of being deliberately non-communicative. "I was in Iraq, in the service, killin' ragheads. Then I came home, caught a multiple homicide beef and was in jail, too many years, nothing but prison food. Then I was in Africa. No frickin' Subways in Africa. So no, I ain't never had no subs."

"Huh?" The guard looked nonplussed, as though this was

genuinely new and unusual information. At a crossroads opposite a Shell gas station they stopped at traffic lights. Now they had a choice to make: carry straight on up the road, or go past the gas station on to Farm to Market 356.

Neither Johnny nor the guard knew it but there were eyes glued to an iPad screen in Huntsville, waiting to see if the convoy took that turn. If it did, then Congo was being taken on the scenic route, up to the junction with Highway 19, then taking 19 all the way south-west into Huntsville. But when the lights turned green the patrol car leading the convoy kept going on along Route 190 toward the Trinity Bridge until it was heading out on the earthworks that carried the highway most of the way across the lake, just a few feet above the water, toward the high, white concrete swoop of the bridge itself.

"Guess you'll never get to have a Subway now," the guard said. "No offense, but . . . you know what I mean."

"Yeah, I know," said Congo. "Question is: do you?"

Thirty miles away, on the northern edge of Hunstville, right by the cemetery, Janoris Hall pumped his fist. "Yeah!" he shouted. "We got you now!" He looked around at the other Maalik Angels who were waiting for the signal to start the operation. "We are in business. They have taken the 190, now we're gonna meet them along the way, have ourselves a rendezvous. All right, now, gather around . . ."

The Angels all clustered around Janoris Hall and Donny Razak like footballers in a pre-game huddle. Janoris paced around the tight little circle in the middle of the huddle, with Donny shadowing him like a boxer in the ring. "We got an opportunity right here, today!" Janoris shouted, throwing a punch at Razak as the other Angels cheered. There were more punches, more cheers as Janoris went on, "It's a once-in-a-lifetime opportunity! An opportunity to make history! We gonna do something ain't never been done before. We gonna do it . . ."

"Do it!" the other Angels shouted back, getting into the tribal rhythm of call-and-response that had come over on the slave ships from the barracoons of West Africa to the cotton fields and gospel churches of the American South.

Janoris pumped his fist. "And again . . ."

"Do it!"

"And again . . ."

"Do it!"

"Gimme Congo on three . . . and a one!"

"One!"

"Two!"

"Two!"

"Three!"

"Congo!"

They all leaped as one into the air toward the center of the circle and slapped their outstretched hands together. Then Janoris Hall looked around at the faces that surrounded him and said, "Let's go get this sucker."

A minute later the road to the cemetery was deserted. The trucks and the SUVs were on the road, heading for the intersection with Interstate 190.

On the TV screens, the overhead images of the convoy were giving way to shots of the crowds gathering outside the Walls Unit. There were human rights campaigners protesting against the death penalty, and victims' groups and law-and-order hardliners shouting, "Die, Johnny, die!"

Network reporters flown in from New York and LA were checking their hair and make-up before they went onscreen, and that was just the men. The women remained virtually shrink-wrapped to preserve their doll-like appearance right up to the moment they went live on camera and pretended that they'd been reporting the story for the past several hours. Traders had set up food trucks selling gourmet ribs and chilli.

And for every individual who had a professional reason to be standing outside the walls of a state penitentiary in Texas, there were a hundred more who were just rubbernecking, waiting for the chance to say they'd been there, the night they stuck the needle into big, bad Johnny Congo.

In the command center, Tad Bridgeman, boss of the Offender Transportation Office, was talking to one of his officers, who was riding shotgun in the passenger seat of Johnny Congo's minivan.

"How's the prisoner? Any trouble?" Bridgeman asked.

"No, sir," came the reply, "good as gold. Last I heard, he "n" Frank were having a conversation about sandwiches, if you can believe that."

"Won't be no sandwiches where that boy's going," said Bridgeman. "Except grilled ones, maybe. They'll grill Johnny Congo too."

"Ain't that the truth!"

"Well, you keep me posted, son. Anything happens, I want to be the first to know."

"Yes, sir."

Major Bobby Malinga of the Texas Rangers was growling at the television screens. "Jesus H. Christ, can we just get away from all the nonsense outside the gates? I want to see where the convoy's at."

Chantelle Dixon Pomeroy laughed sweetly. "Why, Major, that wasn't what you were saying a few minutes ago when you were begging me to take that helicopter right out of the sky."

"Yeah, well, if it's gotta be up there, I want to see what it's seeing."

There was a knock on the door and a uniformed police officer came in. His eyes darted around the command center till he saw Chantelle. "Sorry to bother you, ma'am, but there's a heap of reporters'd like to speak to you, get the Governor's opinion on what's going on here today. What do you want me to tell them?"

"That I'll be right out." She picked up her phone and had

a thirty-second conference with the Chief of Staff in Austin, hardly saying a word beyond, "'K, 'K, I hear you, got it," before a final, definitive, "Ooh-Kay." Then she put the phone back in her handbag and took a small folding mirror out. She checked her face, checked for any stray auburn hairs and then snapped the mirror shut again. As she slipped it back in her bag, she looked at Bobby Malinga and gave a little shrug. "Girl's gotta look her best," she said. Then she headed out of the command room to spread the word from the Governor of Texas.

Just as she was about to say her piece, the media sped away, like a flock of starlings suddenly flying up from a telephone wire. D'Shonn Brown had just arrived at the Walls Unit. He was the only friend or relative of the condemned man who'd be witnessing the execution. Everyone wanted to hear what he had to say about it, even in preference to the Governor of Texas.

About eight miles out of Huntsville, at the junction with Farm to Market 405, Route 190 bends right, and on that bend there's a big open parking lot with a Valero gas station and an eatery called Bubba's, catering for local folk and anyone who needs a break from the road. Janoris Hall, in the passenger seat of the Merc ML63, led four of the SUVs and all three trucks into the lot. Just like Bobby Malinga, Janoris had been frustrated by the lack of overhead TV pictures from the helicopter cam, but in the last couple of minutes the news show's director had evidently tired of the scenes outside the Walls Unit and cut back to the Congo convoy. Janoris had been cursing and banging his hand in frustration against the black leather trim around the satnav as his vehicles were stuck behind one slow-moving truck or RV after another. Though they'd blazed along the highway whenever the road was clear, the obstructions kept coming and he was terrified that they'd see the patrol car, the minivan and the BearCat cruising by them on the other side of the road with nothing they could do to stop them. But

51

the moment he saw the pictures, and the map the TV news station kindly provided in the corner of the screen, he realized that they were going to make it. But it was going to be close.

As they were pulling into the lot around Bubba's, the convoy was only two or three miles away, heading toward them at an even seventy miles per hour. Janoris had numbered all the SUVs, calling them Congo 1 to 5. Naturally he was in Congo 1 and now he sent Congo 2, which was one of the Range Rover Sports, up the road, with instructions to radio in whenever they saw the convoy, then to turn around as soon as possible and follow it back toward the rest of the waiting Maalik Angels. "But don't go past the Peterbilt," he added.

Janoris barely got all his remaining vehicles formed up in the correct order when his phone rang and he heard a voice say, "We seen 'em. No more'n a mile away, be with you in less'n a minute. We can see the chopper, too."

Janoris looked in the direction from which the convoy would be approaching. The road ran dead straight up to the brow of a low ridge about a quarter of a mile away. The moment the convoy appeared over that ridge, that's when the action would begin.

"First two trucks to your starting position. Congo 3 slip in right behind 'em," Janoris ordered. "Congo 5, Bobby Z, do your thing, my man."

The two massive Kenworth T800s rolled up to the exit that led on to the right-hand lane of Route 190 and came to a stop, side by side, their fenders hanging over the edge of the blacktop, with the second Range Rover Sport on their tail. Anyone else who wanted to get out was going to have to wait.

Congo 5, the Audi Q7, had parked around the back of Bubba's. Now a man got out of it, carrying a heavy black tube about five feet long. He positioned himself on the far side of the Q7's bulky nose, went down on one knee and hefted the tube on to his shoulder. Then he pointed it east and raised it up to the sky.

* * *

In Houston a bored director cut away from the overhead shot. There was only so much screen time anyone could give to a shot of three motor vehicles driving along an unexciting stretch of highway. His last instructions to the cameraman were, "Let me know if you see anything interesting."

At that moment, Janoris Hall saw the patrol car crest the brow of the hill. Traffic was light and there were no vehicles between him and them. That was perfect. "Wagons roll!" Janoris called into his phone mike and the two dumper trucks eased out of the lot. They started lumbering down Route 190, one in either lane, barely doing thirty and completely blocking the westbound side of the highway. Congo 3, the Range Rover, moved forward and took its slot in the middle of the exit, right by the side of the road.

Now Janoris leaned down low and peered upward through the windscreen. Yeah, there the helicopter was, hovering over the cars like a mama bird watching over her fledglings. "You see that, Bobby?" he asked.

"Yeah, man, just lining her up," came the reply.

"Don't go too soon, bro. Gotta let the dumpsters do their thing." Janoris looked up the road. The convoy was practically opposite him now. "Go Congo 3." The Range Rover slipped on to Route 190, staying in the outside lane, not going too fast. Behind it, the driver of the police patrol car signaled left and led the convoy into the inside lane. Congo 3 sped up to maintain position right next to the patrol car.

"Go Congo 4, go Peterbilt," said Janoris, and the Porsche led the truck out on to the highway.

The helicopter was right above them now.

The patrol car driver had realized that the trucks up ahead were blocking his way. He turned on the flashing lights on his roof and hit the siren. The trucks didn't budge. He was going to be right up their rear ends any second, so he slowed a little, forcing the minivan and the BearCat to lose momentum, too.

Up above, the cameraman's eyes had been caught by the flashing light. He patched a message through to the TV news studio. "We got something happening here, coupla dump trucks blocking the way. The state troopers must be pissed, 'cause they've turned on the lights."

"OK, keep tabs on it, we'll cut to you if anything happens."

Then something happened. The cameraman muttered, "What the hell . . . ?" as the two trucks veered left, one behind the other. Then he shouted, "Are you getting this?" as the lead Kenworth crossed the yellow center line and stopped right across the oncoming, eastbound lanes. The second Kenworth curved around the far side of the lead truck, stopped, then began reversing back the way it had come to block the westbound carriageway on which the prison convoy was travelling.

Down behind Bubba's, Bobby Z pulled the trigger on the FIM-92 Stinger anti-aircraft missile launcher that was resting on his right shoulder, launching a 22-pound missile that shot into the sky at more than twice the speed of sound. Its sensors locked into the exhaust pipes placed just above and to the rear of the chopper's passenger compartment. Impact was less than a second later.

No one aboard the helicopter even knew that anyone had fired at them. They were all blown to pieces: alive and well one second, dead and gone the next.

The feed to Houston went dead. So no one in the studio or watching on TV ever saw what happened down on Route 190.

The patrol car driver figured he could lead the convoy past the trucks by slewing right and going down the grass verge. He assumed that the Range Rover driver was bound to hit the brakes when he saw a cop screaming across his front. But the Range Rover didn't slow down. It stayed right where it was as the patrol car slammed against it and stayed there as sparks flew, metal ground against metal and the front panels of both vehicles crumpled.

Now both trucks were lined up diagonally across the highway, parallel with one another, but slightly apart.

The dumpsters began to lift, the tailgates swung open and rock-hard, abrasive rubble crashed down on to the road, forming an impenetrable roadblock and behind it a killing ground.

Congo 3's driver, knowing what was about to happen, timed his move perfectly. He swung right, skimming past the Kenworth blocking his carriageway with inches—and milliseconds—to spare. The patrol car, trying to follow him, was hit by an avalanche of concrete, brick and stone and was sent spinning off the blacktop and smashing into the pine trees that grew just beyond the highway's edge.

The driver of the minivan containing Johnny Congo was suddenly faced with a choice. He could crash into the truck, or the rubble. He slammed on the brakes, yanked the wheel to the right and went skidding broadsides into the raised, emptied trailer.

Inside the back of the minivan, the impact of the crash sent the guard hurtling across the compartment, just missing Johnny Congo as various parts of his anatomy smashed into the bench, the steel sides of the minivan and the metal grating across the windows.

Congo himself, not knowing what the snatch-plan was, but seeing that whatever was going to happen was happening now, had braced himself for the impact. His hands were gripping the chain that held him to the floor and his huge biceps were tensed. Even so, his arms were nearly ripped from their socket as the crash happened and if his head hadn't been tucked down by his knees it would have been knocked off by the guard's flying body.

When the minivan finally came to rest, the guard was lying like a discarded toy, his limbs all askew on the minivan floor, still just breathing but completely helpless. As for Johnny Congo, he felt bruised, battered and almost torn in two. But that aside, he was fine.

Then he smelled gas vapors seeping into the back of the van and suddenly he was screaming, "Get me outta here!" and shuffling across the compartment, away from the side that had hit the dumper truck. He was planning to holler as loud as he could and batter against the side of the van. But as he got to the side window and peered through it, his shouts stopped dead in his throat as he saw what was happening outside.

Burning debris from the helicopter had fallen to the earth like fiery boulders from a volcano. The main rotor assembly had cut a swathe through the pines. A severed head was bouncing along the road like a bowling ball. Small fires had broken out in half a dozen places and something big and very heavy had pretty well flattened the cabin of a massive truck that was blocking the highway behind the convoy, just like the two in front had done.

The BearCat had come to a halt with its flat, black fender and armor-plated nose almost touching the minivan. Behind it Congo could see a fancy white Porsche SUV. Someone was getting out of it carrying what looked like about eight inches of gray plastic piping, attached to four short, skinny legs. Behind the first guy, two more brothers were emerging from the Porsche. They were carrying mean-looking guns, with rotating drum magazines slung beneath them like old-fashioned Tommy guns. *Yeah!* thought Johnny Congo, *that is more like it.*

The Krakatoa is a very simple but brutally effective weapon. It consists of a short length of tubing, closed at one end by a plastic disc, held by a locking ring and filled with high-explosive RDX powder. A fuse wire runs through the plastic disc into the explosive powder.

At the other end of the tube, another locking ring holds a

shallow copper cone, shaped like a Chinese coolie's hat, whose point faces inwards, toward the RDX powder.

One of these weapons was placed on the ground, directly opposite the rear of the BearCat. The man who'd put it there stepped back a couple of paces, taking care not to stand directly behind the Krakatoa. He was holding a switch attached to the other end of the fuse wire. He pressed the switch. The Krakatoa erupted and the heat and force of the explosion turned the copper disc into a molten projectile that rocketed forward and smashed into the BearCat with the force of an anti-tank missile. The rear end of the armored personnel carrier disintegrated. It was impossible to believe that anyone, even if they were wearing body armor, could possibly be left alive inside it, but just to make sure the gunmen opened up.

They were holding the Atchisson Assault Shotguns, otherwise known in their present-day form as AA-12s, which may just be the deadliest, most destructive infantry weapon on earth. The AA-12 holds up to thirty-two rounds of 12-gauge ammunition, which it fires at a rate of 300 rounds a minute. Emptying two magazines into a confined space filled with human beings has the same effect on them as throwing them into a gigantic Magimix. They aren't just killed. They're obliterated.

The gunmen slammed new drums into their weapons and strode toward the minivan. The man who'd operated the Krakatoa ran back toward the Porsche and caught a long set of bolt cutters someone threw to him from the car.

The leading gunman was right up alongside the van now. He slammed the palm of his hand on the door panel. "You in there, Johnny?" he shouted.

"Damn straight, now get me out!"

"You all right?"

"I won't be, you keep jabbering on like that."

"You'd better get away from the door, bro."

A second later the entire lock assembly was smashed to pieces

57

by a single burst of fire from the AA-12. The doors flew open and a great, predatory grin spread across Johnny's face as he saw the bolt cutters in the hands of the Maalik Angel who was climbing up into the minivan. It took just seconds for the cutters to break apart the leg irons hobbling Johnny's feet, the chain attaching him to the floor of the van, the belly chain around his waist and the links from that to his wrists. Johnny stretched his arms wide, both hands touching the sides of the minivan. He rolled his head to loosen up his neck and shoulder muscles. Then he called out through the door of the van, "Now gimme that gun."

Johnny caught the AA-12 with one hand as it was thrown to him. Then he turned to confront the agony-racked and whimpering Offender Transportation Office guard who lay huddled on the floor behind him. "How d'ya like this sandwich, you motherf—"

The rest of the word was lost as the shotgun blast echoed around the confined space of the minivan. Johnny took a look at the smashed red mess that used to be the guard's face, chuckled to himself, then climbed out of the van and on to the burning highway.

"Car's waiting for you up ahead, man," the chain-cutter Angel said.

"Gimme a moment," Johnny replied. He walked around to the front of the van. As he got there, the guard in the passenger seat was trying to get the door open.

"Here, let me give you a hand with that," Johnny said.

He opened the minivan door. The dazed guard fell through it on to the road. Johnny watched him trying to get to his feet for a couple of seconds, then he blew him away: three shots in less than a second that picked up the guard and threw him against the minivan like a doll being hurled aside by a spoiled child.

Johnny looked into the cabin. He couldn't decide if the driver was dead or merely unconscious. So he fired another three more rounds into him just to put an end to any doubts.

Then he let the Angels lead him to the Range Rover that was waiting on the far side of the trucks. It raced a mile back down the road and then veered off into an open field where another helicopter was coming in to land. Johnny was bundled into it and it took off again immediately, swooping low over the highway battle zone, where the Angels had set off the timers attached to the Jerrycans in the truck cabins, so now the trucks were all ablaze, belching flames and smoke.

Traffic had begun to pile up on either side of the barricades formed by the trucks and the rubble they'd been carrying. Customers were running out of Bubba's to stare at the mayhem. In the confusion the Angels piled into Congos 1, 2 and 5 and speed away eastwards.

About five miles out of Beaumont Congo 5 in which Johnny was riding turned into a field where a short field take-off and landing Cessna 172 was waiting for him with its engine ticking over. Johnny transferred into it and the pilot immediately gunned the engine and took off. As soon as they were airborne Johnny made a request of the pilot who gave him a puzzled frown; then he grinned and said, "Sure, why not? I guess you must be real hungry," and radioed ahead.

Back at the Walls Unit, a nervous prison governor was explaining to Johnny Congo's attorney Shelby Weiss and his family friend, the well-known entrepreneur and philanthropist D'Shonn Brown, that the execution was being postponed. It appeared that the convoy carrying Johnny Congo to Hunstville had been ambushed. Congo himself had disappeared. There was no trace of him, alive or dead, at the ambush site. Nor was it clear what the exact purpose of the ambush had been.

"What's that supposed to mean?" asked Weiss impatiently.

"I guess it means that we don't know if Congo was taken by friendly gangbangers who wanted to free him, or enemies who wanted to kill him."

"I want to speak to the governor," said D'Shonn Brown.

"I am the governor."

"No, I mean the Governor of Texas. I want to speak to him now. I want to know what's happening here and what he plans to do about it."

So did the entire national and regional media, who were besieging the operational command post, demanding that Chantelle Dixon Pomeroy come out and explain how the Texas judicial system had so catastrophically failed to deliver a condemned man to his execution.

"Do you even know where Johnny Congo is?" one reporter demanded.

A look of panic flashed across Chantelle's face before she recovered her usual self-possession. "I'm afraid that is sensitive information and I can't speak to that point at this time."

"There's nothing sensitive about a simple yes or no. Do you know where he is?"

"Ah . . . I can't . . . that's to say it's not appropriate . . ."

"You don't know, do you? The most wanted man in Texas has missed his own execution and you have no idea at all where he might be. Isn't that so?"

"Well, I wouldn't put it that way at all," blustered Chantelle Dixon Pomeroy.

But she didn't have to put it any way. It was obvious to everyone holding a mike, or aiming a camera, or watching at home on TV: Johnny Congo had got clean away.

When the Cessna 172 carrying Johnny Congo landed at the private aviation terminal of Jack Brooks Regional Airport, it immediately taxied to where a silver Citation X jet waited on the hardstand to receive him, with all its engines warming up.

Johnny climbed on board and an elegantly uniformed blonde stewardess was waiting for him at the top of the boarding ladder. She led him to the rear cabin where an impeccable dark gray suit, white shirt and deep blue silk tie, with black silk socks, shoes and belt were laid out on the bunk.

Showing no emotion whatsoever, the stewardess helped him out of his prison garb, which was emblazoned with the Death Row "DR." She carried it away discreetly and left him to change into the suit.

When he was fully attired Johnny checked the contents of the crocodile-skin briefcase that lay on the opposite bunk. He hummed with satisfaction as he counted the wads of $100 bills, which totalled $50,000, and the bearer bonds to the value of $5 million. There was also a smartphone untraceable to him and a number of passports, including a diplomatic one from the state of Kazundu in the name of His Majesty King John Kikuu Tembo.

Johnny made a regal figure as he emerged from the rear cabin and went forward to the lounge of the Citation. Having been given the statutory two hours' notice of the Citation's flight plans the U.S. Customs and Border Protection Service had sent an officer to process the flight and His Majesty King John graciously allowed her to stamp his passport with an exit visa.

Johnny had stipulated the hire of a Citation X for the reason that it was the fastest commercial jet in the skies. The aircrew had been told to expect African royalty as the passenger and they were suitably respectful. Shortly after take-off, as the Citation was speeding south across the Gulf of Mexico, the pretty brunette who was a member of the cabin crew giggled as she plucked up the courage to speak directly to him, "Excuse me, Your Majesty, but we were informed that you had a special request for your in-flight meal this evening."

Then with a flourish she set before him a bone-china plate on which lay a long sandwich, filled with meat and cheese and oozing mayonnaise.

Johnny Congo gave the girl a smile that pleased, excited and terrified her in just about equal proportions. "Right on!" he said. "I've been looking forward to my first Subway ever."

He took a rapacious bite, and beamed contentedly as his cheeks bulged and his mouth filled to overflowing. Then he lay back in the cream leather chair and chewed contentedly.

He was free and now he could concentrate every ounce of his strength and every cent of his enormous wealth on the complete and utter destruction of Hector Cross.

As they left U.S. airspace, Johnny Congo mused aloud, "Not Hector Cross alone. I am going to get that skinny bitch Jo Stanley who he's been screwing and also his itty-bitty baby girl. I am going to make Cross watch as I off them slowly, with tender loving care. Only then will I start working on him."

Night had fallen and Route 190 was no longer a war zone. But if anything the chaos had only increased in the aftermath of Johnny Congo's escape. Banks of floodlights lit up the road all the way from the gas station to the two burned-out dumper trucks, surrounded by their discharged cargoes of rubble that marked the point where the trap that caught the prison convoy had sprung shut. In truth though there was little need for any additional illumination: not with the headlights and multi-colored roof lights of ambulances, fire trucks, tow trucks and a host of police vehicles all attending the scene.

Every cop from Polk, Walker and San Jacinto counties had been called in to marshal the traffic that had piled up on either side of the blockage. Drivers were being directed away to a hastily arranged set of diversion routes, but not before every single one of them had been told to show their driver's license, provide contact details and describe anything that they had seen, or even better recorded during the brief, bloody, one-sided battle. Everybody who'd been at the Shell gas station or Bubba's was also processed. As a result, more than two dozen witnesses had been asked to stay behind to be interviewed at greater length by the detectives, and numerous phones and tablets containing still photographs and video footage had been collected.

Pretty much every image they contained had been already uploaded on to one social media platform or another by the time the first squad car arrived at the scene—this was the twenty-first century, after all—and the best footage was already being played on TV stations across the nation. The entire media corps that had been gathered in Huntsville for the execution had decamped to Route 190 to report on the events that had prevented it, and other news organizations had still more personnel and equipment hurrying to this stretch of the East Texas highway.

To add to the hullabaloo, the number of law enforcement agencies present at the scene was multiplying like viruses in a petri dish. The Governor had requested assistance from the FBI and called out the Texas State Guard, but no clear chain of command had yet been established and so the usual turkey-cocking was taking place between representatives of the various local, state and national organizations, all jostling to make sure that they took any credit that was going for any shred of success, while avoiding the looming shitstorm of criticism and blame that would pound down on anyone deemed in any way responsible for the afternoon's disaster. Anyone like Major Robert Malinga of the Texas Rangers, for example.

"My God, Connie, did you ever in your life see anything like this?" he asked as he picked his way between the charred remnants of the shot-down helicopter toward the wreckage of the BearCat. A few yards away a young cop, not much more than a kid, was slumped on his knees by the side of the road, throwing up into the grass. Just beyond him a dismembered head, still wearing the headphones of a helicopter pilot, was wedged between the branches of a pine, like a kid's soccer ball in a suburban garden.

"I did a tour in the Pech Valley, Afghanistan," the woman walking alongside Malinga said. "Things got real kinetic there. Saw buses hit by IEDs, markets after T-men had blown themselves up. This is right up there with the best of them."

63

Lieutenant Consuela Hernandez was Malinga's second-in-command. Every time she went home, every other woman in the family—her sisters, mother, grandmother, aunts, cousins, all of them—would tell her how pretty she would be if she only made an effort. But making an effort, just so she could find some slob to spend the rest of her life with, the way all those other women had done, was not Connie's style. She had served six years as a Criminal Investigations Special Agent in the U.S. Military Police Corps before joining the Rangers. Within a week of arriving at A Company, she'd already convinced Malinga that she was a good cop. The one thing he couldn't understand was why she was a Ranger. "The MPs have always been a great place for a woman to get ahead. But I hate to say this, the Rangers haven't had the greatest reputation when it comes to gender equality."

"I know," Hernandez said. "That's why I'm here. Just wanted the chance to piss you all off."

For a fraction of a second, Malinga had feared that he'd been landed with a professional ball-breaker, the kind who was only ever one off-color joke away from a sex-discrimination suit. Then he noticed the sly smile playing around the corners of Hernandez's mouth, realized she was yanking his chain and burst out laughing. From that moment on they'd got along just fine.

"Now I really do feel back in the Pech," Hernandez said, looking at the BearCat.

The back of the armored personnel carrier had been obliterated. The rear axle had collapsed so that the whole vehicle had slumped toward the ground. A couple of crime scene investigators were working their way through the vehicle. In the light from their torches, Malinga could see the blackened corpses of the SWAT personnel who'd been sitting in the back of the carrier when it had been attacked. Every one of them had been wearing helmets and body armor, but their bodies had been ripped apart by the sheer ferocity of the assault.

"What the hell hit them?" Malinga asked one of the CSIs.

"Everything," the investigator replied. "First, there was some kind of projectile that was powerful enough to blow through the armor on the rear of the vehicle like it wasn't any thicker than a tin can. Then someone just let rip with an unbelievable barrage of shotgun fire from no more than twenty feet. We've counted almost sixty twelve-gauge cartridges on the road and they must've been fired unbelievably fast. No one inside had time to fire a single round."

"They weren't in any condition to shoot," Hernandez said. "Even if the blast hadn't killed them, they'd have been totally stunned and disoriented. Talk about a flash-bang."

"Any trace of the perpetrators anywhere? Fingerprints, DNA, anything?" Malinga asked.

The investigator shook his head. "Not that we've found. There's a limit to what we can do here, so we'll take the vehicles away for examination. But my bet is we'll be lucky to find anything at all. They torched the trucks they rode in on. Whoever they were, they sure knew what they were doing."

"That they did," Malinga agreed. Walking away from the BearCat, he spoke to Hernandez. "You know the single most common denominator among convicted criminals? Stupidity. Sure, they're sociopathic, liable to have substance-abuse issues, have an exceptionally high rate of clinical depression, all that good stuff. But above all, they're dumb. Not these guys, though. They were real smart, or the guy in charge of them was. And they had money. They had trucks, getaway vehicles, automatic weapons, ground-to-air missiles, for Chrissakes."

"That's some serious coin," Hernandez agreed.

"So the question becomes, was Johnny Congo rich and smart enough to put this together from jail, or was there someone else who did it for him?"

"Smart and rich, huh?" Hernandez mused. "I don't know whether to arrest this paragon or marry him."

*　*　*

65

Jo Stanley was lying asleep next to Hector Cross in the master bedroom of his London home, a charming old mews house, impeccably decorated in a restrained, masculine style, just a stone's throw from Hyde Park Corner, when she was woken by the buzz of her phone against her bedside cabinet. She rubbed her eyes as she blearily made out Ronnie Bunter's name on the screen. "Hey, Ronnie," she murmured, trying not to wake Cross. He stirred and for a moment she was worried, but then he grunted and rolled over, taking half the duvet with him as he fell back to sleep.

"Hi, look, I'm sorry to be calling you now," Bunter was saying. "I guess it must be pretty early in England."

"Quarter to five in the morning."

"Oh, maybe I should call back later . . ."

"No, it's OK, I'm awake now. Hold on, I'm just going somewhere I can talk." Jo got out of bed and tiptoed across to her bathroom. She closed the door behind her, turned on the light, groaned at her pallid, un-made-up, early-morning face in the bathroom mirror and said, "So, how are you?"

"Oh, you know, getting by."

Obviously, he wasn't. "And how's Betty?" Jo asked.

"Not so good," Bunter said sadly. "Her condition's gotten a lot worse. That's kind of why I called you."

Jo frowned, concerned as much by the exhaustion she could hear in her old boss's voice as the news he was bringing her: "How do you mean?"

"Well, I guess I'm going to have to take a step back, away from the firm, so I can spend more time with Betty, whatever time she has left . . ."

"Oh, Ronnie, that's such a beautiful thing to do," said Jo, "putting Betty first like that. God, I think you've got me shedding a tear!"

She reached for a face towel and dabbed it against her eyes as Bunter said, "I guess that means that Brad will be taking over."

Jo forgot all about her tears as she absorbed the thought of such a radical, unexpected changing of the guard. "OK-ay-ay . . ."

"You sound kinda skeptical about that idea."

"No, not at all, Brad's a great attorney."

"But he's not the right person, I get it. And I don't necessarily disagree. Maybe I should make someone else senior partner . . ."

"But, Ronnie, you can't do that. I mean, this is a family business. Your daddy started it. You took it on. If Brad didn't take over from you, that's basically telling everyone in Texas law that you don't think your boy is any good. Brad would never forgive you till the day he died. You'd lose him as a son. He has to get the job."

"Yeah, you're right," said Bunter without much enthusiasm. "Maybe I'm just being old-fashioned. I guess the way Brad practices law is more in tune with the way the whole world is these days."

"I guess."

"But, Jo, there's something else I have to tell you, and you're not going to like it."

Jo was struck by an icy feeling of dread as she realized that whatever Bunter was about to tell her was the real reason he had called now, rather than waiting for a more sociable time of day. "Go ahead . . ." she said.

"Johnny Congo's escaped. I just saw it on the TV news. Someone—they don't know who just yet—ambushed the convoy taking him to Huntsville for the execution."

"Oh God, no . . ." Jo leaned her back against the wall and slid slowly down till she came to rest on the marble tiles of the bathroom floor. She could hear the sound of footsteps outside the bathroom. Hector must have woken up. Jo held her head in one hand, her eyes screwed shut as she lowered her voice and asked, "What happened? Does anyone know where he is right now?"

"No, they don't even know for sure that he's alive. But in the absence of a body, we have to assume he is."

Jo said nothing. Bunter broke the silence. "I'm so sorry, Jo, I know what a shock this must be to you."

Her voice was cracking as she said, "It's my fault."

"No, don't you go thinking that. How could you possibly be to blame for what happened today?"

"Because it wouldn't have happened if I'd let Heck kill Johnny, when he had the chance. He wanted to do it, but I said no."

"Of course you did. You believe in the rule of law, as you should."

"But what good is the rule of law if people like Johnny Congo can defy it, and get away with their crimes?" Jo asked, feeling as though all her most cherished beliefs suddenly counted for nothing. "I was the one who wanted to play by the rules and now that monster is out there . . ."

"Listen, Hector's beaten Congo once, he can do it again. He'd never blame you, either. He's a better man than that."

"He'd never blame me out loud, no. But deep down inside, he'll know that he was right, and that Catherine Cayla's in jeopardy because I wouldn't let him trust his own instincts."

Jo was crying again now. She cursed under her breath, looked around for something to wipe her face and pulled some toilet paper from the roll as she heard Bunter saying, "Listen, Jo, I know how tough it must be for you right now, but sweetheart, take some advice from an old man who's seen a lot in his time. Don't rush into anything. Take your time to process what I've just told you, and give Hector time to do the same thing too. Believe me, things'll work out better that way. You'll be a lot stronger facing up to this as a couple than as two individuals."

Jo shook her head, as if Bunter could see her. "No, I can't . . . I have to leave. Being with Heck is like living beneath a volcano. When the volcano's quiet and the sun's shining, life is wonderful. But you know that the volcano's going to erupt some day, and when it does, your whole world will be destroyed. I thought I could deal with that, but now Congo's free and I feel so scared . . . I can't live like that any more."

At the very moment she was talking about leaving Cross, the one thing Jo suddenly wanted more than anything else in the world was to feel his arms around her and to lean her head against his chest. There was a pause before Bunter said, "Well, if that's really how you feel, you'd better come on back to the firm. If you and Heck are meant to be together, you'll find your way to each other again. But until you do, come back to Houston, back to the office. It'll be good for you, and good for us too."

"But I already quit."

"Did you? I don't recall getting a formal letter of resignation from you. And I damn sure never fired you."

"I guess not," Jo admitted. "But if you're not going to be there, what am I going to do?"

She got up and examined herself in the mirror again. Her complexion still looked just as pale as it had before and her hair was a mess, but now she had red, watery eyes as well. She resolved that she wasn't going to leave the bathroom until she'd made herself look a hell of a lot more presentable. If she was going to leave Hector, she didn't want him to remember her looking anything at all like this.

"Be my eyes and ears," Bunter was saying. "The doc wants me to stay away as much as I can, but that's going to be impossible unless I know for sure what's going on."

"You want me to spy for you? I can't see that being too popular."

"No, I don't want you to spy for me. But you can represent me, like an ambassador, making my views known, and at the same time relaying back other people's opinions to me. And of course, you can continue your work as a legal assistant. You're damn good at the job, Jo. Folks'll be glad to have you around."

"Thanks, Ronnie, I really appreciate that. And I guess I'm

going to hold you to it, too. I'm coming home to Houston. I wish more than anything else in the world that I weren't. But I've got to leave Hector . . ." She gave a deep, despairing sigh. "And now I've got to find a way to tell him."

Their lovemaking that night had been especially intense and satisfying for both Hector and Jo Stanley. Afterward he fell into such a deep and dreamless sleep that he did not hear Jo leave the bed or the bedroom. When he woke again he heard her in her bathroom. He checked the bedside clock and found the time was not yet five in the morning. He roused himself and went through to his own bathroom.

On his way back he paused by her closed door and heard her busy on the telephone. He smiled and thought that she was probably calling her mother in Abilene. Sometimes he wondered what they still had to talk about after phoning each other almost every night. He returned to the bed and soon drifted off into sleep once more.

When he woke again it was seven o'clock and Jo was sequestered in her dressing room. Hector slipped on his dressing gown and went through to the nursery. He returned to the bed with Catherine in his arms wearing a fresh diaper and clutching her morning bottle. He propped himself on the pillows and cradled Catherine in his lap.

He studied her face as she drank. It seemed to him that she was growing more beautiful and more like her dead mother Hazel with every passing day.

At last he heard the door to Jo's dressing room open. As he looked up the smile melted from his face. Jo was fully dressed and she carried her small travelling valise. Her expression was somber.

"Where are you going?" he asked, but she ignored the question.

"Johnny Congo has escaped from prison," she said. Hector felt the ice forming around his heart.

70

He shook his head in denial. "How do you know this?" he whispered.

"Ronnie Bunter told me. I have been on the phone with him half the night, discussing it." She broke off to cough and clear her throat, and then she looked up at him again and her eyes were swimming with misery. She went on, "You will blame me for this, won't you, Hector?"

He shook his head, trying to find the words to deny it.

"You will go after Johnny Congo again," she said with quiet certainty.

"Do I have any choice?" he asked, but the question was rhetorical.

"I have to leave you," Jo said.

"If you truly love me you will stay."

"No. Because I truly love you I must go."

"Where to?"

"Ronnie Bunter has offered me my old job back at Bunter and Theobald. At least there I can do something to protect Catherine's interests in the trust."

"Will you ever come back to me?"

"I doubt it." She began to weep openly, but went on speaking through her tears: "I never imagined there could be any other man like you. But being with you is like living on the slopes of a volcano. One slope faces the sun. It is warm, fertile, beautiful and safe there. It is filled with love and laughter." She broke off to choke back a sob, before she went on. "The other slope of you is full of shadows and dark frightening things, like hatred and revenge; like anger and death. I would never know when the mountain would erupt and destroy itself and me."

"If I can't stop you from going, then at least kiss me once more before you go," he said, and she shook her head.

"No, if I kiss you it will weaken my resolve, and we will be stuck with each other forever. That must not happen. We were never meant for each other, Hector. We would destroy each

71

other." She looked deeply into his eyes and went on softly, "I believe in the law, while you believe you are the law. I have to go, Hector. Goodbye, my love."

She turned her back on him and went out through the door, closing it softly behind her.

There were two people Major Bobby Malinga wanted to talk to right away: the only two people outside the prison system who he knew for sure had been in contact with Johnny Congo after his arrival at the Polunsky Unit. And both fitted the description of "smart and rich." The first of the pair to fit Malinga into his busy schedule was D'Shonn Brown. Malinga went to his private office. It was large, decorated with the kind of minimal, modern, tasteful understatement that screamed serious money far more cleverly than a gaudy display of lurid marble and gold ever could. The personal assistant who led Malinga in was an impeccably mannered woman whose plain, knee-length charcoal skirt suit and white silk blouse were both tailored to fit her trim figure perfectly, but without the remotest hint of titillation.

Though Brown had met a great many celebrities, business leaders and senior politicians, he did not display any photographs of those encounters on his walls. His diplomas for his undergraduate degree from Baylor, his master's from Stanford Law and the state bar exams of both California and Texas, framed behind his desk, were the only overt sign of ego. And they were there for a very obvious and even necessary purpose. Several academic studies have shown that even the most liberal Caucasians harbor unconscious assumptions about the intellectual abilities of young African-American males. This was just a way of reminding visitors to D'Shonn Brown's office that however smart they were, he was almost certainly smarter.

Malinga took off his hat. He was of the opinion that a man's office was as personal to him as his house and courtesy demanded the removal of headgear in both places. There was no hat stand, so he placed the hat on the desk, sat down opposite Brown and looked at the impressive display behind him. "You sure spent a lot more time in school than I ever did," he said, going the self-deprecating, Columbo route.

Brown shrugged noncommittally, then asked, "What can I do for you, Major?"

"You came to Huntsville for Johnny Congo's execution," replied Malinga, getting out his notebook and pen. "How come?"

"He reached out to me, through his attorney Shelby Weiss, and asked me to be there." Brown sounded relaxed, open, like an honest citizen with nothing to hide, doing his best to assist the police with their investigation.

"So you're a close friend of Congo's?"

"Not really. I hadn't seen him since I was a kid. But he was tight with my brother Aleutian, who was killed last year. As far as I'm aware, Johnny Congo doesn't have any family. So I guess I was the only person he could think of."

"Did he ask you to do anything else, aside from come to his execution?"

"Johnny didn't ask me anything directly. But Mr. Weiss told me that he had expressed a wish for me to organize his funeral and also a memorial party in his honor."

"And you did this?"

"Of course. I found a plot for Johnny's grave, arranged flowers, a mortician and so on for the funeral and made preparations for the party, too. My assistant can give you all the details."

"Even though you hardly knew the man?"

"I knew my brother and he knew Johnny. That was good enough for me."

"Who was paying for all this?"

"Johnny paid. He arranged for me to be given money through Mr. Weiss."

"How much money?"

"Two million dollars," said Brown, without missing a beat, letting Malinga know that a sum like that was no big deal to him.

Malinga wasn't nearly so cool about it. "Two million . . . for a funeral . . . you gotta be kidding me!"

"Why?" Brown asked. "Whatever you or I might think of Johnny Congo's crimes, and I don't deny that they were heinous, he was a very wealthy man. As I understand it, his lifestyle in Africa was extremely lavish. So he wanted to go out in style."

"And for that he needed two million dollars?"

"It's not a question of need, Major Malinga. No one needs to drop a million bucks on a wedding, or a birthday party, or a bar mitzvah, but there are plenty of people right here in this city who would do that without blinking. Hell, I've been to parties where Beyoncé was the cabaret, and there's your two million, just for her. Johnny had the money. He wasn't going to be spending it where he was going. Why not use it to give his guests a good time?"

"OK . . . OK," said Malinga, just about accepting Brown's logic. "So what happened to this money?"

"I opened a special account, just for Johnny's events. Some of it I spent, and again I can provide you with any receipts or documentation you require. The rest is still in the account, untouched."

"And you knew nothing about Congo's escape plans?"

"No, I knew about his plans for his funeral. And I had two million very good reasons for believing they were serious."

"So this all came as a total surprise to you?"

"Yes, it did. I drove up to Huntsville, steeling myself for the experience of seeing a man die before my eyes—not something I've ever seen before, thank God. First I knew about any escape was a reporter sticking a mike in front of my face and asking me what I thought about it, live on TV. I didn't have a clue what she was talking about. Felt like a damn fool, if you really want to know."

74

"And none of that two million was used to buy the weapons, transportation or personnel used to free a convicted murderer and kill fifteen police officers and state officials?"

Brown looked Malinga straight in the eye. "No, absolutely not."

"Did Mr. Weiss say anything to you that indicated the money should be used for such a purpose?"

"What?" For the first time Brown raised his voice. "Are you seriously suggesting that one of the state's most respected criminal attorneys, together with a prominent businessman who is himself qualified to practice law, would have a conversation about the illegal seizure of a convicted killer?"

Malinga did not raise his. "I'm not making any suggestions, Mr. Brown, I'm asking you a question."

"Well, the answer is an absolute, categorical 'no.'"

"OK then, here's another. Did you have any communication with Johnny Congo, aside from what you heard from Mr. Weiss?"

"Again no. How could I have done? Prisoners awaiting execution have a very limited ability to communicate with anyone. And if Johnny had ever tried to speak or write to me, I imagine they'd have a record of it at the Polunsky Unit. Do they have such a record, Major Malinga?"

"No."

"Well, there you go." Brown exhaled, letting the tension out. In his previously calm but authoritative style he said, "I think we're done, don't you? I appreciate that you've got a job to do, Major Malinga. So I'll make this as simple and straightforward as I can. I had nothing whatever to do with Johnny Congo's escape. I had no knowledge of any plans for such an escape. I was not involved in financing any illegal activities or purchases on Johnny Congo's behalf. None of the money given to me to fund Johnny Congo's funeral and memorial event has been used for anything other than the purpose for which it was intended. Are we clear on that?"

"Guess so."

"Then I wish you good luck with your ongoing investigation. My assistant will show you out."

Cross had a way of dealing with the pain that could hit a man when a woman had ripped his heart out through his chest, thrown it to the floor and then harpooned it with a single stab of her stiletto heel. First he sealed it up inside an imaginary thick lead box; then he dropped it, like radioactive waste, into the deepest, darkest recesses of his mind. Once that was done, he got back to work.

Cross was already bearing down hard on his emotions and turning his thoughts to the two issues that would be dominating his life for the foreseeable future: the security of Bannock Oil's Angolan operations, and the hunt for Johnny Congo. Now that his arch-enemy was at large once again, Cross knew that he would have to go back to war. Sooner or later, Congo would come after him, and when he did, there could only be one winner, one survivor.

He called Agatha, the personal assistant who'd been a secretary, confidante and unfailing ally to Hazel for years before transferring her allegiance to him. "John Bigelow wants me to talk to some State Department official called Bobby Franklin, but he never gave me a contact number. Call John's office to get it, then call Franklin to set up a Skype meeting in the next couple of days."

"Of course," Agatha replied with her usual unflappable efficiency.

"Thanks. And then I need to talk to Imbiss and the O'Quinns, but in person. So please track them down and wherever they are in the world, tell them they need to be in London by lunchtime tomorrow."

"What if there aren't any flights?"

"Send a plane. Send one for each of them if you have to. But they have to be here."

"Don't worry, sir, they will be."

"Thank you, Agatha. If anyone else said that, I'd think they were probably bluffing. But I can absolutely count on you getting my people here. None of them would dare say no to you."

"Thank you, sir."

The thought of having his best people around him raised Cross's spirits. Dave Imbiss didn't look like a man you'd want beside you in the heat of battle. No matter how hard he worked at his fitness, he still had a plump, fresh-faced demeanour. But that appearance was deceptive. Imbiss's bulk was all muscle, not fat. He'd been awarded a Bronze Star for heroism in combat when serving as a U.S. Infantry captain in Afghanistan and he had brains as well as brawn. Imbiss was Cross Bow's resident techie, a master in the dark arts of cyber-warfare, surveillance, hacking and all-purpose gadgetry. Paddy O'Quinn was leaner, edgier, a quick-witted, hot-tempered Irishman who'd served under Cross in the SAS until he'd punched a junior officer whose decisions under fire were threatening to cost his entire fifteen-man troop their lives. That mutinous blow saved those soldiers' lives, cost O'Quinn his military career and made him the first name on Cross's list when he began recruiting for Cross Bow.

Paddy O'Quinn was as tough as they came, but he had met his match—and more—in his wife. Anastasia Voronova O'Quinn was a beautiful blonde who looked like a supermodel, fought like a demon and could drink any man under the table. Nastiya, as her friends were allowed to call her, had been trained in the arts of subterfuge and deceit by the FSB, the Russian security agency that was the post-Communist successor to the KGB, while the Spetsnaz—Russian Special Forces—had taught her how to inflict pain and, if necessary, death in a myriad different ways. As good as his men were, Cross believed that he could still more than match them. But even he would think twice before picking a fight with Nastiya.

Together they had already beaten Johnny Congo once. Now they would do it a second time. And then they'd never have to do it again.

D'Shonn Brown had said nothing remotely incriminating. There was as yet no evidence whatever to suggest that he had done anything wrong. On that basis, any suggestion that he had been involved in Johnny Congo's escape could reasonably be taken as unjustified and even racially biased. But Malinga couldn't shake a feeling that hung around the back of his mind like an itch that needed scratching: a cop's intuition that he had just witnessed a slick, proficient, shameless display of lying. He wasn't going to voice that suspicion publicly just yet. He wasn't that dumb. But still, it meant that he could approach his interview with Shelby Weiss primed for any hint that Johnny Congo's attorney had something to hide.

If Brown's working environment was an exercise in contemporary design, Weiss's was far more traditional: wood panelling on the walls; bookshelves full of august legal tomes; all the vanity portraits that Brown had conspicuously avoided. The one thing they had in common was the framed diplomas. But whereas D'Shonn Brown's education had been as close to Ivy League as you could get west of the Appalachians; Weiss took a perverse pride in the fact that he had studied his law in the relatively humble surroundings of the Thurgood Marshall School of Law at Texas Southern University, a public college right in the heart of Houston on Cleburne Street. He wanted people to know that however slick he might look now, he'd started out as a blue-collar kid, working his way up from nothing by ability, determination and damned hard work. Juries lapped it up. Malinga had seen the Shelby Weiss Show enough times in enough courtrooms not to give a damn, one way or the other.

"This is a change," Weiss said as he shook Malinga's hand.

"I've cross-examined you enough times, Bobby. Don't recall that you've ever asked questions of me."

"First time for everything," Malinga said, settling into a padded leather chair that was a lot more comfortable than the ones in front of D'Shonn Brown's desk. "So, Mr. Weiss," he went on, "can you confirm that you visited Johnny Congo at the Allen B. Polunsky Unit on the twenty-seventh of October?"

"I can."

"And what was the substance of your discussion with Congo?"

Weiss grinned. "Oh, come on, you know perfectly well that client–attorney privilege prevents me from answering that question."

"But you discussed his legal situation in general?"

"Of course! I'm a lawyer. That's what we do."

"So how would you characterize his legal situation at that point? I mean, were you confident of being able to delay his execution?"

"Well, the man was a convicted killer, who'd used up all his appeals on his original charge before absconding from the State Penitentiary, spending several years on the run and then being apprehended. What would you say his chances were of a stay of execution?"

"Worse than zero."

"Precisely. Anyone can figure that out, including Johnny Congo. Nevertheless, anyone is entitled to the best defense, again including Johnny Congo. So I assured him that I would use my very best endeavors to keep him out of the chamber."

"And did you use those endeavors?"

"Absolutely. I made every call I could think of, right up to the Governor and beyond. Burned a lot of favors and, believe me, I'm not exactly Mr. Popular right now, not after someone turned Route 190 into a war zone."

"Did Congo pay you for doing that work on his behalf?"

"Sure he paid me. I don't represent a man like that *pro bono*."

"How much did he pay you?"

"I don't have to tell you that." There was a glass jar of brightly colored jelly beans standing on Weiss's desk. He unscrewed the lid and tilted the open jar in Malinga's direction: "Want one?"

"Nope."

"Suit yourself. So, where were we?"

"You were explaining how you couldn't tell me how much Johnny Congo paid you."

"Oh yeah . . ."

"But you can confirm that you paid two million dollars on Johnny Congo's behalf to D'Shonn Brown, and don't tell me that's privileged because I know it ain't. D'Shonn Brown is not your client. Any conversation with him or payment to him constitutes admissible evidence."

Weiss popped a couple of jelly beans into his mouth. "I wouldn't insult an experienced senior officer like you by pretending otherwise. Yes, I gave Mr. Brown the money. You can ask him what he did with it."

"Already have. I'm more interested in what you said when you gave it to him."

"I just passed on Mr. Congo's instructions."

"Which were?"

"Let me see . . ." Weiss leaned back and gazed upward as if Johnny Congo's words might be written or even projected on to the ceiling. Then he focused back on Malinga. "As I recall, Mr. Congo wanted Mr. Brown to gather up all the people he used to hang out with back in the day, so that they could pay their respects to him and see him off." Weiss chuckled to himself.

"What's so funny?" Malinga asked.

"D'Shonn Brown's a sharp kid. He told me that Johnny's buddies wouldn't be able to see him go, but they'd sure see him coming, seeing as most of them were already dead. I could see his point. But that didn't alter Mr. Congo's wishes. He basically wanted to have a lavish funeral, with a service in a cathedral

80

and a long line of hearses and limousines, followed by a party with Cristal champagne and Grey Goose vodka—he specified those brands."

"And this was going to cost two million dollars?"

"Evidently. Congo wanted Mr. Brown to, quote, 'lay it on real thick' and he wanted to 'impress upon him'—and that's another direct quote, I remember being struck by the formality—that this was all the wish of a dying man."

"And what conclusion did you draw from these instructions?"

"That they were exactly what they appeared: a convicted criminal with a lot of money wanting to give society the finger one last time."

"You had no reason to doubt that Johnny Congo was planning to attend his own funeral?"

"Well, he was laying out a fortune on it, and the state of Texas was absolutely determined to execute him, so no, why would I?"

"He'd got away before."

"All the more reason that people like you were going to make sure he didn't again. Are we done?" Shelby Weiss had suddenly lost his carefully worked air of relaxed bonhomie, just the way D'Shonn Brown had done.

"Almost," said Malinga, more than ever certain that there was something both of them were hiding. "Just one last thing I want to clear up. How come Johnny Congo called you?"

"Because I'm a good lawyer."

"Yeah, sure, but how would he know that? He'd been out of the country for years."

"I guess word gets around. And I was already a successful attorney when he was originally locked up in Huntsville, you know, before his first escape." Weiss put an emphasis on "first," just to remind Malinga about the second one. Then he said, "I didn't act for him at that point, but I certainly defended other guys on Death Row. No reason he couldn't have known about me."

"Have you ever, at any time prior to these past few weeks, represented Jonny Congo?" Bobby Malinga asked.

All the question needed was a one-word answer. It wouldn't have taken a second. But Weiss paused. He was about to say something, Malinga could see it, but then had second thoughts. Finally he spoke. "The first time in my life that I represented a man called Johnny Congo was when I was asked to come and meet him at the Allen B. Polunsky Unit on the twenty-seventh of September. There, is that specific enough for you?"

"Thank you," said Malinga. "That'll do just fine." He smiled as he got up. He shook Weiss's hand again and thanked him for his co-operation. And as he left the offices of Weiss, Mendoza and Burnett he felt more certain than ever that D'Shonn Brown and Shelby Weiss had played some part in Johnny Congo's escape.

You know, if someone had tossed a grenade into that bowl, it couldn't have spread the mess wider than Missy Catherine here managed," said Cross, sounding genuinely impressed at the havoc Catherine had brought to the simple business of eating her supper. There were spatterings of her chopped-up spaghetti and bolognese sauce all over the walls and the floor of the Cross Roads' compact kitchen, the table in front of Catherine's high chair, the chair itself and the tray that slotted on to it; not to mention her onesie, her plastic bib and, most impressively, her face, whose most noticeable feature was a huge, gummy grin, ringed by a magnificent spread of orangey-red sauce covering her chin, nose and chubby cheeks.

"She was putting on a special show for you," said Bonnie Hepworth, the nanny. She had known Catherine since the day she was born: she had been the maternity nurse on duty on that day of overwhelming joy, mixed with unbearable sorrow, when a baby had entered the world and her mother, fatally wounded by an assassin's bullet, had left it. Cross had been touched by Bonnie's warm heart, her kind smile and her un-

82

failing combination of patience, efficiency and sound common sense. He'd made her an offer she couldn't refuse. The patients of a Hampshire hospital had lost a first-rate nurse. Catherine Cayla Cross had gained a nanny who would never let this bereaved little girl lack a single moment of love and care.

"If that was the show, I dread to think what she's planning for the encore," Cross said.

"Chocolate pudding. Wait till that starts flying. You ain't seen nothing yet!"

Cross laughed, gazing in wonder at his daughter, his darling Kitty-Cross. How had she done it, he wondered? How could a tiny little person who had only just learned to say her first words fill his heart with so much love? He was helpless in her presence, yet the tenderness of his love for her was equalled by the fierceness of his determination to keep her safe.

Now that Johnny Congo was at large once again, Cross knew that he would have to go back to war. Sooner or later, Congo would come after him, and when he did, there could only be one winner, one survivor. This time, though, Cross would be alone on the battlefield. Jo's decision to leave had ripped open the emotional wound that she herself had helped heal. Cross wondered if there would ever be another chance to find someone new. One of the reasons Jo had left was that she thought he would blame her for Congo's escape. The truth was, he blamed himself much more for exposing her to the death, the pain and the harsh cruelties that were his inescapable companions.

"Mr. Cross . . . Mr. Cross!" His reverie was broken by Bonnie's voice. "There's a Skype call for you . . . from America."

Cross looked at his watch. In all the fussing over Catherine's dinner, he'd completely lost track of the time. "Snap out of it, man!" he told himself. "Work!"

He went into his study, sat down in front of the monitor and did a double-take. Bobby Franklin was not the middle-aged white male he had been expecting but an elegant African-American woman, whose fine features and lovely hazel eyes were given a scholarly touch by her tortoiseshell spectacles. That must have been the information that went missing when he'd lost contact with Bigelow, that afternoon on the Tay. To judge by the grainy image on the screen in front of him, Franklin was in her early to mid-thirties. "Hi," he said, "I'm Hector Cross."

A smile crossed her face. Cross frowned uncertainly. Had he said something amusing?

"Excuse me, Mr. Cross," Franklin said, "but there's something on your face and it looks a little like spaghetti sauce."

Now it was Cross's turn to grin, more from embarrassment than amusement. "That's my daughter's supper. I was crazy enough to try feeding her this evening. Where is it, exactly?"

"On your cheek and chin . . ." She paused as he dabbed at his face. "No, the other side . . . there you go!"

"Thanks. Hope that hasn't totally destroyed my credibility as a security expert."

"Not at all. And it's made you much more interesting as a man."

Cross felt the electrical charge of that first contact between a man and a woman. How strange to experience it through a pair of screens, thousands of miles apart. Pleased that the loss of Jo Stanley hadn't completely beaten him down, Cross looked at Franklin for a moment, just to let her know that he'd heard her.

"Speaking of interesting, you don't look much like an average Bob," he said.

She smiled again. "It's Bobbi, with an 'i,' short for Roberta."

"Well, I'm glad we've sorted that out," said Cross. "Now we should get down to business . . ."

"Good idea . . . so, do you know much about Africa, Mr. Cross?"

"Well, I was born in Kenya, spent the first eighteen years of my life there and the only reason I'm not a full Morani warrior of the Maasai tribe is that although I've undergone all the initiation rites, I've not been circumcised. So yes, I know a bit."

"Oh . . ." Franklin said, wincing. "Sounds like I should have done my homework before we met."

"Don't worry. It's quite a relief that Uncle Sam doesn't know everything about me."

She smiled. "Oh, I'm sure he does. I just hadn't asked his archives the right questions. But I'm glad to hear about your past because it makes my job today a whole lot easier. You'll understand the first thing I want to say, which is this: Africa isn't poor. The great mass of Africans is still very poor. But Africa itself is very rich. Or, at least, it could be."

"You mean if corrupt leaders didn't keep all their people's wealth for themselves and siphon off most of the aid given to them by guilt-ridden suckers in the West?" said Cross, who liked the way Bobbi Franklin thought almost as much as the way she looked.

"Well, I'd put it a little more diplomatically, but, yes. Let me give you some examples to illustrate the point: stop me if I'm telling you things you already know. You're going to be operating off the coast of Angola, so would you care to estimate how much oil those offshore fields produce, in total, per day?"

"Hmm . . ." Cross thought, his mind now fully focused on his job. "Our rig at Magna Grande will produce around eighty thousand barrels a day when it's going flat out. There are lots of other rigs like it. So I guess the total would be, what, twenty times as much?

"Not bad, Mr. Cross, not bad at all. Angola produces one point eight million barrels of oil a day: so yes, just over twenty times your rig's production. The nation's oil exports are currently running at about seventy-two billion dollars a year. And there's about three hundred billion cubic meters of natural gas down there too."

"That sounds like they have around a trillion dollars of reserves."

"And that's why I say that Africa's rich. Granted, Angola's not as blessed with oil reserves as Nigeria, and it doesn't have the incredible mineral wealth of the Democratic Republic of Congo. But it's got Africa's first female billionaire, who just happens to be the President's daughter. And I hope Bannock Oil gives you a decent expense account when you're out there because a couple of years ago the Angolan capital, Luanda, was named the most expensive city on earth. A hamburger'll cost you fifty bucks. Go to a beach club and order a bottle of champagne—that'll be four hundred. If you decide you like it and want to rent a single-bedroom apartment, the best ones go for ten grand a month."

"And I thought London was expensive."

"Here's the biggest sign that things have changed. Forty years ago, Angola was just declaring its independence from Portugal. Three years ago, the Portuguese Prime Minister paid a visit to Luanda. He wasn't coming to give Angola aid. He couldn't afford to. Portugal was bust. So the Prime Minister wanted aid from Angola."

Cross gave a low whistle. He'd always thought there was something condescending, even racist, about the western liberal assumption that black Africa was a helpless basket case of a continent, pathetically grateful for a few crumbs from the white man's table. Now those tables had turned. But there was one vital element missing from Bobbi Franklin's account.

"Just out of curiosity, how rich is the average Angolan?" Cross asked. "I'm assuming they don't eat too many fifty-dollar hamburgers."

"You assume correctly. More than a third of Angola's population, which is roughly twenty million people—no one knows the exact figure—live below the poverty line. Less than half of them have access to electricity. So even though they're sitting on gigantic energy reserves most of them depend on a mix of wood, charcoal, crop residues and animal manure for their cooking fires. This is a classic case of a rich African country filled with dirt-poor African people."

Now they were getting to the heart of the discussion. "How angry are these people?" Cross asked. "Are they ready to take violent action against the government or foreign businesses? They do in Nigeria, after all."

"Yes, they certainly do." Franklin nodded, and Cross was momentarily distracted by how sexy she looked pushing her glasses back up to the bridge of her nose. He tried to snap his mind back to what she was saying.

"Nigerian oil production can drop by up to five million barrels a day because of terrorist and criminal activity. As I'm sure you know, there are regular attacks on the oil industry's infrastructure. There's also a major problem with 'bunkering.' That's the local name for cutting a pipe and stealing the oil it's carrying, kind of like siphoning gas from a car, but on a much larger scale. Add to that the bitter religious conflict between the Muslim and Christian populations and the presence of powerful terrorist groups like Boko Haram and you can see that the danger of large-scale civil unrest in Nigeria is extremely high. It's no wonder, really, that several of the major oil companies have either already pulled back from their Nigerian operations or are seriously considering doing so."

"So could the same happen in Angola?"

"Not as easily, for a number of reasons," Bobbi Franklin said. "Angola was torn apart by war for more than forty years: first a struggle for independence against the Portuguese that ended with independence in 1975, and then a civil war that didn't end until 2002, having killed about one and a half million Angolans. The ruling party, the MPLA, has been in power since independence and the President, José Eduardo dos Santos, has held office since 1979."

"Must be a popular guy," said Cross.

Franklin picked up on his sarcasm and ran with it. "You know how it is: African leaders have a way of staying in office a lot longer than your average western leader. At the last elections, the MPLA won seventy-two percent of the vote and one hundred and seventy-five of the two hundred and twenty seats in parliament. Folks in Angola just can't get enough of 'em."

"That's because the MPLA is doing such a terrific job of giving them money and food, and electrical power."

"Or it could be because the elections are a long way from fair and the government spends a higher proportion of its budget on defense than any other state in sub-Saharan Africa. And there's not going to be a military coup, either, because President dos Santos is head of the armed forces. There's no religious dimension to worry about because, bluntly, Islam is not an issue in Angola. Just over half the population is Christian, the rest follow traditional African religions."

"So Angola's relatively peaceful?"

"These days, sure, and the other advantage you have operating there is that your installations are way out to sea. A lot of the Nigerian ones are in the waters of the Niger Delta, much closer to the mainland, so they're a helluva lot easier for the bad guys to attack."

Cross frowned. He'd been told to expect a warning, but all he was getting was good news. "So what's the problem?"

"I thought you'd never ask," said Franklin.

You're a cool operator, aren't you? thought Cross, feeling increasingly annoyed with himself for not getting on a flight to DC and conducting the meeting in person. But now she was talking again. "You see, there's one last hangover from the civil war: the province of Cabinda. It's separated from the rest of Angola by the narrow strip of territory that links the Democratic Republic of Congo to the Atlantic Ocean. Cabinda still has a rebel movement that calls itself—wait for it—'The Front for the Liberation of the Enclave of Cabinda—Forças Armadas de Cabinda,' or FLEC-FAC for short."

"I'm tempted to put another vowel between the 'F' and the 'C' there."

Franklin laughed, a deliciously feminine giggle that delighted Cross. *Gotcha!* he thought triumphantly.

The State Department analyst swiftly recovered her professional poise. "The rebels have offices in Paris and in Pointe-Noire, which is in the Republic of Congo—"

"Which is not the same as the Democratic Republic of Congo," Cross interrupted.

"Exactly. The Republic is much smaller and used to be ruled by the French. The Democratic Republic is massive and used to be ruled by the Belgians. Cabinda's squeezed in-between the two of them. But here's the thing: almost half of all Angola's oil is situated in what would be the territorial waters of Cabinda if it were ever an independent state. And the entire population of Cabinda is less than four hundred thousand people. So it could, potentially, be a very, very rich little territory."

"Sounds like a place worth fighting over," said Cross.

"You got it. Now, how closely have you been involved in the Bannock Oil operations in Angola?"

"Not at all closely. My wife, Hazel Bannock Cross, was murdered last year. She died giving birth to our daughter. As you can imagine, I've had other issues to deal with."

"I quite understand. I'm very sorry for your loss," Franklin said, sounding as though she meant it.

"Thank you. So, you were going to talk about Bannock's Angolan operations?"

"Indeed. You see, the Magna Grande field where your colleagues have just struck oil is actually located in Cabindan waters, and it will add more than ten percent to Cabinda's daily production of oil. As it is, all that money goes to Angola. But if Cabinda were independent, fields like Magna Grande would be making this hypothetical small nation even richer. Our concern at the State Department is this: sooner or later someone is going to figure that backing the rebels in Cabinda in exchange for a share of future oil revenues could be a very smart investment.

Cabinda is vulnerable because it's really small. You could fit it into the state of Texas ninety times over. To put it in British terms, it's about the size of your county of North Yorkshire."

"So unlike Iraq or Afghanistan, it's not a large area for an army to seize or to hold."

"Exactly. And because it's separated from the rest of Angola, the only way that the Angolans can get men and supplies into Cabinda is to fly them in, through Congolese airspace, or to ship them up the coast. Which would make it hard for President dos Santos to respond to a take-over bid. The National Air Force of Angola has a maximum of five Russian-built Ilyushin-76 Candid transport jets, though we doubt that more than two or three of them are currently airworthy."

"I know the Candid," said Cross. "The Soviets used them as their main transports in Afghanistan. Typical Russian kit: simple but tough. Easy to hit with missiles and guns but damn hard to bring down."

"But if you're a Cabindan rebel leader, you only have to bring down a handful of planes and the Angolans are screwed," Franklin pointed out. "And if you've got powerful backing, who's to say you won't have better missiles than the ones we gave the Taliban, back in the day?"

"You make it sound like the U.S. is getting back in the business of funding insurgency operations."

"No we're not, and certainly not this one. But other people soon might be because FLEC-FAC has just got itself a hotshot new leader called Mateus da Cunha. He is of Portuguese extraction but was born in Paris, France, on the twenty-eighth of March 1987. His father, Paulo da Cunha, went into exile there, along with other Cabindan rebel leaders. His mother, Cécile Duchêne da Cunha, is French. Her family are all wealthy left-wing intellectuals. Très chic, but très communiste, if you know what I mean."

"Typical bloody Frogs!" huffed Cross.

"Typical Brit to say so," Franklin parried.

"Typical Kenyan, if you don't mind."

Franklin's brows knitted in puzzlement. "You know, it's a little weird for me, an African-American, to be talking to you, a white Anglo-Saxon Protestant male, and find myself wondering: Is he more African than I am?"

"I may well be," Cross replied. "And we may both be more African than Monsieur Mateus da Cunha. Tell me about him."

"Well, he had about the most elite education any French citizen can receive. He got his bachelor's degree at the Paris Institute of Political Studies, then mastered at the National School of Administration in Strasbourg."

"Makes a change from all the revolutionaries who were educated at the London School of Economics."

"Yes, and the result is that this kid is connected. He's part of the French and European Union establishment. He knows how to carry himself in the smartest salons of Paris. And he is actively looking for people to invest in Cabinda. He's very slick, very persuasive. He never even suggests that what his investors are really paying for is the means to help him win a war. He simply describes the untapped potential of this pocket-sized piece of Africa. His favorite line is that Cabinda could be Africa's Dubai: a tax-free playground, funded by oil, fringed with beaches and basking in the tropical sun."

"You sound like one of his sales team."

"Anything but! My point is, Mateus da Cunha's determined to do what his father never could and create an independent Cabinda."

"With him as President-for-Life."

"You got it."

"And a large chunk of the oil revenues siphoned into his bank account."

"There you go."

"But before he can do that," said Cross, seeing where this

91

was all heading, "he has to start some kind of uprising. And the best way to let the world know that he's serious would be to blow the hell out of some fancy new oil rig, way out there in the Atlantic."

"That's right, but it's a delicate balance. He wouldn't want to wreck too many of them, because oil is the source of his money, long-term, and he doesn't want to scare people away. One way it might play out is an attack takes place and da Cunha blames it on rogue elements within the independence movement. He tells everyone not to worry, he can deal with these hotheads, but it would sure help if he could tell them that the world is listening to them and respecting their need for freedom and independence."

"This sounds like an old-fashioned protection racket."

"Exactly. Then, da Cunha hopes, the world gets the message and tells Angola to let Cabinda go."

"At this point huge amounts of money appear in a bunch of Swiss bank accounts, held by senior Angolan politicians and military commanders, just to make sure they sign on the dotted line."

"That's a possibility. And then Mateus da Cunha's got himself his own private African kingdom."

"Which can be done," Cross said. "I've seen it. So are you telling me that there's a clear and present danger of this happening any time soon?"

Franklin gave a shake of her head. "No, I wouldn't go that far. But there's a real possibility of unrest that might affect oil installations off the Angolan coast. So I'm advising you, as the Bannock Oil director with responsibility for security, that it would be sensible to take precautions."

"Anything specific you have in mind?"

"Well, any threat you face is going to come in by sea or by air. I'm not aware of any terrorist attack anywhere involving helos. But there are many, many instances of pirate and terrorist attacks made by boat—from the attack on the USS *Cole* off the coast of Yemen in October 2000, to all the Somali pirates who are still operating to this day."

"I've seen that, too." Cross was tempted to add: I've led a raid on the coast of Somalia that wiped out a nest of pirates, destroyed their base and freed two billion dollars' worth of captured shipping, but thought better of it. Instead he said, "I think I've got a rough idea of what we're going to need, in terms of personnel, equipment and training. Thanks for giving me the heads-up on what we can expect out there, Ms. Franklin."

"Please," she said sweetly, "call me . . ." She paused teasingly and then said, "Dr. Franklin. I have a PhD, after all."

Cross laughed. "It's been a pleasure, *Doctor* Franklin. And, if you don't mind, you can call me Major Cross. Until we meet in less formal circumstances, that is."

"I'll look forward to that," she said, and then the screen went blank.

Hector Cross leaned back in his office chair. "Well," he said to himself, "that was more interesting than I'd expected." He looked at the monitor, and even though the lovely Dr. Franklin could no longer see or hear him he added, "And I'll look forward to meeting you very much, too."

It was something Weiss said," Malinga told Connie Hernandez when they were going over the interviews, back at Company A headquarters. "I asked him if he'd ever previously represented Johnny Congo, prior to now, and he thought awhile then said . . ." Malinga looked at his notes to get the phrasing absolutely correct, "OK, here it is. He said this was 'the first time in my life that I represented a man called Johnny Congo.' Doesn't it strike you as odd, the way he said that?"

"You know lawyers," Hernandez replied. "Always trying to twist words."

"Yeah, they do. But only when there's a reason for not giving the straight answer. He didn't say he'd never represented Johnny Congo. It was 'a man called Johnny Congo.' Not even 'the man called Johnny Congo.' It was 'a man.'"

"A man, the man, what's the diff?"

"Because 'a man' could be called something else. Don't you get it? He didn't represent a man called Johnny Congo. But he did represent a guy with another name . . ."

"Who was actually Johnny Congo."

"Maybe."

"But how would he not know that the two people were the same guy? He was his lawyer."

"What if he never actually met the first guy? What if it was all done by phone calls and emails? Think about it. Congo was out of the country, in Africa or wherever. He couldn't come back, couldn't even use his real name. But he hires Weiss, Mendoza and Burnett to work for him, using an alias."

"OK," said Hernandez, starting to become a little more convinced. "So we go back to Weiss, ask him what the deal was."

Mendoza shook his head. "No. I don't want to alert him. But here's what you can do for me. Call the Marshals. See if you can speak to anyone who was on the crew that brought Congo back from Abu Zara. Find out anything they know about where he'd been before that, any aliases he might have used. See, if Congo used another name to deal with Weiss, he might have used it to get out of the country, too. And if we know how he got out, we might just be able to figure out where he's gone. And then maybe we'll catch the son of a bitch."

Hernandez had once dated a guy who'd been on the U.S. Marshals Gulf Coast Offender and Violent Fugitive Task Force. It hadn't ended well. If she'd never said another word to him in her life she wouldn't have complained. But needs must, so she gave him a call.

Her old date wasn't any happier to hear from Connie Hernandez than she was to speak to him. He couldn't help her directly, but just to get out of the conversation he put her on to someone else who might, and three more degrees of law enforcement separation later she found herself talking to one of the men who'd lifted Congo out of Abu Zara.

"This is off the record, right?" the Marshal insisted.

"Sure, whatever, I'm just looking for a lead. Where I get it isn't an issue."

"OK, so this whole Abu Zara thing was just weird. I mean, there was no formal extradition. We just get the call that an escaped murderer who's been wanted, like, forever is sitting in a cell somewhere no one has ever heard of. But the Sultan who runs the place is happy to let us have the killer as a favor to his good buddy, some Limey dude who caught him."

"Caught him where?"

"We weren't told. Africa somewhere was all we heard."

"How about the Limey? Did they tell you anything about him?"

"The man could throw a punch, I can tell you that much. Knocked Congo out cold with one shot, and that evil bastard was a beast."

"What? A civilian hit a prisoner in your custody and you just let him?"

"Wasn't that simple. We flew into Abu Zara and were told to go to the Sultan's private hangar. Man, it was vast. The guy basically has his own personal airline. Anyway, we get there and the Limey has this team with him, guarding Congo—all high-end mercenary Joes, ex-Special Forces. So they hand Congo over and suddenly Congo goes apeshit, starts trash-talking the Limey, cussing him out, real filthy language, and we're trying to restrain him but it's like trying to tie down Godzilla. Then Congo says he killed the Limey's wife, says she was a whore and the next thing we know—bam!—Congo's out, I mean stone cold out, right there on the hangar floor. Unbe-frickin-lievable."

The Marshal started laughing at the memory. Hernandez was just about to butt in, but before she could he suddenly said, "Wait! I just remembered something. While Congo was screaming, he said the guy's name, the Limey."

"Which was . . . ?"

"Wait, it's just coming to me. Began with 'C.' Like, ah . . ." The Marshal tried to bring the name back to his mind: "C-C-C . . ."

"Christ . . ." sighed Hernandez frustratedly.

"That's it!" the Marshal exclaimed. "Cross, his name was Cross! Guess that word-association thing really does work, huh?"

"Thank you," said Hernandez, with a whole new tone of genuine gratitude. "You've been a very, very great help."

"Well, I guess I'm glad to have been of service," the Marshal said, sounding a little surprised by the sudden change in her attitude.

Hernandez hung up. It sounded like the Marshal hadn't followed the story of the murder of Hazel Bannock Cross. Well, that wasn't surprising. Plenty of cops didn't have time to worry about other people's cases and Bannock Oil's PR people had done everything they could to minimize coverage of the tragedy. But even if Hernandez was hardly the girly type, she still needed to go to the hairdresser, just like any other woman. And one time she'd sat waiting for her stylist to start work, reading a trashy glossy weekly that happened to have a story headlined: "Tragic Death of Hazel Bannock . . . and Miracle Birth of Her Billionaire Baby." So she knew exactly who Cross was. Now she just had to find him.

Cross was in his office, just getting ready for his afternoon meeting with Dave Imbiss and the O'Quinns, when the phone rang. "I've got a Tom Nocerino from Bannock Oil Corporate Communications, in Houston, holding for you," Agatha informed him. "He says he needs a quote from you about your role in the Angolan project. He said it was for the investors' newsletter."

"I've not heard of that before."

"It's new apparently. Would you like to speak to him, or shall I ask him to call back?"

"Might as well get it over and done with. Put him through."

"Thank you so much, sir, for sparing me your time," Nocerino began in a voice sticky with sycophancy.

"So this is just for a newsletter, right? I'm not going to see it on my newsfeed one morning because someone's stuck it in a press release and the whole world's been treated to my opinions?"

"Absolutely not, Mr. Cross. I can assure you, sir, this is purely private and in-house. It's a way of keeping valued investors in the loop, making them feel they've got a relationship with Bannock Oil that's more than just financial."

"I've not heard of this before."

"No, sir, it's a very new concept. In fact, this will be the first edition. But the idea came right from the top."

"From John Bigelow?" Cross asked, thinking to himself how typical it was of the veteran politician to be more concerned with the appearance of things than the practicalities of them.

"Yes, sir," Nocerino replied. "Senator Bigelow believes very strongly in the importance of reaching out to the people and institutions that have put their faith and their trust in Bannock Oil."

"And their money . . ."

"Yes, sir. That too."

"OK then, what do you need?"

"Just a few words about your role as Director of Security, in relation to the Magna Grande field. We don't need anything too specific, just something about how excited you are by the potential of Bannock's Angolan operations and how you're determined to ensure that our employees and our corporate assets are kept completely secure. If you'd rather, I can draft a statement for your approval."

"No, if I'm going to have words against my name, I'd rather say them myself. So, can I start talking?"

"Go ahead, sir."

Cross took a second to collect his thoughts, then began dictating: "'The development of the Magna Grande field offers Bannock Oil a fantastic' . . . no, 'a unique opportunity to, ah, establish our presence in the increasingly significant West African oil industry. As Director of Security it's my responsibility to ensure that all our installations and, most importantly, all our employees and contractors are properly protected from any possible threats against them. As I speak, I'm about to go into a meeting with my most senior staff to discuss the various challenges we're likely to face, and how best to prepare for every eventuality. We've had many years of experience working on Bannock's operations in Abu Zara . . .'" Cross paused. "Hang on, make that 'working together on Bannock's operations,' et cetera. OK, new sentence: 'With the full support of the Abu Zaran authorities, we've maintained a security cordon that has kept people safe and oil flowing at all times. Now we're moving into an offshore environment, so it's going to be tough. It's going to be very hard work. But our commitment to doing the best job to the highest standards will be just as great as ever.'"

It all sounded like undiluted bullshit to Cross's ears. But then, was it really so different to all the stirring, inspirational pep talks he'd given to his men before they'd gone out on missions, in war and peace alike? Sometimes you just had to tell people what they wanted and needed to hear.

"How was that?" he asked.

"Great, Mr. Cross, just great," Nocerino enthused.

This was why Cross hated to work with yes-men. There were times when any leader needed subordinates who had the guts to point out where he might be about to go wrong. He said nothing, running his words back in his mind, looking for any possible hostages to fortune.

Nocerino must have sensed Cross's uncertainty. "Don't worry, sir. That was exactly what I needed," he said. "Have a nice day."

No sooner had Cross put the phone down than it rang again. "Yes?" he asked.

"I have another call from America," Agatha said. "It's a Lieutenant Hernandez from the Texas Rangers, investigating Johnny Congo's escape."

"You'd better put him through, then."

"Actually, Lieutenant Hernandez is a woman."

"A female Texas Ranger?" Cross smiled. "That sounds interesting."

"Unusual, that's for sure," Agatha noted. "And everyone's here for the meeting."

"Tell them to come through to my office."

"Certainly. I have Lieutenant Hernandez for you now."

The line was switched. "This is Hector Cross, how can I help you, Lieutenant?" he asked.

"Well, anything you could tell me about Johnny Congo would be a help."

"Can you be a little more specific?"

"Sure. I'm curious about the time Congo spent in Africa, prior to his being reapprehended a few weeks ago. We have reason to believe that he originally hired his attorney here in Houston using an alias, and we think he might have used the same identity to get out of the country."

"Sounds to me like the simplest thing would be to ask the attorney," Cross observed.

"That could be difficult. You ever tried asking a lawyer something he doesn't want to tell you?"

Cross laughed. He was warming to this call a lot more than the last. "So, what can I do for you that the lawyer can't?" he asked, waving Dave, Paddy and Nastiya into the room and

99

pointing in the direction of the table at which he liked to hold team meetings.

"Just tell us anything you know about Congo's activities during his years outside the U.S.," Hernandez replied. "I don't know if you're aware of this, but very little's been said here in the States about exactly how Congo came to be arrested in Abu Zara—like, for example, how he came to be there in the first place. But I have been able to establish that you had Congo in your custody and then handed him over to the U.S. Marshals. So is there anything you can tell me, anything at all that would help us figure out how he escaped and where the hell he is now?"

"Hmm . . ." Cross hesitated. "This is where I'm going to have to sound like a lawyer. You see, I very much want to help you in any way I can. Believe me, no one wants Johnny Congo despatched from the surface of the earth more than me. And no one is more pissed off that he escaped the punishment he so richly deserved."

"But . . . ?" Hernandez interjected.

"But there were certain, ah, unconventional aspects to his capture which could, if described in detail, lead to possible allegations of—how should I put it?—less than fully law-abiding activity."

Cross could see smirks spreading across the faces of his friends. Even Nastiya had abandoned her normally fearsome expression and was trying hard to suppress a giggle.

"Listen," said Hernandez bluntly. "I couldn't give a damn what you had to do to get that scumbag to Abu Zara. My jurisdiction doesn't extend outside the state of Texas, and what happens in Africa stays in Africa. All I want to know is, what do you know that could help me?"

"Here's what I can tell you. Johnny Congo had set himself up as the ruler of a place called Kazundu. It's the smallest, poorest, most godforsaken spot on the entire African continent and he and his partner Carl Bannock turned it into their own private kingdom."

"That's Bannock, as in Bannock Oil?"

"Yes, the adopted son of Henry Bannock."

"And by 'partner' do you mean business or personal?"

"Both. And before you ask, no, I don't know where Carl Bannock is right now. He's dropped right off the map."

"Actually he dropped right out of a crocodile's arse, more like," quipped Paddy O'Quinn, under his breath.

"Do you know of any aliases Congo used when he was in Kazundu?" Hernandez asked, oblivious to the childish amusement her conversation was causing.

"No. But I can tell you this. Kazundu is a sovereign state that issues its own passports. Congo and Bannock almost certainly acquired Kazundan passports for themselves, diplomatic ones probably. And I doubt that too many other citizens of Kazundu left Texas en route to an overseas destination in the immediate aftermath of the escape. So if you can find a Kazundu passport on any passenger manifest, anywhere, chances are that's Johnny Congo."

"Thank you, Mr. Cross, that's a very great help," said Hernandez. "Just one other thing. We get the impression Congo had access to significant amounts of money. Did you get that impression, too?"

"Significant is way too small a word, Lieutenant. Johnny Congo has access to huge amounts of money. He can buy anything, bribe anyone, go anywhere."

"You have any idea where he might have gone?"

"Not a clue. But I aim to find out. And when I do, I—"

"Don't tell me," said Hernandez. "There's a limit to the amount of less-than-law-abiding activity I can ignore in one day."

The moment her conversation with Cross was over, Hernandez contacted the U.S. Customs and Border Protection's Houston field office at 2323 South Shepherd Drive. "Do me a favor. I'm working on the Johnny Congo investigation. We think he may have tried to leave the country in the immediate aftermath of his escape, using an alias. So I need a check on all persons leaving any of the ports of entry covered by your office, for any overseas destination between sixteen hundred hours and twenty-one hundred hours on the fifteenth of November. Look for anyone carrying a passport from Kazundu."

"Ka-where?" asked the official on the other end of the line.

"Kazundu. It's the smallest nation in Africa, spelled Kilo-Alpha-Zulu-Uniform-November-Delta-Uniform. It's possible Congo was travelling on a diplomatic passport. Also the guy is loaded, so chances are he didn't go scheduled. Look for private planes and yachts."

"If he went by boat, he could have gone aboard anywhere, sailed out to sea and we wouldn't have known about it."

"Yeah, but the sea option is a long shot. I mean, boats are slow. And wherever Congo was going, he'd have wanted to get there as fast as he possibly could. So try airports, and specifically private aviation first."

An hour later Hernandez had her answer. She called Bobby Malinga: "I've got good news and bad news."

"Well, I guess that's better than all bad, which is all I've got so far."

"The good news is that I know Johnny Congo's alias. He called himself, get this: His Excellency King John Kikuu Tembo."

"You're kidding me!"

"Nope."

"And CPB fell for it?"

"The man's passport said 'King,' what are you going to do?"

"OK, so we've got a name. How about the flight?"

"He left Jack Brooks Regional Airport, south of Beaumont, on a Citation business jet. The plane was chartered from an outfit called Lonestar Jetcharters by a Panamanian corporation, and here's the first piece of bad news: there's no legal requirement in Panama to register the identities of shareholders in offshore companies."

"So we have no way of knowing who hired that jet?"

"Not unless they were real careless when they communicated with Lonestar, no. And my second piece of bad news is, I know where the jet was going. Trust me, you're not going to like it."

Hector Cross had been thinking about Johnny Congo's movements, too, talking it over with Imbiss and the O'Quinns. "You're a wanted man. You know that if you ever get caught and taken back to the States you're going to be executed. But the good news is, you've got almost limitless resources. What are you going to do?"

"Me, I would prepare," said Nastiya. "I would have Plan A, Plan B, Plan C. Money, passports, identities—all safely hidden, all ready for when they are needed."

"Me too," Cross agreed. "Carl Bannock was a sick, psychopathic, murdering bastard and Johnny Congo still is. The way the two of them lived in Kazundu was so decadent and depraved it made the Emperor Caligula look like a Mormon Boy Scout. But they weren't stupid. You're right, Nastiya, they must have had a plan, or plans, for breaking out of custody then getting away from the States. Next question: where would Congo want to go next?"

"The death sentence had been imposed in Texas, so that's where Congo was going to be taken and that's the starting point of any escape," said Dave Imbiss. "No way he'd want to get on a regular scheduled flight: too risky, too little control and there's no need because he can afford to go private. I don't think he wants to have to refuel, because if the plane's on the ground, stationary, it's too easy a target, so you're looking at a radius of around three thousand miles, max, from take-off point. So that's all of Mexico and Central America, the Caribbean and the

103

northern half of South America. I'm guessing, but the furthest major city he could reach would probably be Lima, Peru."

"Unless he flew north," Paddy O'Quinn pointed out. "The Canadian border's only a couple of hours' flight time from Houston. And that's a very big country for a man to get lost in."

"It's also a country that's on good terms with the United States," said Cross. "If I were Johnny I would want to go somewhere that isn't going to cut a deal with Washington to send me right back to the execution chamber."

"Or somewhere that has a powerful enough criminal network to make the government illegal. There are plenty of people in Mexico who could shelter Congo for a price," Imbiss said.

Cross nodded thoughtfully. "Fair point. But does one criminal ever trust another? And would you want to be in a Mexican drug baron's debt? Congo needs to feel secure. And that means having a government watching his back."

"Cuba," said Imbiss decisively. "Gotta be."

"No, too many Americans," Nastiya objected.

"In Guantánamo, maybe. But the base is cut off from the rest of the island. And you won't find any Americans there."

"Sure you will." Nastiya grinned triumphantly. "When I was in the FSB we went to Cuba for training in tropical conditions— and also so the senior officers instructing us could have good time lying by pool, drinking rum, screwing Cuban girls. In Havana we were shown the Swiss embassy. It's a big building, almost the biggest embassy in Havana, and all this for little Switzerland? No. One-quarter of the building, or maybe less, is for the Swiss. The rest is what they call the 'American Interests Section' of the Swiss Embassy. In other words, unofficial American Embassy. And you know how everyone knows that? Because there is company of U.S. Marines in Havana, guarding Swiss Embassy. They have their own residence, the Marine House. Best steaks, best beer, best big-screen TV in all Havana."

"And you know that because . . . ?" Paddy asked.

"Because I am a girl who loves a man in uniform, darling," Nastiya teased, pouting at her husband. "Seriously, Hector, Congo would be crazy to go to Cuba. The whole island is under constant surveillance: satellites, spy planes, signal intercepts. Congo could not last a day there without being found, even if Fidel Castro himself hides him under his own sickbed."

"So it's not Canada, it's not Mexico, it's not Cuba," said Cross, getting up from his desk and walking over to a table that was easily big enough to seat six for dinner, half of whose surface was taken up with a single, enormous hardback book that was actually slightly longer than the table was wide. "*The Times Comprehensive Atlas of the World*," said Cross as the others got up to join him. "Forget all that internet nonsense, this is still the best way of finding places on our planet." He opened the book and started turning poster-sized pages until he came to an image of Central America. "Right. This is southern Mexico and here's the border with Guatemala and Belize. I'm going to keep turning pages until we've been through every country or Caribbean island, one by one, and worked out a shortlist of possible refuges for a killer on the run. And once we've got a shortlist, we'll start thinking about how to find and catch the bastard."

They'd been talking for an hour, and had come up with four possible destinations when Cross received another call. "Lieutenant Hernandez," Agatha told him.

"Just wanted to say thanks for your help," Hernandez said. "Turned out you were right. And since you've already apprehended Johnny Congo once and shown your desire to hand him over to the appropriate federal authorities, I've decided, upon due reflection, to change my mind and share the information we've ascertained with you."

"Because you have faith in the fact that I'm a law-abiding individual who knows how to do the right thing?"

"Exactly," said Hernandez. "That's what I'm counting on."

"So what have you got?"

Hernandez gave Cross the details of Congo's alias and means of transport. Then she said, "You want to know where the Citation was headed?"

"Very much."

"Caracas, Venezuela."

"And it could get there on one tank of fuel?"

"With a thousand miles to spare. Get there fast, too, the Citation cruises at over six hundred mph. You know how folks like to eat late in Latin America?" Hernandez asked.

"I'd heard that, yes."

"Well, King John Kikuu Tembo made it into downtown Caracas in time for dinner."

"Then I hope he choked on his food," said Cross. He put down the phone and turned his attention back to his team. "We have two priorities now. The first is to track down exactly where in Venezuela Johnny Congo, or whatever he's calling himself now, is hiding before the U.S. authorities grab hold of him. He's got away from them twice. I'm not willing to risk him doing it a third time. I'll take charge of this myself. It's personal business and I'll pay for any costs that are incurred."

"So you are planning on going out to Caracas?" Dave Imbiss asked.

"Not immediately. You remember when Hazel was murdered how Agatha drew up a list of the top private detectives in every country where there was anyone who had ever threatened her, or had reason to want her dead? We'll do the same this time, find the best man—"

"Or woman," Nastiya interjected.

"Or woman in Venezuela and get them on the case. They'll have local knowledge and contacts we can't match. Just to be on the safe side, get people working in the border areas of Colombia, Brazil and Guyana. I don't want him slipping into a neighboring country without us knowing about it. As and when someone finds Congo I'll go out and deal with him."

No one asked what Cross meant by that. There was no need.

"If you want a hand, when the time comes, you can count on me for anything you need," Paddy O'Quinn said, "and I'm sure that goes for all of us. It's time that bastard paid for what he did to Hazel."

"Thanks," said Cross as the other two murmured their agreement with Paddy. "Now, back to company business. Bannock Oil has a multi-billion-dollar investment a hundred miles off the Angolan coastline and it needs protecting. I've had an unofficial briefing from someone at the State Department in Washington and it seems that we may be heading into stormy water."

Cross gave a brief outline of the information Bobbi Franklin had given him. "What it amounts to," he concluded, "is that we need to be thinking about this on two levels. The first is the development of a basic defensive strategy that will enable us to deal with any threat that we're likely to face against the rig, or *Bannock A*, or both. And the second is an intelligence operation, looking at anyone who might carry out an attack, starting with Mateus da Cunha. Paddy, you've got Special Forces experience, so I'm putting you in charge of defensive planning. Talk to some of our old chums down in Poole. They've been training on North Sea rigs for donkey's years."

"You mean you're making me talk to the bubble-heads? Jaysus, Heck, that's a lot to ask of a Hereford man."

"Now, now, Paddy, don't insult the SBS," Hector cautioned him, barely suppressing a grin as he pretended to be stern. "I've heard they've got one or two half-decent fighting men. Even if they are only tarted-up bootnecks."

"Excuse me," said Nastiya, "but what are you talking about?"

"Have I not told you, darling, about the fierce rivalry between the two main elements of the United Kingdom Special Forces? You see, Major Cross and I were, as you know, proud to serve in the SAS, the first and still greatest of all the world's Special Forces, and that's an Army unit, based in Hereford. But the

Royal Navy, feeling left out, decided it wanted a force of its own. So it took a slice off the Royal Marines and called that the Special Boat Service and packed them off to Poole, where they could play all day at the seaside. We call them bubble-heads on account of the bubbles coming from their diving suits. And we call Marines bootnecks because . . . do you know, I have absolutely no idea why we do that, but we do. And each unit despises the other, until threatened by an outsider, like a Septic, for example . . ."

"For Septic tank read Yank," Dave Imbiss explained wearily.

"In which case," O'Quinn concluded, "we join forces and become the Lads, and you'd better not mess with us or you'll live to regret it."

"You say this to a woman trained by the Spetsnaz, who can chew you up and spit you out like they eat for breakfast?" Nastiya asked contemptuously.

"That's enough!" Cross commanded. "I spend too much time with an actual infant to have any interest in dealing with you three acting like two-year-olds. Stop pissing off your co-workers, Paddy, and give me your first thoughts about defending the Bannock Oil installations in Angolan waters."

Paddy spoke for nearly an hour from the notes he had worked up. As he listened Hector congratulated himself—not for the first time—that he had grabbed Paddy before he had been snapped up by any other company. When he finished speaking Hector nodded. "All of that makes good sense. Let me have your notes to forward on to the Bannock Board. They are going to have to make provision for all that extra equipment. Once we've got that in motion, Paddy, you and I need to start planning precisely how many extra men we're going to need down in Angola, what our protocols are going to be in terms of crisis response, and how we're going to get them all trained up. Next item on the agenda: intelligence-planning. I am giving that job to Dave, as usual, because he's the man we need to plant a bug or hack a system, and Nastiya, because she's the only person in this room who's actually been a spy for a living. So, Mrs. O'Quinn, where do you think we should start?"

"With da Cunha, since he is the only person we know who is a potential threat. And it is wise of you to ask the advice of a woman, Hector, because this job requires the feminine touch."

"Such as . . ."

"Such as seducing Mateus da Cunha. He is a man who wants to conquer and rule a country, so he is, by definition, even more of an egotist than any other, normal man. He has also been brought up in France, so he will have a French attitude to infidelity."

"And what a fine attitude that is," said O'Quinn cheerfully. "I sincerely hope that you are not proposing yourself for the role of seductress."

"I hadn't thought about it, darling. But now you mention it . . . it might help me pass a rainy afternoon," deadpanned Nastiya.

"What's good for the goose is just as good for the gander," Paddy suggested, and his wife winked slyly at him.

"Don't fuss yourself. Home cooking is good enough for me."

"Mostly because I'm the best cook in the house!" Paddy laughed.

Nastiya ignored him, and went on smoothly: "Da Cunha's record tells us that he is highly intelligent, sophisticated and also disciplined enough to succeed at a very high academic level. But I suspect that he is also a vain, arrogant, privileged young man who cannot resist boasting to people, and to women in particular, just how brilliant he is and how great he is going to be in the future."

"I am following you." Hector nodded. "But we'll need covert surveillance on da Cunha and a properly worked-up cover for Nastiya, Dave. If da Cunha meets a woman who promises him sex and money, the first thing he'll do is thank his lucky stars.

The second will be to hit Google and check her out. So make sure Nastiya's cover has online back-up."

"Got it," Imbiss assured him.

"Then unless anyone else has anything they need to say, our meeting is temporarily adjourned. You all know what you have to do. Give me an hour to get things moving in Houston, and then we can go and get something to eat. I'm paying."

Yevgenia Vitalyevna Voronova, known as "Zhenia" by the multitudes of her male friends who admired and adored her, and even by her few female friends (who were more cautious in their approval), kissed Sergei Burlayev, her partner of the evening, goodnight and clambered out of the Ferrari 458 Italia that Sergei's father had given him to replace the one he'd written off in a crash six months previously. She set off across the concrete floor of the private underground car park, teetering just a little unsteadily in her 10.5-cm-high heeled Chanel pumps. With the self-satisfaction of one who is just slightly tiddly, Zhenia congratulated herself on the skill with which she had matched her shoes so perfectly to the color of Sergei's car, which was now roaring back up the ramp and out into the streets of the Moscow International Business Center.

She reached the express lift and slid her personalized key card into the slot at the second attempt. The doors opened, Zhenia tottered in and gratefully leaned against the wall of the lift, snuggling into her coat of jet-black, wild-caught Barguzin sable as she was whisked more than seventy floors up the bizarre, apparently random structure which was the Moscow Tower.

Zhenia giggled when she recalled how proud her papa had been when he managed to get a penthouse right at the top of what was, for a short while, the tallest building in Europe, and how his pride turned to fury when it was promptly overtaken in height by the Mercury City Tower, right here in the Moscow IBC. Papa had stood at the five meter-high windows that wrapped around his living room, watching the Mercury Tower go up, raging at the fact that he had been beaten to the penthouse there by one of Vladimir Putin's favored henchmen. One word from the President's office had been all it took to ensure that no other offers for the property were considered.

The lift pinged, the doors opened and Zhenia stepped out into the Voronov family's entrance lobby. Its design had always displeased her. The wall directly opposite the lift was mirrored from floor to ceiling, an admirable idea in her view, except that the important business of examining her own reflection was made extremely difficult by the huge stone fireplace that stood right in the middle of the wall.

Still, this was no night for complaining. Sergei had taken her to Siberia, a restaurant-cum-club on Bolshaya Nikitskaya where it cost 25,000 roubles just to book a table. Lots of their friends had been there and they'd all eaten gloriously, drunk extravagantly, danced wildly and generally laughed, flirted and delighted in the joy of being young, beautiful and rich. The only disappointment had been that she had not been able to bring Sergei back to the apartment. Zhenia had harbored steamy fantasies of dragging him back home and exploring every position in the *Kama Sutra* and all fifty shades of gray with him.

That was always possible when Papa was away and Mama was too drunk to take any interest in her surroundings. However, tonight she had had to be satisfied with a quickie in the cramped back seat of the Ferrari, trying frantically to keep pace with Sergei's mercurial libido rather than be left dangling high and dry at the end. She had managed to reach the summit with just seconds to spare and was feeling so satisfied with her achievement that she decided to have one last nightcap.

Zhenia had first tasted Bailey's Irish Cream during her years studying History of Art in London and been utterly seduced. There was bound to be a bottle in one of the fridges behind the splendid marble-topped bar in the living room. Zhenia dropped her coat and her clutch bag on the lobby floor and stepped out of her heels, knowing that the servants would pick up all her belongings and put them neatly away. Then she made her way to the living room wearing nothing but her little red party dress.

"Where have you been, you little slut?"

The words were slurred and spiced with malice. The man who spoke them was sitting at the bar in a shiny gray suit. His shirt, which swelled around the mound of his monumental paunch, was so tight at the collar that the layers of fat drooped over it. Despite an expensive series of transplants and the application of a wide range of gels and sprays, there was more pink bald scalp in evidence on the top of his head than thin gingery-gray hair.

"Good evening, Papa." Zhenia studiously ignored the question.

"I said, 'Where have you been?'" Vitaly Voronov was the man known throughout Russia as the Woodpulp Tsar for the fortune he had made chopping down trees and turning them into paper. "But I know the answer: you have been rutting like a bitch in heat with that bone-idle wastrel Sergei Burlayev. Don't deny it. You smell like a whorehouse on Saturday night."

"And you, my darling Papa, smell like a pathetic old drunk who's just had a bellyful of the cheapest potato vodka he can find," Zhenia snapped back at him. She had drunk just enough that night to have abandoned her usual caution. "You are sitting at a bar stocked with every fancy brand there is, and yet you drink that peasant urine. Look, you even kept it in a paper bag just like a true *moujik*! Didn't Mama teach you how to use a glass?"

"You want to know why I drink this?" Voronov said, getting up from the cream leather bar stool and advancing toward his daughter, his hand still around the bottle in its brown paper overcoat. "I drink it because it reminds me of the old days, that's why. When I was poor, and I grew up in an apartment that wasn't half . . . no, not even a quarter the size of this room. Six of us, squeezed in there, my daddy coughing his lungs out after twenty years down the coal mine. My mum cleaning the blood and God knows what off the sheets in the hospital laundry, then standing in line for hours, just to buy a loaf of bread and a couple of cabbages, if she was lucky."

"Yeah, yeah, I get it, Daddy. Life was tough. You had to work and fight for everything you ever had. Blah-blah-blah . . ."

"Don't you talk to me like that, you spoiled little bitch," he shouted, making her recoil from his flying spittle and the stench of his alcohol-drenched breath. "And you still haven't answered my question."

Zhenia faced her father. "If you really want to know, I've been at a club with Sergei and some friends, and then Sergei brought me back here like a gentleman. I gave him a little goodnight kiss and then I came up here."

"You're lying! You have been screwing him—"

"No!" she protested. And then she stopped, as if struck by a revelation. She stared at her father's face, really peering at it, and then she burst out laughing. "Oh my God! I've only just got it! Now I know why you've been up all night drinking, why you want to know about my sex life and why you're always telling me that I'm a whore. I know what you want from me, my darling Daddy. I know exactly what you want, you filthy old peasant."

Voronov stepped forward, his face contorted with fury, squaring up to her, just as he would to a man he was about to fight. "All right then, slut," he snarled, "if you're so clever, if you know so much with your fancy education, go ahead, tell me . . . what am I thinking?"

There was a devil in Zhenia, an aggressive, fighting spirit that came straight from her father she hated so much and it seized her now. She stared right back at her father, provoking him, taunting him, matching his brute, male presence with the womanly power of her youth, her beauty, her body and her scent and purred, "Here's what I think, darling Papa," Zhenia paused again, just to add to the tension, and then she said the words that would change her life, and many others forever. "I think you're jealous of Sergei. You want to screw me yourself."

Her father hit her across the face with the flat of his hand, putting all his great strength into the blow. Zhenia's vision exploded with pain and the force of the impact wrenched her head to one side, taking her body with it and tearing at her neck muscles as she was sent spinning to the floor. Voronov stood over where she lay, moaning in agony on the floor. He was aiming wild, drunken kicks at her stomach, shouting filthy abuse at her. She was curled up into a foetal position trying to protect herself.

She had no idea how much time had passed when, through the fog of semi-conciousness that had fallen over her like a dark cloak, she heard a woman's voice somewhere far away screeching, "Stop it! Stop kicking her, you bastard! Leave her alone!"

She realized dimly that it was her mother, Marina Voronova. She almost laughed through her pain as she thought, *Mama has come to watch someone else get beaten up for a change.*

Voronov stopped kicking her as he turned to face his wife, shouting, "Shut up! Shut your stupid mouth. One more word and you'll get a taste of my boot also!"

Her mother was screaming back at him, "I hate you, you bastard, I hate you!"

Some tattered shreds of her own survival instinct warned Zhenia that this was her opportunity to escape. She stumbled to her feet and desperately tried to break into a run.

Her father yelled, "Come back here, you little slut! You are going to suffer for the things you said about me," but before he could chase after her, he was crying out in alarm as Marina launched herself at him, raking his face with her long, manicured nails, knowing that she could not hope to overcome her powerful husband, but desperately trying to buy Zhenia time to escape from him.

Zhenia staggered back into the lobby, where a Filipina maid was just gathering up her coat, bag and shoes from the floor.

"Give me those!" Zhenia shouted.

The maid looked around in surprise that turned to shock when she saw Zhenia's face. She stood there, dumbly, staring at the blood spurting from Zhenia's nose.

"Give them to me!" Zhenia insisted, her voice rising in desperation as she snatched everything from the terrified servant and then raced to the door of the lift. She hammered at the button with the side of her right fist, in which she was clutching the ankle-straps of her shoes.

"Come on, come on!" Zhenia pleaded. She could hear the sound of her mother sobbing in the living room and her father shouting, "I'm coming for you, Yevgenia! You won't get away from me!"

Not daring to turn around she heard his footsteps pounding over the marble floor. Where was that damn lift?

"I'm going to smash your lying mouth. I am going to break your jaws so they will never be able to put them back together again. I am going to mash your face so that no man will ever look at you again . . ."

Then the lift pinged, the door opened and Zhenia almost threw herself into it, pressing the "doors closed" button again and again.

She looked around and her father was only a few paces away, filling her whole field of vision.

The doors began to close. Voronov forced himself between them, pushing them apart with his bare hands.

Zhenia hit him with the heel of her shoe, bringing it down on the back of his right hand. Voronov howled in pain. He pulled his hands away. The doors closed, and the lift plummeted back down the shaft, carrying Zhenia to safety.

She didn't have her car keys in the tiny evening bag, nor the internal passport that was essential for almost any official transaction in Russia, nor even her driving license: just her lipstick, some tissues, a packet of ten Marlboro Lights, a min-

115

iature going-out purse that contained her black Amex card and 5,000 roubles in cash, and last, but most importantly, her mobile phone.

Zhenia closed the bag, shrugged on her coat and stepped back into her shoes. It was only when she straightened up that she caught sight of her reflection in the lift wall. Her left eye looked puffy and swollen, as did her cheekbone, which was already starting to color with the beginnings of an ugly bruise. There was blood coming from one of her nostrils. She suddenly realized that her neck was aching and that even the slightest movement of her head sent shooting pains through her strained muscles and ligaments. She felt sick and disoriented and when the lift reached the ground floor and the doors opened it took Zhenia several seconds to gather her thoughts and find the will to walk out into the reception.

The next few hours passed in a semi-conscious blur as she called Sergei again and again without ever getting an answer, leaving endless messages begging him to come and rescue her and then gazing in bewilderment when he finally texted her: "Your dad called mine. We can never talk ever again. S."

She wandered the streets, wondering why her father hadn't come after her, or sent his security men to grab her, only slowly understanding that he'd chosen another, crueller form of retribution as one dear friend after another turned their back on her. The Woodpulp Tsar had put the word out to his fellow oligarchs, calling in favors or making threats, as each one required, but always making sure that they got the same message: his daughter was a non-person and no one was to have anything to do with her until she crawled back home and begged for his forgiveness.

It took Zhenia till dawn to find one contact her father couldn't get to. Andrei Ionov had been a rebel since they were in kindergarten together. He left home for good when he was eighteen, rejecting his privileged upbringing and working, mostly

116

unpaid, as a freelance journalist for a series of anti-government websites and magazines, somehow managing to stay out of jail as one avenue after another was closed down. When she called him he gave her an address in Kopotnya, an infamously lawless and impoverished district in the south-east corner of the city, jammed up against Moscow's ring-road, the MKAD.

"Are you sure this is where you want to get out, miss?" the cabbie asked her as he dropped her—Chanel shoes, fur coat and all—outside an old Communist-era apartment block, on a street of cracked paving stones and patchwork tarmac. Dawn was just breaking as she walked, still dazed and only vaguely aware of her surroundings, into the courtyard at the center of the block. She saw high white walls that were filthy, peeling and pockmarked. The surface of the yard was just beaten-down earth and rubble, from which three spindly, leafless trees were trying to grow between the cars parked wherever their drivers could find a few square meters' space. Laundry was flapping from the railings of the balconies: cheap clothes in vile colors, and sheets so filthy it was hard to believe they'd ever been washed. She heard a voice call down from one of the balconies, "I'm up here!" and somehow managed to make her way up a stairwell that was strewn with rubbish and stank of vodka and urine to a door where Andrei was waiting to greet her.

Zhenia slept for little more than an hour and woke with a splitting headache, feeling more nauseous than ever, and when she saw her swollen, discolored face in the mirror she burst into tears of misery and despair. She was about to give up, surrender and crawl back on her knees to her cruel and twisted father and her hopelessly dysfunctional mother when she remembered one last possible source of help: the half-sister, ten years her senior, whom she'd never really known, still less liked. But they had exchanged occasional birthday emails, and Zhenia's sister had always attached her phone number to the message, each time with a different overseas dialing code.

Zhenia knew that this was her only chance. Her only hope of survival.

It was three in the morning in London and Anastasia Vitaly-evna Voronova, known as "Nastiya" to her friends, was still asleep when the phone rang.

"Yevgenia?" she said, once she'd woken up, using her half-sister's full name because she simply didn't know her well enough for pet ones, and barely recognizing the muffled, desperate voice on the other end of the line. To her mind, Yevgenia had always been a spoiled, pampered little princess, the child of the trophy wife her father had acquired when he'd found himself seriously rich and wanted to shed any trace of his years of impoverished mediocrity, his first wife and daughter included. But as she listened to Zhenia's story, Anastasia felt, for the very first time, as though they were truly sisters. For, though she had seldom been the victim of her father's brutality, she had witnessed it often enough. It was the sight of her mother's helplessness that had first fired Nastiya's determination never to allow any man to beat or bully her; from that had come the hunger, drive and unflagging willpower that had made her the woman she was today. The discovery that her own sister had been attacked was enough to waken long-buried feelings and reopen emotional wounds that she had thought were long since healed.

"Don't worry," she told Zhenia. "I'll take care of everything. First, I want you to go to my mother's apartment. I'll let her know you're coming."

"But will she let me in? I mean . . . he left her for my mother."

"Believe me, when she hears what he did to you, she'll be only too glad to help. We'll get you a doctor and you'll need a brain-scan to make sure that you've not got anything more serious than concussion to worry about."

"How can I pay? He's bound to have stopped my Amex card."

"I said, don't worry. I can pay for everything, and if you want, when this is all over, you can get me a little present—nothing fancy—in return."

"I'd like that," Yevgenia said, almost crying at the relief of being in touch with somebody who was kind to her. Then she remembered the darkness that was still out there. "But . . . but what are we going to do about Papa?"

"Nothing," said Nastiya. "Ignore him completely. Do not acknowledge his existence. Let the bastard sweat. But if the day ever comes when he threatens you again, let me know. I will make sure that whatever we do about Papa, he will never, ever forget it."

Somehow she knew that her big sister really meant every word said. When Nastiya broke the connection and her phone went dead Yevgenia stared at it for a while and then she whispered, "I love you, Nastiya, like I have loved nobody before you."

Shelby Weiss did not appreciate being made to look like a fool by an overgrown gangbanger like Johnny Congo. Of course he'd understood that even in these days of wanton excess among the very rich, two million bucks was a ridiculous price to set aside for a funeral. So he would bet his two million bucks to a nickel that D'Shonn Brown was not really as squeaky-clean as he always claimed. It was also safe to say that Congo had never struck him as a man who would compliantly walk right into the Death House without a fight. But it had never for one second occurred to Weiss that Congo and Brown would turn U.S. Route 190, the goddamn Ronald Reagan Memorial Highway no less, into the East Texas answer to the Gaza Strip. And he really didn't like having Bobby Malinga come into his office the day after and treat him like some kind of suspected gangbanger himself.

On the other hand, one message had come through loud and clear from the whole experience: Johnny Congo had money, lots and lots of money. And though, as Weiss now realized, he had made a lot of it in various unsavory business ventures in the heart of Africa, the original source of his wealth was the income his partner Carl Bannock enjoyed as a beneficiary of the Henry Bannock Family Trust. Weiss let the thought of that trust percolate through his mind for a while and his subconscious work at it, the way he did when he was planning a courtroom strategy, letting a sequence of thoughts line up like wagons behind a locomotive until he had a long train steaming down the track, heading full speed toward his destination.

The Bannock Trust, Weiss reasoned, was a gold mine, not just for its beneficiaries, but also for its legal administrators, who could charge sky-high fees that were just the merest drop in the torrent of Bannock Oil bounty. Weiss himself had never crossed the line and actually stolen from a client, but it occurred to him that a lesser man might be able to skim six- or even seven-figure sums from it every year without anyone ever needing to find out.

At the present time, the trust was administered by the firm of Bunter and Theobald. Old Ronnie Bunter had not only been a close personal friend of Henry Bannock, he was also as fine and decent a man as had ever stood at the Texas Bar, a Southern gentleman of the old school for whom all who knew him felt nothing but affection and admiration. His wife Betty had in her time been a perfect Texas Rose and long after she ceased to practice law, she was a towering figure in the legal community, organizing charity events, supporting those members of the profession who had fallen on hard times, or who had simply become too old or infirm to look after themselves. All three of Weiss's ex-wives had simply adored her. But the word was poor Betty was suffering from dementia and her loving husband, being the kind of man he was, had given up full-time work in order to devote himself more fully to care for the woman he loved, and who had sacrificed so much for him.

As a result, effective control of Bunter and Theobald had passed to Ronnie and Betty's son Bradley, who was, in Shelby Weiss's eyes, a genuine freak of nature. Here was a guy who had had it all. Not only were his parents rich and influential, they were also loving, attentive and devoted to their children. Brad himself was handsome, healthy and strong. Yet despite all these advantages—blessings for which the young Shelby Weiss, coming up the hard way, would have killed—Brad Bunter had somehow managed to become an ocean-going, weapons-grade, 24-carat shitweasel. The man was deceitful, treacherous, greedy, ambitious and filled with an undeserved sense of entitlement. Moreover, he was a notorious spendthrift, with a passionate attachment to fast women, slow horses, losing teams and white Colombian powder. His parents, being too decent themselves to even imagine that their son could be the man he was, had somehow never seen through his shiny veneer of surface charm, and Brad had always been smart enough to play nice with them, or as nice as he could manage, anyway. So when Ronnie Bunter's peers had tried to tell him the truth, he had waved them away.

But everybody in the business knew that Brad Bunter was a second-rate oxygen-waster and it would surely not be long, Weiss reasoned, before someone took advantage of that fact. That someone, he decided, might as well be himself.

He called a private detective whom he had often used to check out his clients' stories and find incriminating information to use against their opponents. "I want you to do a number on Bradley Bunter," Weiss said. "He's the acting senior partner of his dad's law firm, Bunter and Theobald. I need to know who he's screwing, what he's snorting, how much he owes, and to whom, and what the vig is. And a word of advice, take a big shovel. Believe me, you're going to dig up a ton of dirt."

A week later, having received a full and very informative report, and having the strong sense that he would be pushing at an open door, Shelby Weiss picked up the phone, was put through to Bradley Bunter's office and said, "Brad, it's been too long. I just wanted to say, I'm so sorry to hear that your dear mother is unwell. Please send her my kindest regards. Listen, I don't know if this is a good time or not, but I have a business proposition, and I think you might be interested to hear it. Let me buy you a drink and tell you what I have in mind . . ."

Brad Bunter couldn't believe his luck when Shelby Weiss offered him a million-five in cash, a partnership in a new, enlarged firm with his name in its title and a massively increased annual remuneration package in return for merging Bunter and Theobald into Weiss, Mendoza and Burnett. The other junior partners in Bunter and Theobald burst into applause when Bradley presented the equally sweet deals, relative to their current earnings, that were on the table for them.

"Here's to the Hebrew!" Brad toasted, downing a double Jack Daniel's at the bar to which he and his colleagues had retired to celebrate their imminent good fortune.

"The Hebe!" they all chanted, even the ones who were, in fact, Jewish.

The toasts continued: "Here's to the Wetback! Here's to the WASP!"

At the Bunter family home, however, the news of the proposed merger was received very differently. "I'm so sorry, Ronnie," Jo Stanley said as she relayed the details of the partners' meeting to her boss. "The deal's going to be accepted. They were unanimous."

"I can't believe it," Bunter said. He looked suddenly older, shrunken and more fragile, as though he had received a physical blow. "It's not possible. Are you sure it was Brad that suggested this? My own son, throwing away our family firm . . . It's not possible."

"I don't know what to say, Ronnie," Jo said, moving closer to him, wanting to offer him some kind of comfort, but unable to hold out any hope. "From what I could make out it all happened very quickly. Shelby Weiss came to Brad with a deal, he jumped at it and, well, I guess it was just too rich for anyone to say no to it."

"I could veto it," Bunter said, regaining a flicker of energy. "I don't get to the office much these days, but I'm still the senior partner, I could do that."

"What would be the point?" Jo asked. "Brad would hate you. The others would quit. You'd still have Bunter and Theobald, but there wouldn't be anything there. If you want to preserve your legacy, Ronnie, the best thing you can do is demand a partnership in the new firm. They won't say no to you. And screw every last dime you can out of Shelby Weiss. If he's going to take your firm, make him pay. And think of Betty . . . this way she won't ever want for anything and neither will you."

"I guess so," said Bunter regretfully. "But to see it all go like this: three generations' work, lost in an instant. It's hard to take, Jo . . ."

She patted his hand, saying nothing, knowing from the look on Ronnie's face that he was thinking about something and trusting that he'd share it with her soon enough.

"You say Weiss was the man behind this?"

"That's right. Bradley was very insistent about the fact that he had Weiss's personal assurance for all the terms he was offering."

"I've never liked him, you know. Shelby Weiss, I mean. Oh, I know about his hard-luck story, how he worked his way up from nothing and I admire him for that. He knows his law, too, there's no doubt about that, and he can put on a helluva show in court. If he'd been born a hundred years earlier, he'd have been selling snake oil at county fairs and making a good living at it, you can bet."

Jo laughed. "Roll up! Roll up! Just a dollar a bottle!"

"Exactly, my dear, a dollar a bottle indeed. So what's he peddling now, eh? What's got him so excited that he's willing to throw millions of his firm's dollars at a stuffy old law firm like Bunter and Theobald? What do we have that he wants?"

"Why do I get the feeling that you already know the answer, Ronnie?"

Bunter laughed. "Ah, Jo, you know me too well! Let me

elucidate . . . I don't have to tell you that Weiss was the lawyer representing Johnny Congo in the time between his arrival here in Texas and the appalling disaster of his escape. Now, Betty gets tired very easily these days and needs to rest, which means I have a lot of time on my hands. So I've filled some of it by doing a little digging into the events of that terrible day. I still have a few old friends around the place, codgers just like me . . ."

"Those codgers run the state, Ronnie, as you very well know."

"Not as much as they used to, but never mind. My point is, I have it on good authority that Congo, the professional and personal partner of Carl Bannock—wherever he may be—gave Weiss a great deal of money, millions of dollars in fact, a significant proportion of which ended up in Weiss, Mendoza and Burnett's bank account. Just a couple weeks later, here comes Mr. Weiss, knocking on our door, using that very same money, I dare say, to present an offer that makes no financial sense, unless . . ." Bunter left the sentence unfinished and gave Jo a look inviting her to finish it.

"Unless he knows just how much money there is in the Henry Bannock Family Trust."

"And he wants to get his greedy hands on it," Bunter concluded. "Very well," he went on, his energy now fully restored. "Here is what we are going to do. I will take as much money as Weiss is desperate enough to give me, and in cash. I will demand an emeritus partnership at the merged firm, with full rights to view the company accounts and attend partners' meetings, or have a representative attend them on my behalf. As before, you will be that representative. I want you to watch Weiss like a hawk. Keep an eye on everything he does and let me know the instant you get any hint that he is trying to interfere with the administration of the trust. Henry Bannock was my dear friend and I promised him that I would make sure that all his descendants would be able to enjoy the fruits of his labors."

Bunter looked Jo in the eye. "I may not be able to preserve

my legacy. But I'll fight till the very last breath in my body to preserve Henry Bannock's."

Among the many things Johnny Congo and Carl Bannock had learned through experience was this: If you wanted to buy political influence or protection, always go to the socialist governments first. It had nothing to do with the rights or wrongs of any political ideology; it was more a matter of psychology. "In life, a certain proportion of people realize that they are superior to the common herd," Carl had theorized, one hot, lazy, drug-fuelled afternoon in Kazundu.

"Amen to that, bro," Congo had agreed.

"Now, a country like America is filled with opportunity for someone who knows they deserve more than those around them, and who understands that the dumb masses deserve to be ripped off, screwed over and trampled underfoot, just for walking around, the way they do, like big, fat cattle too shit-stupid to know they're heading for the slaughterhouse."

"They got it coming, no doubt about it."

"Say you're someone who wants to take advantage of the opportunity afforded by the pathetic state of the mass of humanity. If you come from a nice, prosperous home, get a good degree, know how to present yourself properly, well, then you can go to Wall Street and make a killing. Did you know that ten percent of Wall Street bankers are clinical psychopaths?"

"Only have to see that *American Psycho* movie to know that, babe." Congo laughed. "Christian Bale cutting up all the rich white girls. Whoo-ee! The Batman getting his evil on."

Carl smiled. "Ha! Plenty of opportunity for being bad and getting away with it in Hollywood, too! But a man like you came up a different route. You didn't have the advantages that the kind of guy who ends up as a banker enjoys. You came from the street. So you committed what the law calls crime. But, let's get real, there's no moral difference between someone dealing drugs and someone selling securities that turn out to be worthless junk. They're both doing wrong, if you care about that. It's just that one of those people is wearing a suit, sitting in a fancy office, and the other's on a street corner, wearing a wife-beater and dirty jeans."

"One's white and the other's black, man, that's the frickin' difference."

"I'm white. Look where I ended up."

Congo laughed. "Only 'cause you met me, baby. I remember it like it was yesterday, the new boy, all sweet-assed and innocent, being brought to my cell to get his lesson in prison manners. Well, I taught you good. Made a man of you."

"You put me in the prison sanatorium. I had internal bleeding, my rear end all shot to pieces." Carl gave a wry smile. "Hard to believe that was the start of a beautiful friendship."

"Gotta start somewhere. So, 'bout these bankers and gang-bangers, what's your point?"

"My point," said Carl, drawing the smoke from some locally grown weed deep into his lungs, "is they've got a million ways to thrive in America, or anywhere like it. But in a communist country, like a people's republic or whatever, the State controls everything. So the only way the superior individual can screw the people is by ruling them, being a politician. So that's where the people like us end up. And that's why we can always make a deal in a place like that."

"Plus, they hate the U.S.A. And when they find out we're on the run from Uncle Sam, it's like, my enemy's enemy is my friend."

"And if my enemy's enemy has millions of my enemy's dollars they like it even better."

Venezuela was the proof of that. Carl and Congo had flown in, put some serious coin in a few very well-placed back pockets and the result had been a pair of Venezuelan passports and an assurance that although an extradition treaty between Venezuela and the United States had been in force since 1923, there was no chance that they would ever be handed over to the gringos as long as the United Socialist Party of Venezuela was in power. And they intended to stay in power for a good long while yet.

And so, having left the U.S. as a ruler of Kazundu, Congo flew into Caracas as Venezuelan citizen Juan Tumbo. That was where he was now, sprawled in a leather recliner with a Montecristo No. 2 Cuban cigar clenched between his teeth, a magnum of Cristal in an ice bucket on the floor beside him and a heap of coke on a mirror on the side table: that and a big, fat tube of lubricant.

Congo had spent three weeks in the godforsaken Texas death cell. He'd been much too close to death for comfort. Now he wanted to live it up. He'd got R. Kelly on the sound system, laying down some old school R 'n' B, telling his woman how her body was calling for him. And as Congo got into the music, feeling the slow, sexy rhythm, there were two bodies calling for him, too: perfect young bodies with flawless café-au-lait skin and tumbling blond hair the color of dark, sweet honey. Carl watched them dancing to the music, mirroring each other's movements. Their every facial feature was drawn as perfectly as if God himself had said, "This is what I want humans to look like." And what made them even more extraordinary was that they were identical. Looking from one to the other, Congo was unable to detect a single imperfection. There was not the slightest facial blemish to mark one out as different to the other, not a solitary hair on their heads cut to a different length or colored a contrasting shade.

In Houston, it was past nine in the evening and Tom Nocerino was putting the finishing touches to his newsletter, before sending it upstairs for final approval. The section on the Magna Grande oilfield of Angola was looking all right now, he thought. He'd finished with Hector Cross's quote, boiled down to three short, snappy sentences, bam-bam-bam: "It's going to be tough. It's going to be hard work. But we're going to get the job done."

You can't beat a good old-fashioned triad, Nocerino thought, sipping a cup of coffee as he gave the draft one last read-through.

The only section he was worried about concerned another big, new venture Bannock was undertaking. Once again it was an offshore field, but in the Arctic waters of the Beaufort Sea, off the north coast of Alaska: about as far removed as you could get, in terms of both distance and environment, from Angola. The Bannock board had sanctioned the purchase of a drilling barge, the *Noatak*, whose double-hulled construction was specially designed to withstand the pressures of Arctic pack ice. Resistance to compression also dictated that she was shaped like a giant steel soup bowl, 250 feet across. The *Noatak* was about as mobile in the water as a soup bowl, too, since she possessed no engines of her own. The board of Bannock Oil had decided that the multi-directional thrusters that would have provided the barge with the power to move and manoeuvre were too expensive to fit. They were, in any case, an unnecessary extravagance since Bannock had already acquired a $200-million icebreaking supply tug, the *Glenallen*, which was purpose built to tow huge, floating oil rigs into the waters off the North Slope of Alaska, anchor them in place and then keep them supplied with everything that the rigs or the men aboard them might need, under any conditions. She was more than 350 feet long, weighed almost 13,000 tons and her four Caterpillar engines produced more than 20,000 horsepower. Why buy more engines when those monsters were already available?

There was just one thing stopping Tom Nocerino from spinning the story of a weird but wonderful drilling barge and a state-of-the-art icebreaking tug into the kind of upbeat story that the investors' newsletter demanded. After a spring and summer of exploration, Bannock Oil's vessels and personnel had yet to find any oil under their particular patch of the

Beaufort Sea. The geologists' reports were unequivocal. There were billions of barrels down there somewhere, it was just that they hadn't yet found the right place to drill for them. But now, though the *Noatak*'s entire reason for being was that she could keep working through the winter, the *Glenallen* was towing her back around the far north-western corner of Alaska, en route to the mooring off Seattle where she would spend the next several months.

This ignominious retreat was being made to evade the levies that the state of Alaska imposes on any oil-drilling operations present on its territory or in its waters on 1 January of any given year. Tom Nocerino had to find a way of changing "We spent hundreds of millions of bucks, we couldn't find any oil, so now we're getting out before they tax us" into "Alaska—it's going great!"

It wasn't going to be easy, but he'd been seeing an incredibly hot tax attorney for the past couple of weeks and he was certain this would be the night she'd agree to have sex with him. So he was going to find the right words, get them approved by Bigelow and press "Send" on the newsletter mailout before he left work, or die in the attempt.

High above the Arctic Circle, the *Glenallen* was towing the *Noatak* through the Chukchi Sea, the body of water that lies between the Beaufort Sea and the Bering Strait that separates the westernmost point of the United States from the far eastern tip of Russia. The two ships were harnessed together by hawsers thicker than a fat man's waist, held by a massive, solid steel shackle aboard the *Glenallen*. In the calm waters that had prevailed so far, they had maintained a slow but steady progress during which the fact that the barge weighed more than twice as much as the tug that was towing her had not been an issue. But now the barometric pressure was dropping, the wind was rising and the ocean swells were building. The crew of the *Glenallen* didn't need a weather forecast to tell them that a storm was coming: that much was obvious. What they didn't know, however, was what would happen when it struck. Left to her own devices, the *Glenallen* had the size, strength and power to cope with almost anything the oceans could throw at her. But now she was handicapped by the huge, graceless, helpless craft that followed in her wake. The men on both ships just had to pray that handicap wouldn't prove fatal.

The storm came roaring out of the Arctic in a fury of wind and ice, whipping the waters of the Chukchi Sea into a maelstrom. The waves piled one upon another, reaching higher and higher into the sky as if they were trying to grab the snow-laden clouds and pull them back down into the depths from which they'd come. These were conditions whose elemental savagery mocked the puny efforts of humankind to survive, let alone master the forces of nature. The air was cold enough in itself, some twenty degrees centigrade below freezing. But the winds that surged as high as eighty miles per hour made it feel more like fifty below. No man could look barefaced into the teeth of such a storm and survive, for the blast of freezing air laden with water droplets that had frozen as hard as buckshot would shred his skin and pulp his eyes. Yet somewhere out on the heaving black wastes two unlikely vessels, tied to one another like blind mountaineers in an avalanche, were making their slow, desperate way through the tempest.

Without the *Glenallen*, the *Noatak* was completely at the mercy of the ocean beneath her and the weather above, yet her size and helplessness were now in danger of destroying the very craft on which her own survival depended. As the *Glenallen* tried to climb up each successive, towering wave, the deadweight of the *Noatak* pulled against her, dragging her stern so low that water flooded over it, cascading down into the body of the hull. Then, as the tug rushed down the far sides of each foaming wall of water, so the barge charged after her, looming out of the snow-filled darkness like a runaway express train.

The *Glenallen*'s skipper could not cut the umbilical cord between his ship and the *Noatak*, for then the barge would be swept away on the waves and it would surely be lost, along with its fifteen-man skeleton crew. Yet if the link were kept, the *Glenallen* might go down too, for the high, triangular drilling tower at the dead center of the barge was acting as a combination of sail and metronome. The flat metal panels that shrouded the bottom third of the tower caught the wind, which thereby pushed the barge before it. And as the *Noatak* sped forewards, so the forces of wind and water made the tower swing back and forth in an ever-increasing arc, taking the hull with it. Meanwhile the snow and sea spray dashing against the metal structure of the tower froze in layer after thickening layer of ice, which became heavier and heavier, exaggerating the effect of each metronome swing, plunging the decks of the barge beneath the churning water. With every extra degree of motion, the top of the tower came closer to the water surface, hastening the moment when the *Noatak* would be unable to bob back to the surface after each successive wall of water had crashed over her. And should the barge go under, the *Glenallen* would be dragged down with her to the grave.

It was left to Mother Nature to cut the Gordian Knot with a succession of surging waves that caused the tether between the two ships to be pulled tight in a sudden, convulsive jerk, then to sag as the tug and barge were drawn together, only to be snapped tight again as they were pulled apart. The first time this happened, the shackle held firm against the incredible force exerted by the barge. But with every successive tightening the force on the shackle increased and the mountings holding it to the *Glenallen*'s aft deck juddered and loosened, only by fractions of a millimeter at first, but then more and more until they snapped.

The shackle—120 tons of steel—smashed its way along the

131

deck, leaving a trail of damage in its wake until it finally flew off the tug's stern and plunged into the depths of the Chukchi Sea.

The barge was swept away like a cork in a rushing stream, picked up by the waves and carried in the direction that the nor'westerly wind was driving them, straight toward the Alaskan shoreline. There was absolutely nothing that the fifteen men aboard the *Noatak* could do to fight the waves or steer away from the coast. All they could do now was pray for a miracle to deliver them, knowing that if it did not come they were surely doomed.

When the shackle had been torn from the *Glenallen*'s deck, and with it the cables that linked her to the drilling barge *Noatak*, the tug's skipper had sent out a distress call. It had been picked up by the *Munro*, a U.S. Coast Guard cutter that was on patrol, more than 150 miles to the northeast. There was no way that the *Munro* could reach the stricken barge in time to rescue the fifteen crewmen who were still aboard her. But she did have a Dolphin search and rescue helicopter that might be able to make it. Heedless of the danger of even attempting to fly through a storm of this magnitude, the chopper's four-man crew raced to their aircraft and took off into the wild and merciless night.

The *Noatak* was less than five miles from shore when the Dolphin emerged out of the darkness and snow and took up its position hovering like a fragile metal dragonfly over the bucking, plunging, oscillating barge. The best that the helicopter crew could hope for was to lower a man on to the *Noatak*'s landing pad and pray that he could grab the rig's crew members one by one as they let go of the rails to which they were clinging and made their way across the fatally unstable pad, perched at the very edge of the barge's upper deck, with no shelter from the wind as it came howling through the drill tower's rigging. Should a crewman slip before he was safely clipped to the harness dropped from the helicopter there was nothing but the flimsy

132

railing to stop him plunging into the sub-zero waters where the cold would certainly kill him, even if drowning did not.

One by one eight men ascended from the hell of the barge to the heavenly embrace of the helicopter. But then the pilot signaled that the Dolphin could take no more weight onboard and the helicopter disappeared off into the night. The seven men still left aboard the *Noatak* had a rational, intellectual grasp of what was happening. The Dolphin was flying to the *Glenallen*, which had closed to within a mile, and the process would be repeated in reverse as the *Noatak*'s crew were lowered on to the tug's landing pad, grabbed by its crew and taken below. But it was one thing to be told that the helicopter would return and another to believe that it could when all the time the coast was getting ever nearer. Even when the Dolphin had taken up its station above the landing pad once again, the tension did not ease for a moment. The swinging drill tower might at any moment strike the helicopter's rotor blades like a stick shoved between the spokes of a bicycle wheel, but to far deadlier effect. The coast was somewhere out there in the impenetrable night, coming closer and closer all the time, yet the crew of the Dolphin could not rush, for haste would only lead to mistakes.

The last seven men had to wait their turn, beating back the fear that was taking an even tighter grip of their minds and bodies, resisting the urge to fight their way past the men whose turn to be rescued would come sooner than their own. One by one, they rose into the sky. Wave by wave the inevitable impact of the barge against the shore came closer. Finally only the captain of the *Noatak* remained and he was still hanging in mid-air when the curtain of snow in front of the Dolphin's cockpit parted for a moment and the light picked out a blackness that somehow seemed more solid than what had been there before. It took the pilot a second or two to compute what he was seeing and then he was pulling the Dolphin up and away, praying that both the helicopter and the men hanging beneath it would miss the rock-face that had suddenly appeared before them and now threatened to flatten them like insects against a windshield.

Only seconds later the *Noatak* smashed into the jagged promontory. Its hull comprised two thick layers of steel, specifically designed to resist the crushing grip of Arctic pack ice. But even that steel proved no defense against the harsh, unyielding rock. The hull ruptured, the water flooded in and the drilling barge *Noatak* sank beneath the pounding waves, with only the drill tower rising above the water's surface to mark its passing.

In Houston, John Bigelow, Chief Executive and President of Bannock Oil, had been up all night, following developments in the northern wastes from the comfort of his home office. Shortly after three in the morning he got the call he'd been dreading from Bannock's office in Anchorage, Alaska.

"I'm sorry, Mr. Bigelow, but we lost the *Noatak*. I assure you, sir, that we did our best, the Coast Guard, too, but this was a helluva storm. For this time of year, we've not seen anything like it this century."

Bigelow maintained his air of unruffled command throughout the next few minutes as he established the extent of the losses, both human and material. There was little environmental damage beyond the wreckage of the barge itself, that at least was something to be glad of. But when the call was finished he walked unsteadily to his drinks cabinet and poured himself a very large Scotch. He took one gulp and then set the glass aside, unfinished, as he slumped into a chair, held his head in his hands and asked aloud, "My God, what have I done?"

The early-morning sun was slicing through the semi-opened slats of the bedroom blinds and Congo was sitting up in bed, watching TV. A young girl lay on the rumpled sheets beside him. She rolled over in her sleep so that her head was level with his naked crotch. Then with one hand she reached out reflexively and cuddled his genitalia.

134

"Not now." He pushed her hand away. "I'm trying to concentrate, for Chrissakes!"

The girl rolled back to where she'd started and dropped into deep sleep again. Johnny Congo had been awake all night, too jacked up on all the coke he'd snorted to be able to sleep. Now he was curious to know if his escape was still making any waves, so he'd turned the smart TV to CNN, keeping the volume down low because he didn't want the little bitch beside him to wake up and start whining at him for her money. Next he opened up a screen within the screen to check all his and Carl's email accounts. And then it wasn't just the drugs that were keeping him wide awake.

It began with Congo finding a Bannock Oil newsletter that had been emailed to Carl in his role as the sole remaining adult beneficiary of Henry Bannock's trust fund. The two words "Hector Cross" leaped out of the screen at Congo as if they'd been written in neon the size of the Hollywood sign. There the white Limey bastard was, bragging about how he was going to keep the Bannock installation in Angola safe and sound and Congo found himself laughing aloud at the way his bitterest enemy had delivered himself into his hands.

"Now I know just where to find you, white boy," Congo murmured happily, his wired mind so filled with random, half-formed ideas about how to revenge himself on Hector Cross that he did not at first pay much attention to the breaking news story about an oil-drilling barge sinking off the coast of Alaska. But then he thought he heard someone say the words "Bannock Oil," so he put the news on to full-screen, turned up the volume loud enough to hear clearly and focused on the news story as it slowly took shape, each new reporter or talking head adding one more small piece to a puzzle that was still a long way from being completed.

The element of the sinking that most troubled Congo was its possible effect on Bannock stock. Cross's attack on the palace

135

complex he and Carl had built for themselves in Kazundu had left Carl dead and their buildings in ruins. When Congo had been captured and thrown in jail, the various criminal enterprises he had run alongside Carl all fell to pieces. That left the Bannock Trust as his sole source of cash, but the trust was largely funded by the dividends earned by the company stock that formed the great bulk of its capital value. If Bannock Oil suffered, so would the trust and so would Congo.

Congo felt put-upon, paranoid, convinced that the sinking of a barge in Alaska was somehow, in ways he could not quite work out, part of a scheme to rob him of the money that was rightfully his. Money was what this was all about, so he flicked channels until he got a network that was all about money: Bloomberg.

By this time it was six in the morning. The daily *Bloomberg Surveillance* show was just starting, and it was opening with helicopter footage of a searchlight, sweeping across storm-tossed waters. This had to be the sinking. Congo sat right up in bed and prepared himself to watch the show.

It was eleven o'clock in London and Hector Cross was finishing his third mug of coffee that morning as he worked on his pitch to the Bannock Oil board for the funds he would need to buy a military surplus ship. Aside from the brief glimpses of a kiddies' TV show that he'd caught while attempting to shovel some breakfast down his little girl's pretty but uncooperative mouth, Cross had deliberately stayed away from all media or means of communication. He was about to put in a request for several million of Bannock Oil's dollars and he had to get it right first time, so he didn't want anything to distract him. Then his iPhone pinged to alert him of an incoming message. Cross ignored it, but a minute later, programed to take offense when ignored, the phone pinged a second time and he could not help himself glancing at the screen. The sender was one of his contacts, named as "JB Private Office," which meant Bigelow, or Jessica, his senior personal assistant. The message was so brief that it was all contained within the alert. It simply read: "Urgent. Turn on Bloomberg Surveillance NOW. CEO interview re Noatak."

Cross frowned with annoyance. The word "Noatak" rang a bell, but he couldn't remember why. Still, if it was important enough for Bigelow's office to contact him at five in the morning, Houston time, he'd better find out what the fuss was all about. He switched on his office TV, found *Bloomberg* on the Sky box and saw a middle-aged man whose thinning gray hair, horn-rimmed spectacles and bow-tie gave him the air of a college professor rather than a morning TV presenter.

"So," the man was saying, "market-makers are waking up to two major stories that could have significant impact on early trading on the Dow this morning. We'll be returning to one of them momentarily, the loss of Bannock Oil's Alaskan oil-drilling barge *Noatak*."

Cross gasped out loud. Now he knew why the message had been so insistent. He went online, looking for more information, while the presenter continued, "But before that, you can bet Slindon Insurance CEO Thornton Carpenter didn't enjoy opening his inbox this morning, because it contained one of Seventh Wave Investment's founder Aram Bendick's legendary flamings."

Cross was only vaguely aware of a photograph of a balding, pugnacious white male in a suit filling the screen as the presenter continued, "Bendick has made billions thanks to his hyper-aggressive, extremely personal attacks on corporate bosses, made in the form of personal emails that he simultaneously releases online. His strategy is to force company boards to ditch their existing strategies and run their businesses the way he sees fit, and which usually involves aggressive cost-cutting measures that boost short-term profits and stock prices but, say critics, including many of Bendick's victims, leave previously healthy businesses hollowed-out and easy prey for competitors."

137

Now an image of a letter with a few lines superimposed in much larger type appeared. Cross had gone on to the BBC News site and was working his way through the several stories that had already been posted about the sinking. He was only catching the odd word as the voice from the screen informed more attentive viewers that, "Bendick's letter accuses Carpenter of, quote: 'running Slindon for the benefit of himself and his fellow senior executives, rather than shareholders . . . wasting millions on golf tournament sponsorships that gave board members the opportunity to hobnob with top golfers and golf groupies, but did nothing to promote the Slindon Insurance brand' and 'indulging in orgies of over-eating, over-drinking and obscene overspending, only barely disguised as strategic-planning retreats for senior decision-makers.'

"Mr. Carpenter has yet to respond to these allegations, but Aram Bendick joins us now from his New York City apartment—good morning, Mr. Bendick."

"Good morning, Tom."

So now Cross had half the presenter's name, at least.

"Slindon Insurance profits were up three percent last year, the company paid record dividends to stockholders, and that was all on Thornton Carpenter's watch. So why the attack on him now, and why make accusations that some might say have nothing to do with his performance as CEO?"

Bendick's reply was as confrontational as his appearance. In an abrasive "Noo Yoik" accent he sneered, "Because they've got everything to do with his performance, which is lazy, ineffective and lacking in any clear vision for the future of the business he's supposed to lead."

"And this is because Slindon—like a lot of major corporations—sponsor a PGA tournament? Really?"

"Yeah, really. Look, you said the company's profits were up three percent. Their three closest competitors averaged over five. Why? Because their CEOs and their boards and their executives were thinking about growing their markets and cutting their costs, not about buying Bermuda shorts and suntan oil for a five-day, all-expenses-paid luxury holiday in Hawaii, dressed up as a chance to think outside the goddamn envelope—excuse my language but this kind of corruption, because that's what it is, really offends me."

"So you stand by all your comments in the letter?"

"I wouldn't have written them if I didn't."

"And what do you want to see happen next?"

"I want, and expect, my fellow stockholders in Slindon to demand—and get—major changes in corporate policy. And if that means changes in personnel, so be it."

"And do you have any other corporations in your sights right now?"

"Always, Tom . . . always."

"So, Aram Bendick laying it on the line there, the way he usually does. We'll be following this story as it develops and as soon as we get a response from anyone at Slindon, you'll have it. Now to Alaska, where a Bannock Oil drilling barge sank at around eleven last night, local time."

Now Tom had Cross's complete attention as he continued, "This marks the latest in a string of setbacks for Bannock and a number of other oil companies trying to open fields in the Beaufort and Chukchi seas, north of Alaska. They've been dogged by the difficulty of working in one of the most hostile environments on the planet, and by constant criticism and hostile lobbying from Green campaigners opposed to any further exploitation of Alaskan oilfields. I'm joined by Maggie Kim, noted Wall Street petrochemicals analyst and founder of the Daily Gas blog and newsletter. Maggie, what effect do you see this disaster having on Bannock Oil, going forward?"

Maggie Kim was a Eurasian woman who could, Cross thought, be damn good-looking if she ever took that stern "take me seriously" expression off her face and risked an occasional smile. But once she started talking he forgot all about her looks. This woman clearly knew what she was talking about, and it wasn't good news for Bannock Oil.

"As you say, Tom," Kim began, "the *Noatak* is not the first drilling barge to be lost in Alaskan waters. On New Year's Eve 2012, the Shell barge *Kulluk* ran aground and had to be scrapped. A little over a year later, Shell halted its entire drilling program in the Alaskan Arctic, which had cost around five billion dollars to that point and announced an immediate six-hundred-and-eighty-seven-million-dollar write-off. Now, a loss like that is a serious blow, even to Shell which regularly ranks among the world's three largest corporations. But a business like Bannock, which is much smaller, is correspondingly less able to withstand such a shock."

"So was Bannock biting off more than it could chew, going into the Alaskan Arctic in the first place?"

Kim nodded thoughtfully. "That's certainly a valid question. For the past several years, first under the leadership of Hazel Bannock, widow of the company's founder Henry Bannock, and her successor as President and CEO John Bigelow, Bannock has had an aggressive, high-risk, expansionist policy. And I have to admit that it's worked up to now. Hazel Bannock bet the farm on what industry experts believed was a played-out oilfield in the Arab Emirate of Abu Zara and hit an untapped subterranean chamber filled with five billion gallons of sweet and light crude. Now Bigelow and the Bannock board are playing double or quits, because they're also opening a field off the West African state of Angola. The company won't release precise figures for its combined investment in Alaska and Africa, but it has to be close to ten billion dollars."

"Well, Bigelow lost his chips on one half of their bet when that barge sank last night. Can he and Bannock afford it if both bets go down the pan?"

"You know, I hesitate to give you a definitive yes or no on

that right now, without knowing the exact numbers. But I can tell you for sure that John Bigelow's got to be praying that nothing goes wrong in Angola. And when I think about all the security issues that have plagued the oil industry in West Africa—bombs, corruption, even hijacked ships—I've got to wonder if Bannock can possibly survive another disaster like the one last night."

"Thank you, Maggie, and to answer the points that you raised, I'm joined now by John Bigelow himself. Good morning, Senator. I guess I should first ask you, have all the crew from the *Noatak* been recovered safely?"

"Good morning, Tom," said Bigelow, who looked as exhausted, anxious and tense as any other 62-year-old man would do who'd been dragged from his bed in the early hours to be told that one of his ships had just sunk. "I'm delighted to be able to report that thanks to the hard work and courage of the fine men and women of the U.S. Coast Guard, all fifteen members of the crew were taken off the *Noatak* before she sank and are safe and well. And can I also say how glad I am that you led with that question, because our concern right now, as a company, is for our people, not our bottom line. At times like these, human lives matter much more than dollars and cents."

"That's very true, Senator, but like it or not, dollars and cents will very quickly become the issue. Maggie Kim has just been giving us her view that you have been playing double or quits, trying to develop two fields simultaneously . . ."

"Yes, I heard that."

"Is she right?"

Bigelow faked a smile and gave a hollow, joyless chuckle that made Cross wince: if a man's laughter was that unconvincing what did that say about his words? "Well, you know, Tom, I've enjoyed listening to Maggie over the years. She's always got something to say, that's for sure. But she's in business, just like we are, and hers consists of saying things that will grab people's attention. Mine is running a profitable, stable, successful petrochemicals business, and that's what I plan to keep doing."

"With due respect, Senator, you didn't answer my question: has Bannock's ambitious development program left it over-extended?"

"My answer to that is very simple: no. With respect to our Alaskan operations, the *Noatak* was fully insured, we will be able to commission a replacement and the oil will still be waiting when operations begin again. As for Angola, as I'm sure you know, Tom, I served for many years on the Senate Committee on Foreign Relations, so I know a little about global affairs and have a great many contacts upon whom I can call for advice. And from everything I have been told, I can assure you, Maggie Kim and your viewers that the situation in Angola is nothing like that prevailing in Nigeria, where the government faces a serious threat from Islamist militants. Those people do not exist in Angola. The government is secure, the country is peaceful and there is no cause for alarm."

"Well, that's bloody well asking for trouble," Hector Cross muttered to himself.

"So you're confident that your bets on Alaska and Angola will pay off?"

"They're not bets, Tom, that's what I'm saying," Bigelow replied. "They're sensible, pragmatic investments made on the basis of known oil and gas reserves. And, yes, those investments will provide Bannock Oil and its shareholders with a significant return on their capital for many years to come."

The interview ended and Cross switched off the TV. He wondered whether it was even worth writing the funding request. John Bigelow had done his best to put up a strong defense. But Cross knew him well enough to be able to recognize when the Senator was saying what he actually believed, or just toeing the party line.

* * *

Meanwhile, in Caracas, Johnny Congo was feeling like he was watching a lottery draw and all the numbers on his ticket were coming up one by one: the news that Cross would be working on Bannock's Angolan project; then the hedge-funder that liked sticking it to corporate bosses; then the Bannock oil rig going down. Somewhere in all that there was a way of nailing Cross once and for all. He couldn't quite figure it out yet, but it was there all right, no doubt about that. What he needed now was something to distract and relax him, so that his subconscious could work on the problem and figure out an answer, and that something was lying right beside him.

He stretched out his right arm and gave the sleeping girl beside him two rough shakes. She woke up, raised herself on one elbow and looked at him through groggy unfocused eyes as he pulled the sheet down to his knees.

"Put your mouth over here, girl. Time you got back to work."

Well, gentlemen, the hot news that I wish to share with you is that Mateus da Cunha is holding a reception at his French grandparents' apartment in Paris to launch a foundation he is setting up, officially to raise awareness of Cabinda and promote the cause of independence in that country. Unofficially, I believe it's a front for his plan to gain control of Cabinda by force." Nastiya O'Quinn was addressing the meeting of Cross Bow Security high command which she had asked Hector Cross to convene. She was sitting on Hector's desk and the rest of the team were spread out around the room in front of her, draped in various attitudes of relaxation over the furniture. Nastiya was wearing a tight-fitting skirt which had rucked up above her knees to reveal her calves. No matter how often they had been presented with this view it still demanded their full attention. But now, as one, they raised their eyes to her face.

"So fasten your seatbelts, ladies and gentlemen, we are about to take off," Hector cut in. "As you will recall from our previous discussions, the oil reserves in the province of Cabinda could be worth two or three hundreds of billions of dollars." There was a general murmur of interest and excitement and her audience sat forward on their seats.

Nastiya nodded. "Some estimates put the amount even higher, especially if oil ever gets back to a hundred dollars a barrel. I have been invited to the da Cunha reception not as Nastiya O'Quinn, but as Maria Denisova, an investment consultant, whose clients are Russian oligarchs and other ultra-high-net-worth individuals from the former Soviet Union. Although the Duchêne family is known for its tradition of liberal, even radical opinions, it's one of the oldest and richest families in France. So this will be a very smart occasion, attracting the cream of Parisian society, as well as many guests from across Europe and even the United States. On the other hand, it will also be a money-raising event. Now I will hand you over to Dave Imbiss to give you further details. If you please, David." She flashed her famous smile at him across the room.

"I've put together the legend for Miss Denisova," Dave Imbiss told them. "I've set up her company website, along with a trail of newspaper articles, social media pages, and photographs of Nastiya with men whom da Cunha will certainly recognize. We're also working on setting up a Moscow office, with an email address and a phone that will be manned by old contacts of Nastiya's."

"I plan to go to Moscow in the next few days to put everything in place. I will also be hiring a personal assistant, who will act as the receptionist if anyone calls the office or visits it."

"I'm concerned about security," Hector cut in. "Can you trust these contacts of yours and some dolly-bird receptionist to sound convincing if da Cunha gets in touch, and to keep their mouths shut at all other times?"

"I met these friends of mine when we were all being trained in the arts of espionage, so yes, if you can trust me, you can trust them too. As for the receptionist, I do not know the term 'dolly bird,' but I have someone in mind and, yes, I am confident that she can be relied on, too," Nastiya told him forcibly.

"Fair enough. Now, can you get an invitation to this party?"

"I already have one. I called up da Cunha's office, as Maria Denisova. I explained who I was, what I did, and how much money my clients had to spend on interesting investments that offered above-average returns. They put me straight on the list."

"Will you need Dave to be with you in Moscow, or Paris?"

"I can make sure you're tracked all the way, so if anything goes wrong I can get you out of it," Imbiss assured her.

"No, that's all right, Dave. Moscow is no problem and you've got equally important work to do here, helping Hector to get the Caracas job set up. As for Paris, I can look after myself there, too. Just get me the smallest video camera you can find, show me how to set it up and I'll be fine."

"You're not making a sex tape are you?" said O'Quinn, trying and failing to make it sound like a joke.

"Don't worry, my darling," said Nastiya, talking for once as a loving wife rather than a tough professional. "You know how it is: I may have to blackmail da Cunha. The best way of doing that is to have damaging material that he would never want publicized. Would it embarrass him to be seen having sex with a white woman? No. But if that woman had slipped Rohypnol into his drink, knocked him out and then created footage that appeared to show him tied up while she whipped him, then I think he would tell her almost anything to stop the world seeing him humiliated that way."

"Ah, that old whipping routine," said O'Quinn, nodding in understanding. "It always works. The men'll say anything. For example, I said, 'Will you marry me?' when you did it to me."

When she got to Moscow, Nastiya went straight from the airport to the Sadoyava Plaza office building, a prestigious

145

location just a couple of hundred meters from Tverskaya Street, where many of the world's smartest designer names had their flagship Russian stores. She rented a serviced suite on the fourth floor, where all the building's short-let office space was located, and made arrangements to have it accessorized with equipment, decorative displays and furniture that would be appropriate for a business serving high-net-worth clients.

With that element of her cover secured, she made her way to her mother's apartment, where Yevgenia was staying. The three women hugged and kissed, laughed and cried. She was delighted to discover that the swelling on her sister's face had subsided and any remaining traces of bruising could be concealed by make-up. The two of them spent the rest of that first day together talking, beginning the task of filling in the gaps left by all the years they'd spent apart, and getting to the point where they could call one another Nastiya and Zhenia without feeling at all uncomfortable. Zhenia did not know it, but she was being tested, or more precisely auditioned for the role of Maria Denisova's personal assistant.

"Oh! My first real job!" said Zhenia excitedly the following morning when Nastiya told her that she had a role set aside for her in the da Cunha operation.

"Well, it's your first real fake job," Nastiya pointed out. "But this is a very important pretence. I need to know that if anyone comes looking for my business, they will find one that is credible enough to make them trust me. I will have a couple of my colleagues from the old days—"

"Do you mean spies? Papa once said that you'd become a spy."

"Never mind that, all you need to know is that they are good men, completely trustworthy and tough enough to keep you safe. All you have to do is learn the whole of Maria Denisova's legend: who she is, what she does, who her clients are—everything."

"I can do that," said Zhenia, "but what am I going to wear?

146

I mean, wouldn't a personal assistant go around in, I don't know . . . business clothes? I don't have anything like that."

"Then we'll buy you some."

"Oh good! But there's still one other thing that worries me. You said that I have to know all about Maria Denisova's clients."

"That's right. And if anyone wants to speak to them, you must make the connection."

"But who are they? This business of yours doesn't really exist. How can it have clients?"

"Because our darling father is going to give them to me."

"Are you sure?" Zhenia asked dubiously. "I don't think he'll want to give you anything."

"And I don't think he's going to have any choice in the matter. Give me his number. It's time I said hello after all these years."

Voronov was intrigued by the prospect of meeting his long-lost daughter, and interested when she said she knew where he could find her younger sister, who was still missing. He summoned her to his dacha, just outside Moscow, where he lived when the demands of business weren't keeping him in the city.

Nastiya had no intention of giving her father any excuse to degrade her with the same kind of insults he had hurled at Zhenia, and she certainly didn't want to provide him with the slightest encouragement to develop any incestuous feelings toward her as he had done with Zhenia. So she put her hair up into a very casual chignon and donned an impeccably tailored, slim-fitting trouser suit by Jil Sander that played with the idea of a man's double-breasted jacket without being in the slightest bit butch. This she teamed with a pair of flat brown brogues that were not only chic, but also had artfully hidden steel toecaps. As a fighting outfit, this gave her complete ease of movement, and a dash of hidden danger. But by pulling her hair up off her face and neck, she merely revealed the perfection of her bone structure, while the trouser suit was cut so cunningly that it constantly hinted at the figure it was apparently disguising.

She was met outside her hotel by a chauffeur-driven black Maybach limousine. The driver, she saw at once, was trying to hide a gun in a shoulder holster beneath his uniform jacket. The fact that she had found it so easy to spot reassured her. It suggested that he was far from first-rate and, if the need arose, could be dealt with relatively easily. Nastiya smiled sweetly as he opened the door for her, deciding to play the role of the pretty little woman: one of her great pleasures in life was seeing the look of surprise on the face of stupid, thuggish men when they realized, too late, that she was not at all what she seemed.

They drove out of the city and into the woods where, in decades gone by, the Party bigwigs had built their dachas, or country cottages. Today, all those relatively humble buildings had been knocked down, replaced by grotesquely oversized mansions, temples of bad taste for men with ill-deserved fortunes, hidden behind endless kilometers of high walls, watched over by security cameras as if the men and women beyond them were prisoners of the State, rather than its owners. Finally, the Maybach turned off the road and drove up to an ornate wrought-iron gate, guarded by a sentry box. The limo stopped by the box, the driver conferred with the guard and the gates swung open. The tree-lined drive that greeted them twisted and turned around an open landscape dotted with trees, classical follies and even a lake with an ancient stone bridge at one end that hardly seemed Russian at all. Then Vitaly Voronov's country cottage came into view and Nastiya suddenly found herself gripping her hand to her mouth to stifle her giggles. The building in front of her would have been instantly recognizable to hundreds of millions of people around the world, for it was an apparently perfect reproduction of Highclere Castle, the stately home in Berkshire, England, best known as the location of TV's Downton Abbey.

"My God," Nastiya whispered to herself, "the crazy, drunken pervert thinks he's the Earl of Grantham."

The car scrunched up the last stretch of gravel and came to

a halt before the main entrance. The driver opened the passenger door and Nastiya walked up the front staircase to the massive, studded wooden doors that opened, as if by magic, at her approach. She steeled herself for the moment when she and her father would clap eyes on one another for the first time in more than fifteen years. But when she stepped into the great hall, the first person she met was her stepmother Marina.

Marina was exceptionally beautiful—Nastiya saw at once where Yevgenia had got her looks. However she was so impeccably dressed, groomed and painted that she seemed less like a living person than a precious object. But there was a look in her eyes that Nastiya recognized at once, for she had seen it in her mother, many years ago. It was the despairing, broken look of a woman who has had the joy of life beaten out of her, whose soul has been ground down by violence and abuse. At once, any hostility or suspicion Nastiya might have felt toward the seductress who had taken her father from her vanished, replaced by a fierce determination to defend a woman who was herself defenseless.

Marina did not say hello. Instead, she stepped forward, took Nastiya's hands in hers and, in a voice that was little more than an anguished whisper, asked, "How is she?"

"She is safe and well," Nastiya assured her, leaning forward to kiss Marina on the cheek. She paused when their heads were side by side and murmured, "And you will be too. I promise."

Then they stepped back and Marina raised her voice to the normal pitch of one woman greeting another and said, "You look so chic, my dear. You must tell me where you found that divine suit. Doesn't she look lovely, darling?"

Vitaly Voronov grunted noncommittally as he walked into the lobby. He was wearing a tweed shooting jacket and a pair of plus-fours that were clearly the work of a Savile Row tailor, yet even the skill of the craftsmen who had cut and sewn them could not disguise the vulgarity of the mustard-colored checked pattern that Voronov had chosen, or the fact that the man inside them was a crude, uncultured boor.

"You didn't tell me Anastasia was so beautiful," Marina added. "You must be very proud."

Voronov ignored his wife completely and looked at his oldest daughter with an indifference that bordered on contempt. Nastiya was mortified by how deeply the little girl in her was hurt by the total absence of love in his voice. She told herself that she should never have been so stupid as to expect even a shred of paternal affection from a pig like him.

"Go," Voronov said to his wife, dismissing her with a wave of his hand.

One more reason to hate him, thought Nastiya, watching her stepmother vanish obediently into the depths of the vast house.

"Follow me," Voronov said, leading Nastiya into one of the reception rooms that led off the hall. However faithful the architects had been to the exterior of Highclere, they had paid no attention whatsoever to its interior decoration. The homely grandeur of family portraits, antique furniture and great bookcases filled with leather-bound volumes had been replaced by a vulgar profusion of black marble, glittering mirrors, gleaming chrome, gold knick-knacks and white leather furniture that seemed more appropriate to a sheikh's bordello in downtown Riyadh or a bachelor pad for a Colombian cocaine baron than a family's country home.

Voronov sat himself down in a large armchair, indicated that Nastiya should take a similar one opposite his and picked up a telephone handset from a side table. "You want a drink?" he asked.

"No thank you."

"Your loss. Give me a bottle of vodka. No, not that gutrot, the good stuff." Voronov put the phone down and looked at his oldest child. "So what do you want? Because if you want money, you can just piss off. You aren't having any from me."

"No, Father, I don't want money."

"Good. So what is it then?"

A waiter in a white jacket—also covering a weapon, Nastiya noted—placed a tray on the table beside Voronov. Nastiya saw a heavy crystal tumbler and a silver ice bucket from which protruded the neck of a vodka bottle. The waiter then reached for the bottle, swathed it in a gleaming white napkin and poured it into the tumbler, all the way to the top, before replacing the bottle in the bucket. He then disappeared without a word.

Nastiya watched the little performance and let her father have a good long drink before she spoke. "There are a number of things that I want from you, Father, and they will not cost you a single rouble. But before I explain precisely what they are, I want to ask you a question: do you want to die?"

Voronov put down his glass and looked at her as if she were talking gibberish. "What kind of stupid question is that? Of course I don't want to die."

"Good, because you will die, and I will be the one who kills you, unless you do exactly what I say."

Voronov burst out laughing. "You? Kill me? Don't make me—"

But he never finished the sentence. Somehow—for Voronov could not possibly have explained how she'd done it—Nastiya covered the gap between them before he was able to move. She pinned him down with a crushing grip on his throat.

"I assume that your security people are watching on closed-circuit TV," she told him.

Voronov made a squawking sound and flapped his hands weakly.

"You will agree that I could have killed you and been gone from the house before they reached you. You see, Papa darling, I was trained by the Spetsnaz." She released her grip on his throat and slipped gracefully back into her chair. "When your useless buffoons arrive, tell them there's nothing to worry about. Just a little spat between a father and his daughter. If you say anything else, I will not be so kind the next time and, believe

151

me, your guards will not be able to save you, or themselves. So, I can hear them coming . . ."

By the time the bodyguards burst into the room, Nastiya was sitting with her legs demurely crossed and the first thing they heard was her laughing prettily and saying, "Oh Papa, you're so amusing!"

The lead guard stopped in the doorway. "Is everything all right, sir?"

Voronov opened his mouth to speak, discovered that he could emit no more than a harsh, painful croak and waved them away with a desperate grin.

"You should have paid more attention to me, Father," Nastiya said as the door closed behind the last guard. "Then you would have known about the work that I've been doing and the skills I've picked up along the way. But since you've now learned from experience what I'm capable of, I'll tell you what it is you're going to do for me."

She got up from her seat, walked toward Voronov and was delighted to see him cringe away from her as she approached. "Here," she said, "let me be a good daughter and pour you another drink. You'll feel better with this inside you."

As her father drank, gasping at first as the alcohol went down his bruised throat, Nastiya listed her demands. "Firstly, you are going to give me everything Yevgenia needs to get on with her life, including her internal and international passports, her driving license, the keys to her car—I assume it's where she left it in the garage beneath the Moscow Tower—her laptop and tablet and three large suitcases filled with her belongings. I have a list of what she needs. Give it to your staff and we will pick it up from the tower this evening, at the same time as we pick up her car."

"Forget it," Voronov rasped. "I'm not giving that ungrateful little bitch the dogshit off the bottom of my shoe."

Nastiya gave him an indulgent smile, as if talking to some-

152

one with a tragic mental handicap. "No, you're going to give her everything. Do you need another demonstration, just to remind you what I can do?"

Voronov looked at her. Perhaps he was trying to work out if her threats were real. Or maybe he was wondering how the little girl he'd left behind more than twenty years ago had somehow turned into a trained killer. Nastiya really wasn't bothered either way. She stared right back at him until he cracked and said, "What else do you want?"

"You are going to call two of the richest, most powerful people you know. I don't care where they live: Moscow, St. Petersburg, London, New York, Paris—doesn't matter. They just have to be rich, trustworthy and willing to do you a personal favor. You're going to tell them that you have a new mistress. Her name is Maria Denisova. She used to work in a bank, but now she wants to set herself up as a financial adviser, finding unique investment opportunities that offer massive potential rates of return: from companies that are way undervalued, to new artists who are about to hit the big time. You are indulging her in this foolish ambition because the happier you make her, the happier she wants to make you, and we all know how she can do that.

"So now this mistress has found a man with investment potential. His name is da Cunha. She needs to be able to tell him that she is working for other ultra-high-net-worth individuals. All you need your friends to do is to be ready to take da Cunha's call and to reassure him that Maria Denisova can be trusted. If he tries to sell them anything, they should tell him that they'd rather everything went through Miss Denisova."

"Who is this da Cunha?" Voronov asked.

"A Portuguese, with an African father who has big development plans in West Africa."

Voronov suddenly perked up. "Really? Should I invest with him?"

Nastiya answered his question with a question of her own.

153

"When you get an email from Nigeria, asking you for money, do you send them the cash?"

Voronov nodded. "OK, I get it. So what's your interest in this da Cunha, then?"

"Professional. I can't say any more than that. If I did, it would only give me another reason to kill you."

Voronov laughed. "That's funny!"

"No . . . it's not. And just to be clear, da Cunha will be given your name too, so if he contacts you, reply to him in the way I have outlined. So now, please, you have two calls to make. Start dialing."

It took Voronov five attempts to find the two men Nastiya needed: he'd already used up a lot of goodwill having Yevgenia shut out of Moscow society. But in the end he persuaded a newspaper magnate based in London and a retired petrochemicals tycoon now taking it easy at a palatial villa in Cyprus to act as referees for his fictional mistress. "If she ever gets sick of you, Vitaly," the oil boss said, "tell her to give me a call. She can forget her little finance business. Just lie in the sun all day and screw me all night. Then she'll know what a real man feels like!"

Voronov gave a forced laugh and ended the call. "There." He looked at Nastiya. "Are we done now? I'd like to get on with my life. Without you in it."

Nastiya did not answer him immediately. She looked deeply and steadily into the eyes of her father and she saw there the confirmation of what she had known about him all along. Vitaly Voronov, for all his boasting and manly posturing, was a craven coward. She, her mother and her half-sister had nothing more to fear from him, ever.

"Yes, we're done," she replied to his question at last. "But there's one more thing you should know. If I ever hear that you've laid a finger on Yevgenia, Marina or any other woman unfortunate enough to enter your life, I will hunt you down and kill you. No matter where you are in the world, no matter how many men you hire to protect you, I will terminate your miserable existence. Now, could you tell your driver to get the Maybach? I need a lift back into Moscow."

While Dave Imbiss and Nastiya O'Quinn had been setting up the da Cunha sting, Hector Cross had been thinking about the other matters on his agenda. It had not taken him long to work out that while the sinking of the *Noatak* had created one problem it might then have immediately solved it. After all, there was now a perfectly good, ocean-going tug with nothing to do in the Arctic any more. So why not take it down to Cabinda in the Atlantic to act as his floating headquarters on the Magna Grande offshore field?

Then one morning, soon after Nastiya's return to London, Hector Cross summoned the team and told them, "I received a report last night from our investigator in Caracas—his name is Valencia, by the way. Guillermo Valencia. He and his people have been carrying out surveillance on the Villa Kazundu, or as I like to think of it 'Chateau Congo' for the past two weeks, and he's done a damn good job. So, this is what we know . . ."

Cross pressed a key on his computer and an image appeared of a large house and its grounds, seen from above. "The villa is part of a private estate, built on a hill overlooking Caracas. The house is built against the hill and partly dug into it: from the huge garage that's actually dug into the rock at the basement level to the bedrooms on the top floor. It's in the highest, and therefore smartest row of houses, with just a short, steep stretch of scrubland above it before you get to the ridge that runs along the top of the hill. So this shot is taken from that land and you can see that it's a very handy vantage point, one we should make use of."

Cross pressed the key again and a grainy, zoom-lens image of a large African-American, dressed in swimming shorts and an open towelling robe, sitting astride a recliner by the pool, with an iPad on the cushion between his two thighs and a phone pressed to his ear.

"I don't have to tell you who that is," Cross said. "The reason Valencia made a point of sending it to me was that he said Congo spends a lot of time on the phone, or his iPad. In other words, he's in touch with people in the outside world, and he's talking to them for a reason."

"I guess you're the reason, Heck," Dave Imbiss said.

"That's one possibility, yes."

Now three photographs of men in identical black suits, edited together into a single image, popped up onscreen. "Congo shares the property with three groups of people," Cross continued. "The first are his security guards. They work in shifts of three at a time: one in the gatehouse and two patrolling the grounds. These men work for a security company, so they don't have any personal loyalty toward Congo. They're used to Congo being away, so they've become very slack in their procedures and Valencia says they don't look like they've sharpened up much since Congo arrived back. Finally, they're not expecting trouble. A lot of the residents on this estate are connected to the Venezuelan government, so if anything ever happened to them or their property, it would be taken very seriously indeed. They'd probably bring in SEBIN—short for Servicio Bolivariano de Inteligencia Nacional—the political police, who've been doing the dirty work for every Venezuelan government, whether hard right or far left, since 1969. And no small-time crook in their right minds would want to screw with them.

"One last important point about the guards: they're armed, but only with pistols, rather than any fully automatic weapons. Turns out the gun-control laws are surprisingly strict in Venezuela. All guns apart from licensed hunting weapons are banned for private citizens. So the guards carry pistols, keep them well hidden and the local police turn a blind eye. So now the second group of people at the house: domestic staff."

Cross pressed the key several times in quick succession and a series of images of men and women in different uniforms flashed by. "There's about a dozen in all: the housekeeper, the chauffeur, plus assorted maids, cooks, gardeners and car-mechanics, some of them resident at the property, others just part-timers. Our only interest in them will be making sure they don't get in our way."

"So how are we going to do it?" asked Paddy O'Quinn.

"Very carefully," Hector answered him. "This isn't like charging into Africa, landing a bloody great plane filled with trucks and ordnance in the middle of nowhere and blasting away anything that moves. We'll be operating in a guarded house in a fancy neighborhood, in the capital city of a relatively wealthy, sophisticated western nation. So, just for a start, we can't take any weapons into the country. In fact we're going to be completely unarmed when we breach the perimeter—which reminds me, something I forgot to say earlier: there's an alarm system, a good one: cameras, motion sensors, pressure pads, panic buttons, the works. The feed from the CCTV cameras goes to the gatehouse. All the alarms are connected to the local emergency services. And one final thing: the doors to the house itself have all got keypad locks, each with a different code, and no one apart from Congo knows all the different codes."

"Excuse me for repeating myself," said O'Quinn, "but once again: how are we going to do it?"

Cross grinned: "Easy. So gather around, children, and I'll tell you how . . ."

Hector needed three men for the Caracas job, so he made a quick trip to Abu Zara, where Cross Bow's main operational base was located: there and back in under twenty-four hours. He spoke to half a dozen of his best men, telling them that he was looking for volunteers for an off-the-books mission, making it very clear that this was highly risky work that could end up with any or all of them in jail, or in the ground. More than once he was asked, "Are you going after Congo?" He didn't reply to the questions, which was all the men needed to know. They all said they were up for it and so Cross drew lots, selecting Tommy Jones, Ric Nolan and Carl Schrager, who were veterans of the Parachute Regiment, SAS and U.S. Army Rangers respectively. They were booked on to separate flights that would take them on three different routes to Caracas. They were all staying in different hotels, just as Paddy O'Quinn and Hector himself would be doing.

Before he returned to London, Cross gave them a thorough briefing on precisely what he had in mind. Valencia had by now managed to get hold of the original architect's plans for Chateau Congo and the men were given PDF copies and told to memorize them before they left Abu Zara, because they weren't taking anything with them that could possibly link them to the property. On the night of the operation, they wouldn't be carrying any form of ID.

"If anyone's KIA, they'll have to be put into an unmarked grave," said Cross bluntly. "But I'll know, and I'll make sure your loved ones are looked after."

The final instruction he gave them was to make sure they would be able to dress for action head to toe in black. "It's stating the bleeding obvious, but don't wear it all on the flight, or stick it all in the same case. I don't want you walking into immigration at Caracas looking like a bloody SWAT team. Wear a black T-shirt, pack the black trousers—that's pants to you, Schrager."

"Yeah, he is pants and all," bantered Jones.

"Balaclavas go in the carry-on. Roll 'em up so they look like socks. Right, any questions?"

Cross dealt with a few queries about the practicalities of the journey to Caracas and how to make contact when they got there. He listed a few items of civilian equipment that should be brought for use on the night. "Right, gentlemen," he concluded. "Next time I see you, it'll be in Caracas on the night of the mission. Good luck . . . and good hunting."

The Duchêne apartment was located on the first and second floors of a mansion block on the Avenue de Breteuil, within a stone's throw of both the Eiffel Tower and the Invalides. It was the epitome of Parisian elegance and sophistication. The building looked out on to a broad, tree-lined esplanade that provided a delicious sliver of parkland—immaculate lawns and paths made for slow, romantic strolls—running beside the avenue. Nastiya stood on the edge of the esplanade, in the shadow of the trees and watched for a few minutes as a stream of limousines disgorged the evening's guests. The men were mostly dressed in anonymous suits and ties, though a few signaled their intellectual leanings in the slightly longer hair that was immaculately swept back off their foreheads and over their ears; the shirts daringly unbuttoned to mid-chest and the casually draped velvet scarves that kept those exposed, middle-aged ribcages protected from the winter chill. The women, of course, were as fanatically dieted, groomed, coiffed and couture-clad as Paris, that most fashionable of all cities, demanded.

Nastiya paid particular attention to the women. She was looking for signs of competition: single, predatory females who might have their own reasons for wishing to seduce a rich, handsome African leader-in-exile. Having made her assessment, she emerged from the trees, picked her way across the road and went through an arched gateway lit by flaming torches that led to an inner courtyard on to which the main entrance to the building opened. A line of guests awaiting admission trailed down the low flight of broad stone steps that led up to double doors, both open. These were flanked by a pair of black-suited security guards, complete with earpieces and, Nastiya noted, guns holstered beneath their jackets. Every so often a guest would be asked, very politely, to step to one side to be frisked. Just inside the door, two more female operatives were casting an eye into all the women's bags. Finally another pair of younger, prettier women in matching cocktail dresses were checking guests' names and IDs against a list. The very visible security precautions only added to the cachet of the event. They suggested the presence of something genuinely dangerous: an idea of liberty by which a government might be threatened and against which it might act. And that, she knew, would only serve to flatter the guests and make them feel all the more daring for attending.

Nastiya made her way past all the various checks and into a hallway floored in white marble on which exquisitely patterned Persian rugs had been laid. The magnificent staircase that rose up from an atrium to the first floor was marble, too, with an iron balustrade whose pattern was picked out with dashes of gold. Family portraits, lit by electric candelabra, lined the walls of the atrium, as if to remind anyone who wished to enter the Duchênes' apartment that this was a family that could trace its line back through the centuries and would surely endure for centuries more to come. Waiters stood poised at the top of the stairs, bearing silver trays on which glasses of champagne sparkled invitingly. Nastiya took one and walked into the main salon. All the furniture, bar a few antique armchairs, had been removed to allow maximum space for guests to mingle, talk, admire themselves in the full-length mirrored panels set into the wood-panelled walls, or wander out through the three sets of French windows on to a terrace surrounded by stone balustrades and warmed by patio heaters.

A small dais with a microphone had been placed at the far end of the room, in front of a grand marble fireplace which was now flanked by a pair of loudspeakers on stands. Nastiya had just completed a circuit of the entire room and terrace when she saw a man who she knew to be almost eighty walk up onto the dais. This was Jérome Duchêne, the family patriarch. *Now I know where da Cunha gets his looks,* Nastiya thought to

160

herself, for Duchêne could easily be taken for a handsome man in his sixties. He was still blessed with a full head of silver hair and slim enough to carry off an ensemble of a midnight-blue velvet dinner jacket with satin lapels, open white silk shirt and narrow-cut black evening trousers. He walked up on to the dais, tapped the microphone to check that it was on and, speaking in French, said, "Ladies and gentlemen, it is with great pleasure and a father's pride that I present to you my grandson, Mateus da Cunha!"

There was a polite ripple of applause, followed by something that seemed like a mass intake of breath as the women in the room caught sight of their host. It was partly in the fluid, athletic way he strolled up on to the dais. His suit and shirt were both black, but his skin was a perfect, smooth café-au-lait and his features seemed to combine the strength of African features and the refinement of Nordic ones to create a perfect combination: a vision of what humanity would look like in a post-melting-pot age. He was tall and very obviously in excellent physical shape beneath his perfectly tailored clothes. But there was something more that became apparent the moment he looked around the room and was only underlined when he started to speak. It was that quality which can be called charisma, stardom, leadership, even charm, but which amounts to the ability to make oneself, without the slightest obvious effort, the center of everyone's attention, while at the same time persuading every individual, male or female, that you are talking directly to them, that you are as fascinated by them as they are by you and that their wellbeing matters even more to you than your own. Da Cunha had it, and knew it, and every single person in the room soon knew it, too.

Da Cunha held out his hands, palms up, as if reaching out to everyone in the room. "My friends . . . my dear friends . . . first I must begin by begging your forgiveness. Here, in the capital of France, the city of my birth, I am speaking to you in English.

It is, I know, an inexcusable treason . . ." He gave an almost bashful, apologetic smile that provoked a ripple of laughter. "But there are people here tonight from many nations and it is, perhaps sadly, a fact that English is the language they are most likely to share."

It's also, thought Nastiya, the language in which your French accent makes you sound the most charmingly seductive.

"So," da Cunha continued, "thank you all for coming tonight. Simply by being here you are expressing your belief in the dream of an independent, prosperous, peaceful nation of Cabinda. And how perfect that we are sharing this dream in the city where the greatest of all rallying cries for people yearning to be free was born: *Liberté, égalité, fraternité!* That freedom, that equality and that brotherhood are what I desire for my people. But those blessings cannot be secured without the support of the outside world, a support that is moral, political and—yes, I cannot deny it—also financial. And so tonight I am announcing the creation of the Cabinda Foundation, a non-profit organization that will campaign for the cause of a free Cabinda. The foundation will hold events to raise money and awareness of the political situation in Cabinda, but also, more importantly, to educate people about the beautiful land of my forefathers.

"Now, I know what you are thinking . . ." da Cunha paused, looked around the room and again let the hint of a smile play around his lips. "Where the hell is Cabinda?"

This time the laugh was louder, an outburst of relief that he had acknowledged what all but the African experts were thinking, and forgiven them for thinking it.

"I will tell you. It sits on the west coast of Africa, just five degrees south of the equator, surrounded by much bigger, more powerful countries. One of these countries is Angola, which claims Cabinda as its province even though there is, as a matter of fact, no common border at all between Cabinda and Angola. This geographical reality is supported by historical precedent.

Cabinda has been recognized as a distinct entity, separate from Angola, since the Treaty of Simulambuco of 1885, which was agreed between King Louis the First of Portugal and the princes and governors of Cabinda. The treaty also stated, and I quote: 'Portugal is obliged to maintain the integrity of the territories placed under its protection.'

"So we are not asking for something new. We are demanding that the imperialist Angolan government, along with the entire global community, recognize a Cabinda that has existed for more than a century. So, you may ask yourself, what kind of place is this country of which, until this evening, I had never previously heard? Why should I care about it? What reason can there be for investing money in this Cabinda project?

"Well, mine is a small country, but it produces seven hundred thousand barrels of oil a day, generating enough revenue to provide an income of a hundred thousand dollars a year for every man, woman and child in the state. Think of the houses, the schools and the hospitals that could be built for those people. Think of the clean water they could drink and the roads, the airport, the telecommunications network that could be created for their benefit and that of overseas visitors and investors."

Again, da Cunha paused to survey the room, but this time it was not for comic effect. "And consider this: a nation state that has a population of about four hundred thousand and an income of forty billion dollars does not need to levy income tax, sales tax or property tax on its citizens, or anyone else. And to anyone who loves to lie on a sunny beach I say that this is also a country with a tropical climate, one hundred kilometers of undeveloped coastline and no jetlag for anyone flying from Europe because Cabinda is just one hour behind Central European Time.

"My friends, I am talking of a Dubai with rainfall and lush green forests, or a Monte Carlo with oil. This is Cabinda, and I hope, and believe, that its future will be your future, and its prosperity will be your prosperity. Now, ladies and gentlemen, please raise your glasses and join me in a toast . . . to a free Cabinda!"

"A free Cabinda!" a chorus of voices replied as warm applause broke out around the room.

Da Cunha basked in the success of his speech for a moment and then said, "We are fortunate enough to have a number of respected members of the press here this evening. I am happy to take a few questions. But only a very few—this is a social occasion, after all. So if anyone would like to ask me anything, this is your chance."

This was Nastiya's moment. If she could engage da Cunha now and pique his interest, she could shortcut the whole process of getting to know him. But for that to work, she had to be the last person to whom he spoke and thus the freshest in his mind. So she did nothing as an earnest-looking woman, standing directly in front of the dais, raised her hand and said, "Pascale Montmorency, from *Le Monde*. My question for you, Monsieur da Cunha, is this: For many years FLEC-FAC, the organization that you represent, like your father did before you, supported the use of violence as a means to gain the freedom of Cabinda. Where do you personally stand on the question of violent action?"

Da Cunha had given a couple of thoughtful, appreciative nods as the question was asked. Now he replied, "I stand by my personal belief in seeking change by peaceful, political means, so I do not advocate violence. But I understand that when the conditions of life are intolerable, then some people will feel impelled to fight for their freedom. That has been the case for centuries. It was the case for the people of France when they rose up against the House of Bourbon in 1789, and when they resisted the Nazi occupiers of their nation during the Second World War. So I will not condemn those inside my country who wish to fight now, though I do counsel them that their actions must be proportionate and must never be targeted at the innocent. That I can never condone."

164

An unshaven man in a shabby corduroy suit and a loosened tie gave his name as Peter Guilden from the London *Daily Telegraph*, then said, "Isn't that just another way of saying that you don't want to get your hands dirty, but you don't mind if someone else does it for you? Surely you cannot hope to persuade the Angolan government to give away the most valuable province in their entire country, just by force of argument."

Nastiya could see that the question irritated da Cunha, but the flash of anger in his eyes was swiftly replaced by humor as he smoothly replied, "How is it that a nation as polite as Britain can produce an institution as rude as the British press?"

Guilden pressed on, ignoring the laughter around him. "We're not rude, Mr. da Cunha, just independent. As a lover of freedom, surely you welcome that."

"Up to a certain point," da Cunha said, with a very French shrug of the shoulders and pouting of the lips, earning more smiles from his audience. "But to answer your original question, I don't believe that violent action is an essential prerequisite for regime change, or national independence. I think there comes a point when the injustice of a situation becomes intolerable to the whole world and change is then the only possibility. Violence did not end apartheid in South Africa. The Berlin Wall came down without a shot being fired. And neither South Africa nor East Germany had oil, which, as we all know, has a way of making the West pay attention. One last question . . ."

This was Nastiya's moment. She fixed her most dazzling smile on her face, stuck up her hand, prayed that da Cunha would notice her and was relieved to discover that she, too, could still attract attention when she wanted to.

"The lady over there, in the green dress," da Cunha said, looking straight into Nastiya's eyes.

"Maria Denisova," she said, looking right back at him. "Forgive me, Monsieur da Cunha, I am not a member of the press, but I do have a question to ask you."

He gave her a charming smile, revealing perfect, dazzling white teeth and Nastiya could actually feel the envy-laden female stares boring into her back as da Cunha said, "I am proud of my Cabindan blood, but I am also half-French and it is therefore quite impossible for me to turn down a request from a beautiful woman. Please, madame, ask your question."

"Actually, it is mademoiselle," Nastiya purred, flirting shamelessly and provoking even more silent rage.

"All the more impossible for me to say no, then."

"Very well. My question is this: you are the leader of the political movement for freedom in Cabinda and the creator of the Cabinda Foundation. Can we assume, then, that you will be the first leader of a free Cabinda? After all, you will go to so much trouble on Cabinda's behalf, it would only be natural."

Nastiya had, in the sweetest possible way, effectively accused da Cunha of wanting to stage a coup d'état, and she could sense the sudden tension in the room and, for a second time, the pattern of suppressed anger, swiftly followed by apparently lighthearted humor.

"What a question!" da Cunha exclaimed. "Are you sure you're not really an English journalist?" He let the laughter subside before he continued, "I will answer you like this: I am not a prince in exile, waiting to be acclaimed by his people. I am a man who dreams of bringing freedom and democracy to a homeland from which he has long been excluded. By that same token I must accept the will of the Cabindan people. If they one day choose me to lead them, that would be the greatest honor I could ever receive. If they do not, then the knowledge that I helped give them the right to choose will be enough of a reward. Benjamin Franklin was never the President of the United States of America, but his place in history is just as secure as those who were. I would be honored to be Cabinda's Benjamin Franklin."

It was a mark of his arrogance that da Cunha could compare himself to one of America's Founding Fathers, and an equal proof of his charisma that his audience responded with rapturous applause. Da Cunha bowed his head in thanks; then he stepped down from the dais and made his way straight to Nastiya.

"Are you sure you're not a reporter?" he asked with another dazzling smile calculated to set any female tummy fluttering.

"Quite sure," Nastiya said, reminding herself that she was just as adept at manipulating the male of the species. "But I admit that I had a reason for asking my question."

"Apart from attracting my attention?"

"Maybe." Nastiya produced a little shrug and pout of her own.

"So what was your reason?"

"It was a practical, business issue." The words and her straight-forward, no-nonsense tone were not what da Cunha had been expecting. "As I informed your office, I act as a representative and consultant to a number of very wealthy individuals. My job is to seek out interesting investment opportunities, like the work of a young artist who's about to become a star; or a property that's not officially for sale, but whose owner is open to offers . . . or a country that does not exist yet, but which could make a great deal of money for anyone bold enough to back it from the start."

"And you want to know whether I am a safe investment?"

"Exactly. My clients need to know that you will be in a position to deliver your promises once Cabinda is free. They don't want someone else coming in and saying, 'Sorry, the deal's off.'"

"Someone who doesn't owe them anything, you mean?"

"That's one way of putting it. So, my question stands: What guarantee can you give that you will achieve independence for Cabinda, or that you will lead the new nation when it wins its freedom?"

"Hmm . . ." da Cunha paused, and Nastiya could see that for once he wasn't performing, or trying to create a particular effect. He was genuinely weighing up the degree to which he should take her and her potential backers seriously. "Those are certainly important questions," he finally said, "and they deserve serious answers. I must attend to my other guests now and I am busy in meetings with potential supporters all of tomorrow and most of the day after. So perhaps you might join me for dinner, two days from now, and I will do my best to give you the right answers."

"That sounds like a delightful idea." Nastiya smiled, just to let him know that she wasn't all just business, and da Cunha replied in kind.

"Then dinner it is," he said.

Just as the capital of Mexico is Mexico City, so the capital of Cabinda—in fact, its only sizeable town—is also called Cabinda. It stands on a promontory that juts into the Atlantic like a stunted thumb. Jack Fontineau had been in Cabinda for less than a month and already he was so sick of the place that it was all he could do to stop himself walking out of his stifling office—where a single ancient fan, too old and decrepit to rotate at any speed, was all that stirred, let alone cooled the air—across the plain of dirt and dust littered with rusting containers and washed-up hulks that served as a dockside, on to the single long jetty at which ships of any size could berth and right into the shark-infested sea.

It was ten at night, which meant four in the afternoon back home in Houma, Louisiana, where his office at Larose Oil Services, his Chevy Silverado and the house which he shared with his wife Megan and their three kids were all not just air-conditioned, but damn near refrigerated. Jack could be there now if he hadn't been foolish enough to accept what his boss Bobby K. Broussard swore was both a promotion and a great opportunity. "Go out to Africa, it's the new frontier," the lying bastard had said. "We want you to set up our office in Angola."

Jack knew guys that had worked out of Luanda, and they said it was all right. There were decent hotels, beach clubs, bars where you could get any kind of imported booze you wanted. Sure, the prices were insane, but what did that matter when you were on expenses? But Jack wasn't sent to Luanda. No, B. K. had figured out that most of Angola's oil was up to the north, off Cabinda. So if Larose Oil Services could get into Cabinda ahead of the other companies that provided services for offshore rigs they'd have a captive market. It was only when Jack got to Cabinda that he discovered there was a reason everyone else was still in Luanda. The place was a dump. Most of the houses weren't much more than shacks, and a three-story building with rusty metal windows and filthy whitewash peeling off the sides of crumbling walls was the locals' idea of a luxury office complex.

As for running a serious offshore supply operation here, forget it. The government had plans for a fancy new port and oil terminal a few miles up the coast from the city. They'd put up a website with maps showing where the deep-water jetties, the rig-repair dock and the warehouses would be. But they'd yet to stick a single shovel in the ground, or cement one brick on top of another. A man could die of old age around here, waiting for things to get done. Forget *mañana*, that was way too soon for your typical Cabindan. But Jack couldn't make the folks back at head office understand that, any more than he could get them to appreciate that he was six hours ahead of Louisiana time, which was why he'd ended up starting his working day around lunchtime and then staying at work till eleven o'clock at night, or even midnight, just so he could be on the end of the line when someone tried to call him. It was marginally less hot working evenings, too, which helped.

So now he was getting ready for another call from head office in which he'd try to explain why he wasn't anywhere near hitting his new business targets for the quarter and pray that they'd send some other sucker out to take his place, even if it meant getting fired. Better that than taking a walk off the end of the jetty.

* * *

There were five men in the ancient Nissan Vanette driving down the Rua do Comércio, the main road that runs along the Cabindan waterfront. They wore a combination of jeans, cargo pants and calf-length shorts. One of them had a Real Madrid football shirt, another sported a Manchester United crest on his T-shirt. He had a baseball cap on, too, the peak pointing sideways. All five of the men were armed with guns or machetes, though they weren't expecting to have to use their weapons because this was only meant to be a symbolic operation: a wake-up call to the authorities to pay attention and take their demands seriously, or the next time people would get hurt. The message would be sent by the very basic IED—not much more than a block of C4 explosive, a detonator and a timer—that was sitting in a canvas bag in the footwell of the front passenger seat. The van pulled off the road and drove across an open expanse of unpaved ground to a cluster of small warehouses and offices, slowed down so that the driver could pick out the sign he was looking for and then came to a halt. There was a brief burst of conversation as the men debated whether they'd found their target, agreed they had and then geed one another up with shouts of encouragement and exhortations to have courage and get the job done. Then they piled out of the Vanette, looked around to make sure that no one was watching and headed for the warehouse door.

Listen, B. K., you can set all the targets you like, but they don't mean shit once you get out to a place like this," Jack Fontineau said into the telephone. "Most people don't have any kind of presence here at all, and the ones that do aren't authorized to make decisions, so we've got a better chance of getting their business in Luanda, or even back home than we do here . . . Yeah, yeah, I know that this is where the oil is, but . . . Hold on, I think I just heard something. Gimme a second, will ya? I'm just going to check it out . . ."

* * *

170

The five amateur bombers were surprised to discover that the side door to the warehouse was unlocked at this time of night, but it made their job a lot easier. Once inside they received a second shock. One of the men was carrying a torch, but the moment he switched it on it was apparent that far from being filled with supplies for offshore rigs, the warehouse was virtually empty. In fact, the only object of any significance was a brand-new Toyota Land Cruiser sitting just inside the main goods entrance. They stood pondering the significance of this for a moment and then someone pointed toward the far end of the warehouse, about thirty meters away, where there was an office with its lights still on. Through the window they could see a white man, talking on the phone. Then he put the phone down, got out of his chair and walked toward the office door. Someone hissed a warning at the man with the torch and he turned it off. Now the only light was coming from the office and in the semi-darkness the men raced to hide behind the hefty bulk of the Land Cruiser.

Jack Fontineau had a torch, too. He picked it up as he walked toward the door and switched it on as he stepped out on to the warehouse floor. He wasn't entirely sure what he'd heard, just a combination of noises and a flicker of light in the corner of his eye that added up to a sense that there was someone else in the building. There it was again, a pattering sound like running feet. He swept the torch very deliberately from left to right across his field of vision and then back again and it was on that second sweep that he saw something—or someone—scuttling behind his Land Cruiser.

"Who's there?" Fontineau called, wishing he'd got more than a torch with which to defend himself. "Come out. I know you're there."

He walked forward slowly, not really wanting to go any further, but forcing himself to stay calm, breathe steadily and keep going. There was nothing to worry about, he told himself.

Anyone could see there wasn't anything here to steal apart from the Land Cruiser and they were welcome to that. He wasn't going to risk his own safety for the sake of a company car.

Then he heard another sound. Fontineau stopped in his tracks and frowned as he tried to place where the sound had come from. He shone the beam to his left but saw nothing. Then he swung it back the other way, to the right . . .

. . . and saw a man, no more than a couple of paces away. He was young, black, a head taller than Fontineau and built like a cruiserweight. The man was moving right at Fontineau and raising his right arm. Fontineau saw a flash of metal, glinting in the torchlight. He tried to shout, to beg for mercy, but before he could even form the words the man had hurled his arm back down, plunging the blade of his machete so deep into the side of Jack Fontineau's neck that his head was almost severed from his body. As Fontineau fell to the ground, a geyser of blood erupted from the terrible wound, covering his attacker's arm, chest and face and spattering across the bare concrete floor of the warehouse and the Land Cruiser's white bodywork like paint flicked on to a bare canvas.

Now the other four members of the bombing team emerged from behind the vehicle, shouting and gesticulating in a mixture of excitement, bloodlust and panic until their leader, who had the canvas bag with the bomb in it, called for silence. The voices subsided as the leader took out the bomb and placed it inside the rear of Fontineau's car, close to its massive 138-litre fuel tank. He set the timer and then pointed toward the warehouse door. It was time to leave.

The five men were back inside the Vanette and heading out of town on the Rua do Comércio when the bomb exploded. A cheer rang around the interior of the battered old vehicle. They had done their job. Now they would get paid.

* * *

172

A bomb that's planted in an empty warehouse in an obscure African city is not a news story. But a bomb that's planted in a warehouse that's empty except for an American, whose charred, dismembered body is found in the smouldering ruins, well, that's a whole different matter. Jack Fontineau's death was made all the more dramatic by the fact that he was on the phone to his boss in Louisiana when the attack took place. Bobby K. Broussard was soon besieged by reporters and, with a suitably mournful, emotionally stricken expression on his face, he told them: "Jack said, 'Give me a second, I'm just going to check it out.' Because that's the kind of man Jack was. He didn't shy away from danger. He didn't leave it to other people to risk themselves for him. He faced up to his responsibilities, like a man. And in the end that bravery cost him his life. Now our thoughts and our prayers are with Jack's wife Megan and their three darlin' children."

Megan Fontineau was a former cheerleader at Louisiana State and she made sure to face the cameras looking her beautiful, blonde best, with glamorous designer shades that she removed to reveal her tearful, cornflower-blue eyes. Her two daughters were both as pretty as pictures and Jack Jnr, aged eight, was a photogenic, all-American, gap-toothed little scamp. Their pictures hit every TV network, front page and news website in the western world.

Pretty soon the media were doing background stories on Cabinda and reports were coming out of Paris of a rebel leader called Mateus da Cunha, who was half-French, sophisticated and looked great on camera. He gave the world's media the same line he'd given the guests at his reception: he wasn't in favor of violence himself, but he could understand the frustrations that led other people to take up arms in their struggle against oppression. One starstruck CNN reporter called da Cunha "a new generation's Nelson Mandela" and the phrase started to gain traction as other commentators picked it up and ran with it.

* * *

In Caracas, Johnny Congo laughed out loud when he heard that. "Mandela, my ass!" he chortled at the TV screen. Congo knew a scam artist when he saw one. Da Cunha didn't disapprove of violence; he loved it, any fool could see that. In fact, Congo was prepared to bet the man had set the whole thing up himself. Plus, the story concerned Angola and oil, two subjects currently of great interest to Congo, who went online and checked da Cunha out. Soon he'd learned all he needed to know about the Cabinda Foundation and the struggle for independence from Angola. This, he realized, was the final thing he'd been waiting for, the last nail he'd hammer into Hector Cross's coffin.

Congo called a satphone number that belonged to Babacar Matemba, a West African paramilitary commander, whose political, criminal and homicidal activities had been funded by the sale of blood diamonds and coltan, a metal essential to the electronics industry that, ounce for ounce, is the next best thing to gold. In the days when Johnny Congo and Carl Bannock had been running their own private kingdom in Kazundu they'd helped Matemba smuggle his contraband goods on to the global market. Now it was time to get back in touch.

The two men exchanged greetings. Congo told Matemba about his escape from Death Row and assured him he'd soon be back in business. "In fact, that was what I was calling you about. I wondered if you could spare me some men. I need experienced fighters, good enough to train other people, so they've gotta be smart. I need the best and I'm willing to pay real well, maybe make up for some of what you've not been getting from Carl and me lately."

"What do you want my men to do?" Matemba asked. He listened while Congo told him and then said. "I like the sound of that, Johnny."

"Me too, Babacar. Me too."

The next call Congo made was to the Cabinda Foundation. "I want to speak to da Cunha," he said.

"May I tell Monsieur da Cunha who is calling and what it concerns?"

"My name is Juan Tumbo. I want to donate money to your foundation. A lot of money."

The call was put right through. Ten minutes later, the Cabinda Foundation had a major, anonymous donor and Johnny Congo knew exactly how he was going to destroy Hector Cross, and make a shedload of money doing it, too.

As an ex-Marine, Congo was well acquainted with a lot of men who had been trained to a very high level in the arts of sabotage and destruction, and had practical battlefield experience of putting their training to work. As a former convict and career criminal, he also knew a large number of individuals who had a total absence of scruple or conscience and were prepared to cause any amount of material damage or physical harm if the money was right. In a few particular cases, which Congo valued highest of all, these were one and the same men. Chico Torres had served in the Marines as a combat engineer. His particular genius was for blowing things up, on land, on sea—hell, if you found a way to get Chico to Mars, he'd blow the shit out of that, too.

Chico was all ears when Congo got in touch and told him all about his new-found interest in the Angolan offshore oil industry. He asked a few pertinent questions about the specific nature and scale of Bannock's set-up at the Magna Grande field, then told Congo, "Yeah, I can see the weak link in the chain. Think I know how to break it, too. Just need to do some detailed investigation, get my numbers right, you know what I mean. Gimme a few days, I'll get back to you, man."

Johnny Congo had not been the only interested party calling the Cabinda Foundation in the aftermath of Jack Fontineau's death. Nastiya knew that a man like da Cunha needed to be challenged, taken by surprise and kept a little off-balance. So, having watched his stellar appearances on the world's news networks she called his office and informed his secretary that she had made a booking for them both at Sur Mesure, the Mandarin Oriental's own restaurant, famed for the avant-garde "molecular cooking" of its head chef Thierry Marx. Da Cunha kept the appointment, but soon tried to reassert control by suggesting that he was already entirely familiar with his surroundings.

"Monsieur Marx is a great enthusiast for Japan," da Cunha said when they had been seated in the extraordinary, cocoon-like dining room, whose walls were swathed in loosely draped, cream-colored fabric, piled and gathered like crumpled paper. "He takes a holiday every year in a Buddhist monastery there, and holds a third dan in judo and a fourth in ju-jitsu."

"Really?" said Nastiya, putting down the champagne glass from which she'd been sipping. "Then I advise him not to fight me. He would lose."

Da Cunha laughed. "I'm sure! Women never fight fair!"

"Oh, but I was being quite serious. He would have to be much, much better than that to stand any chance of winning." She gave da Cunha a sweet, innocent smile and, almost girlishly said, "I could kill you, too, right now, before you even had a chance to get up from the table. But don't worry, I would have to be very upset indeed before I became that violent, and I'm feeling great, right now. This Krug is delicious! It really is the best of all the great champagnes, wouldn't you say? And it goes so well with this starter."

The starter, consisting of a single, immaculate quail's egg wrapped in spinach and a disc of foie gras, surrounded by a ring of spinach jelly, had been placed in front of them. Nastiya attacked it with great enthusiasm, but da Cunha just picked at his dish.

"I hope I haven't ruined your appetite," she said.

"No, but I admit my mind is not giving the food the attention it deserves."

"Why not?"

"Because I am trying to decide whether you are the most intriguing, intoxicating, dangerous woman I have ever met, or the biggest bullshitter of all time."

Nastiya smiled. "Maybe I'm both. Maybe it's my bullshit that makes me so dangerous."

"Ha! Time to stop talking and eat."

For the next ninety minutes, as the nine courses of the tasting menu followed one another—each a small, perfect experiment in the art of capturing flavor at its most intense in a myriad different forms and textures—they talked about their lives. Nastiya worked on the principle that the best covers are those that contain as much truth as they can fit, so she spoke about her former life as an FSB agent. "Though I sometimes tell civilians I was trained by the KGB," she said. "No one knows what 'FSB' is, so it's easier to use a name that everyone has heard before."

"Then it's true, what you said about being able to fight and kill?"

"Yes, but honestly"—she reached out and delicately laid the tips of her fingers on his arm—". . . I'm really not going to try and prove it tonight."

"That's a pity," da Cunha said. "It might add a touch of excitement. After dinner, perhaps . . ."

"We'll see . . ." She left the merest suggestion of an invitation hanging in the air. Da Cunha's expression showed that he had taken the hint, but he was smart enough not to push the point. Instead, he got down to business.

"So, what qualifies you to seek out interesting investment opportunities and why on earth should wealthy clients take your advice?"

"I don't know . . . What qualifies you to set yourself up as the first leader of an independent Cabinda? Please, I know you had to answer the way you did in public. But you don't want to be Franklin. You want to be Washington—without the possibility of ever losing an election."

"Did I say that? Answer my question . . ."

"Well, apart from my combat skills"—she had not mentioned the word "sex," but somehow they both knew that was what she meant—"I speak a number of languages fluently, I'm trained to gather and assess intelligence, I have contacts around the world who alert me to possible opportunities and as a woman I have advantages that a man does not. If I were male, you would not have been so willing to let me ask you a question, nor so keen to approach me immediately afterward, nor so ready to extend an invitation to dinner."

"I can't deny it," said da Cunha with a smile.

"Finally, I am Russian and do not have the pathetic western obsession with human rights and non-violence. So why don't you tell me what you really intend to do, how much money you need to do it, and what you will give in return for that money?"

"Well, Miss Trained Russian Agent, if you were in my situation, what would you do?"

There was a pause as a new course was brought to them, accompanied by a fresh glass of wine. Nastiya waited until they were undisturbed again and then replied, "I would create instability. I would do everything I could to make western oil companies and western governments believe that they can't be safe in Cabinda as long as it is a province of Angola. So I might start by, say, attacking the offices of an American company that supplies oil rigs."

"Ah yes, that was a very unfortunate incident. I believe that an American executive was among the casualties. You understand, of course, that I was not involved in any way."

"Pah!" Nastiya gave a flick of her hand to wave his weasel words aside. "Weren't you listening? I told you I'm not squeamish. But perhaps I didn't make myself clear. I work for oligarchs, and you know how they made their money, every single one of them? Crime. Sure, they weren't all Russian mafia, though some were. But they stole state assets, or bribed someone to sell them at a fraction of their real value, or forced the original owner out of the business. Men like that will not think you are a bad guy if you fight to get what you want. But they will think you are a pussy if you stand on the sidelines, wringing your hands and telling the world that you are frightened by a drop of blood."

There was no humor or flirtation in da Cunha now. His eyes bored into hers and his jaw was set as he leaned toward her and lowered his voice to a rumbling growl. "Then go back to these men and tell them that I wouldn't be frightened by an ocean of blood. Tell them that I need money for personnel, weapons, training, housing and supplies. I must also fund a major international public relations and lobbying campaign that will win over media opinion-formers, buy the support of key politicians and force governments to recognize Cabinda. And I need to do just enough for the people that they, and the outside world, think that their lives will improve in an independent Cabinda."

"What about the Angolan government?"

"Simple. I will make it hell for them to keep Cabinda, and very worthwhile for them to let it go. Everyone has their price, and if we have to put ten million, or a hundred million, or even a billion dollars into the bank accounts of the President and his key military and political allies, then that is what we will do because the prize is worth so much more."

Nastiya sensed that this was the real Mateus da Cunha: a man of limitless ambition, naked greed and an absolutely ruthless will. Her professional self now saw him as an enemy to be taken seriously and even feared. Her moral compass told her that he had the potential to commit acts of great evil to achieve what he wanted.

She had anticipated the evening ending in some kind of sexual advance from him, so it came as no surprise when, at the end of the meal, he did not so much ask as tell her, "Come back to my apartment. We can finish our discussion in comfort."

At this point she had planned to reply, "No, I can't wait that long. My room is much closer." She had a well-stocked bar from which to pour him a drink and the powdered Rohypnol to slip into it. The hidden camera was pointed at the bed, waiting to capture whatever humiliating pose she could draw him into. But now she realized that it simply was not safe for her to invite him up. For once in her life she could not count on her ability to remain in total control of any sexual situation and she was not prepared to risk her marriage, her job and the faith that Cross had placed in her. So she smiled as she declined: "That's a very tempting invitation, but no. Another time, perhaps."

Da Cunha shook his head with a sigh. "So, you've led me on and then you disappoint me. I must be losing my touch." He paused, looked at her and then gave a very Gallic shrug. "Ah well, perhaps we have both deceived one another. You see, the truth is, I don't need any money from your investors, not at this moment. I've found a backer who can fund the first stage of my campaign. But I don't want your people to lose interest because there may be opportunities for more investment later. So I'll tell you something that will make them all a great deal of money. They must do nothing for a month. Then go short on Bannock Oil. Tell them that whatever the price of Bannock stock is, they must bet on it going lower. Start slowly, but build their positions: tens, even hundreds of millions of dollars, all staked on Bannock dropping. Tell them from me, they won't regret it."

Nastiya could hardly believe her luck. He had just given her as much information voluntarily as she could have hoped to extract from him by blackmail. Perhaps it was true and good deeds really were rewarded: that truly would be a surprise.

They walked together out of the restaurant and into the hotel foyer. "You're quite sure I can't tempt you?" da Cunha said before he took his leave.

"On the contrary, I'm sure you can tempt me," Nastiya replied. "But I am equally sure that I can resist temptation."

He looked at her and nodded, a half-smile playing around the corners of his mouth as he said, "Tonight, perhaps. But there will be another night. And then we will see just how strong our resistance really is."

While Nastiya was in Paris, Cross had taken a brief break from his work preparing Cross Bow's deployment at the Magna Grande field to visit an old friend and comrade-in-arms, Dr. Rob Noble. He was a former Army medic and Hector had met him when they were both serving members of the SAS. Rob now had a flourishing practice in Harley Street, providing all manner of health-boosting, anti-aging, sex-life-enhancing treatments to rich patients, who were very rarely ill, but almost always in need of the latest, most fashionable prescription drugs. He made a great deal of money doing a job he realized was of no social benefit whatever, which explained why the bulk of his profits went to fund free clinics for mothers and children in conflict zones around the world.

Noble's experience, both in the Army and out of it, had led him to the view that there were people walking the planet who did so much harm to others that they needed culling. When Hector Cross gave him a brief introduction to Johnny Congo's CV, Noble readily agreed that this was a man who perfectly fitted his criteria for swift and terminal removal from the scene. "Though I'd rather not supply you with the poison to do it, if that's all right," he added. "I've taken the Hippocratic Oath, after all, promised not to give anyone deadly medicine and all that."

"Don't worry," Cross reassured him. "I'm just looking for something that'll knock someone out quickly and painlessly, then leave them with as little recollection as possible of what happened to them when they wake up."

"Hmm . . ." Noble considered the problem. "You do know, of course, that there's no such stuff—outside of an operating theater—as an instant knock-out drop. Still, I should be able

181

to put something together for you. Come back in a couple of days and I'll have it ready for collection. Half a dozen doses should be enough for you, I hope?"

"More than enough. And I could use a few morphine ampoules, too, in case anyone gets hurt who's not meant to be."

"Consider it done."

Two days later, Cross returned to Harley Street to be given two small plastic cases, each containing six ampoules. One box had a small red cross on it, the other did not. Each ampoule bore a prescription label, describing it as insulin, with instructions for use.

"You've just developed a case of diabetes," Rob Noble told Hector. "The first ampoule in each box really does contain insulin, just in case any customs man is minded to test it. The other ampoules in the Red Cross box are morphine, as requested. The ones in the plain box contain a subtle blend of party drugs, funnily enough. I've combined a four-thousand-milligram dose of gamma-hydroxybutyric acid, otherwise known as GHB Juice or Liquid G, which should induce unconsciousness about as fast as anything around, and mixed it with ketamine, a tranquillizer much prized by blithering idiots who like to mess with their brains for its ability to create a dissociative, otherworldly effect—like a less extreme version of an LSD trip, I suppose. It also induces amnesia, so it should do the trick for your purposes. As a combination they should leave the recipient feeling very, very strange, but providing their general health is all right, the dose shouldn't prove fatal."

"Thanks, Rob, you're a genius," Cross told him.

"I would agree with you wholeheartedly. But does the Nobel Prize Committee ever give me a call?"

Cross returned to his office to find Nastiya returned from Paris. "So, did you get anything out of da Cunha?"

Nastiya nodded. "Yes."

"And . . . ?"

"Da Cunha says that he is trying to achieve freedom for Cabinda by peaceful means, but he is lying. He will do whatever it takes to control the country and its oil revenues and he is looking for backers to fund his military and PR campaigns and pay the bribes he needs to persuade politicians to do what he wants. At first he was very interested in the possibility of using Russian money, but when we met for the second time he made it clear that he already has someone who has enough money to pay for the early stages of the struggle."

"Did he say who it was?"

"No, but he did say who his next target would be. He was worried that my clients would feel snubbed by his refusal of their money now. So as a gesture of good faith he asked me to pass on a message to them, telling them to invest heavily in short positions, against Bannock Oil."

"You're sure it was Bannock Oil?"

"Absolutely, he was very insistent that Bannock stock would plummet in value."

"Did he say when?"

"Yes. He told me to tell my people not to do anything for a month, but then to attack Bannock with as much money as possible."

"That's great work, Nastiya. You've delivered the goods once again. It's just a pity the package stinks."

Cross told Agatha to put him on the next available flight out of Heathrow to Washington DC. He called Bobbi Franklin and invited her to dinner at Marcel's, on Pennsylvania Avenue, just a five-minute cab ride from the State Department.

"This is very short notice," Franklin said, though she sounded as though it was a pleasant surprise. "Business or pleasure?"

"Both."

"I'm intrigued. I'll see you there."

* * *

Congo's bomb-making buddy Chico Torres was as good as his word. Within days, he'd produced a detailed plan of attack; a quantified list of all the materials Congo would have to supply so that Torres could assemble the ordnance that the job would require; and the specifications of the delivery system and personnel needed to convey the right package to the right place at the right time to produce the effect that Congo desired. "If you want, man, I can see the whole operation through from planning to execution. If I get the Benjamins, you'll get the bang, you know what I mean?"

Congo and Torres concluded their financial negotiations satisfactorily. The price and the time-schedule were set. Over the next few days, Congo started the recruitment process for the men who would work with Torres on his side of what was swiftly becoming a much bigger, more intricate and potentially devastating scheme than even Congo had initially envisioned. Further discussions with Babacar Matemba and Mateus da Cunha put flesh on the bones of their half of the deal. Now Congo just needed to sort out the financial pay-off that his military actions were designed to create. So he put in a call to Aram Bendick, worked his way through the army of gatekeepers Bendick employed to keep casual callers off his back and finally got through to the financier himself.

"I like your work, dog," Congo said, having introduced himself as Juan Tumbo. "Badmouthing the CEOs, driving the stock down, picking up assets for a song—gotta love that, right? So I looked you up on that Forbes list of billionaires, saw you at eight-point-two bill, ranked hundred and sixtieth. Man, that's gotta hurt, don't it? Y'know, not even being in the top one fifty."

"Those figures are wildly inaccurate," Bendick said testily.

"Yeah, well, reporters, right, what do they know? But let me ask you something: however many billions you got, you can always use a few more, am I right?"

"Where are you going with this, Mr. Tumbo? I'm just online now, looking at the exact same list as you; only difference is, I don't see your goddamn name anywhere. So you better tell me why I should listen to any more of your shit, or this call ends now."

"You don't see me on no list because I don't wanna be there. I keep my business to myself. But now I'm telling you, Mr. Bendick, I can double your money. So now you're going to say, bullshit, how can I do that? I'll tell you that, too, when we meet, but first I'm assuming you can follow the money going in and out of your Seventh Wave Funds, yeah?"

"Of course."

"So check out your U.S. Special Situations Fund. You seeing that on your screen?"

"Yeah, what of it?"

"In about ten seconds the amount invested in that fund is gonna rise by fifty million dollars. Wait for it . . ."

"Got it!" For the first time, Bendick sounded interested, enthusiastic even, about the way the call was going.

"There you go, that was me. I just gave you fifty mill—boom! Consider that a proof of funds. Now, when we gonna meet? I wanna tell you how we make billions."

Hector Cross came to his feet with a genuine smile of welcome when he saw the maître d' escort Bobbi Franklin across the crowded restaurant to their table. Not only was her face even more elegantly beautiful without her glasses, she had the figure to match, and unless she made a habit of going to work in little black dresses, heels and pearls, she'd bothered to change for dinner. That was a most promising sign.

They got the business out of the way before the meal was served. Cross told her about the threat he believed the Bannock operation in Angola was facing, and how the information had come into his possession.

"Is there any chance da Cunha was bullshitting?" Bobbi asked. "Guys will say almost anything to impress an attractive woman."

"She said, speaking from years of experience . . ."

Bobbi laughed. "Hey! I thought we were keeping it strictly business until the food arrived! But thank you for the compliment, anyway . . ."

"You're welcome, and no, I think he meant it. Da Cunha believed that Maria Denisova represented some seriously wealthy, powerful individuals. He wouldn't have wanted to make enemies of them by giving false information. The question is, what can anyone do about it?"

"Well, we can talk to the Angolan government and ask them to redouble their security efforts. I can have a word with our friends in Langley, see if they can take a real close look at Mateus da Cunha, but he has French citizenship and our European allies have become very sensitive indeed about us conducting intelligence operations against their nationals."

"How about the military? Can we get any naval protection?"

"It's tough. We're facing multiple threats in the Middle East, South-East Asia, Eastern Europe, and this is happening after years of defense cuts. If you had information about a specific threat, at a particular location on a given date, that might be enough to prompt some action at the Pentagon. But if all you know is that something may happen, somewhere at some point, well, that's not going to do it."

"So what you're basically saying is that we're going to be on our own."

"Sounds like it." She took a sip of wine while Cross digested what she had said and then added, "I hope you're not going to blame the messenger."

"No, I'm not going to blame the messenger for being so honest, I'm going to ask her to do what she can, just to make people aware of the threat. And then I'm going to say: Forget

186

about Cabinda, and oil, and threats of violence. Tell me about yourself."

The rest of the dinner was pure pleasure. Bobbi Franklin was bright, full of humor and as genuinely interested in him as he was in her. For the first time in a very long while, he was able to relax, forget about the cloud of violence and danger that seemed to be permanently looming over him and just enjoy the company of a woman who mixed brains, beauty and sheer niceness in apparently perfect proportions.

When the meal was over, she allowed him to escort her back to her apartment, but left him with just a kiss, albeit a very pleasurable and lingering one at the door.

"I like my men to work just a little bit to get what they want, even if I want it too," she said.

"I'm not afraid of hard work," he said. "But I won't be able to do much for you for a while: not till this Cabinda business is sorted one way or another."

"I understand. But you know where to find me in future. And I'm not planning on moving."

In the morning Cross flew from Washington to Houston. In his Bannock Oil office he gave John Bigelow a more detailed version of the briefing he had provided Bobbi Franklin.

"I wanted us to meet face-to-face and in private because I need to give you my considered, professional opinion," Cross told him. "Bearing in mind the losses that the sinking of the *Noatak* have already inflicted on the company, and the irreparable damage that could be caused if we suffer a similar loss at Magna Grande, I believe that we should scale down and even cease operations in Angolan waters until the precise threat facing them has been identified, analyzed and dealt with."

"That's out of the question," Bigelow said. "We have to go ahead with Magna Grande and it has to be a success."

"Respectfully, I disagree," Cross said. "The revenues from

187

Abu Zara are still rock-solid. If we scale back costs across the board, live within our means and just let the wounds from Alaska heal, we can still survive."

"And what will the shareholders say if the best I can promise them is lower revenues and profits? I've already got that vulture Bendick writing public letters accusing me of incompetence."

"Speaking as both a director of Bannock Oil and the father of a girl whose entire fortune is dependent on the prosperity of Bannock Oil and the long-term strength of its shares, I'd say forget about Aram bloody Bendick. The man's a bloodsucker, but he can't destroy this company. Mateus da Cunha can, particularly if he's being bankrolled by Johnny Congo."

"But why would Congo want to destroy Bannock?" Bigelow asked. "He's Carl Bannock's buddy and as much of a disgusting lowlife as Carl is, he lives off the proceeds of Bannock Oil, too. So what interest would he have in hurting his own livelihood? Look, I appreciate you coming to talk to me, Heck. You think we face a threat, and I hear you. But you're the best goddamn security chief I ever met in my life and I trust you and your guys to do a great job, keeping our investment in Magna Grande safe. You just head out to Africa and do what you do best. We're going to extract billions of gallons of oil, the shares are going to go nowhere but up, Bendick's ass is going to get the kicking it deserves and you, my friend, will get the thanks of a very grateful corporation."

Well, at least I tried, Cross told himself as he headed back to his hotel. His next stop was Caracas. And now he realized that the hit on Johnny Congo wasn't just a matter of personal revenge. The future of Bannock Oil could hang on removing the threat that Congo posed.

It was just past midnight in Caracas, Venezuela, as a gray Toyota Corolla paused for a moment about 500 meters from the entrance to the Villa Kazundu and Tommy Jones, all in black, just as Cross had specified, slipped out of the passenger seat on to the roadside. There were no other cars to be seen or heard and the neighborhood where the villa was located boasted few streetlights, for the men who owned the properties behind the high walls and thick hedges valued their privacy more than road safety—they paid their chauffeurs to worry about that. So it was easy for Jones to slip across the road and on to the dirt track that ran uphill on to the bare terrain beyond the final row of houses. He turned and jogged along the hillside, parallel to the road, until he reached the vantage point, first established by Guillermo Valencia, where one could look down on to the Villa Kazundu and its grounds. Jones then lay down, his head pointing downhill, and removed a state-of-the-art thermal-imaging camera from a thigh pouch. He turned it on, checked that the Bluetooth link to the transmitter on his belt was working, lifted the camera's viewfinder to his right eye and began scanning the property. One after another two human shapes appeared in shades of white and gray against the darker background of the foliage around them: the security guards patrolling the grounds. Jones spoke in little more than a whisper.

"Are you seeing this, boss?"

"Crystal clear," Cross replied. "How about you, Dave?"

"It's all good here," came Imbiss's reassuring voice from London. "I've hacked into the villa's camera and alarm systems and am ready to disable them on your command. The entry code on the front door keypad has been changed to zero-zero-zero-zero. Thought I'd keep it simple for you."

"My tiny mind and I thank you for that. Do you have any readings from inside the house, Jones?"

The camera panned across to the villa itself. It was sensitive enough to penetrate basic domestic brickwork, but the three figures that now appeared on the screen were little more than vague, pale gray blobs. "Reckon that's the master bedroom, boss," said Jones.

"Good," said Cross. "Let's hope the master stays there, preferably asleep. We go at oh-three-hundred, as planned. Keep me updated if anything changes between now and then."

"You got it, boss."

The rented Toyota, with Paddy at the wheel made another pass along the road, barely pausing as Hector, Nolan and Schrager got out and ran to the point on the Villa Kazundu's perimeter where the three of them would go over the wall. Each man had been assigned a specific guard and knew exactly where to find him. They were all dressed in black and wore latex gloves to prevent them from leaving fingerprints. Hector ordered Nolan and Schrager to inject an ampoule of Rob Noble's patent concoction into their guard's neck, allowing enough time for him to become incapacited. Next, they were to take the guards' handguns: these would be used to shoot Congo, giving the police no connection between the murder weapons and the assailants. Third: rendezvous by the main entrance to the house. Then the real fun would begin.

Jaime Palacios had been manning the gatehouse for five hours, three more to go. This was the job reserved for the senior operative on the shift: partly because the gatehouse guard had to greet people going in and out of the property; partly because he also had to watch the bank of mini-screens that displayed the views from the security cameras; and partly because he could spend the whole shift sitting down, instead of walking around the grounds. Since there had never been the slightest threat to the villa or its occupants, this was about the easiest work a man could get, and thus much prized by all the agency's longest-serving men.

Palacios had drunk a little rum, watched porn on his Samsung Galaxy TV, picked his nose, scratched his backside and occasionally contacted the two other men who were working the night shift with him, ostensibly for an update on the security situation, but mostly just for a few seconds' conversation. He had not worked with either of his colleagues before. They were both new to the agency, unlike Palacios who'd been coming up to the Villa Kazundu for almost six years, on and off. In that time, he'd seen some pretty crazy things happening there. He knew for sure that Señor Tumbo and his *maricón* boyfriend had powerful friends and that they liked to be entertained by men, women and anything in-between: the freaks he'd seen pass through these gates looked wilder than any stars of any porno he'd ever seen. He hadn't been up to the property since Señor Tumbo had been living there alone, but he'd heard stories of wild orgies, to which the security guards like him had been invited and given their pick of the girls to enjoy.

Nothing like that had ever happened to Palacios, so he had to make do with the low-grade filth he downloaded from the internet. At that moment he was so absorbed with it that he had not noticed the CCTV screens going blank, or the black-clad figure slipping silently through the open gatehouse door and coming up behind him. He hardly even felt the prick of a needle going into his neck.

For a few seconds, Palacios struggled against the powerful hands that covered his mouth to prevent him crying out and held him tightly to his chair, but then his head began to swim and he dropped into a state of deep unconsciousness.

Jones had warned Hector about Johnny Congo's change of location within the building, which had been revealed both by the concentration of blobs on the thermal imager's viewfinder and the music coming from the living room.

"It sounds like he has the usual females keeping him company."

"I don't want any collateral damage," Hector told his men. "No one fires without a clear line of sight on Congo. If you can, grab a girl each and get her out of the way. Leave Congo to me." He waited for their nods of acknowledgement, then said, "OK, then, let's do it."

Cross led Nolan and Schrager across the forecourt and up the steps to the front door. The code that Dave Imbiss had changed worked. They were in.

The room in which Congo was sequestered with the girls was across from the entrance hall, to the right. The door to the room was ajar. Cross moved silently to the door and slipped a mirror on a telescopic handle out of his leg pocket. He squatted down on his haunches, extended the handle until the mirror was just beyond the edge of the door, about a meter off the floor, and studied the image it revealed.

He had a view of the back of a leather sofa and beyond it the torsos of two girls, dancing with one another, their bodies pressed together in a blatantly sexual bump-and-grind routine. At first Hector could not work out Congo's exact position, until he saw the top of his head, the skin almost the precise shade of deep, dark brown as the leather on which he was sitting. His scalp was protruding an inch or so above the top of the sofa.

But from this angle Hector's view was partially obstructed. He couldn't see the girl's faces, or get any more of a sense of the room as a whole unless he tilted the mirror upward. But if he did that there was a strong chance of catching the light from the ceiling and alerting the quarry to his presence. Silently he signaled to his men: indicating that Nolan should move to his right and Schrager to his left. Then he raised his fingers and counted down: three—two—one—go!

Hector burst through the open door into the room beyond. But almost immediately his speed faltered, because he'd seen what had previously been hidden from him. This was the mirror hanging over the fireplace. And as Cross saw the mirror, so his prey saw his image in it. With the reflexes of a wild animal Congo sprang instantly from the sofa. He dived across the room and grabbed hold of the nearest of the two naked dancing girls. Twisting her arms up behind her back, he spun the woman around to face Hector Cross, holding her in front of him as a shield. The second woman shrieked when she saw Hector and the pistol he was pointing at her; then she turned and darted away through the open glass doors behind her and vanished into the dark interior of the house. Johnny Congo continued to face Hector, still holding the first blubbering female before him as he backed away toward the open doors through which the other girl had disappeared.

"Put the girl down!" Cross snarled.

Congo threw back his head and laughed. "Oh, I recognize that voice. Screw you, Cross, I ain't putting no one down. But all three of you bastards had better drop those pieces on the floor right away or I slit this bitch's throat!"

"Cut her then," said Cross with feigned indifference. "Go ahead. Do it . . . But if she dies, you die a second later. Believe me, I'll take that deal."

Cross saw the girl's eyes widen. She'd understood what he was saying. He had not expected that.

Congo didn't flinch. "You haven't got the balls for it. You'd have shot her already if you had. Put the gun down, Cross." He nodded at Nolan and Schrager: "Them too . . ."

"That's not going to happen, Congo."

"Then we got ourselves a stand-off, don't we?"

All the time Congo was edging backward, getting closer to the open door. As he moved he bobbed and weaved his head, like a boxer evading punches, making himself a harder target to hit. But no matter how much his head might move, Congo's eyes were locked on to Cross, darting only occasional glances at the other two men. He knew who was the danger man.

Cross moved with him, standing off five meters from him, meeting Congo's stare and returning it, holding the pistol out in front of him, two-handed, aiming at a point just above the girl's forehead. If the shot was clear for even a fraction of a second, he was determined to take it.

But by now Congo was directly in front of the glass door and barely a pace in front of it. From the plans of the house that Hector had studied he was almost certain the door led to the main kitchens and, beyond that, the servants' quarters. In that area of the house, the rooms were far smaller and more numerous, linked by a maze of corridors and stairs that ran up toward the bedrooms on the first floor and down toward the garages where he knew there were at least two fast cars and a Suzuki 500-cc motorbike parked.

That was where Congo was certainly heading. He could run full pelt to the garage and once he was there and in a car, or on the motorbike, he'd be gone, and the last chance Hector would have of stopping him would be Paddy O'Quinn. But Paddy would have a hell of a job to intercept Congo in the darkness. He would have to be in exactly the right place at exactly the right time.

So it was up to Hector to stop him now. But Hector was running out of time. He calculated the odds against him. There was only one way of doing it: firing at the girl's legs. At this range a 9-mm bullet would drill its way right through her and into Congo. The girl had great pins. It would be a crying shame to wreck one of them. But better a bad wound and a lifelong limp than a knife in the throat. And better one wounded hostage than a killer back on the run.

Hector's aim never wavered, but in his head he was visualizing the precise moment in which he'd bring it down and fire, shin-high, at the girl. He breathed in and then slowly out. When he reached the fullest point of the next breath, he'd fire.

Congo was almost inside the frame of the door. It had to be now. Cross started breathing in. Then Congo did the unexpected. He stabbed the girl low down in her back and her scream of agony distracted Hector for an instant. In that brief

194

flicker of time Congo lifted the girl as easily as if she were a rag doll and hurled her at Hector's head. Hector flinched and his shot was blocked by the girl's flying body. But now Congo was fully exposed to both Nolan and Schrager.

They fired together but an instant before the shots rang out Congo somersaulted backward and their shots flew high. They had both been aiming at his head. Congo landed in a perfectly balanced crouch. Immediately he used all the power of his massive legs to throw himself sideways; with the speed and agility of a big wild cat he dived behind the heavy door frame. The back-up shots fired by Nolan and Schrager came a second too late. They smashed clouds of white splinters from the wooden frames. But Johnny Congo was gone. Stunned for a moment by the speed with which it had happened, they heard his footsteps pounding on the concrete stairs as he raced down to the garages on the lower level of the rambling old house.

Bitterly Hector realized how cunning Congo had been. If he had killed the girl outright, Hector could have ignored her. But wounded, she demanded his attention.

"Nolan! Deal with her," Cross shouted. He looked at the girl, and spoke in Spanish. "You want to live? Then do exactly what he says." Then he glanced at Schrager. "Schrager! On me." He was already running as he barked one more order, "Jones! Get to Paddy's car. Go!"

Congo had less than ten seconds' start. But if Cross couldn't get to him before he reached the garage, it might as well be ten hours. Cross ran into the passage that led to the kitchen. It was pitch black. He pulled out his phone and turned on the torch. Another two seconds lost. Ahead of him he heard a crashing sound.

Now he ran: down the corridor, left through the swing doors and into the kitchen. Cross saw four staff: two chefs and two in maid's uniforms standing in a terrified huddle to one side of the room. Now he knew what sound he'd heard. Congo had pulled down a rack of metal shelves that had been stacked with pots and pans. There was a clear way through the chaos to the far end of the kitchen, but it was slow. More time lost.

Cross kept moving. He heard a burst of muttered expletives behind him as Schrager trod on an upturned pan, but ignored it and kept moving. On the far side of the kitchen the passage forked: one way, right, to the servants' quarters; the other, left, to the staircase that led down to the garage. Cross turned left and was almost at the top of the stairs when he heard running footsteps at the bottom.

There were three flights of stairs, arranged in a zig-zag. Cross didn't bother running, he just jumped each flight, landing on the levels, spinning around in a one-eighty then leaping down the next flight. He landed at the bottom of the stairs, stumbled and fell on to the bare concrete floor of the small lobby between the stairs and the door to the garage.

As Cross hit the floor, driving the air out of his lungs, the door above his head was shredded by an extended deafening burst of close-range submachine-gun fire that ripped through the air at precisely the level where Cross would have been if he'd been standing. Schrager jumped right into the blizzard of steel and aluminum rounds that reduced his ribs to kindling, snapped every bone in his arms and pulped his head into a shapeless, faceless pink and crimson blob in the instant before he dropped down beside Cross, stone dead.

Cross ignored the corpse beside him. His mind was on the bullets that had hit it. They had been fired by a weapon that could not sustain more than two seconds' fire without running out of ammo, which meant that Congo almost certainly had to change the magazine, which in turn gave Cross the time he needed to get up on to his hands and knees, hurl himself at the door, crash through it and then go straight into a roll that took him away from the center of the door and the line along which Congo would be aiming, once he'd reloaded.

196

Cross ended the roll in a low, crouching position. His gun was in his hand and he swung it through an arc, looking for Congo. But there was no sign of him. The garage was huge, with spaces for at least twenty cars, most of them filled. Cross's ears were still ringing with the sound of the gunfire. He couldn't hear Congo as he ran, bent low beneath the roof lines of the vehicles to either side of him.

Then suddenly there was the whirring sound of an engine starting up, bright white Xenon headlights bloomed directly opposite him, dazzling him, disorienting him, and then the lights grew even brighter, and he was aware of them bearing down on him. Cross fired four fast shots, aiming between and slightly above the retina-searing blaze of light; then he threw himself out of the way as two-and-a-half tons of supercharged V8 Range Rover roared past him and out on to the ramp.

He stood up, placed his hands on his knees and panted for breath. Now it was down to Paddy O'Quinn and Tommy Jones in the gray Toyota Corolla.

Johnny Congo cut the Range Rover's lights as soon as he hit the ramp that led up from the garage to the Chateau Congo forecourt. They'd served their purpose by dazzling Hector Cross, but from now on they'd only mark his position for his pursuers. As he burst out of the gate of the property and turned hard left on to the road downhill, leading back into the city, he saw a pair of lights appear in his rearview mirror. Congo took the first right and looked again: they were still there.

"Fine!" He nodded. His blood was up. "We know just how to deal with you," he whispered.

From the moment that Congo and Carl Bannock had first arrived in Caracas, they'd started planning what to do if they ever had to leave it in a hurry. Anything could happen. A new, less sympathetic government might be elected, or just seize power: Latin American countries had a history of revolutions and military coups, so that was always a possibility. The U.S. government might decide that they wanted Congo back in custody badly enough to make their pursuit of him more aggressive. Or a fellow criminal might just decide to take them out for business reasons: if the word got out about the money they were making from coltan and blood diamonds it would be enough to tempt a saint, let alone a sociopath.

Having spent many years at Huntsville, first observing the obvious inadequacies of the wardens who guarded him and then learning how to control them by a brutally effective system of bribes and threats, Congo took it for granted that the men guarding him and Carl were equally unreliable and open to persuasion by his enemies. So Congo had devised a complex series of exit strategies. His recent experience in Kazundu, where he and Carl had been caught napping by Hector Cross's airborne military assault, followed by Carl's death and his own narrow escape from execution, had only deepened Congo's determination not to leave anything to chance. He'd gone back over his plans in exhaustive detail, making sure that all his escape routes, within the house itself and beyond, were still operable, with weapons cached throughout the building so that everything he needed would be available to him, no matter how extreme the circumstances.

Even so, Congo had spent enough time playing football and fighting in the Marines to know that it didn't matter how good the coach's playbook might be, or how thoroughly a mission was planned, there were always times when the unexpected happened, a whole new kind of shit hit the fan, the play broke down and you just had to improvise your way out of trouble with the resources that were available. So when he was caught unawares, with no firearm within reach, he'd grabbed the knife in one hand and the woman in the other and taken it from there. Not killing her, that had been a nice touch. He wouldn't have thought of it if he hadn't recognized Cross's voice and known that he was too pussy to just let a bitch bleed to death without doing something to save her. So that was the second time Cross had paid for being soft: seemed like the honky asshole just hadn't learned his lesson.

Had it killed him, though? That's what Congo wanted to know. He'd heard two sets of footsteps coming after him, but only one man came through the door into the garage. Someone had been shredded by his two-second burst from the FN P90 Personal Defense Weapon that had been waiting for him just inside the door and no one could survive that, no matter how much body armor they were wearing. Congo almost hoped Cross had been the survivor. Killing him blind on the far side of a closed door would not give him much satisfaction. He wanted to see Cross die in front of him and he wanted to make the process as slow and painful as possible. However, right now Congo had his own survival to think about.

Once outside the Chateau Congo grounds, his black Range Rover, which boasted dechromed black wheels, fenders, radiator grill and running boards, simply melded into the darkness around it. Knowing the roads as well as he did, Congo was able to drive with his foot flat on the accelerator, even without lights, making turns so late that the driver pursuing him had to slam on the brakes, losing valuable momentum and falling far enough behind that Congo was able to turn off the road on to a heavily shaded stretch of driveway that led to a pair of gates set back from the road without being seen. He cut the engine and watched as the chasing car raced past, waited fifteen seconds for it to disappear around the next bend and then pulled back on to the road and drove off in the opposite direction.

Now Congo was heading for his safe house, which was an apartment above a fried-chicken restaurant in a working-class area of the city. The apartment looked to all the world like just another dirty, badly maintained, down-at-heel fleapit. But while Congo had done nothing at all to improve its appearance, he had installed steel doors and bulletproof windows. Amid all the jumble of TV aerials on top of the building, he'd installed dishes providing him with satellite phone and internet access. He'd worked out escape routes from the front, rear and over the neighboring rooftops. And if he ever got hungry, he could always count on plenty of fried chicken.

Congo parked the Range Rover at a reserved space in a downtown car park. He unclipped an interior door panel beside the driver's seat, reached into the hidden storage well and removed a waterproof plastic pouch. It contained the IDs and money that had been in his safe-deposit box in Zurich, plus other bearer bonds and documentation that he'd had waiting for him at the villa. Now in possession of everything he needed to get anywhere in the world, Congo took a bus to within a half mile of the safe house and walked the rest of the way. Over the next twenty-four hours, he'd select one of a number of possible combinations of boat and plane that would take him across 180 miles of Caribbean water to the island of Curaçao in the Dutch West Indies, or a short distance further to its neighbor Aruba. Both islands possessed international airports open to scheduled and private flights and were thus ideal jumping-off points for the longest stage of his journey. Congo knew exactly where he was heading and what he would do when he arrived there. The only issues left to be determined were exactly how he'd make the journey, and what identity he would adopt along the way.

Back at the villa, Cross had just got back to his feet when the sound of Dave Imbiss's voice on the radio cut through the ringing in his ears caused by the burst of FN fire that had taken Schrager down.

"The Caracas police have had a report of gunfire in your neighborhood. I don't get the feeling that they're taking it too seriously, but a squad car's been despatched to check the property out. Get out or bluff it out, those are your two options," Dave told him.

"How long have I got?"

"Five minutes tops. But call it four minutes: three to be safe."

Cross was on the move at once, running out of the garage and back the way he'd come, straight past Schrager's remains. There were blood spatters all over the wall and fragments of balaclava, hair, skull and brains smearing the floor and the stairs. Cross ignored him: forget the dead; the only ones that mattered now were the living. He spoke into his mike once again: "Nolan, how's the girl?"

"I've given her a morphine ampoule and that's calmed her. I'm getting a bandage on her now, but she's still bleeding heavily. Needs a doctor, that's for sure. Did you get the bastard?"

"No. He reached the garage before we could cut him off. Schrager is down. I'm on my way back up to you."

By the time he got to the kitchen it was empty. The servants must have heard the gunfire and scarpered. In the living room, Nolan was taping up a bandage that was wrapped around the stabbed girl's waist. "It's not safe for you here, understand?" He told her in Spanish, and she nodded mutely.

Cross turned back to Nolan. "Take her down to the garage. Get the biggest motor you can find. There should be keys somewhere. If not, just take it the old-fashioned way. She goes on the back seat. We will drop her wherever she wants. Schrager stays where he is. Got it?"

"Yes, boss."

Cross started the stopwatch on his phone. He wanted to know, to the second, how much time he was using. There was just one thing he needed to do before they left. If he couldn't get Congo he wanted one of his communications devices. He'd already scanned the living room to see whether Congo had left a laptop, tablet or phone there, but could see no sign of either. There was an office marked on the plan, on the far side of the hall. Cross was on his way there when Imbiss came on the air again: "The cops are getting closer. Less than three minutes. You need to get out."

"Got it."

Cross went into the office, turned on the light. He could see a desk, but it was bare. Congo had to have a laptop, or an iPad; everyone did. Where the hell would he use it? Cross thought about his own routine. Since he'd been living alone, he seemed to turn off his laptop, last thing at night, the way he always used to turn off his bedside light. Maybe Congo was the same. His bedroom was upstairs. Cross looked at his watch: thirty-eight seconds gone.

He took the stairs at a run, expecting at any moment to hear the sound of an approaching siren. When he got to Congo's bedroom, the light was already on. Cross didn't think anything of it. Congo was the kind of guy who'd leave lights on everywhere. He could afford the electricity bill easily enough and he wasn't going to lie awake at nights worrying about global warming, either. Cross swept his eyes around the room. The bedclothes were strewn all over the place and he caught the sight of blood on the crumpled bottom sheet. He didn't see anything he was looking for, though, and there wasn't time to start searching cupboards and drawers. He was about to leave when he heard a sound from across the room. The doors to what looked like a walk-in wardrobe were open and Cross was certain someone was inside. He raised his gun, walked soundlessly across the room to the wardrobe, paused behind one of the doors and then stepped into the wardrobe.

The girl was there. She'd put on a T-shirt—one of Congo's presumably, for it was so big that it looked like a dress on her—but nothing else; and she had a holdall in one hand, but she wasn't filling it with clothes. Instead she was holding a great fistful of gold and diamond jewelry: necklaces, bracelets, watches—men's and women's alike. There was a wall safe behind her, its door hanging open. She gave a startled little squeak when she turned and saw Cross pointing a gun at her, but then straightened up, squared her shoulders and glared at him, defiantly.

"We earned it, what he did to us." She paused, waiting to see how Cross would react.

Cross nodded. "OK." He lowered the gun, looked at the watch. One minute, nineteen seconds. The voice in his ear sounded again.

"A minute before they get there."

"Did he have a computer, a phone, anything like that?" he asked.

The girl nodded. "An iPad. Look by the bed."

"Go down again to the garage. Wait there. We will give you a ride into town. . . wherever you want to go." She nodded again, then picked up the holdall and headed for the door.

Hector found the iPad where she had told him it would be.

As he ran back down the stairs to the garage a car horn bleeped ahead of him, followed by a quick flash of headlights. Nolan had found and been able to start another black Range Rover. Hector ran toward it, and saw the girl waiting beside it.

"Get in the back!" Cross ordered her. Then he spoke on the radio to Dave Imbiss again. "Which way are the cops coming, Dave?"

"Up the hill, approaching the house from the left, as you leave the gates. So turn right and pray to God you can be out of sight before they get there."

"Right at the gates," Cross said to Nolan.

"If we beat them to it," Nolan muttered.

The twin sheets of solid steel were looming before them. Cross prayed that the car had some kind of transponder that would make the gates open automatically, but they were getting closer and closer and still nothing was happening. The Range Rover slowed as Nolan hit the brakes.

"Keep going!" Cross barked.

"But, boss . . ."

"I said give it the gun, damn you!"

Nolan took his foot off the brakes, inhaled sharply, muttered, "Here goes nothing," and hit the gas. The Range Rover surged forward. The gates were filling the windscreen, a gleaming metal wall, closer and closer still.

And then, when even Cross was bracing himself for the impact, they slid open and the Range Rover raced through, almost scraping its paintwork against the bare steel on each side of the chassis. Nolan spun the wheel right and the car surged up the ramp and around the bend. Cross had been watching the rear mirror all the way, but he saw no sign of a police car's flashing lights. He relaxed, slumped back in the passenger seat and only then realized that he'd not heard from Paddy O'Quinn.

"Paddy, are you there? Do you have a tail on Congo?"

"Sorry, Heck, the bastard was driving a black car along unlit roads without his lights on. We had him and then . . ." O'Quinn sighed. "We didn't have him any more."

"Damn! Well, keep looking and let me know if you get even a sniff of him."

Cross closed his eyes and gathered his thoughts. The primary aim of the mission had failed and he'd lost a good man, one with a wife and kids at home, which made it even worse. Congo had escaped and all Cross had to show for his night's work was Congo's iPad.

When they dropped the wounded girl on the outskirts of the city she limped away without another word, and without looking back.

The police arrived at the property belonging to Juan Tumbo just as the steel gate to the underground garage slid the final few centimeters back into the closed position. They were unable to enter the property, or to rouse any of the security guards or other employees. They could, however, hear the distant sound of dance music coming from the house. When they checked with their station commander they were told that although the house, like all the others in the neighborhood, was equipped with security cameras, alarm systems and panic buttons, none of them had been sounded. Nor had there been any further reports of gunfire. If a weapon had been discharged, the chances were that it was the owner, fooling around or trying to impress a woman.

"Forget it," the officers in the patrol car were told. "If someone reports a crime tomorrow, then we will investigate it."

When morning broke at the villa, the staff held a meeting. None of the guards had any idea what had happened. They were still deep in what ketamine-users know as the "k-hole," a place where people lose their sense of time, place, identity and reality, where their memory is wiped away and their mind is beset by hallucinations. The rest of the staff agreed that Señor Tumbo had been alive and well when he left the building, so if he wanted to come back, he would. In the meantime, there was the mutilated body of a stranger to dispose of. All of them agreed that it was not wise to trouble the police with such a trivial matter. And the head gardener named César was given the job of burying it as deeply as possible in the furthest, least accessible corner of the property, while the others got to work cleaning up the mess.

When they thought about it, the staff of the villa realized that they were actually in an ideal situation. Everyone in the neighborhood was accustomed to Señor Bannock and Señor Tumbo being away for months at a time. The supermarket where they bought their food kept an account that was paid automatically by a bank somewhere in America that also handled all the utility bills. The garage was filled with cars and there was a credit card for the petrol. If they all just kept quiet and told anyone who asked that the owners were away on business, they could keep living in luxury for as long as they liked.

The police therefore received no further reports from the villa, and saw no reason to return. So far as everyone was concerned nothing of any note had taken place at all.

Hector called the royal palace in Abu Zara City, asked to speak to His Highness the Emir and, once he'd given his name, was put straight through to the Emir's private office. A few moments later, he heard the voice of the ruler of Abu Zara.

"I am so glad that you called, Hector. I was very sorry—in fact, disgusted to hear that the Americans allowed that animal Congo to escape. I can only imagine how you must feel, after all that he has done to your family. If there is anything I can do, you have only to ask."

Most Englishmen, confronted by an offer like that, instinctively refuse it, not wanting to put the other person to trouble on their account. But what might pass for good manners in England would constitute a profound insult to a man like the Emir, who would not take kindly to the refusal of an offer of help. Cross knew that, and so had no compunction about replying, "Thank you, Your Highness. Your concern means a lot to me and, as it happens, you could be a real help."

"I am delighted to hear that. What is it that you require?"

"A few days ago I discovered where Johnny Congo was hiding in Caracas. My men and I attempted to seize him, but he escaped. I am very concerned that my daughter Catherine Cayla may once more be in danger. I would like to move her immediately to the apartment in Abu Zara where I know she will be safe. May I have your permission to do that?"

The Emir chuckled softly. "You know that I have, how do you say, a ticklish spot for the young lady in question. Please send her to be a guest in my country forthwith, if not sooner."

"Thank you, Your Highness. I'm very grateful indeed for your kindness."

Catherine Cayla, accompanied by her nanny Bonnie Hepworth

and her entire entourage, took off the following morning and flew directly from London Heathrow to the little Gulf State where the Bannock Oil security headquarters were situated.

They were immediately installed in the apartment on the top floor of a building whose other occupants were all senior politicians or members of Abu Zara's vast royal family. As a consequence the building was a virtual fortress, from the razor wire that guarded its perimeter to the security systems that monitored every square millimeter of every floor and the steel baffles, designed to deflect any rocket grenade or missile fired from the ground below, that protected the windows of the Cross apartment.

The place had been created as a safe house for Catherine Cayla, where she could live without Cross having to worry about her. Her trust fund took care of the phenomenal cost of upkeep.

Ten days had passed since the Caracas operation. Cross and O'Quinn were back in London and preparations for the offshore assignment at the Magna Grande field were in full swing when Nastiya's phone started ringing and she saw Yevgenia's name pop up on the screen.

"I just had a call from da Cunha," her younger sister said.

"Did you give him the numbers that Papa got for us?" Nastiya asked.

Yevgenia giggled. "He didn't seem awfully interested in them. He was much more interested in your private number."

"I hope you didn't give it to him—the real one."

"No, I told him I'd get in touch with you and let you know he'd called."

"Good."

"So are you going to call him?"

Nastiya knew that her sister was smiling in a conspiratorial, gossipy sort of way as she asked the question. She replied in what she hoped was a flat, businesslike fashion: "Why? I found out what I needed to know. There's nothing to be gained by talking to him again."

"He sounded very sexy," Yevgenia wheedled. "You know, with his French accent . . ."

"To some people, maybe."

"Well, I thought he was very charming."

"Yes, he's got charm all right . . ."

"Oh, so you do like him!" Yevgenia exclaimed, delighted to have caught Nastiya in her trap.

"I didn't say that."

"Come on, admit it, you think he's sexy."

Nastiya decided it was time to show who was in control. "Let me remind you, little sister, that I am a married woman and I love my husband, so even if I can see how other women might think a man was attractive, that doesn't mean that I find him attractive myself."

"Well, then, tell me what another women would see when she looked at Mateus da Cunha?"

"Hmm . . ." Nastiya wondered whether to end the conversation right here and now. But Yevgenia was her long-lost sister and one of the things sisters did—or so Nastiya assumed—was swap tittle-tattle about men, so she went along with Yevgenia's question. "Well, another woman would see a man who's about one meter eighty-five tall . . ."

"Ooh, I like that! It means that even in my highest heels I still have to tilt my head up to kiss him. Does he have a good body?"

"I think it's clear that he takes regular exercise, yes."

"And is he black? I've never had a black boyfriend. Papa would go crazy!"

"He's mixed race: his mother is French. So his skin is paler than a full-blooded West African and his facial features are more Caucasian: narrower nose, thinner lips."

"What about, you know . . . down there? Is that African? I hope so!"

Almost certainly, Nastiya thought, but what she said was, "How should I know?"

"Oh, don't play the innocent with me, big sister! I bet you know exactly how big he is!"

"I haven't a clue."

"Then I'll just have to find out for myself!"

Now Nastiya really was concerned. Yevgenia wasn't nearly ready to take on a man like da Cunha. "No, Yevgenia, don't do that," she said. "Listen to me, this is serious: Mateus da Cunha is very handsome, very clever, very charming and he knows exactly the effect he has on women."

"Mmm . . . yummy!"

"But he's also a very dangerous, ruthless, cynical bastard. The only thing he really cares about is power and he'll do anything to get it. Do you hear me?"

"Yes, and it's all good!"

"No, really it's not. You know how Papa hurt you? Well, that was nothing, nothing at all next to the damage da Cunha could do."

"All right, all right, I get it," said Yevgenia, sounding like a sulky teenager.

Nastiya seized her opportunity to change the subject. "Good, now I have something else I wanted to talk to you about. I was thinking that maybe you could come to stay with me in London for a few days. I'd love you to meet Paddy and some of the people I work with. We have to go to Africa soon, but before then, maybe?"

"Yes please! I haven't been to London for ages and I have so many friends who live there."

"Good, then it's settled. Now all we have to do is agree on the date . . ."

Aram Bendick was hot, sweaty and jet-lagged, and his temper, abrasive at the best of times, was verging on the volcanic.

209

He'd got on a Gulfstream G500 in New York City that flew to Cape Verde—whatever the hell that might be—for a refuel. "Just a precaution," the pilot said. "We could get where we are going on a single tank, but only just."

"So where the hell are we going?" Bendick asked and the pilot just smiled and said, "I'm sorry, sir, but I'm not at liberty to divulge that information."

Bendick would never have got on the plane at all, and certainly not without his usual six-man bodyguard, every man of them ex-Mossad, if it hadn't been for the second tranche of $50 million that Juan Tumbo had placed in an escrow account with the words: "If you don't get back to New York within seventy-two hours of your take-off, that money gets sent to your lawyers. You can tell 'em what to do with it. Even if your plane lands just one minute after that time, you still get the money."

The first fifty million had arrived in his fund, exactly as Tumbo had promised. The second was checked out by his lawyers and they were satisfied it was legit. Bendick figured he had a lot of enemies, but none of them were crazy enough to throw away a hundred mill just so they could kill him. So he got on the plane at three in the afternoon, worked all the way to Cape Verde, then ate dinner at the start of the second leg, watched a movie and finally crashed for three or four hours. He was woken just before they landed at a two-bit excuse for an airport some place where no one had heard of air-conditioning and the immigration officials made the obstructive jerks on the desks at JFK look as smooth and charming as George freakin' Clooney.

The clocks told him it was eight in the morning, but it was already hot and humid and it was a blessed relief to discover that the Range Rover waiting for him outside the terminal had air-conditioning and comfortable seats to soothe him. Bendick would have grabbed some much-needed shut-eye, but the road was so full of potholes it was like trying to sleep on top of a bouncy castle. So he forced his weary, bloodshot eyes to stay open and looked out at a giant slum, where all the buildings looked like they should have been condemned decades ago and the streets were filled with people carrying possessions and merchandise on their heads and milling around like they had nothing better to do with themselves. What in God's name, Bendick wondered, would make a man who could spend tens of millions just to get a one-to-one meeting live in a dump like this? As to where the dump was, he figured it had to be Africa, just from the fact that just about everyone he could see was black, and the city was built on the sea, because they'd flown in over the water to land. Beyond that he knew squat.

The Range Range drove uphill through the outskirts of the city before arriving at a black wrought-iron gateway, reinforced with painted steel panels behind the ironwork, set into a high concrete wall. There were two armed guards on the gates, but they recognized the car as it approached and had the gates open right away, so that Bendick could be driven right on through. Within the compound he discovered an entirely new world of sprinklers playing over lush green lawns and uniformed gardeners tending to the dazzling flowerbeds. As the car pulled up outside the entrance to a grand, colonial-type mansion white-gloved servants hurried to open the passenger door, greet Bendick with a smile and lead him to a cool, airy suite of rooms, where heavy shutters kept the heat of the sun at bay while a ceiling fan provided a cooling breeze. An hour later, once he'd showered, changed and finished a light breakfast, perfectly prepared to his exact specifications and eaten on a shaded balcony overlooking the gardens, Aram Bendick was ready to meet his host.

He was led downstairs, back across the entrance hall and into a private study. A black man was sitting behind a desk at the far side of the room from the door. He had a beard and short, tightly curled hair, both streaked with gray, and although he looked broad-shouldered and imposing when he was sitting down, it was only when the man got to his feet that Bendick appreciated the sheer scale of him. The man was a mountain on legs.

"I'm Juan Tumbo," he said in an African-American voice that seemed to rumble up from the bowels of the earth, taking Bendick's hand in a bone-crushing grip. "Good of you to come'n see me, 'Ram—hope you don't mind me calling you that, now that we're business associates. They lookin' after you here? The place is only a rental, servants come with the building."

"They looked after me fine, Mr. Tumbo, and if my wife was here she'd say the house was quaint, but that city out there's gotta be the shittiest, most godforsaken dump I ever saw," Bendick began. "Makes East Harlem look like Monte frickin' Carlo, you know what I'm saying? And, excuse me for asking, but where the hell am I anyway?"

Tumbo smiled, entirely untroubled by Bendick's aggressive, abusive style. "Cabinda City, capital of the great state of Cabinda. And yeah, the city's 'bout as bad as you say, but come on over here to the window—see the ocean out there? Underneath that water they got some of the richest oil and gas deposits in the world: billions of barrels of it." Tumbo smiled. "Tens of billions, in fact."

"So, what, you dragged me halfway across the world because you want me to invest in some kind of oil project?" Bendick sneered. "Screw you, I got a million others I could choose from."

Tumbo moved closer to Bendick, looming over him. "You want to mouth off, trying to impress me with what a big swinging dick you got, or you want to make some serious coin? I don't want you to invest in an oil project, I want you to invest against it. I mean, you know how to make money on a stock that's going down, right?"

Now Bendick was a little more interested. "Yeah, and I got a fifty-thousand-square-foot mansion in East Hampton, a two-

212

hundred-and-eighty-foot yacht, a gazillion acres in Montana and a three-floor, sixteen-room apartment on Fifth Avenue to prove it. What's the play?"

"The play is, I got a bone to pick with a dude name of Hector Cross. This motherfucker killed the one person in the world I ever truly cared for, fed him to the crocodiles. Fed him alive."

"You're shitting me," said Bendick, at the same time thinking, *Is this brick shithouse telling me he's a goddamn fairy?*

"No, that's the literal truth," said Tumbo. His voice had lost its calm, well-spoken tone and taken on a harsher, cruder note. "Cross turned my man into breakfast for a pair of frickin' purses with teeth. Now, I'm not happy 'bout that. Fact I want to kill the son of a bitch. But, see, the more I think about it, the more I ask myself whether killing him is enough. The answer I get is no. I wanna see him suffer. I want him brought down low. I want him to know what it's like to be poor, feel humiliation, be afraid for hisself and his family, feel it deep in his bones. That's where you come in, 'cause the more Cross loses, the more you and me win."

"How are you planning on doing that, exactly?"

"By poisoning the well that provides Cross and his kid with all their money: Bannock Oil. See, I got a lot of information about that particular corporation: inside information, shit that don' get made public. I know exactly how to hurt Bannock and Cross as well, hurt 'em in a way that'll take eighty, ninety percent off the share price and make Cross about as popular as a leper with a bomb. Way I figure it, you can bet against Bannock on the way down, then use the money you make to buy the whole damn business at ten cents on the dollar, five if you're lucky."

"So why me? Why don't you do the whole deal yourself?"

"Well, let's just say I value my privacy. Plus, I checked you out. I saw how you operate, bad-mouthing corporations and executives, throwing any crazy shit you can find at them, all over the internet, the media, dragging chief executives through the mud. I like your style, man."

"OK, but what do you want from the deal, aside from screwing Cross over?"

"Half the money, that's what."

"And if I say no?"

"Then your wife's a widow. So, you in?"

"You making me an offer I can't refuse?"

"No, I'm making you an offer you'd have to have garbage for brains to refuse."

Bendick shrugged. "Is that what you think? You haven't told me what the deal is. All you said is you want to hurt Hector Cross, like I could give a shit about that, and you're gonna bring down Bannock. But you haven't said how you're going to do that, and I can tell, just by listening to you, that you don't have the first frickin' clue about the best way to profit from a corporate meltdown. So go ahead, big boy, tell me what you really got to offer me."

Tumbo didn't say anything. He just looked down at Bendick and for a moment the financier was truly afraid that he'd gone too far. The way Tumbo was gritting his teeth, like he was really struggling against a powerful inner impulse, it was possible he might just forget about all the money he had riding on Bendick's safe return.

Finally, Tumbo spoke. "Don't you ever, ever disrespect me like that again, 'cause if you do, I'm going to rip your ugly kike head right off of your scrawny white neck . . ." He raised his hands, the fingers spread, and then he bunched his fists, just inches from Bendick's suddenly sweating face. "You don' know how lucky you are, boy. I've killed men for way less'n you just said. But I'm working on my anger management, trying to turn over a new leaf, so I'm gonna take a deep breath, count to ten and then I'll tell you as much as you need, or wanna know."

Bendick didn't say anything. For once in his life, there was nothing he could say to help him get what he wanted. He just had to zip it and let this very large, very angry man take his time, let him count to a hundred if it made him feel better.

Luckily, ten seemed to do the trick. Tumbo exhaled slowly, breathed in again and then said, "Bannock Oil lost a rig up in the Arctic, right?"

"Right," said Bendick, only too happy to be in agreement for once.

"So that means they lost money twice over, once from the cost of the rig and a second time from all the oil they can't be drilling no more. Right?"

"Uh-huh."

"Now, what if the same thing happened right here, in Angolan waters? What if they lose another rig, and they lose the chance to make money from getting to all that sweet African crude? I mean, once is bad enough, but twice? C'mon! They gonna be screwed."

"In theory, yeah, but the Bannock board already know the risk they're facing and they've taken steps to protect themselves. Bigelow's been on TV, spoken to the *Wall Street Journal*, given briefings to all the top financial bloggers just letting everyone know there's never been an offshore field in history had the kind of defensive systems they're putting in place here. Listen, you're not the only one around here knows about Bannock Oil. You think when I go after a corporation I don't get dossiers on all its top people? Hector Cross is in command of the whole operation, and he knows what he's doing. He's kept the oil flowing out of Abu Zara for years and if any wise guys ever try to disrupt production there, Cross and his men just whack 'em. What makes you think he's gonna mess it up, just because he's killing Africans instead of Arabs?"

"Let's say I got my reasons," Tumbo replied. "I'd like to tell you what they are, but you don't want me to do that."

"Why not?"

"It's for your own protection. If'n you don't know what's going to happen, you can't be responsible or accountable when

215

it does. You can say, 'Hey, I didn't know they was gonna do that. I just figured, Africa's a dangerous place, something might go wrong and I'm going to be ready when it does.' And no one can do anything, 'cause you'll be telling the truth. But if certain, ah, unfortunate events take place, and you knew about them all along, then that might make you an accomplice, or a conspirator, and you don't need that, my friend, 'cause believe me, you'd be easy meat the moment you stepped inside a jail."

"This is you giving me deniability, huh?"

"Exactly. Now, one more thing: you suggested I was manifesting ignorance about the ways and means of making money from a corporate meltdown. Go ahead, then, enlighten me."

"OK," said Bendick, relieved to be back on his own territory. He gave Tumbo a brief lecture in the basics of leveraged trading. First he talked about stock options: how it was possible to pay for the right to buy stock at a set price, at a set future date, if you thought the stock was going to rise above that price; or pay for the right to sell at a set price, at a set future date, if you thought it was going to fall below that price. But Tumbo was not impressed.

"I know that long and short shit, man. 'Put options' and 'call options' ain't no more than a fancy way of calling up a bookie and placing a bet. What else you got?"

"Well, do the initials CDS mean anything to you?"

"I know they are one letter away from a TV network, that's for sure."

Bendick laughed politely, not wanting to offend. "Yeah, CBS, that's a good one . . . but it's not what I had in mind. A CDS, or credit default swap, is basically a form of insurance. Say you loan someone a million bucks and you think to yourself: Man, what if that sonofabitch goes bust and can't pay his debt? . . ."

"Then I go around there and whup on him till he pays me, or dies, I ain't bothered which," Tumbo said casually.

"Or . . . or you could buy a credit default swap," Bendick suggested. "Basically, it was invented as a way of insuring a debt.

216

So you loan the million bucks, then you go to someone else, who sells you a million-dollar CDS, in return for an annual premium, just like a regular insurance policy. You pay them a set amount every year for the full term of the agreement. If the money you loaned is paid back, then you've spent the premium money, but you don't care because you were probably getting more in interest from the guy who took your money."

"Damn straight I am."

"But if the guy who took your money defaults, then the one who sold you the CDS has to pay you the million you just lost. It's exactly like an insurance company paying you if your car is written off or your house burned down, except for one big difference. In regular insurance, you can't insure something you don't own. I mean, say you live next to a guy and you know he's a smoker, plus he gets wasted every night. You figure, sooner or later he's gonna burn his damn house down. So you know something the insurance company doesn't know and if you could buy insurance on this neighbor's house, then you'd collect a ton of cash when the house burned down. You with me?"

"All the way."

"OK, so, back to that burning house . . . the problem here is, you can't buy that insurance, not if you don't own the house. But, and here's the thing, you don't have to own shit to buy a CDS. If you think a business is going to fail, you can buy a CDS secured on that business—strictly speaking, on its corporate bonds—and when it goes under, you collect on the full value of the CDS. Now, if you're looking at a triple-A-rated corporate bond, then the premium rate is real low, not much more than ten basis points—that's one tenth of one percent. So you can buy a billion dollars" worth of coverage for a million bucks a year. That means you stake a million to win a billion."

"Oh, I like those odds."

"Yeah, well, they won't be so good for Bannock. The whole world knows it's had a rough ride lately, so the premium will be higher, maybe even as much as one hundred bps, which is one percent, so now you're staking ten mill to make that billion. But that's still terrific odds, am I right?"

"Damn straight."

"And here's the real beauty of it: Bannock doesn't have to go bust. Suppose it gets hit real bad, so it's not flat out on the canvas, but it's definitely taking a standing count. Well, then the premium price of a CDS goes up and up, in line with the risk. I mean when it looked like Greece was gonna default on its loans, the price of a CDS on Greek government bonds went up to ten thousand bps. That was one hundred percent, the full value of the loan, payable every year. So if you're holding a billion-dollar Bannock CDS with a really low premium, someone who's got Bannock bonds and is in danger of losing every cent of them is gonna pay you a whole lot of money to take that CDS off your hands, just so they're covered if Bannock goes under. Still with me?"

"Oh yeah, I sure am," Tumbo purred. "And I'm thinking to myself, maybe you should take that hundred mill I put into your fund and into that escrow account and go buy every cent you can of credit default swaps on Bannock Oil for me, and as many as you want for yourself with your own money, too."

"No, that's not how it's going to work," Bendick said. "What's going to happen is I'm going to put your money into those CDSs and we're gonna split the proceeds fifty-fifty."

Tumbo looked at him, frowning, then burst into laughter. "You're kidding me, right? You're just busting my balls, 'cause you can't possibly be serious 'bout taking half my money offa me, just to be my damn broker."

"Absolutely I am. My guess is, you would have a hard time as an individual finding anyone willing to take your business. They might want to know your real name for a start. So I'm taking a risk, right from the off, and I need to be compensated. In addition to that, I operate very publicly and if people see me, the famous Aram Bendick, taking a massive short position against Bannock Oil, they're gonna think they should be in on the action, too. So the price of Bannock CDSs will rise and the price of Bannock stock will fall and I'll have created a self-fulfilling prophecy. So I figure that's worth half your money. Plus whatever I put in for myself, as well."

"You're forgettin' two things," Tumbo said. "In the first place, none of this happens unless something goes wrong for Bannock out at sea on that rig, and you ain't having nothin' to do with that. And second, you really don't want to mess with me. I mean, I thought we established that already. But still, I'm gonna be generous. You can have ten percent of my action, plus whatever you add for yourself. I'm in for two hundred mill. That's pretty much all my spare capital, but I have faith in this proposition and I know you won't let me down, now, will you?"

Bendick gulped. "No, I won't, but I must have twenty-five percent of the upside. Hell, that's pretty much standard hedge-fund rates."

"Fifteen, and I ain't going any higher."

Bendick thought about it. He was getting $30 million worth of CDS action for nothing more than being himself—maybe $3 billion in potential profit on a single deal. What kind of fool said no to that? "I'm in," he said.

"Then we got a deal. Now I'll get you back on that plane. The sooner you land in New York, the sooner you can start buying that CBS, CDS, whatever-you-call-it shit, and the sooner you'n'me start making money."

Five minutes later, Bendick was back in the Range Rover, heading for the airport, wondering what the hell he'd got himself into, and how the hell he was going to get out the other side.

The Cross Bow operation at Magna Grande would require two complete teams of boat crews and armed security personnel, so that they could operate a three-weeks-on/three-weeks-off rotation between the offshore field and dry land. There wasn't enough room at sea to train both groups simultaneously, so Cross and his core staff would have to spend six weeks on the water, so that they could make sure everyone was up to standard. Meanwhile, they were working sixteen-hour days, selecting enough top-class personnel from existing Cross Bow staff and contract operatives to man this operation without stripping their operations on Abu Zara bare. They also had to find and recruit men with the specialist skills required for maritime work, which was another way of saying ex-SBS, Navy SEALs and Marines, as well as sorting out the complex logistics required to provide all the supplies needed by a large number of people on a long-term mission at sea.

At the same time, studying detailed schematics of the *Bannock A* and the oil platform, they had to work out strategies for dealing with all the various crises that could possibly occur aboard two of the world's biggest floating petrol-bombs. Every conceivable contingency from a long-range missile strike to a single man with a bomb was considered and appropriate responses prepared. New equipment was required, including drysuits that could be worn in the water and on the installations, and the special carbon-fiber helmets whose streamlined shape and ridged surface made them resemble giant shells that are used by waterborne Special Forces.

All Cross Bow's standard weaponry had to be reviewed in the light of the particular problems caused by operating in an environment where a singe stray around could spark a fatal conflagration. Under those circumstances the use of firearms had to be a last resort and even then they would have to use ammunition with less penetration, and thus less stopping power than Hector would normally consider acceptable. Furthermore, if the rig or the FPSO ever fell into the hands of terrorists any operation to recover them could well involve a swim, which severely limited the weight of gear that anyone could carry.

By far the best option in these circumstances was the Ruger Mk II semi-automatic pistol. Though its moral standing had been somewhat diminished by its popularity among hitmen, who loved it for its reliability and the lack of mess caused by the lightweight .22 rounds it fired, the good guys liked the Mk II as well. The U.S. Navy SEALs used its long-barreled AWC TM-Amphibian "S" format, which came with a built-in suppressor and a love for water so great that the makers even suggested pouring a tablespoon or two into the suppressor to make it super silent. In this Special Forces format the Mk II was accurate to seventy meters, an excellent distance for a pistol and far more than was ever likely to be needed in the confines of an oil platform or ship. It weighed just 1.2 kilos, which was much lighter than any rifle, and was still small enough to be holstered against the body or leg without impeding the ability to swim. Cross put in his order without delay, sourced ammunition and holsters and then left the world of gun-dealers for one final, essential requirement: a large box of condoms.

As he told Agatha, who was far too unflappable to be shocked by the arrival of a gross of contraceptives, "I don't care how amphibious this gun is supposed to be, a man should always keep both his weapons dry."

Just in case conventional methods were not enough, Cross did have one last trick up his sleeve, and to discover how to play it he needed another long session in Harley Street with the ever-reliable Rob Noble. From there he returned to the office for yet more hours of planning. Well after midnight, Hector and Nastiya were scraping the last bits of food from the cartons of Chinese take-aways scattered between them on the conference table when she said, "You need a break, just a little time away from all this."

"No, I can't," Cross said automatically. "There's too much to do."

"But you can't do it all yourself. Why don't you come to lunch with me and Paddy on Saturday? You've never even been to our house, and we've had it ever since we got married."

"If I take any time off this weekend, it'll be with Catherine Cayla. Nanny Hepworth is bringing her across from Abu Zara."

"Well, bring her too! We have some friends who have a little son. Maybe she can meet her first boyfriend."

"Over my dead body!" said Cross with mock indignation, his mood lightening up a little.

"Don't worry, there'll be plenty of women to act as chaperones. Come on, it'll do you good. And there's someone I want you to meet—someone who's done you a big favor."

Despite himself, Cross was intrigued. "Really, who's that?"

"My sister Yevgenia. She was Maria Denisova's personal assistant on that da Cunha business, and if it wasn't for her, I'd never have thought of persuading my father to get some of his associates to be my imaginary business clients."

"You know, I'd been wondering how you did that."

"Aha! Well, you can ask Yevgenia all about it, and if you ask her very nicely and are very charming, she may let you call her Zhenia and then you'll know that you are her friend."

"Is she as dangerous as you?"

Nastiya laughed. "With a gun or her fists, no. In other ways . . . possibly. Come on, Mr. Spoilsport! We're only in Barnes, so you won't have to come far."

"Barnes!" Cross exclaimed, as if the charming south-west London suburb were some barely civilized, distant corner of the globe. "But that's miles away."

Nastiya laughed. "It's five miles, Hector, that's all! Catch a train at Waterloo. You'll be here in no time."

"If I do come, I'll drive."

"If you drive you can't drink, and then it's not so much fun for you. Take a taxi."

"I'll think about it," Cross prevaricated. But Nastiya was a hard woman to refuse. So at one o'clock on Saturday afternoon he paid off a cabbie and walked up the path to the front door of the O'Quinns' terraced house in Barnes.

He had Catherine, still strapped into her portable baby seat, in one hand and a bag of essential nappies, toys, and spare clothes, specially packed by Bonnie Hepworth, in the other. Nastiya bade him a cursory hello and then swooped on the little girl, whom she had adored almost from the day she was born, billing, cooing and then unstrapping her from the seat and carrying her off into the living room to be admired by the other female lunch guests.

"Now you've dropped me right in it," said Paddy O'Quinn, who'd appeared at Cross's side, wearing a chef's apron and carrying a very welcome Bloody Mary, made hot and spicy, exactly as Cross liked it. "I'll be getting earache all night about why don't we have a baby? Believe me, boss, it isn't for the want of trying."

"Thanks, Paddy, but I don't need to hear the sordid details of your sex life," Cross said as he took a sip of the Bloody Mary and cast his eyes around the room. The O'Quinns had invited some near-neighbors called the Parkers over to join the lunch party, along with their two-year-old son Charlie, who was currently toddling across the room, sporting a spectacularly runny nose, toward the corner where Miss Catherine Cayla Cross was holding court.

"So, I understand that there are two women present that I don't know and one of them is your sister-in-law," Cross said to O'Quinn. "I'm guessing it's not the one currently wiping her little nipper's snotty nose, which leaves the one in the skintight jeans . . . Just as a general observation, they really know how to turn out beautiful women in the Voronov family, don't they?"

"Oh, you've noticed, have you?" Paddy smiled. "Now, if you'll excuse me, I have a joint of beef to check."

As Daddy Parker joined the clean-up operation on Junior, Hector took a proper look at Yevgenia Voronova. She very clearly came from the same stock as Nastiya. Cross could see it in the cool, blue eyes set beneath quite straight eyebrows that suggested strength of purpose and character. And yet

Yevgenia was quite different, too. Her body, though beautifully proportioned, was a fraction fuller and softer, more curvaceous than Nastiya's lean, athletic figure, but this did not strike Cross as any kind of disadvantage. Yevgenia's rich chestnut hair was parted to one side of her face and fell across her forehead and down in glorious waves that broke over her shoulders before tumbling down her back. Her nose was fine and straight, tilted upward from her mouth. And oh, Cross mused, what a mouth that was.

Nastiya O'Quinn had walked over to Cross while he was carrying out his inspection. He kissed her casually hello and then nodded in her sister's direction and said, "She's almost as good-looking as you are."

Nastiya smiled. "You're a very flattering English gentleman, but Yevgenia is ten years younger than me and, as the French say, '*ravissante*.'"

"We say 'ravishing,' same thing. And yes, she is. So, you're a woman, you tell me . . . are they real?"

"What, Zhenia's breasts?" Nastiya looked outraged at the very suggestion. "One thing I can tell you about the women in my family, Hector: we don't need any help in that department!"

"No, not them, her lips."

Nastiya smiled. "Ah yes, they are magnificent: so full, so soft. I must confess I envy her a little for that mouth. The way she always has just a little pout, it's as if she's kissing the world."

"I never knew you were so poetic, Nastiya."

She gave a dismissive shrug and then went on, "So are they real? Well, I can tell you that her mother has exactly the same lips, so either they both went to the same surgeon or they were both blessed by the same genes. Why don't you go and ask her?"

"I couldn't do that!" Cross protested.

"Why not?"

"It's rude, that's why."

Nastiya looked at him skeptically. "Oh, and it's not rude to talk about my sister behind her back? Ha! You go and ask her, like a man, or I will tell her that you asked me."

"Very well, you give me no choice," said Cross. "I have no option but to go and talk to your stunning sister. It's a tough job, but . . ."

"Enough." Nastiya laughed. "Go!"

Yevgenia was on her haunches, playing a little game with Catherine, holding a toy monkey in front of her, and moving it every time she tried to grab it, producing shrieks of childish laughter. Cross stopped a couple of feet away, just to watch, and then Yevgenia registered his presence, got to her feet and introduced herself, adding, "But since you are Nastiya's boss, and also one of her closest, most trusted friends, then you are my friend too, and you can call me Zhenia."

The way she said her name made it seem as soft and sensual as a woman's hand running across mink.

"Then you'd better call me Heck," he replied. "You've already met my daughter Catherine."

Zhenia's face lit up. "Oh, she's so adorable! Nastiya told me all about her, and she's even sweeter than I dreamed she would be."

"Thank you." Cross smiled at the child and said, "I love her more than I've ever loved anyone else in the world . . . apart from her mother, of course."

Zhenia's brow crumpled into a sympathetic frown. "Yes, Nastiya told me about Hazel, too. I'm so sorry . . ." A brief silence fell and then she brightened up. "So! You were talking to Nastiya and both of you were looking at me . . ."

"Was it that obvious?" Cross asked.

"A woman always knows when she is being studied."

"Which must be most of the time, in your case."

"All the time," she sighed. "Anyway, I could see Nastiya giving you orders—she loves giving orders, that one!"

Cross laughed. "Yes, but sometimes she forgets who's really in charge."

225

"And that's you?"

"Yes," he said with calm, unforced authority.

"Even so, Nastiya gave you an order . . ."

Cross nodded ruefully. "That's true. I asked her a question about you, and she told me I should just come over here and ask it to you, instead."

"And . . . ?"

"My exact words were: Are they real?"

Zhenia looked down at her cleavage. "What, these?"

"That was pretty much her reply, too, but I was talking about your lips. They're extraordinary."

"I know," she said and pursed them together in a silly duck face that made them both laugh. "So, you think maybe I had fillers or implants? Hmm . . ." She pursed her lips thoughtfully again, making her natural pout just a little bit more apparent. "You know, there's only one way to find out for sure . . ."

Cross looked at her coolly, letting her wonder whether he'd call her bluff and kiss her, enjoying the unmistakable charge of flirtation in the air.

Then the mood was broken by a cheerful cry of "This way, everybody!" as Paddy summoned them to join him in the kitchen-diner, built in a conservatory that looked out on a small but well laid-out garden. As Nastiya directed each of her four guests to one of the chairs arranged around a rustic kitchen table, Paddy proudly declaimed the menu: "Today we have a fine joint of prime English beef, cooked medium rare, nice and pink in the middle and maybe just a drop of blood for you, boss. With that there are roast potatoes, Yorkshire pudding, and a fine selection of vegetables, straight from the freezer, courtesy of Mr. Birdseye, because I love you all dearly, but I'm not after scraping carrots and podding peas all morning. If you drink enough of that Chilean red that's waiting for you on the table, you'll never know the difference anyway. Meanwhile, baking away in the oven there's a splendid apple pie and the custard will be made fresh and not from a packet, that I promise. Ladies and gentlemen, luncheon is served!"

The Bell 407 helicopter was 300 miles northwest of Cabinda City, close to the maximum extent of its range, when the pilot called out to his single passenger, "There she is, right up ahead of us, just where she should be. Man, that's one strange-looking boat!"

Johnny Congo looked out across the calm Atlantic waters until he saw what the pilot was pointing at: a ship shaped like a paper dart, or an old Delta-wing bomber, with a sleek narrow prow that flared outwards toward a broad, squared-off stern. As they flew closer, Congo could see that it was a trimaran, with three hulls bound together by a single deck, like three piers beneath a bridge. Now he made out a tall, triangular A-frame structure that rose from the main deck, just forward of the stern. A bright yellow craft of some kind was suspended from the A-frame and men, still ant-size at this distance, were clustered around the frame as it tilted backward, carrying the craft over the stern and then lowering it into the water.

By the time the process was completed, the helicopter was preparing its final approach to the vessel, heading straight toward the superstructure that rose in three decks, each smaller than the last, like a gleaming white ziggurat. A crewman wearing white shorts and a navy blue sleeveless shirt was standing on the bow deck, guiding the helicopter in to land, and now Congo could see the "H" painted on the bow deck that marked the landing pad. The pilot brought the Bell into a perfect, smooth touchdown and cut the Allison turboshaft powerplant as the crewman ran in under the rotors and secured the skids to the deck and then remained by the helicopter as the entire pad started to sink into the ship's black hull. It settled with a barely perceptible or audible bump on the floor of a large hangar and it was only then that the pilot undid his seatbelt and invited Congo to do the same.

As he climbed down on to the hangar floor, Congo saw a short, muscular figure in combat fatigues and a khaki T-shirt striding toward him. "Chico! My man!" he said, holding his hand out straight so that Chico Torres could reach up and high-five it. "This is some boat you got me, bro."

Torres laughed, his teeth gleaming behind his close-cropped goatee beard. His head was shaved and tanned a deep nut-brown and his whole body exuded a tough, compact muscularity. "Welcome to the *Mother Goose*, baby," he laughed. "She's one of a kind, and this is her maiden voyage. Quite a way to start, huh? C'mon, I'll give you the guided tour . . ."

Congo followed Torres out of the hanger, down a passageway and then up a flight of stairs that led to a hall, which opened on to a series of lavishly decorated living and dining rooms, culminating in an outdoor space where anyone sitting at the bar only had to swivel their stool to look past the sunloungers and the plunge pool all the way across an aft deck big enough to fit a tennis court to the A-frame that was lifting the odd little yellow craft back out of the water.

"So, *Mother Goose* is the Triton 196, so-called because it's one hundred and ninety-six feet, or sixty meters in length," Torres said. "For the first hundred and twenty feet she's your basic superyacht, designed to appeal to your basic, bored billionaire, plus his buddies and babes. These people, they've seen everything, done everything, what else is left? Answer: what happens in the last seventy-six feet. Check it out."

Torres opened a hatch that led on to a steel ladder, going down. They descended back into the hull, through another hatch and into a hanger that looked like an even bigger version of the one that the Bell was sitting in. In any normal superyacht, this would be where the "toys," as owners like to call them, were kept: launches, jetskis, sailing boats, windsurfers and the like. But the *Mother Goose*'s toys were a little different.

"Here's the main attraction," said Torres, "one of two Triton 3300/3 mini-submersibles—guess you saw the other one hanging from the A-Frame as you came in. We're practising getting 'em in and out of the water, as fast and as smoothly as we can. Funky-looking, ain't it?"

"No kidding," said Congo, walking around the sub.

The gleaming yellow hull was U-shaped like one of the inflatable neck-rests people buy when they're flying long haul, economy, and are desperate for anything to get the muscle spasm out of their necks. In the middle of the U, a spherical cabin, made entirely from transparent acrylic thermoplastic, nestled like the passenger's head in his neck-rest. The sub was so tiny—just thirteen feet long and nine wide—it looked as though Congo could just pick it up and throw it across the hangar. He was looking at it now with doubt and disappointment etched into his features. "This is it?" he asked. "A frickin' Yellow Submarine? That's our secret weapon?"

Torres laughed. "Better believe it. This baby can go down to a depth of one thousand meters—that's three thousand three hundred feet. She can operate underwater for twelve hours, non-stop. By the time we've finished working on her, she'll be more than capable of doing exactly what you asked me to do. So say hello to your little friend, Johnny C. And don't worry, she's gonna pack a real big punch."

Cross sat down and cheerfully helped himself to a classic English lunch, washed down with a very drinkable Chilean Cabernet Sauvignon. The Parkers turned out to be Mike, a witty, self-deprecating but obviously brilliant lawyer, and Caro, his art-curator wife. They were planning a safari holiday in Africa to celebrate their fifth wedding anniversary and were delighted to discover that Hector was not only a fount of information on the

229

subject, but a fully fledged Maasai warrior. Then Zhenia fielded endless questions about life in Russia and its strange and often frightening foreign policy with charm and intelligence.

The gathering was alive with warmth, laughter and a sense of relaxed, everyday family life, as one parent or another—Hector included—had to get down on their knees to deal with their child, or sit at the table with an infant on their lap, keeping pudgy little hands away from the stems of wine-glasses. It struck Cross that he had never really known this kind of normality. For most of his adult life he had either been a soldier or the boss of a security firm. His working life had been spent in barracks and messes, with little attention, if any, paid to home comforts. Then he'd met Hazel Bannock, been plucked from his Spartan existence and plunged into the life of the super-rich, with all the private jets, personal servants and sprawling homes that entailed. But the fact was, Paddy's roast beef, which came straight from the local supermarket, tasted just as good as any he'd been served at a duke's stately home, and the wine—which cost thirty-five quid for half a case from a cut-price booze merchants—went down just as readily as Château Lafite did at a hundred times the price.

Cross could tell that Zhenia was loving it also. All the money in the world hadn't compensated her for having an abusive father, but here, in this normal, everyday world, she seemed completely relaxed, bubbling over with fun and laughter. The relationship between her and Nastiya was deepening before his eyes: two sisters who'd lost one another for so many years weaving a connection that had made both of them happier. Now Caro Parker was chatting about the ice rink that was erected every winter in the courtyard of Somerset House, on the banks of the River Thames, just a stone's throw from the Savoy, saying how much she wanted to go, but was Charlie still too young for it, when he wasn't even three yet?

"Too young?" Nastiya protested in horror. "In Russia children skate before they can walk. If a mother waited until her son was three before putting him on the ice, all the other mothers, they would say, 'Why have you been so cruel to your little one?'"

"Let's go skating right now!" Zhenia exclaimed. "Come on, Nastiya, let's show these British how a Russian can skate!"

"I'll have you know I'm not British, I'm Irish," said Paddy with mock dignity.

"And I'm not British, I'm Kenyan." Cross struck a Napoleonic attitude of defiance. Then it occured to him for the first time ever that while he was a splendid shot, a strong runner and swimmer, a master of several martial arts, who could freefall parachute, ski, climb mountains and survive in almost any environment on earth, he had never in all his life gone ice-skating. It wasn't something that Kenyan-born children tended do, growing up on the African savannah. A second later he realized something else: he did not want to make a fool of himself in front of Yevgenia Voronova.

Damn it, man, don't be ridiculous, Hector told himself. *The girl's not yet twenty-five; you're practically old enough to be her father. In her eyes you're an old man.*

He thought of Bobbi Franklin. She was gorgeous, she was smart and she was completely age-appropriate. But she wasn't here, and Zhenia was, and suddenly Paddy was on the phone ordering cabs and Cross was gathering up all the huge number of items Nanny Hepworth deemed essential before she'd allow Catherine out of the house.

"I've yomped across the Brecon Beacons with packs lighter than this," Cross muttered to himself as he shoved yet another stuffed toy into the bulging baby-bag, and Zhenia was pleading with him to sit next to her in the cab, "So that I can spend more time with baby Yekaterina—my Tsarina Catherine the Great!" And there they were, speeding through West London, the streets already dark, though it was only five in the afternoon, dropping the baby off at Cross Roads where Bonnie Hepworth was waiting to sweep her away for her bath, and then heading on to Somerset House, just the two of them.

Neither said much. Zhenia was too busy looking out at the glittering shop windows and Christmas decorations and Cross was perfectly content just to watch her. When they reached Somerset House, Mike Parker was waiting, clutching a fistful of tickets and saying, "We're in luck! Normally you have to book weeks in advance, but they had some spare places for the next session. The others are all putting on their skates, even Charlie!" he added, leading them to the cabin where the skates were issued. Zhenia grabbed hers and went off to find Nastiya, with whom she was soon deep in conversation, chattering in Russian at a million miles an hour and giggling conspiratorially at regular intervals.

"Are you any good at this, boss?" O'Quinn asked, nervously, as the two of them laced themselves into their boots.

"I don't know, old sport," said Cross breezily. "Never done it before in my life."

"I don't know about you, but I think I'm about to make a complete tit of meself."

"Nonsense! We're men. We're proud veterans of the SAS. There's nothing we can't do!"

"Speak for yourself . . ."

Cross tried to approach the situation logically. He'd done a fair bit of Arctic warfare training, which involved endless miles of cross-country skiing, which involved travelling across flat snow, instead of ice. And now he came to think about it, he'd been given a pair of roller skates when he was a boy. If you put those two skills together, you practically had ice-skating.

"Absolutely," Mike Parker agreed, when Cross put this theory to him. "The key thing is not to lift the skates up and down. No plonking! Just ease your leading foot on to the ice, slide forward and outwards, then do exactly the same thing with the other foot. Nothing to it."

Parker stepped out on to the ice and set off at a steady, unspectacular, but relaxed pace. Well, that looked easy enough, Cross thought.

Then Paddy O'Quinn tiptoed nervously out, took a couple of terrified steps, desperately waving his arms for balance, and fell flat on his backside, cursing furiously all the way.

Finally it was Cross's turn. Don't plonk. Slide forward and out. Now the next foot. Suddenly he was moving. It was hardly a Winter Olympic medal-winning performance. But he was upright and he was moving and—bloody hell!—he was coming to the end of the rink and now he had to turn left, to follow the anti-clockwise direction in which everyone was circulating. He took a moment to take in his surroundings, for the rink was surrounded on all sides by the splendid neo-classical façades of one of London's most magnificent old buildings. But then an unexpected crisis suddenly reared its ugly head: How did you turn? Answer: Cross didn't. He just slid into the barrier at the end of the rink, held on for dear life, turned around to face the rink and then leaned up against the barrier, casually surveying the scene and doing his best to look as though this was all entirely intentional.

But where was Zhenia? On their way out of the house she'd grabbed a bright red fleece beanie and a short, black Puffa gilet, cinched in at the waist to ensure that no one could fail to notice her figure, even when covered in quilting. The hat, at least, should be easy to spot under the dazzling floodlights. Cross scanned the crowd, one stranger's face after another, until he suddenly spotted her, darting across the ice, weaving in and out of slower skaters, hotly pursued by Nastiya. The two of them looked exultant, laughing at the sheer joy of doing something that was clearly as natural to them as breathing. Then Zhenia saw him. Cross waved and she waved back, changing course to skate straight at him, flat out, her eyes never leaving Cross's until she came sliding to a stop in a shower of ice, so close to him they were almost touching.

Zhenia spun to her left, facing in the same direction as the circulating skaters, held out her right hand and said, "Come on. I'll help you."

Cross was not used to seeking assistance from young girls, but he swallowed his pride and said, "Thanks. I may need it."

He took hold of her hand and then gasped as he was suddenly hit by a physical shock, a power surge he felt right to the depths of his being. He looked back at her and she smiled as if to say, "Yes, I felt it, too," but then her expression changed and she called out, "Come on! Follow me!"

He let her pull him out into the crowd and responded as she guided him with her hand, towing him around the corners and showing him how to get into a nice, even rhythm on the straights. They completed a lap, and then another. Cross didn't tell her that he'd been doing fine on his skates for a while now, gaining confidence every time he negotiated a turn or managed to slow down of his own accord, but the feel of her hand in his was so magical he just didn't want to let go. Then, on the third lap she pulled away a little, only keeping her fingertips very lightly touching his. The occasional brushing of her skin against his was even more thrilling and when she took her hand away at the end of the circuit and said, "You're on your own now! Follow me!" he felt like an addict whose drug had been taken away. But then he discovered that there was something new to excite him: the sight of her perfect bottom, caressed by skintight denim, swishing to and fro in front of him.

Cross set off after it like a donkey after a dangling carrot, seriously aroused now, wishing he could grab that fabulous body, press his mouth against her perfect lips and breathe in the scent of that tumbling chestnut hair. But how could he make a pass at Zhenia with Nastiya and O'Quinn, both of them his employees, watching him? Nastiya would kill him . . . or would she? She'd invited him to lunch, after all, telling him that he should meet Zhenia. She'd even told him to go and ask the girl an obviously leading question. Was Nastiya setting the two of them up? Or was it that she simply couldn't imagine he would ever actually stoop to seducing her baby sister?

In the end, when the session had ended and they'd all taken off their skates, it was Zhenia who spoke out. "Take me for a walk, Hector. Show London to me."

"Isn't Nastiya expecting you to come home with her?"

"Nastiya is not my mother. And anyway"—she flashed a wicked little smile—"she won't mind. She says you are too sad and too alone. You need some happiness in your life. We are Russians, you see. We have a more joyous view of life."

"I'm not actually dying of sorrow," he protested.

"No," she said. "Not now, you aren't."

They walked down the Strand and into Trafalgar Square. A choir was standing beneath the Christmas tree given to London annually by the people of Norway, and singing carols.

"This is so beautiful," she said, looking around at Nelson's column, the National Gallery and the church of St. Martin-in-the-Fields.

"So are you," Cross said, and she turned her head to regard him quizzically, placing it in exactly the right attitude for kissing. Hector hesitated for the smallest part of a second and then took advantage of it.

"You two should get a room somewhere!" a stranger called out to them good-humoredly, prompting laughter from a few other passers-by. It was hardly the most poetic of compliments, but it made Zhenia giggle and cling to him, which in turn boosted Cross's good humor; both of them revelling in the joy of the magic moment when they realized that they wanted the same thing.

They strolled up to Piccadilly Circus holding hands, and suddenly she asked, "Do you live very far from here, Hector?"

"Only about fifteen minutes away," he answered.

"Is your bed comfortable?"

235

"My bed is the most comfortable in the whole of England."

"OK! Then I bet you that I can make it to your house before you." She challenged him with eyes that shone.

"How much?" he demanded. "How much will you bet?"

"A million."

"A million of what?"

"Whatever you want."

"That will do for a start," he agreed and they started to run.

Shelby Weiss was in his den, watching the University of Texas Longhorns take on the Oklahoma Sooners in front of 100,000 fans at the Memorial Stadium in Austin, cracking open his second can of Coors and generally feeling good about life. Then the phone beside him rang and suddenly his Saturday afternoon took a serious turn for the worse.

"Yo, Shelby, how you doing, man?"

The color drained from Weiss's face. Only half-a-dozen words, spoken by a man who hadn't even given his name, but they'd been enough to chill his blood as cold as his beer and scare him absolutely witless.

"What . . . what the hell . . ." he babbled, trying to collect his scrambled thoughts. "For Chrissakes, man, you can't just call me up on my cellphone! What, you've never heard of the NSA? Those guys listen to everything—everything! And you're a wanted felon. Oh yeah, you made the Feds' Ten Most Wanted list. You're a frickin' rock star of crime. And you're calling me?"

"Whoa, easy, tiger." Weiss heard a deep, throaty chuckle that was as scary as a naked blade. "You musta got me confused with some other dude. See, my name is Juan Tumbo, says so right there on my passport. And I'm a law-abiding citizen with no criminal record, no reason for you not to take my call, 'specially when I happen to know you're sitting on a coupla million bucks a buddy of mine advanced you, just in case he should need some legal representation."

"Hey, Johnny . . ."

"Juan. The name is Juan Tumbo. I told you, I got nothing to do with no Johnny. Now, you listen to me, Mr. Weiss. I've been entering into certain business transactions with a guy in New York, Aram Bendick. He's a big-time investor; you may have hear of him."

"The name is familiar to me, yes," Weiss agreed, wondering where the hell this was all heading.

"OK, so Mr. Bendick and myself have entered into a series of financial arrangements. Matter of fact, I've given the man a hundred million bucks."

"Did I hear you right?" Weiss gasped. "One hundred million dollars?"

"Yeah, lotta coin, right? Now, I can imagine that some fools might think: This dumb nigger put a hundred mill in my pocket, I'm'a takin' it all for myself. I don't believe Bendick is that crazy. I think he knows that I might make my objections known, if you understand what I mean."

"Yes, Jo— Mr. Tumbo, I believe I do."

"But it doesn't hurt to take precautions, am I right?"

"Totally."

"So, that being the case, I'd like you to pay a visit to Mr. Bendick, talk to him about the situation and draw up contracts, specifying exactly what he's going to do with my investment, and how he's going to make sure that I get the best possible return. And I mean the best possible. Not an OK deal. Not a good deal. The best."

"When I make a deal for my clients, it is always the best it can possibly be."

"Good. So you fly up to the Apple tomorrow, go see Bendick bright and early Monday. He'll lay out what it is we have in mind. My guess is, you'll want a piece of the action. So if you want to buy in, be my guest."

One thing Shelby Weiss prided himself on was that he could

always smell money and now he was getting a real good sniff of it. "Tell you what," he said. "How about I forgo my fee and just take a percentage of any profits?"

Silence fell. Five seconds went by . . . then. "Hello?" Weiss called. "Hello? Mr. Tumbo? You still there?"

Finally he received an answer. "Yeah, I'm here. I just been breathing deeply, counting to ten, trying to calm myself down. See, I thought I already mentioned the two million bucks you got in your account."

"But they weren't paid by you, were they, Mr. Tumbo?"

"Listen to me, Mr. Weiss. Listen carefully now, 'cause this is important. I'm gonna give you a chance now to save your own life. All you have to do is go to New York and cut a deal for me, the best deal you can possibly get, just like you said. You want to try to make your own deal with Aram Bendick, on the side, be my guest, it'll make you rich. Now you do that, everyone's happy. You don't do that, well, cast your mind back to the events of, what was the date now? Yeah, November fifteenth. Think about the people that died that day. Consider, if you will, the power and planning and resources it took to carry out an operation like that. Now consider what would happen if that same power and planning and resources was all directed to the task of ripping your head off and stuffing it up your ass, and crucifying your wife, and sticking your children on skewers and—"

"Stop! For God's sake, stop. I'll do it. I'll do anything you want. Just leave my family out of this."

"No problem, Mr. Weiss. I was just pulling your leg anyway, exaggerating a little so's you got my general point, you follow me?"

Weiss threw his empty can of Coors into the bin, jumped up from his desk and strode across the room to his private minibar. Screw beer, he needed something stronger. "Yes," he said, unscrewing the cap on a bottle of Jack Daniel's. "I understand.

I'll go to New York. I'll cut you the best frickin' deal anyone ever got out of Aram Bendick."

"Now, that's the Shelby Weiss I'm used to hearing! You go to New York, take care of business, catch a show. Believe me, brother, you'll be glad I called."

Holding Zhenia's naked body in his arms Hector smiled secretly as he realized that there was no greater proof of youth being wasted on the young than the insecurity that afflicted even this most gorgeous young woman when the critical hour struck, and he found that Zhenia's psychological armor fell away along with her clothing and the fiesty, flirtatious Muscovite socialite became shy and even slightly awkward.

Hector had been very gentle with her. He had undressed her lovingly. He spent time kissing her and stroking her hair, whispering to her how beautiful she was and describing how wonderful it felt to run his hands over her lovely high breasts. Then he kissed her neck and sucked her erect blood-darkened nipples. Very gently he held each delicate bud between his teeth, feeling them swell and harden. Then he was caressing her belly with his lips. He cupped her tight around buttocks in his hands, drawing them toward him so that her thighs fell apart and the secret cleft between them opened shyly before him. Her inner lips were pink and glossy, pouting in shy invitation. When he ran the tip of his tongue deeply between them, she gasped with shock, then clasped her hands around the back of his head and drew him even closer to her.

"Yes!" she whispered. "Like that. Don't stop. Please don't ever stop!"

Later when he awoke the sun was shining through a gap in the curtains. Zhenia was sleeping in his arms, curled up with those firm around buttocks thrust hard into his belly, gripping both his arms firmly by the wrists and holding his hands in front of her to cup her breasts; her breathing was soft as the wind and the smell of her lubricious sex filled his head and heightened his senses.

He was suffused with a sense of warmth and contentment such as he had not known since the death of Hazel Bannock, his wife and the mother of Catherine Cayla. Then as he came fully awake his wellbeing was replaced by a sensation of guilt.

"Cradle-snatcher!" he accused himself silently. "She's a baby." Then he rallied against the accusation and came to his own defense. "An infant is one thing she's not. She is a full-grown woman in her middle twenties: old enough to drive, vote, work, marry, fight wars and have children. When I was her age I had already commanded a platoon of men in combat, shot and stabbed enemies by the score, seen friends and comrades killed and maimed beside me. She's old enough to make her own decisions and she was absolutely party to this one. The jury finds you not guilty." He grinned with self-satisfaction. "And strongly suggests that you do it again just to make certain of your motives."

He could not deny that basic, red-blooded lust for a delicious member of the opposite sex was one of his motives. But it wasn't the only reason he revelled in her presence in his bed.

Zhenia was every bit as smart, funny, feisty and beautiful as her big sister. He was not in any doubt that both girls had inherited from their father the drive, hunger and unfettered ambition that had made him an oligarch. But he would never suggest that to either of them.

Of course, Zhenia wasn't a trained fighter like Nastiya, but she had the spirit and the courage for it: Cross was utterly certain of that. And she made him feel young; rejuvenating him with her lust for life and her sense of fun. He would never have gone skating if she hadn't suggested it, nor would he have been willing to make a fool of himself on the ice without her presence to spur him on. His relationships with both Hazel and Jo had been overshadowed by fear, violence and danger, right from the off, but today had just been fun, from his first sight

240

of Zhenia at that little house in Barnes, to the ecstasy of their orgasmic lovemaking.

Suddenly Zhenia turned in his arms and stared at him, the pupils of her hazel eyes enormous with sleep. "Why so serious, Hector," she mumbled. "What are you thinking about?"

"I was just thinking . . ." He broke off but continued to stare at her enigmatically. She came fully awake and raised herself on one elbow, her expression taunt with consternation.

"Tell me. Is something wrong?"

"I was just thinking that we must do that again immediately to make absolutely certain it was as good as I thought it was the first time."

"Well, then tell me why are you wasting precious time?" she asked demurely.

These contracts . . .' Shelby Weiss began, sitting in Aram Bendick's Manhattan office and trying very hard to act a great deal calmer and more unflappable than he actually felt. "As far as I can see, they are all, ah, predicated on the collapse of Bannock Oil's stock and even of the entire corporation."

"That's correct," Aram Bendick agreed. "As I explained to Mr. Tumbo, the regular put-option trades will become profitable once the stock price drops below the level at which I bought, which it's already on course to do, following my very public attacks on the Bannock board. And the credit default swaps will similarly increase in value as the market starts to see an increased risk of Bannock Oil not being able to pay its debts, so we can either sell them then, or wait to see if the company does, indeed, default. That's when profit would be maximized, obviously. My advice to Mr. Tumbo would be to mix'n'match. Sell some on the way down, take enough profit to eliminate his downside, but then hold on for the really big bucks when and if Bannock Oil does collapse."

"Excuse me for being confused, Mr. Bendick, but are you aware that Mr. Tumbo has a very large personal interest in

241

Bannock Oil?" Weiss replied. "His financial security is tied up with Bannock's." *Not to mention the fact that I just blew every dime my partners and I have got buying a law firm that barely exists without Bannock,* he thought to himself. "Can you explain why he would consent to enter into financial agreements that are predicated on the failure of his greatest asset?"

"Because he'll make far, far more out of Bannock Oil dead than he ever will when it's alive."

"That can't be possible."

"Sure it is. Back in the early Nineties, George Soros made a billion dollars on one trade, betting against the British pound. John Paulson called the property crash of 2007, bought credit default swaps on mortgage-backed securities and made four billion when they all tanked. If Bannock Oil collapses, we're gonna make so much money those guys'll look like two-bit day traders."

Weiss fought hard to keep his jaw from dropping open. "You mean, you're in this for billions?"

"Many billions."

"And what makes you think it's going to pay off? I mean, I'm very aware that Bannock's taken a helluva hit up in Alaska. But word on the street in Houston is they're going to make up for it and more in Africa."

"Let's just say that Mr. Tumbo was very certain that there would be a precipitous fall in the value of Bannock stock. I got the feeling it was a personal crusade for him, that he was going to make it happen. Now, you're the man's attorney, you tell me: can Juan Tumbo make things happen?"

He bust out of the convoy taking him to the Death House: yeah, he can make things happen, Weiss thought. He said, "Sure, in my experience he's a very resourceful individual."

"Then Bannock Oil will collapse and Mr. Tumbo will become much, much richer than he already is."

"Then I guess I don't have any objection to approving the

contracts on my client's behalf." Weiss was frantically running calculations through his mind: *If I remortgage the house, and the condo at Vail, and I empty the kids' college funds, maybe I could raise a mill . . .* "In fact, this deal looks so sweet"—Weiss forced a sickly grin across his face—"well, I might just be tempted to get some of it myself."

Bendick laughed. "Yeah, Tumbo told me you might say that. He also figured it would be a good way of making sure we were all on the same team, aligning our interests, so to speak. So, sure, if you want to join the party, I can make that happen. Just one condition, though: you keep this to yourself. No one, but no one outside the three of us gets to hear exactly what I have in mind. Understand?"

"Believe me, Aram—I hope you don't mind me calling you that, now we're in business together—this one's strictly private."

"Glad we got that clear," said Bendick. "So, you want a Scotch to celebrate?"

He poured the drinks and handed one to Weiss. The mood was much more relaxed, both men feeling certain that they were on to a winner. "Just out of curiosity, what kind of name is Tumbo, anyway? Like Dumbo without the 'D.' I mean, come on . . ."

"Why don't you ask him that question?" Weiss asked.

Bendick laughed. "Oh no! I've met the man. Whatever he wants to call himself, that's just fine by me."

Hector Cross spent three days and nights with Zhenia Voronova before he and his team left for Angola. As he kissed her goodbye at Farnborough Airport he was so physically exhausted that he knew he'd be asleep before the wheels of the Bannock Oil jet had left the ground. But at one and the same time he also felt refreshed, re-energized and filled with life in a way that he hadn't since before Hazel died. Zhenia had worked some kind of magic on him: "Let me be your second spring," she had said, and she had been just that, warming his soul, melting all the winter ice and reviving what had once seemed dead.

"Please come back to me," she whispered as they parted.

"I will, I promise," Cross replied, meaning it with all his heart. He bade farewell to Catherine Cayla, too. For safety's sake, she was being taken back to Abu Zara. Cross told himself that she was still too young to understand what Christmas was, but still it hurt him to be apart from her then, of all times. *Never again,* he swore to himself. *In future, I spend Christmas with my girl.*

On land, Cross was as good a fighter and commander as there was to be found anywhere in the British Army. He'd been schooled at the Royal Military College, Sandhurst; been accepted by the SAS; fought in numerous conflicts (not all of them publicized) on Her Majesty's behalf and then, having left the forces, done battle all over the world with men who had threatened his clients or his family. At sea, although he had some experience of taking on Somali pirates, he was not remotely as well qualified, and he knew it.

Cross therefore wanted the men who would be responsible for protecting Bannock Oil's personnel and property at the Magna Grande field to receive the best possible training for the job, and he included himself in that number. That was why he had asked Paddy O'Quinn to track down some talent from the SBS, which was not only the first specialist waterborne Special Forces unit in the world, but also—in its own eyes, at least—by far the best.

So it was that an initial force of thirty men reported for training duty at the Cross Bow base on the one-time Arctic supply tug *Glenallen*. Alongside Cross were the two O'Quinns and Dave Imbiss. Half of the rest were the smartest, toughest, most reliable men on Cross Bow's books. They were immediately distinguishable from the newcomers because, having long been used to having her among them, they weren't trying to sneak long, lecherous looks at Nastiya. Those that were comprised ten crewmen, all veterans of the Special Boat Service, the SBS, led by a Glaswegian by the name of Donnie "Darko" McGrain.

Darko had been a Class 1 Warrant Officer, the Marines equivalent of an Army sergeant major. He was not physically imposing, being of average height with a scrawny physique apparently comprised entirely of bone, muscle and gristle. But he exuded an air of unrelenting energy, focus, determination and malice that was enough to reduce much bigger, stronger men to quivering wrecks. He made his presence felt from the moment he strode into the briefing room that had been constructed, along with basic sleeping, washing and off-duty quarters within the holds originally intended to carry spare parts, food and other supplies for the Arctic drilling barge *Glenallen* had been designed to support.

The men were sitting or sprawled in a variety of postures in the chairs set up opposite a low stage from which briefings and training lectures would be conducted. Most of them were bantering and joking with one another. Dave Imbiss and the O'Quinns were sitting at the front, deep in their own conversation. Then Cross walked in accompanied by Darko McGrain and suddenly every man, and the lone woman in the room, swung around, eyes front, back straight, waiting to hear what the boss had to say.

"Good morning gentlemen . . . and lady," Cross began. "Four weeks from now all the preparations end and Magna Grande comes on stream. You can't see them, but there are half a dozen oil wells within a few kilometers of here, all ready to feed oil to the rig and from there to the *Bannock A* floating, processing, storage and offloading vessel. There the crude will be turned into the usual range of products you'd expect from a land-based refinery and will then be loaded on to tankers for distribution around the world. So we are watching over an incredible undertaking, capable of generating tens of billions of dollars and, along the way, keeping you lot in work for years to come. But don't think for one moment that this is some kind of easy-going ocean cruise. We've had credible intelligence reports that Cabindan separatists, who want independence from Angola, have targeted this field. They may be planning a spectacular, something that will put them on the world map, the way 9/11 did for al-Qaeda. Our job is to make sure that they cannot and will not succeed. And the only way we can do this is if we are fit, disciplined, well organized and well trained. Some of you have had experience of ocean-swimming, getting on to rigs and large vessels and carrying out counter-terrorist operations at sea. But most of us—and that includes me—know very little about any of that. So we have to learn fast. Therefore let me introduce you to the man who's going to knock us into shape over the next four weeks: Donnie McGrain."

There was a half-hearted smattering of applause as McGrain stepped to the front of the stage and looked out over his audience with a beady, piercing stare. "Right then, let's see just how bad this is," he barked in a Glasgwegian accent as rough as a bag of rusted nails. "How many of ye's have served in the Royal or U.S. Marines, the SBS or Navy SEALs, or anything like that in any other armed forces?"

Six hands went up. McGrain shook his head and spat out an expletive. "Six? Ye'll no' retake a rig wi' six men, Mr. Cross, I can tell ye that for sure." He sighed heavily. "Youse lot with yer hands in the air then . . . Anyone got their SC qualification—that's swimmer-canoeist for anyone who wasn't SBS?"

Two hands remained in the air.

"Have youse bright sparks done any exercises on the North Sea rigs?" McGrain asked; and the two hands were lowered.

McGrain sighed and clutched his brow theatrically. "So ye cannae swim, cannae climb, dinnae know yer way around a rig. But trust me, four weeks from now ye will . . . bah God ye will. And if ye don't, Ah will personally kick ye's up the arse, off this ship and intae the bloody ocean, and ye's can swim yer way back hame. Do I make masel' clear?"

There was a wordless rumble around the room that more or less amounted to a "yes."

McGrain was not impressed. "Ah said, DO AH MAKE MASEL' CLEAR?"

This time the voices replied as one, "Yes, sir!"

McGrain nodded. "Tha's better. But I was a warrant officer, no' a bloody Rupert. So ye dinnae address me as 'sir.' Mr. Mc-Grain will be perfectly adequate."

Five minutes later, McGrain was in the cabin Cross had commandeered as his personal office. Both men had mugs of coffee in their fists. "It won't be easy, Mr. Cross, I can tell you that," said McGrain in a far less broadly Glasgwegian accent. "But you say these are good men."

"The best," Cross replied.

"Well, they'd better be. We've got four weeks to teach them how to swim hundreds of meters, carrying all their gear; how to get aboard the rig and the FPSO; and then how to overcome anyone on board without blowing the whole thing to hell."

"These men work around oil installations all the time. They're well aware of what could happen if a stray bullet hit an oil tank or a gas pipe, as am I. We've already taken precautions to minimize the risk."

"Aye, but it's not just your lads you have to worry about. It's the terrorists, too. A bunch of African guerrillas running around an oil rig, shooting off their AK-47s, is not my idea of fun. See, Mr. Cross, sir, here's what you need to remember. An oil rig is a place where the risk of fire and explosion is so great that you can't take a single everyday electrical device into the production area. Not your phone, not your camera, nothing. Oh, aye, that platform is equipped with all the latest safety features, I'm certain of that. There'll be steel plates between the production and accommodation zones. If there's an explosion, they'll deform and absorb the blast, like the crumple-zone of a car absorbs a crash. And every single drop of paint applied to any metal surface of the rig will be what's called 'intumescent.' That means that when it's exposed to fire, it bubbles up and forms a protective, heatproof layer between the flames and the metal.

"Now that's all fine and dandy, but this is still an oil rig. And oil is highly flammable. And where there's oil there's also gas, which is highly explosive. And even if there's time for some clever laddie to realize that the platform is under attack and initiate the shutdown procedures, ye cannae turn the flow of oil off, just by flicking a switch. It takes three hours, minimum, for the pressure to drop to nothing and if something makes the whole bloody place go bang at any point in those three hours, well, you can have all the steel plates and fancy paint you like, but it's nae going tae make a blind bit of difference."

The *Glenallen* supply tug was a substantial ship, capable of crossing any of the world's oceans in virtually any conditions, but she looked like a little dinghy compared to the towering mass of brutally functional engineering that was the Magna Grande drilling rig. The rig in its turn was dwarfed by the *Bannock A* production facility, which was moored about a mile away. Somehow, Hector Cross and his team had to protect these two huge vessels, using a pair of patrol boats that buzzed around their charges like little birds around a pair of exceptionally ugly hippos. But what if the enemy broke through their defenses, or caught them by surprise and managed to capture either or both of Bannock Oil's prize assets?

Hector Cross had ordered the *Glenallen* to take up a station some 400 yards from the rig. Then he assembled his men on the deck, looking out across the smooth, gentle swell of the ocean toward the subject of this afternoon's briefing. "Take a good look at that rig, gentlemen," he said. "Let's imagine the worst happens.

Suppose a bunch of terrorists have decided to take control of it and they're threatening to blow it up, or kill the crew unless their madcap demands are met. OK, then, how do we stop them?

"Answer: we don't, not unless it's absolutely necessary. In order to recapture a large vessel, or rig, standard operating procedure requires an initial, clandestine insertion of around twenty Special Forces operatives from the water, whose job is to secure the position for a full-scale assault by fifty to one hundred airborne troops brought in by helicopter. So it's way out of our league. But there may come a time when we have no option. As you all know from your own experience, defense cuts have left virtually all western armed forces smaller and more run-down than at any time since the start of the First World War. So maybe the military can't get here in time, or maybe there just isn't anyone available to come to our help. Then we're just going to have to do the job ourselves.

"This afternoon, we're going to set out the basic issues involved in recapturing that rig. Once we're topside on the rig, we'll be dealing with the kind of anti-terrorist operation with which most of us are very familiar. But first we have to get there. And I'll leave it to Mr. McGrain to tell you how that'll be done."

"Right!" barked Donnie McGrain. "This here is what is known as a semi-submersible rig. It's a bit like a bloody great metal iceberg, because most of it is beneath the surface. As you can see, the rig, also known as a platform, has four diamond-shaped legs. Each of these legs has a side-support sticking out diago-nally into the sea, like a metal wall. The part you can't see is the huge, and I mean absolutely bloody gigantic underwater pontoon that the legs and the supports are standing on. That's because the legs, the support and the pontoon have all been flooded with seawater, making them sink down into the sea, leaving just the upper section of the legs and the actual rig structure visible above the water. The pontoons are anchored to the seabed, which is about two thousand five hundred feet

249

beneath us—och aye, it's a long way down—and that's what keeps the whole thing in place.

"Now, if there is an attack on the rig, the chances are it'll happen at night, so as to have the maximum chance of taking us by surprise, and for the exact same reason, any counter-attack against them will also be carried out under cover of darkness. Now, that rig lights up like Las Vegas at night and illuminates the sea all around it. So you will make your initial approach from outside that lit area. You will be dropped into the water, either from this boat that we are on, or from one of the two patrol boats that operate from it, and count yourself lucky you're not being chucked out of a submarine, the way we used to do it.

"Once in the water, you will swim in pairs, staying submerged for as much of the journey as possible. If the sea is rough, the waves will act as cover and reduced visibility will make it harder for anyone aboard the rig to spot you. And dinnae worry: the men in each pair will be linked by a buddy-line, so no one's going tae drift away into the ocean without anyone noticing.

"In order to climb up a leg, the lead man—who for the time being will be me, or one of the other ex-SBS men—will hook on to one of the legs, secure the line to the leg and then start the process of climbing the rig. Now, there are ladders and walkways going up the legs of the rig, but we do not use them, if we can avoid it, because those ladders are the first thing that any terrorist with even half a brain in his wee head will booby-trap. So we start by heading for the spider deck, which is the first deck above water level—you can see it, over there, hanging underneath the main deck of the rig, between the four legs. Tae do that the lead man fires a grapnel, to which a rope is attached. He climbs up the rope, secures the spider deck and then pulls up the rope. While he's doing that the second man in attaches a rope ladder to the rope, so that it's pulled up to the spider deck and up they all go. We also have telescopic lad-

250

ders, with a hook on the end that can, if conditions permit, be extended up to the spider deck without the need for a grapnel.

"Once you get on to the spider deck, you can repeat the process to get on to the main deck. But what if the entrance to the main deck is blocked, or there's some bastard with an AK-47 standing the other side of it? Then the best climber in the team gets the chance to play at being Spidey-man. He hangs on to the underside of the main deck and makes his way to the edge of the rig, using carabiner clips and a rope to create a line the others can use. Then he climbs up the outside of the rig, rolls over the railing, lands on the main deck, shoots the bampot guarding the entrance in the back and whistles tae his pals to come and join him. And if you've got that far intact, then dinnae worry. Compared to what you've just done, the rest of the job's a piece of piss. So does anyone have any questions?"

McGrain dealt with the various inquiries the men had to make, then said, "Right, youse lot. It's been hot, boring work, standing here in yon sun, listening to me blathering on. What you need is a nice, wee, bracing dip. So in you go, right now, shoes off but keep your clothes on, all of them, and give me four laps of the boat. You too, Mr. Cross."

Hector didn't need to be told. He was already climbing up on to the rail and was the first to plunge into the water, twenty feet below. Once their boss had shown willing, the rest of the team could hardly hang back, but still there were plenty of muttered complaints as one after another they jumped into the water and formed a line of thrashing figures, following their leader like chicks after a mother duck.

The twice-daily swims were the bane of the men's lives. A lap of the *Glenallen* was approximately 250 meters, so McGrain had begun Day One of training by ordering two laps per session. Men who thought nothing of a ten-kilometer run found themselves struggling to swim a twentieth of the distance. And then there was the shark factor. Tough, battle-hardened soldiers flinched at the thought of plunging into deep, dark ocean waters, filled with who knew what deadly sea creatures. But McGrain showed no mercy. He forced everyone into the water, like it or not, and had them swimming around and around, upping the distance every day, until they were so exhausted they would have considered it a mercy to be gripped in the jaws of a hungry man-eater and spared the unrelenting slog around, and around, and around the *Glenallen*.

Soon the days and then the weeks started racing by. McGrain began by using the tug as a training ground, getting them used to the idea of being in the water—just in swimming trunks at first—grabbing hold of a climbing net draped over the side of the boat and clambering up to the deck. By week two they were working on the vessels they were going to be defending, learning to climb up the hull of the *Bannock A* as well as the legs of the Magna Grande rig, and now they discovered a new enemy: heat. Combat clothing for this kind of operation was based on a drysuit that could be worn in and out of the water, but drysuits are designed to keep their wearers warm and both swimming a long distance and climbing up the hull of a semi-submersible rig or a giant floating oil refinery are tasks that generate a huge amount of body heat. Even in the cold conditions of the North Sea, overheating can be a serious problem for fighting men. In the equatorial heat off the coast of West Africa the heat factor was a potentially deadly problem and a great deal of time, effort and experimentation was devoted to finding gear that would provide the combatants with all the pouches and webbing they needed, while still being light and breathable enough to keep heatstroke at bay.

Day by day, session by session, whether carrying out fitness drills and practical exercises, or doing classroom work, learning and memorizing the location and function of every important area of the rig and FPSO, the Cross Bow landlubbers were turned into something close to proper amphibious troops. But as the final

252

week began, McGrain was still worried that there were holes in the team's preparations. "They've had it too easy," he told Cross. "The weather's been steady: no high winds, no rough seas, barely even any rain. And we still haven't started night training."

"Are they ready for it yet?" Cross asked.

"Impossible to tell, boss. I mean, you get some fellas and they're tough as nails, but you throw them into deep water at night and when they're ten feet under, and everything's black, and they don't know which way is up, they just go tae pieces. There's only one way you ever find out which ones can hack it and which ones cannae, and that's doing it."

Before Cross started sending his men up a ship's hull and a rig's legs in the middle of the night he had to inform the men in charge of them and get their agreement to what he had in mind. As a long-serving U.S. Navy veteran, Captain Cy Stamford had no objection to letting Cross and his men carry out nighttime exercises on the *Bannock A*. It helped that the two men had worked together before, fighting pirates off the coast of Puntland in northeast Somalia and had developed a healthy, mutual respect.

"Sounds like a good idea to me, Heck," Stamford said. "You don't have to tell me that wars are fought at night, and that means you have to train at night, too. I guess once your guys have learned how to get on to the ship, they're going to have to practice fighting on it, too."

"That's the plan, Cy. I think it'll be good for your crew too. The more accustomed they are to the idea of combat, the easier they'll find it to deal with and keep calm if it ever happens for real."

"I agree. I've got to inform Houston, just as a matter of protocol. But I'll tell them what I'm telling you: this has my complete support. And I'm not the only Navy vet among the men on board. If there's anything we can do, don't hesitate to ask."

"Thanks. If the balloon ever does go up, we'll almost certainly be conceding numerical superiority to the bad guys, so we should definitely talk about how to make the most of you and your men. If we can find a way to include you in training that would be even better."

"Sure, it would make a pleasant change. Life can get dull around here. I didn't go to sea just so's I could sit in the same place, week after week."

"Then I'll see what I can do to liven things up," Cross promised him, feeling grateful to be dealing with someone who understood the realities of his world. But when he made the same request to Rod Barth, the Offshore Installation Manager, more commonly known as "OIM," or just "boss" of the Magna Grande platform, the reception was very different.

"Listen here, Mr. Cross," Barth said, wiping a hand across his perspiring forehead, "I'm an oilman. I'm the guy who makes sure that this baby makes money. I get the oil out of the ground and into the pipelines, 24/7, and I don't appreciate anything that gets in the way of my oil. It's bad enough having guys climbing aound like monkeys during the day—no need to have them doing it at night as well. And if you want them running around my rig in the dark, playing at soldiers, forget it. It's not going to happen, not as long as I'm in charge here, and I don't plan on going anywhere else any time soon."

"Me neither," said Cross, resisting the temptation to grab Barth by his fat, jowly neck, shove him up against a bulkhead and give him a short, sharp introduction to the kind of violence he could expect if a terrorist ever got on board. "My job is the same as yours: to keep the oil flowing. And nothing would stop it more effectively than a terrorist blowing this rig to pieces with you and everyone else who works on it on board."

Barth gave a porcine snort of contempt. "Gimme a break, Cross. We both know that's not going to happen. You tell me when a terrorist last blew up a rig? Oh, wait, you can't, because it's never happened."

"No one had flown two jets into skyscrapers until 9/11, either.

Listen, I have credible information, both from my own sources and the U.S. State Department, that there is a genuine risk of attack. I'm responsible for ensuring the safety of all the people and installations at this field. I'm telling you I need to be able to train my men at night and I'd appreciate your co-operation."

"Here's what I'll do," said Barth. "I'll call Houston. I'll ask the folks at Operations how they feel about the safety risks to our workers and to the equipment on this rig if we've got military exercises being conducted on it at night by a bunch of mercenary hotheads who don't have the first clue about the dangers of offshore oil production."

Cross took another deep breath and then, not bothering to hide the anger simmering beneath his usual steely composure said, "My men are not mercenaries. They're highly experienced ex-servicemen, they're trained to stay cool under pressure and they've spent years working around oil installations in Abu Zara."

"Yeah, sitting in the middle of the damn desert. That's a totally different situation to this. I reckon Houston'll agree with me, too."

Cross sighed. "I didn't want to do this. I was hoping we could come to a civilized agreement. But now I'm going to pull rank. I'm a main board director of Bannock Oil and I can get straight on the line to Senator John Bigelow, the President and Chief Executive, and get his direct order in support of my plans."

"You can call the White House, for all I care. Won't make a bit of difference. Your boys aren't coming on to my rig, ever, and that's all I've got to say."

Cross called Bigelow, who assured him, "Don't worry, Heck, I get it. Of course your people have got to be able to train for every possible eventuality. I'll sort this out right away and get back to you."

Three hours later, Bigelow was on the line, exactly as promised. But what he had to say took Cross completely by surprise.

"I'm afraid it's a 'no,' Heck. Now, before you blow your top, just hear me out. What we've got here is a legal issue. Bannock Oil is responsible for the safety of everyone aboard the Magna Grande rig and the *Bannock A* production vessel, including people who work for the many sub-contractors we've got out there. If any of these people were to be hurt, let alone die as a result of anything that happened during one of your training exercises—which fall outside the parameters of the work and conditions they are contractually obligated to accept—then the company could be liable for millions of dollars in damages. The same applies to your people, too. If they suffer injury as a result of a workplace incident, we could be liable."

"But they work for me. They're employed by Cross Bow."

"Yes, and Cross Bow has been a subsidiary of Bannock ever since your wife bought it off you, and this is a Bannock project, so again we'd potentially be liable. No hazardous activities, Hector, do you hear me? If the seas are rough, don't go swimming in them. Nothing after dark unless there are lights everywhere and safety harnesses are worn."

"For God's sake, John, these men are former soldiers," Cross protested. "They've gone to war. They've risked their lives to protect Bannock's oilfields in the past because that's what they're paid to do. These are men who actually like risking their necks. Believe me, they'd much rather be training and getting some action that sitting around being swathed in cotton wool because of some suit's pathetic obsession with safety."

"It's not an 'obsession,' it's the opinion the legal department has given me after due consideration of the law and our potential exposure. For the record, I cannot ignore that opinion because then I'd be violating all the insurance policies we have in place to cover against possible legal action."

Cross made one last attempt to sway him: "But, John, if the field is ever attacked, and neither my men nor your staff have had any training, we wouldn't be talking about an injury here or there. We could be looking at large numbers of fatalities and millions of dollars' worth of damage to your installations. Seriously, let's get down to dollars and cents. You stand to lose far more from a terrorist assault than you ever will from a training exercise."

"I hear you, Heck, really I do," Bigelow said. "But the way Legal sees it, looking at our past experience and that of other oil companies, the odds of any such assault are so minimal that we can safely ignore them. But the chances of injury or even some kind of emotional trauma caused by exposure to combat training are much higher. Therefore we have to play the odds and say no to your request."

"For God's sake, John, this can't be the right decision. You're putting the whole future of Magna Grande, even of Bannock itself, in danger."

"That's enough, Heck!" Bigelow snapped. "I have a lot of respect for the work you've done for Bannock Oil, and of course I'm aware of your personal ties to the company, but when you talk of the company being in danger, why, that just sounds like scaremongering. You're a better man than that, Heck, and a braver one, too. I'm sorry, but the decision is final. No training of any kind on the rig or the production vessel after dark, and no simulated combat situations, on either facility at any time."

Cross slammed down the phone and sank back in his chair. They could still practice night swimming in the water around the *Glenallen*. They could use the tug as a surrogate training ground. But one of the biggest potential advantages he'd been counting on against any assailant was familiarity with the battlefield, and that had just been thrown away.

Cross prayed that corporate stupidity in Houston didn't lead to defeat in the Atlantic Ocean. He'd always had a sixth sense about what he called "the Beast." It was an evil, malevolent creature that constantly sought ways to attack him and those he cared for. Its face changed from time to time as it found new human carriers for its violent virus, but its essential nature remained unchanging. Recently he had begun to feel the presence of the Beast again. It was close at hand, and that meant Congo had emerged from wherever he'd been skulking since his escape from Caracas. He wasn't far away now, Cross was sure of it, and if he knew how the Bannock Oil suits were conspiring to make his life easier, he'd be laughing. But then Cross brought his mind up short. "Stop whining!" he told himself. "You've faced worse odds, in much less favorable situations, and you've beaten Johnny bloody Congo to a pulp in your time. So get a grip, do your job and make damn sure that whatever Congo or anyone else does, you still win anyway."

The first thing Cross had to do, he realized as his temper cooled, was to eat a slice of humble pie. He gritted his teeth and called Bigelow once more: "I'm sorry if I sounded insubordinate there, sir. There's a chain of command and I have to abide by it."

"That's no problem, Heck," Bigelow replied, his voice oozing the satisfaction he felt at having his place at the top reinforced. "Hell, we all get a little heated from time to time—I know I've done it often enough, fighting for the issues that really matter to me. And if there's anything I can do to help you improve security at Magna Grande, without compromising the safety of our people out there, you just let me know."

"Thank you, John, I appreciate that," said Cross. He'd counted on Bigelow wanting to display his magnanimity, and his power to grant gifts. "Even if we can't train on the platform or the FPSO we really need to be familiar with their layouts. My guys can't do anything to help if they're blundering around like tourists without a map. If we could recce both units in detail—under the supervision of their safety officers, of course—then that would be a real benefit to my team, and to the people and property they're supposed to be protecting."

"That makes sense," Bigelow agreed. "I'll make sure we get it all set up as soon as possible."

"And one other thing," Cross added. "My people are stuck on a tug, 24/7. The food's pretty basic and there's not a lot to do, other than train and sleep, but the rig and the FPSO both have canteens, gyms, movie rooms, pool tables and God knows what else. If we could use those places that would be great for morale, and it would create familiarity between security and operations staff. Believe me, if we're ever in any kind of hostage or combat situation, being able to recognize faces and know which side people are on could be the difference between life and death."

"Well, we can't deprive your people of good food and videos, now can we?" Bigelow chuckled. "Consider it done."

"Thanks, John, I appreciate that," said Cross. What he did not add, but still thought, was: *But all the guided tours, good meals and gym workouts in the world won't mean squat if we have to go into battle without proper training.*

Fail to prepare, prepare to fail: just because that was a cliché didn't make it any less true.

Johnny Congo had agreed the date and time of the attack with Babacar Matemba at the upcountry training base and Mateus da Cunha in Paris. Aram Bendick, meanwhile, had been establishing massive short positions in Bannock Oil stock and bought well over $2 billion worth of Bannock credit default swaps. He'd also been getting nervous. "I spent three frickin' days talking percentages with that shyster of yours, now it's almost a month later and I'm still standing here with my dick in the wind, waiting for something to happen. You'd better make it worth my while soon, man, 'cause I am damn sure I won't stand here much longer."

"Not long now, white boy," Congo assured him. "That dick of yours'll be nice and hard real soon, don't you worry 'bout that."

Now the day had come and it began with good news. "Weather report is showing a low front coming in from the west," Chico Torres told him over breakfast on the *Mother Goose*. "It's gonna get a little rough."

"That a problem?" Congo asked, feeling nervous about the sheer scale of what he was attempting, but not wanting to seem pussy about it.

"No way, man, anything but," Torres replied. "We're gonna be a hundred meters beneath the waves and it'll be smooth as silk down there. Could be an issue getting launched. But if we time it right, we'll go in ahead of the weather, it'll pass right over us and by the time we get to the target they'll be rocking on the surface and we'll still be taking it easy down below."

Congo nodded, but then Torres added a quick postscript. "The only thing bothers me is the birds. The kind of weather we're going to get tonight, a Marine pilot could fly right through it with his eyes shut. But any time you're relying on local talent, you gotta wonder if they can handle it."

"You suggesting an African can't fly a helicopter?"

It suddenly struck Torres that he was talking to a man who'd been born in Africa. *Congo: the clue's in the name you dumb jerk*, he chided himself. "No way, man, not at all. Just, it's a specialist field, you feel me? Night-flying over water in bad weather, low visibility, high winds, all that shit."

"They'll manage, and you know how I know that? Because if they don't manage they're gonna die and ain't no one wants to do that."

"Then we're good to go."

So now they were twelve hours and twenty-four nautical miles away from H-hour and both Triton 3300/3s had been lowered into the water. Now the A-frame was hoisting up a powered submersible sled, laden with a three-ton cargo that weighed almost as much as one of the subs, then swinging it out over the water and bringing it down at a point between them. Towlines were run from the sled to the subs and made fast, with Torres standing on the hull of the sub in which he would be riding, giving instructions and ensuring that the cable which would allow him to control the sled from inside the Triton's transparent cabin was properly connected and functional. Then final wishes of good luck were shouted down from the support ship, the hatches were closed and the two yellow submersibles sank beneath the ocean swell, towing their cargo behind them, and an instant later were completely invisible.

Congo went over the mission's timetable in his head, just in case, even at this late stage, there was something that he'd missed: a factor that hadn't been considered. But if there were such a thing, he couldn't spot it. The subs would travel at three knots for eight hours before setting up their side of the deal, turning around and heading back the way they came.

The *Mother Goose*, meanwhile, would follow a spiral course, at first travelling away from the Magna Grande field before curving around and coming in closer. When she was nine nautical miles from the target, by which time night would have fallen, she'd cut her lights, stop for no more than ten minutes to pick up the subs at an agreed rendezvous point, then move off again, once more moving away from the field. If the weather prevented a quick retrieval, the subs' crews would be brought abroad and the crafts themselves scuttled. By this point, the only thing anyone on any vessel or rig in the vicinity would be thinking about would be the storm and no one would give a damn about the *Goose*, what she was doing or where she was going.

When the subs had turned for home, Congo would call Babacar Matemba and tell him to get his birds and his men in the air. "And then," Congo said to himself, "it's showtime!"

Close to the equator the sun sinks so fast that you can actually watch it move across the sky as it sets. This evening the towering black thunderclouds massing to the west blocked most of its descent, right up to the final moment when it stabbed one last, dazzling beam of light across the ocean, fell beneath the horizon and darkness descended. The storm, however, had yet to hit the National Air Force of Angola base where two Russian-made Mil Mi-35 "Hind" attack helicopters were preparing for take-off. All their markings had been crudely obliterated with black paint. Despite the prospect of worsening conditions, the two crews chatted animatedly as they walked toward their craft. They were happy, as well they should be—every man had been promised $10,000 in cash for a single night's work. The base commander, who was turning a blind eye to the temporary disappearance of the only two Hinds in Angola's helicopter fleet that were actually airworthy, was pocketing $250,000. The Minister of Defense, meanwhile, had confirmed the receipt of $5 million in his bank account in London. London is the preferred financial laundry for corrupt politicians from the developing world, thanks to a capacity for turning a blind eye to dirty money that puts the gnomes of Zurich to shame; a property market that is one of the world's safest investments; and an obsession with the human rights of foreign criminals that is in its own perverse way profoundly immoral. No matter how appalling the accusations against a man may be, or even his proven guilt, it is virtually impossible to deport anyone who can either claim the slightest family contact with the United Kingdom or suggest that he is in fear of the doubtless well-deserved punishments that he faces back home. In the event of a coup, or—less likely—an election defeat, such considerations would be extremely important to the minister concerned.

With all the key players bought and paid for, Johnny Congo knew that he would get what he wanted. Sure enough, he soon received word that the helicopters were in the air, on a course that would take them out to sea and then northeast toward Cabinda. And he had the personal assurance of their commanding officer that the pilots he had chosen, the finest at his disposal, would be more than capable of dealing with the weather.

* * *

The *Mother Goose* met her chicks at the assigned rendezvous. The crew's training proved to be worthwhile because both submersibles were recovered, despite the waves that were already being whipped up by the wind. Radio communication with the subs had been impossible when they were underwater and Congo was desperate to know if they'd been able to carry out their mission as planned.

"Take it easy, bro," Torres told him. "The timer's set, the package is in position A and the target ain't going nowhere. You wanna know if there could be any kinda snafu? Yeah, sure there could. Anything that can go wrong will go wrong and all that shit. But we checked everything, then we rechecked it, then we checked again, just for the hell of it. And it was all good."

Babacar Matemba selected the fifteen men who had performed best in training for the attack on Bannock Oil and brought them to a landing strip just a few kilometers from the Cabindan coast to await their pick-up by the Angolan helicopters. Not wanting to find himself trapped on a rig if things went wrong, he delegated command of the raid to one of his most ambitious subordinates, a tough, merciless killer called Théophile Bembo who had spent fifteen of his twenty-two years on the planet carrying a gun in the service of one warlord or another before settling on permanent employment with Matemba's private army. Té-Bo, as he preferred to be called, thinking the name was "*beacoup plus gangsta*" than the one he'd been christened with, was built like an ebony Adonis, with the heavily muscled physique characteristic of West African men. When not under fire he went everywhere with a pair of bright red Beats by Dr. Dre headphones clamped to his shaven head, nodding to the pounding rap rhythms slamming through his brain and stopping from time to time to bust some moves in front of his admiring comrades and any good-looking women who might be passing.

He was still wearing the phones and listening to Kanye West

as he led seven of his men on to one of the Hinds, both of which had now been topped up so that their fuel tanks were filled to overflowing. Neither Matemba nor any of his men were remotely bothered by Té-Bo's apparently lackadaisical attitude. They knew that when the bullets started flying, the Beats would come off, Té-Bo would snap into warrior mode and their enemies would fly before him like seed husks in the wind.

On the *Glenallen*, Hector Cross finished the bedtime story he read every evening, via Skype, to his beloved Catherine Cayla, then headed up to the bridge, bracing himself as he went against the movement of the boat. The sea was becoming distinctly rough and for the first time since they'd arrived in African waters the wind and rain were making their presence felt.

"Anything I need to know about?" Cross asked the skipper, a Swede called Magnus Bromberg who'd learned his trade in the chilly waters of the Baltic and the North Sea.

"A bit of weather coming through," he said casually. "It'll blow a gale, force eight, gusting nine maybe, enough to make some of your boys seasick, I think. It's OK, my ship and my crew survived the storm of the century unscathed, so this is nothing to worry about, I can promise you that."

"I'll be sure to issue Kwells for anyone who needs them," Cross said drily. "Oh, and speaking of violent sickness, what's the cook knocking up for dinner tonight?"

"Veal Milanese with pasta and tomato sauce," Bromberg replied, smacking his lips. "One of his best dishes, I would say, but it could get a little messy on a night like this. Hard to keep the plate still!"

Cross laughed, thinking of baby Catherine and her astonishing ability to cover every surface for miles around in bits of flying pasta and wondering if he and his men were going to be any tidier tonight. He still had a few duties to complete before he could relax over an evening meal. Though forbidden from conducting exercises on the *Bannock A* or the rig, he had at least obtained permission to have one of his men, unarmed, on watch at all times, both to report any suspicious circumstance and to remain with the vessels' crews if anything did go wrong.

All the vessels on the Magna Grande field could communicate via conventional ship-to-ship radio and for most practical purposes—such as Cross's conversation with Cy Stamford, for example—this was still the simplest way to talk. In addition, however, the oil platform, the FPSO and the tug were all equipped with VSATs, or very small aperture terminals, which were in turn linked to overhead satellites. This meant that not only did they all have high-speed onboard Wi-Fi, but they could all communicate online, in real time with one another, and Bannock HQ in Houston.

Cross had taken advantage of this by giving miniature earpieces to his sentries on duty on the platform or the *Bannock A* through which they could talk to the command post on the *Glenallen* and receive messages in return. His reasoning was very simple. The only time the sentries would really matter would be if any or all of the vessels were attacked. And if that happened, then the ability to communicate without the enemy's knowledge would be essential.

As a matter of operational protocol, all communications with the sentries were handled via their earpieces, which was how Cross, who could receive their messages via his phone, now checked with the men at both locations. He was told by both not to worry. There were no signs of trouble anywhere. "You'd have to be a bloody stupid terrorist to set to sea in this," the man on the Magna Grande platform, an ex-Greenjacket called Frank Sharman, joked.

"Well, a lot of terrorists are bloody stupid, that's why they're terrorists," Cross pointed out.

"Yeah, true, boss, but there are limits!"

"Fair enough," Cross said, but he couldn't help but feel that

Sharman had a point. With any luck they'd have nothing worse to worry about than keeping their veal Milanese on their plates. But in Cross's experience, Lady Luck had a way of slapping a man in the face if he ever took her for granted. And then there was the Beast to think about. He could practically feel its fetid breath on the back of his neck. It was close now, he knew it, and it was getting ready to strike.

The storm was coming in, whipping the rain against the helicopters flying just a few meters above the foaming ocean, daring the waves to hit them. They'd skimmed between passing ships and oil rigs, using them as cover, and maintained strict radio silence for the entire flight. Perhaps that's why the radar operators on duty aboard the Bannock Oil installations didn't detect the approaching aircraft until they were barely twenty kilometers away from their target. Only then was Cy Stamford informed that there were two unidentified aircraft, almost certainly helicopters, approaching on a bearing that would take them directly over his ship and the rig.

"Find out who they are and what the hell they think they're doing," he ordered.

Seconds later, the pilot of the lead Hind was telling Té-Bo: "One of the Bannock ships wants to know our identity and what we are doing in their area. What do you want me to say?"

He received no reply. Té-Bo had eschewed the helicopter's earphones for his trusty Beats and was still getting in the groove. It took frantic gestures by the Hind's crew and a shake of the shoulder from one of his men before he was alerted to the need to respond. He swapped cans, listened as the pilot repeated his question and then just said, "Nothing."

Stamford ordered the request to be resent and the pilot passed it on to Té-Bo for a third time. This time the young guerrilla leader said, "Tell him that you are National Air Force, because that is the truth. Then say that you are on a regular training flight."

266

"At night? In a storm?" the pilot protested. "That is not regular! No one will believe it."

Té-Bo pursed his lips, almost pouting as he thought. "Then say that you are training to carry out a rescue mission in bad weather, at night, because emergencies are more likely to happen on a stormy night—no?—than on a fine day when the sea is calm."

The pilot did as he was told and was happy to be able to tell this moody brat who for some reason seemed to be in charge that the men on the *Bannock A* seemed satisfied by his story.

Cy Stamford, however, was far from convinced. He called Hector Cross. "You aware that there are two helicopters claiming to be from the Angolan National Air Force heading in our direction?"

"Yes, Bromberg's just told me about them. I'm up on the bridge now, keeping tabs on the situation."

"They say they're practising their emergency response in extreme weather conditions. I guess it's possible, but we weren't informed in advance and they didn't exactly volunteer the information willingly."

"Sounds dodgy to me. I'm putting both my patrol boats in the water. If they do turn out to be hostiles, we'll be waiting for them."

"OK," Stamford replied. "But here's some advice from an old sea dog: think real hard about what you're going to do next."

As Cross put his handset down he was doing precisely what Stamford had just told him: thinking. And, as the veteran captain had implied, he wasn't finding it easy to come to a satisfactory conclusion. His problem was not that he lacked the means to defend the rig or the *Bannock A*. His two patrol boats were both armed to the full military specification. At the bow, each carried a Browning M2 .50-caliber heavy machine gun, mounted on a retractable Kongsberg Sea Protector weapons platform and firing control system, complete with smoke-grenade launchers. Aft of the cockpit, they each had a Thales Lightweight Multi-Role Missile launcher, capable of attacking both ships and aircraft. So once they put to sea they'd be capable of destroying the two helicopters at will. The question was: What would they be destroying?

Suppose the two birds really were conducting a training exercise for the Angolan Air Force, and, what was more, an exercise preparing them to come to the aid of offshore oil projects? If an oil company boat blew them and their crews out of the air, the political consequences would be catastrophic and no one would blame the Angolan government if it demanded massive compensation and withdrew Bannock Oil's right to drill in its waters. Even if the men on board were terrorists, how would he ever be able to prove it once they and their helicopters were sitting on the seabed, half a mile beneath the ocean waves?

So he couldn't fire until he had absolute proof that the helicopters were hostile. But the only way he'd get that proof was if they actually mounted an attack on the rig, and at that point he couldn't order sea-to-air rockets to be fired at them for the simple reason that only a madman or a blithering idiot causes a massive explosion directly above an oil rig. That meant that Cross's only course of action was the one he most despised: do nothing. It wasn't even worth launching the patrol boats just yet because if there really were Cabindan terrorists about to mount a raid on the rig, there was no point showing them precisely what he had to fight back with.

In fact the less they could see, the better. Cross turned to Bromberg: "I want to watch those helicopters, but I don't want them watching us, so we need to go dark. No external lights. All windows covered. No lights on up here, either, if you can still handle the ship that way."

"All the controls are illuminated. If I can keep them lit, we can do it," Bromberg replied.

"Then do it."

"What about the men preparing your patrol boats for launching?"

"They can stand down for the time being. But they've got to be ready to move fast when I tell them."

A lesser man might have protested, or asked for clarification, or questioned Cross's authority. Bromberg just took in what had been said, gave the information a moment's thought, nodded and said, "You've got it."

"One more thing," Cross added. "I need to get a sight of the helicopters as soon as possible, but as long as the rig's between us and them, with all its lights blazing, that's impossible. Can you get me a better angle?"

"Sure."

Bromberg gave his orders and the *Glenallen* picked up speed, taking up a new course that sent it to the east of the rig, moving with the wind. Cross went outside, on to one of the small, open weather decks that flanked the bridge, ignoring the driving rain and bracing himself against the bucking and diving of the tug as she rode the increasingly high, foam-capped waves. He was carrying a thermal imager and as he put it to his eye he turned to the northeast, from where the helicopters were coming. Slowly, painstakingly, he tracked from side to side, slightly shifting the vertical angle of his imager to track at different heights, and avoiding the dazzling blaze of light that surrounded the rig as he searched for the faint heat-glow that would signal the presence of an aircraft. His hair was plastered to his head, his clothes were soaked through and he had to stop every few seconds to shake away the rainwater puddling on the thermal-imaging unit. One minute became two.

They had to be really close now. Why couldn't he see them?

And then as he panned once more across the sky, there they were, coming in at such a low altitude that they might almost be stones skimming across the water. They were close enough that Cross could get a clear picture of the shape of their fuselages. To anyone with any military experience it was unmistakable.

"They're Hinds," Cross said to himself.

269

He'd heard of one Hind that was owned and operated by a South African mercenary, but if they were flying in a pair they had to be military. Angola had its own take on the Communist hammer and sickle on its national flag and had always bought the bulk of its military kit from the Russians. So the evidence was overwhelming: these had to be Angolan Air Force helicopters, and that meant it really might be a training exercise after all.

But what if it wasn't? Cross spoke to Frank Sharman on the rig: "Two helicopters, Hinds by the looks of them, are approaching your location. Keep an eye on them. They claim to be on a training mission. If they are, fine. If they show any sign of hostile action, keep me informed of exactly what's happening and await further instructions."

"You got it, boss."

Cross could feel a tightening in his guts and around his throat. It was the first sign of the tension that gripped him in the moments before combat and he knew precisely what it meant. As much as his mind had come up with a perfectly good, rational argument for accepting these helicopters at face value, his instincts had marked them down as threats. He raised his eyes briefly to the waterlogged heavens and prayed that his instincts were wrong, for once.

Té-Bo's boyhood hero was Usain Bolt, and as he grew older one of the things he came to admire most about his idol was the way that Bolt could be fooling around on the track just seconds before the start of an Olympic final, yet when the starting gun fired, he was right into the zone, focused on nothing but his race, instantly ready to run faster than any other human who had ever lived. In the same way, Té-Bo prided himself that he could snap into his own zone, as a warrior and leader, at a moment's notice. So it was that he was now firing orders at the men in his lead helicopter and the one behind, making sure that everyone knew their assignments, and that all of them were as ready as he to wreak havoc on their target and its inhabitants.

One of the Hind's crew pulled open the fuselage door, letting in a blast of rain-soaked air. Many of the men shouted at the sudden drenching, but Té-Bo barely noticed it. So far as he was concerned, the bad weather was his friend, for looking down at the platform he could see that its helipad was deserted. No one would be expecting an incoming flight on a night like this. Now, as its companion took up a station immediately over the derrick, the first Hind came in to land. The second its wheels hit the pad, Té-Bo was jumping down on to the surface of the platform, waving his men down after him and dispatching them to their assigned destinations around the rig. The helicopter rose back up into the air, adding its downdraught to the gale-force wind, and the second bird came in to land.

There was no response from the crew of the platform. How could there be? They had no weapons, so all that they could do was to call for help and then try to find somewhere to hide away until help arrived. But there would be no one to answer their call. Té-Bo's leader, Babacar Matemba, and the other man—the one who called himself Tumbo—had assured him that the Angolan Navy was a joke and there were no Americans for 1,000 kilometers in any direction. They told Té-Bo not to worry. He would seize the Magna Grande rig, do what had to be done and be back on the helicopters, flying back to the biggest pay check he had ever received—enough to buy the love of any girl in the Congo—long before anyone was close enough to stop them. Matemba had always told Té-Bo the truth, so why should he disbelieve him now?

The Hinds had been flying so low that for a short time they were actually out of sight behind the oil platform, but the moment the first of them gained altitude, came into view and darted toward the helipad, Cross knew that while the aircraft

271

belonged to the Angolan Air Force—he was certain of that—they were not on any kind of training mission. Seconds later the lead aircraft touched down on the helipad and men were dropping down from it on to the platform.

At this distance, in atrocious visibility, the new arrivals were little more than blurred outlines. But Cross could see at once that they knew their business. There was no panic, no rushing around, none of the "spray and pray" that he had seen among some Middle Eastern and North African insurgents, who liked to blaze away just for show without the slightest idea of how to hit a target. Instead they moved off the helipad swiftly and with purpose and the reason for their discipline wasn't hard to find. The first man off the Hind had taken up a stationary position on the platform, guiding everyone else toward their individual targets and remaining where he was as his helicopter took off, the other replaced it and another squad disembarked.

Cross heard Sharman's voice coming through his iPhone's earpieces. "First off, boss, the helicopters are definitely Air Force, or ex-Air Force. Someone's tried to paint over the markings, but they missed."

"OK, so now what's happening?"

"I count eight men on each bird," Sharman went on. "They're fanning out across the platform, moving toward the production areas and the accommodation and administration block.

"As close as you can get to the OIM," Cross told him. "Barth likes to throw his weight around, but I seriously doubt his ability to stay calm under fire. You'll have to nursemaid him. So find him. Try his office first. Make sure he doesn't make too many stupid decisions. Try to stop him panicking. And keep me up to speed."

"Yes, boss."

"One other thing . . . These terrorists, rebels or whatever the hell they call themselves, are either going to blow the rig, or take everyone aboard hostage, or both. If you get taken, you won't be able to talk. So take out your earpiece and try to leave it as close as you can to whoever's in charge. The more we can hear, the more we'll know what's going on and what we can do about it. Got that?"

"Yes, boss . . . Wait . . ."

There was something that sounded like a crackle of static in Cross's ear, then Sharman's voice: "The shooting's started. Can't tell exactly where it's coming from. I'll try to find out. Meanwhile, I'm off to deal with that pillock Barth. Hope they do him first."

Cross moved back into the bridge, wiping the water off his forehead and hair as he came through the door. He was greeted by the sound of a frantic, desperate voice emanating from a speaker positioned on the wall. "We're under attack! Can you hear me? It's an attack! Oh God, I can't believe this, they're firing guns! This is impossible! Mayday! Mayday! For God's sake, someone help us!"

"As you can hear," said Bromberg drily, "the Offshore Installation Manager is not responding well to the crisis. I thought it best to put this on speaker. Saves the radio op having to repeat everything."

Sharman's deeper, much calmer voice could now be heard saying, "It's all right, sir, don't you worry. The security people know what's happening. Just relax, and let the professionals take care of everything. Why don't you sit down over here, sir?"

"Get your hands off me!" Barth yelled and then, "Abandon ship! Abandon ship! This is not a drill! We are under armed attack . . ."

"Excuse me, sir."

Cross could hear the sound of some kind of impact, a grunt and then the thump of a heavy object hitting the ground.

"I've given Mr. Barth a sedative, boss," Sharman said. "Christ, there are people running everywhere, they're heading to their muster stations, hang on . . . Oh no . . ."

Cross heard the sound of gunfire in the distance and then

Sharman's voice commanding, "Stay where you are! For your own safety do not, repeat not attempt to abandon ship. Remain indoors and stay still."

Over the next few minutes Sharman gave a running commentary on what was evidently a well-planned, efficiently executed operation, as more Bannock workers died and more and more of those who were still living were herded toward the canteen: the largest internal space on the platform. Then he very calmly said, "I can hear people coming; they're at the door. Uh-oh . . ."

Seconds later there were voices jabbering in what sounded to Cross like French, though he knew that the European language spoken in Angola, including the province of Cabinda, was Portuguese. Sharman's steady, measured tones cut in, "I understand, comprendo: me go with you. Look, hands up, see? I surrender. Whoa! No need to point that at me. I'm coming . . . No fight, OK? . . . I'm coming . . ."

The voice on the tannoy died away as Sharman was led away, out of the range of the radio mike. But Cross still had the feed from Sharman's earpiece as he and Barth were led to join the others in the canteen.

It was time Cross talked to Houston. He walked back into his command post. Dave Imbiss was already sitting there, tapping away at a computer keyboard linked to a large screen.

Cross sat down opposite his own laptop and was about to put a Skype call through to John Bigelow when he heard Imbiss call out, "Hector, quick, you've gotta look! This is streaming live, right now."

Cross spun his chair so that he could see Imbiss's screen. An impossibly young African face appeared. With his headphones around his neck, he could have been any street kid in any city from Los Angeles to Lagos. "This action is being carried out on behalf of the oppressed people of Cabinda," he began, speaking English in a heavy French–African accent. "We demand the independence of Cabinda. We demand recognition by the United Nations and all the permanent members of the Security Council. We demand the return of Cabinda's natural assets to the Cabindan people. We will negotiate only with the President of the United States. Until our demands are met we will kill one person every five minutes. We are completely serious. *Regardez!*"

The young man's face disappeared from view to reveal Rod Barth being held by a man in green combat fatigues while a second pointed a gun at him and a third tied a blindfold around his head. Sharman was nowhere to be seen. Now Barth was being forced down on to his knees, begging for mercy: "No, no! Please, don't do it . . . I can get you anything you want . . . Let me talk to someone . . . please!"

"My God, that's Barth, the Installation Manager," Cross said.

The young man now reappeared in the shot, several feet from the camera, to which he turned once again. "I repeat, we are completely serious. Our demands must be met. Or else, in five more minutes, you will see this." There was a holster on the young man's belt. He unclipped it, pulled out a Sig Sauer pistol, raised the gun-barrel to Barth's temple and fired, blasting an eruption of blood, brain and bone from the far side of his skull.

Cross could hear the sound of the shot in his earpiece, just out of synch with the internet feed, and Sharman groaning, "Oh no . . ." and then shouting out, "No! Don't be daft!" as a confused babble of protests and barked orders was followed by a burst of gunfire, the screams of a wounded man, another couple of shots and then a terrible silence.

On the screen, the kid with the headphones leered into the camera again. "Now you know what we do to people who make resistance. And remember: *cinq minutes.*" Then the screen went dead.

Cross didn't need to call John Bigelow. The President of Bannock Oil was on his laptop screen within seconds of the terrorist webcast ending. "Did you see that? They blew Rod

Barth away! One of our most senior employees! For God's sake, Cross, how could you let a thing like this happen?"

"The attack was mounted using Angolan Air Force helicopters," Cross replied, determined to ignore the eagerness with which Bigelow was rushing to put the blame on him. "I could not fire on them without risking a major international incident."

"But that's impossible! You just heard the guy. They want freedom for Cabinda, from Angola."

"I know, sir. But the fact remains, those are Angolan aircraft with their markings painted over. So either someone's hijacked them—"

"We'd have heard about that if they had," Bigelow interrupted.

"I agree. So either they've been bought by someone, but again, why would Angola sell to rebels? Or they've been obtained by other means, such as bribery. Or someone in the Angolan regime is in league with the rebels. With the money there is to be made in Cabinda, anything's possible."

"So now what are we going to do?"

"Well, the best people to sort this out are the U.S. military. So we need to get on to the Pentagon, immediately, and find out what assets they have anywhere near here. But they'd better be bloody close. The next shooting's due in less than three minutes."

"Leave this to me," Bigelow said, and the screen went dead.

Cross got out his iPhone and wrote a text: "CP now." He sent it to the O'Quinns and Donnie McGrain. Less than sixty seconds later all three were in the room. "We need to start putting an operation together," Cross said. But before he could elaborate Imbiss was saying, "They're back online."

Beats Boy, as Cross now thought of him, repeated his demands. Then he killed another man, in a blue boiler suit this time. Then he said, "Five minutes."

There was a ringing from Cross's laptop: another Skype call from Bigelow, but this time he was sharing the screen with the image of a uniformed man sitting at a desk with a Stars and

Stripes just visible behind him. "Heck, this is Vice Admiral Theo Scholz of the U.S. Fleet Forces Command, he's going to put you in the picture."

"Good evening, Mr. Cross, let me get right to it. I'm afraid I've got nothing but bad news for you. We have forces currently deployed in the North Atlantic, Caribbean and South Atlantic; also the Eastern Mediterranean, Red Sea; but there aren't any surface vessels closer than four days from your current position and a sub would be no damn use to you. The best option would be SEALs. We currently have units in Bahrain, as well as right here in Little Creek. The problem is getting them to you. We have no forward air bases in West Africa. We can try to persuade the Angolans to help us, but even then . . . God, it's a logistical nightmare, you're looking at twelve hours at absolute minimum, probably twenty-four. I guess what I'm saying is—"

"We're on our own."

"Sure looks like it."

"Is there anything the President can do?"

Bigelow butted in. "You must know, Heck, the President of the United States does not negotiate with terrorists."

"Yes, I understand that," Cross replied. "But the most powerful man in the world doesn't sit on his arse doing nothing while a bunch of gunmen led by a murdering psycho who doesn't look old enough to shave kill the American workers of an American corporation. Not if he wants to get re-elected. So maybe someone can think of a way that he can do something, or say something that can stop—"

A shot rang out from Imbiss's screen. Bigelow and Scholz must have been watching, too, because they both looked horrified at what they had just witnessed.

"It was a woman this time, Heck," Imbiss said.

"You've got to do something, Cross, before they kill them all," Bigelow insisted.

Scholz shook his head in despair. "This is terrible, just terrible. Good luck, Mr. Cross. And may God be with you."

"Right, first things first," Cross said as his key people formed a circle around him. "We have to get aboard that rig, despite the fact that we've never climbed it in the daytime, let alone at night, and we've never swum in rough seas or darkness, either. So, Donnie, how many of our people would you trust to jump off a patrol boat, swim a couple of hundred meters to that rig and arrive at the right place in one piece?"

"Mah lot for sure," McGrain replied, "and youse lot probably. No offense, Mrs. O'Quinn, I'm worried about you, being a wee scrap of a lassie in conditions like that, but I'm too bloody scared of what you'd do if I said no."

"You should be," said Nastiya.

"What about the rest of them?" Cross asked.

McGrain shook his head ruefully. "Not many, if I'm being honest. See, you can forget about two hundred meters. If you want to approach unobserved, you'll want to be four hundred away from the platform, minimum. If the boats just make a slow pass, lights off and nae stopping, maybe you can get everyone in the water without being spotted. But any closer than that ye've got nae chance."

"Four hundred meters is too far," Cross said. "In these seas it could take ten or twelve minutes to swim it, even with the wind and waves behind us, and that'll leave another two, maybe three hostages dead. No . . . the platform lights up the sea all around it. The boats will go in as close as they can to the edge of that pool of light and we'll go in from there. So, Donnie, there's you and your SBS lads, and me and my lot. Who are the best of the rest?"

"The two lads who got their swimmer-canoeist badges—Flowers and King—for sure. There's Schottenheimer who was a Navy SEAL. Of the others, you can only count on three: Keene,

278

Thompson and Donovan. I can't guarantee they'll make it, but they've more chance than the rest of them."

"Good, then we'll go into the water in pairs, connected by buddy lines. I'm not having anyone floating off into the wilds of the Atlantic. Donnie, you and me go first. How much time do you need to climb up to the spider deck and drop a line back down for the others to go up?"

"Ah'm no' bothering climbing, sir."

"I'm sorry?"

"Well, the way Ah see it, there's no way any of them terrorists have had the time to start booby-trapping ladders and gantries way down by the water-line. Am Ah right?"

"I've not seen any sign of that," Imbiss agreed.

"On the other hand, the risk of someone getting killed or washed away into the wild blue yonder if we try any fancy stuff, rigging lines and playing at Spiderman, is somewhere between high and a bloody certainty. So Ah say, go up the rig's ladders right up to the final ascent on to the main deck. At that point, yeah, mebbes we can be a wee bit more discreet."

"Are you willing to be first up the ladder?" Cross asked.

"I'd be a bloody hypocrite if I wasn't. So aye, Ah'll put my money where my mouth is."

"How long will you need to get up to the spider deck and check that the way up is safe?"

"Three minutes, max. And one more thing . . . You need tae make sure there's always one of my lads at the bottom of the ladder. There's nae way yon beginners'll get up on to it without someone to catch the wee buggers and pull them up."

"Good point," Cross agreed. "So, we're looking at a three-minute delay after the first pair. After that, we need three groups of four people—that's two pairs at a time—each group two minutes apart. I'll select and task each group at the briefing. And before anyone asks, yes, I know that four of us from London, five of Donnie's SBS people and six of our Cross Bow

279

guys makes a total of fifteen people, and I've just counted out fourteen swimmers, but Dave, I need you here. It's no reflection whatever on your fighting abilities. You don't need to prove them to me. But I need you to work your magic on that keyboard over there. Can you get into the rig's CCTV system?"

"If it's controlled by a computer that's linked to the internet, absolutely," Imbiss agreed.

"Good. Then get inside that computer, mess with the cameras. I don't know if any of the bad guys are watching the monitors, but if they are, I don't want them seeing anything that looks remotely like us lot getting on to the platform and walking around it. But get us the real feed. I need to know where the terrorists are and what they're up to."

Imbiss nodded: "OK, that should be doable. What else?"

"Just monitor all the comms in and out of the platform. If they get instructions from whoever's behind all this; or they make any new demands; or they start killing more people, or fewer, I want to know. And if it ever gets critical and you get the feeling something big's about to happen, I need to know that too."

"How do you want to communicate?" Imbiss asked.

"We'll use the earpieces. We don't have enough for everyone, but we'll divvy them up so that there's at least one per pair."

"And if, by some blessed miracle, we actually swim as far as that bloody great beast of a platform, and climb up the bloody thing, and get to the top without so much as a scratch: what then?" asked Paddy O'Quinn.

"Then all the hours we spent in London planning how to recapture an oil rig from a bunch of hooligans won't have been wasted. McGrain, summon everyone, boat crews included, to the briefing room, on the double. The briefing starts in two minutes and anyone who isn't there when I start talking is going to regret it," Hector replied.

"Yes, sir."

280

"Paddy, give him a hand rounding up the troops," Cross continued. "Dave, I need you to get the CCTV feed from the canteen so we can see what's going on there, and find Sharman while you're at it."

A grainy, monochrome image of the canteen appeared on-screen showing two of terrorists who'd helped kill Rod Barth cradling AK-47s. They had taken up a position by the door and the kid in the headphones was standing in front of them with a big grin on his face. Then Imbiss panned the camera and Cross could see what had cause the little bastard's amusement. A terrorist was dragging a screaming woman through the crowd, accompanied by a mate who was using the club of his AK to beat anyone who tried to obstruct them.

"That's five terrorists so far, but there may be more where the camera can't see them," Imbiss said. "As for hostages, I reckon there's at least seventy. Could be more of them, too. Now, where's Sharman . . . ?"

The camera panned to and fro before Imbiss muttered, "Gotcha!" and zoomed in on one section of the canteen.

Cross saw Sharman's face come into focus and said, "Sharman! This is Cross. I can see you on the security camera. Nod if you can hear me."

Sharman nodded.

"Good," Cross went on. "We count five terrorists. Is that correct?"

There was a shake of the head.

"So there are more. How many more?"

Sharman raised his right hand up to his face and gazed intently as if inspecting his fingernails. His thumb, however, was bent and holding down his little finger. So there were three fingers showing.

"I make that three more men making eight in total. Correct?"

Another nod.

That makes sense, Cross thought. *Headphones has got well over half the platform crew in one place so he needs enough men to be sure he can pacify them.*

"Good work, Sharman," he said. "Hang tight, we're coming to get you."

Sharman gave a discreet thumbs-up.

"Any sign of the other terrorists?" Cross asked.

"I've got one guarding the helipad," Imbiss told him. "I saw some heading toward the derrick, but for some reason the feed is really poor from the production side of the platform and the image keeps breaking up, so I can't see what they're doing. Other than that, I'm getting flashes of guys walking down passages in the general accommodation area."

"I imagine they're rounding people up."

"Well, if they are, they're killing them there and then because I'm not seeing any more people being taken up to the canteen."

"OK, keep me posted if there are any developments. I've got to get this mission under way." Cross left the command post, walked into the briefing room, saw that everyone was there and got straight down to business. He tasked the various members of his team to deal with the helipad, the production area, the residential and administrative block and the canteen where the bulk of the platform's staff were being held hostage. Then he described how he hoped to get into the canteen and take out the terrorists who controlled it while limiting the danger to the hostages. It took less than five minutes—enough for another hostage to lose their life, as he was painfully aware—but by the end of it everyone knew exactly what was required of them. He wrapped it up with an order to the boat crews to get their boats in the water faster than they'd ever done before, and weather conditions be damned.

"I don't care if there's a storm out there. There are people dying on that platform and we are the only hope of saving them. So get that boat in the water, pronto, or I'll kick you in myself and you can swim all the way to the rig!"

* * *

Té-Bo was enjoying himself. Exactly as Commander Matemba and Monsieur Tumbo had predicted, the entire Magna Grande installation was helpless. No one had come to its rescue, and the only signs of resistance had come from a few of the oil workers who had tried to use hammers and wrenches against men armed with AK-47s. That resistance had not lasted long. Some of the shots had sparked small fires, but the rig's automatic sprinkler systems had dealt with them. That was good. The rig would be destroyed, but not while Té-Bo and his men were still on it.

His phone started ringing. It was one of his men, Yaya Bokassa, who'd been sent to the control room to monitor what was happening on the platform. "The screens have all gone dead!" he told Té-Bo. "I can't see what is happening anywhere."

"Sabotage!" announced Té-Bo dramatically. "Someone must have cut a wire, or smashed the cameras."

"Impossible! We have accounted for all the personnel on the rig. And how could they kill all the cameras at once? There must be a malfunction in the system."

"Then make it work again!"

"I don't know how. I need help."

Té-Bo gave a disgusted "Pah!"; he stopped the call and turned to face the hostages. "*Écoutez!* Listen to me!" he called out. "I require any man who knows how works the control room to announce himself now. If you do not, I will kill two of you, right now. You have ten seconds, or I commence to shoot."

Té-Bo began counting down. He had reached "two" when a man called out, "I'm the control room manager. I'll tell you what you need to know. Just, please, don't shoot."

"*Très bien,*" Té-Bo said as the man stepped forward, hands above his head. He spat out a series of quickfire orders in French to one of the terrorists and then asked the man in front of him, "What is your name?"

"Herschel Van Dijk," he replied in a strong Afrikaaner accent.

"So, you say you can operate the control room. Very good. It does not function correctly. So you will make it function. If you do not do this, you will die."

Té-Bo issued more orders to his man and Herschel was led away toward the control room.

It was a minor setback, but overall Té-Bo was still perfectly content. Everything was going according to plan. He looked at the stopwatch function on his phone. It showed four minutes and fifteen seconds. Time to find another hostage to kill.

Cross took the two patrol boats on a course upwind of the platform, pushing the boats right to the very edge of the lightpool, allowing just enough leeway that they'd still be hard to spot if the pilot of the airborne helicopter happened to be looking in their direction. Every member of the team was armed with a long-barreled Ruger. Many had pouches carrying additional, specialist gear. Two of the SBS men, swimming in the same group as Nastiya, were going in as a pair, one of whom had an additional line attached to his waist, next to his buddy line. The far end of the line was clipped to a canister about a meter long. The last thing Cross did before he went in was to tell him, "Whatever you do, look after that thing. If it doesn't get on to the rig in one piece, we might as well just jump back into the water and swim home."

"Don't worry, boss, you'll have it."

"Good. Right, Donnie, time we went in for our evening dip."

On the *Glenallen* Cross had talked about swimming to the platform. Once he was actually in the water it was more a matter of frantically trying to produce something remotely close to a freestyle stroke as the waves picked him up, swept him forward and then plunged him into a churning, foaming vortex. Time after time he struggled back up to the surface, gasped for breath and then started thrashing his arms and legs again, feeling the tug of the line that linked him to the much faster, more experienced McGrain.

To make matters worse, the drysuit, sealed at his wrists and ankles and specifically designed to keep moisture coming in or out, was turning into his own private sauna, trapping all the heat generated by his exertions. Not a drop of seawater had penetrated the suit and yet Cross was soaking wet in his own sweat as his temperature rose. Now he understood something all SBS and SEALs had long known: that heatstroke is as great a danger to a combat swimmer as the sea itself. Cross and all his people were in a race against time to get on to the platform before their body heat got to them.

All the while, the gargantuan bulk of the Magna Grande platform loomed ever more imposingly above them and Cross felt smaller and smaller as the sheer scale of what he had to master became ever more apparent. The massive legs with their side supports looked like an immobile, unyielding quartet of steel cliffs, waiting with cruel indifference for the sea to dash the raggle-taggle band of feeble, struggling humans against them. The waves crashing against the legs were forming eddies and rip currents between them and the ocean was propelling Cross directly into the maelstrom so that he faced a choice between being flattened against a leg like a bug on a windscreen, or being drowned as he was sucked down into the hungry sea.

He thanked heavens for McGrain up ahead of him. "Och, it's no' so bad, sir," the Scotsman had said as the leading patrol boat had manoeuvred into position. "Compared to a bad night on the North Sea this is a bloody millpond."

Now they were close enough that even with the rain and spray battering his eyes, Cross could make out the rusty ladder running down one of the legs that McGrain was aiming for. He saw the SBS veteran turn his head back toward him, though his eyes were focused on something beyond them both. Cross turned, too, to check what McGrain was looking at, and then his blood, so recently close to boiling, seemed to chill to ice in his veins.

A wave was coming toward them. It was higher by far than any they had yet encountered. It was a black wall of water, glinting with the reflected lights from the rig and it seemed as solid as the platform itself; it rose above Cross like a great jackboot, ready to stamp down upon him.

On and on it came, encircling and enfolding Cross. He seemed to be in a long tunnel, whose sides were all water. Then the sides of the tunnel began to collapse as the wave broke and all Cross could do was take one last breath, and pray.

Oohhh, shit!" Donnie McGrain had seen plenty of waves, but never one like this. Where the hell had it come from? It was as if every other wave had been a Transit van and this one was a Chieftain tank. He put his head down, thrust his arms forward in a racing freestyle stroke and kicked hard, ignoring his heaving lungs and aching muscles as he dragged one last burst of speed out of his body. He did not have to look; he could sense the weight of the water arcing over him as he raced the wave to the rig.

The ladder was just a few meters in front of him now. It seemed to be taunting his pleading fingers as he stretched out his right arm and fell just short.

Now he could feel the undertow dragging at him as the wave drew itself up to break with all its might against the human structure that had the impudence to resist its journey across the ocean.

McGrain's left arm wheeled over his body, reached for the ladder . . . and though his fingertips brushed the metal he could not make them stick.

He kicked again as the crest of the wave hit the leg high above him, made one last, desperate lunge and felt his fist clench around a rung as the water flung him against the ladder, knocking the breath from his lungs. Sensing rather than seeing Cross being hurled at the face of the leg, just a couple of meters away from him, McGrain gasped for air and then the weight of the seven seas seemed to fall on him as the wave plunged down, tore him from the ladder and sucked him deep into its grasp.

It wasn't just his own descent that was the problem. McGrain had Cross's weight dragging him down too and he knew that a first-timer, even one as proficient in so many other military disciplines, was bound to feel disoriented when he was plunged under water at night. If Cross started swimming deeper rather than heading for the surface he would drown them both.

But then McGrain felt the line go slack beneath him. For an instant he wondered if Cross had cut the line, not wanting to drag them both down. He was the kind of man who'd do something that insanely self-sacrificial. But then McGrain saw a patch of even deeper, more Stygian black against the gloom of the water, thought: *The pontoon!* and smashed into raw steel for a second time. He tugged on the line and felt an answering tug back. So Cross was conscious. McGrain yanked the line again, this time pulling upward. He prayed that Cross had got the hint, steadied himself against the pontoon, squatted and then thrust upward. Cross came with him and McGrain started kicking for the surface.

He was out of breath and they were still at least ten, probably more like twenty meters below the surface. McGrain ignored the pain in his lungs and fought the screaming voices in his head tempting him to breathe out, expel all the stale gas from his body and suck clean, fresh air back in.

But there was no air, just water. To breathe in was to drown and die. He had to make do with what he had . . . but he so, so wanted to breathe out.

McGrain kicked again and sensed Cross doing the same thing as the line slackened once again. McGrain could feel his oxygen-deprived brain start fizzing like an untuned TV screen.

Blissful, painless unconsciousness was just a moment away. Now it was not his swimming training that he drew upon, but the brutal lessons he had been taught about resisting the pain of torture, blanking out the agony, ignoring all your deepest instincts.

He kicked again, and again, and again, lost in a black, sunless universe in which there was nothing but hurt, and water, and kicking . . . and suddenly his head burst out of the water into the open air and now he could open his mouth and drag the salty air deep down into his starving lungs. He trod water, looked around and saw Cross, behind him, doing the same thing, and beyond him was the ladder, just stuck there imperturbably on the side of the leg as if saying, "Well, where the hell have you been?"

The sea seemed a little calmer now and McGrain had little difficulty grabbing hold of it, climbing a few rungs and helping Cross up after him. "Right," he said, "let's get to the top of this bastard rig."

There was no sign of any hostiles on the spider deck, or any evidence that they had been there. The platform was rectangular in shape and at each end of the long sides there were metal stairways, enclosed in protective steel mesh but otherwise open to the elements, that zig-zagged up the outer sides of the platform. They rose past three lower decks to the main deck itself. The accommodation and administration block stood at one end of the main deck, with the helideck perched on its roof. The various processing functions of the production block were at the other end of the deck, as far away from the living quarters as possible, with the derrick towering up above the platform in-between. Once he was out of the water, Cross had put in his earpiece and was now receiving information from Dave Imbiss once again.

"We've lost another two hostages," Imbiss told him. "Hostiles are still distributed as before: most in the canteen and accommodation areas, some by the derrick—I think they're down near the turntable, right by the drill-string, though the signal's still breaking up. Doesn't look like anyone's expecting company. The hostile by the helipad is the only lookout but he's not the outdoors type—he's spent most of the time trying to get out of the weather. I suggest taking him out first, just in case he starts doing his job."

"Copy that," said Cross. "What about the crews of the Hinds—can they see anything?"

"Doubt it. The ones on the pad won't have a line of sight from their cockpit to anything happening beneath them. As for the bird in the air, if anyone's hanging out the side door, looking down, they could see people moving on open decks, maybe. But the visibility's lousy, so it would be really hard to distinguish us from their buddies and unless these guys are trained air-sea rescue personnel, which I seriously doubt, I don't see them wanting to stick their heads outside the cabin in a storm like this."

"Understood. Any indication of anyone placing IEDs?"

"Not that I can see, but that doesn't mean they're not there."

On one level Cross was pleased by the apparent carelessness of the men who had seized the platform. Their failure to take any of the obvious steps required to hurt anyone mounting a counter-attack had made it much easier for Cross to get his people aboard. But this was very clearly a well-planned and ruthlessly executed operation. So why make such an obvious mistake? And what were the helicopters doing, hanging around when—as he had every intention of demonstrating—they could easily be destroyed? It was plain that whoever had planned this attack had never had any intention of letting it play out for very long. In fact, it had every appearance of being a suicide mission. But to what purpose? Was it just a case of killing as many oil workers as possible and making a mess of the platform? Or was there something else?

That was a question for later. Cross had to focus all his

attention on the here and now. O'Quinn and Thompson had been tasked with securing the helideck. One swift movement of Cross's hand was all the signal they needed to get on their way.

Now the other teams took up their positions at the bottom of their respective stairwells. McGrain was on the far side of the spider deck, ready to lead his team up toward the derrick to take out the hostiles there. Cross and his three men were heading for the accommodation block, with the aim of clearing a route to the canteen. Once there, Cross had to achieve the safe rescue of the hostages and destruction of the hostiles who were holding them. All the men were under orders to minimize the use of ammunition by shooting to kill at extreme close range, with minimum risk to the hostages or the safety of the platform itself. But in order to fulfil those orders, they had to get into the canteen, prevent the hostiles opening fire and simply gunning all their captives down and find a way to get close enough to men armed with AK-47 assault rifles to be able to kill them at point-blank range.

No sane commander would ever sanction such a wildly improbable set of objectives unless he had absolutely no alternative. That was, however, the situation in which Cross found himself. He had one very slender chance of making his plan work. And for that, he was counting on Nastiya.

Paddy O'Quinn was standing behind the stern of an orange lifeboat that was positioned at the top of a slide from which it could be launched into the sea. Dave Imbiss had guided him to that vantage point, barely thirty feet from the foot of the ladder that led up to the helideck. The sentry was huddled beneath the overhang of the deck itself. He didn't look like much of a hostile, more like a scrawny kid who'd got the job no one else wanted and was now as miserable as countless sentries through the ages who've been sent outside to keep watch on wet and windy nights. The lookout was such a pathetic sight that O'Quinn felt genuinely sorry for him, but that did not alter the fact that he represented a potential danger to the mission. And so, resting the long brushed-steel barrel of his Ruger against the hull of the lifeboat, O'Quinn fired twice, secure in the knowledge that there was no way anyone in the helicopter that stood on the helideck with its engine idling could possibly have heard the shots even if the Ruger had not possessed its inbuilt suppressor. O'Quinn had aimed for the kid's heart. Both rounds hit him in the center of the chest and as his body crumpled to the ground, Thompson dashed from his own position, even closer to the helideck, picked the corpse up and pulled it deeper into the shadows.

Making sure to remain under cover, O'Quinn made his way to where Thompson was standing. They were now just a few feet from the bottom of the ladder. Soon they would both be dashing up it, but not yet.

O'Quinn switched on his comms. "Hostile down. Repeat, hostile down. The way is clear. Over."

"Message received and I'll pass it on. Good work," Imbiss replied.

A second later Cross was informed that O'Quinn had dealt with the lookout. Now the other three teams could start making their ways up through the platform and the rescue mission could begin.

There were countless danger spots aboard the Magna Grande rig, but high on the list was the wellhead where the oil being pumped up from hundreds of meters beneath the seabed finally came aboard. So that was one of the key targets for any anti-terrorist mission and McGrain, being the man in the team with the most experience on offshore platforms, was given the job of securing that area, and the drillers' cabin, from which the entire drilling operation was controlled. His team of three other men included Terry Flowers, a Royal Marines veteran who'd qualified as a Class One Ammunition Technician and was thus trained, among many other things, to disable any booby traps or explosive devices that the insurgents might have left along the way. The quartet walked slowly toward their target area, looking like a group of World War I soldiers who'd been blinded by gas. McGrain was in front, with his head down, sweeping a torch from side to side, with Flowers walking behind him, his eyes focused on the beam from the torch. Flowers had one hand on McGrain's shoulder, ready to squeeze hard if the torch lit up anything that might be a trip wire or pressure-plates that could trigger a blast. The other two shuffled along behind, but their attention was concentrated on what was going on around them as they looked for any sign of the terrorists themselves.

They'd stopped three times, all for false alarms, by the time they came to the base of the derrick. McGrain stopped and held up his hand, halting his little column. Then he gave another quick series of hand signals that sent the men fanning out around him: Flowers to his left, the other two to the right. At the bottom of the derrick was an open working area, like a clearing at the heart of a steel forest, where pipes and girders took the place of trees. The drillers' room was some twenty feet or so above them, overlooking the whole area, and at the center of this clearing rose the drill pipe itself: the heart and purpose of the platform.

Two hostiles were crouched at the base of the pipe. They were placing blocks of C4 explosive beside it. And if those blocks should ever go off and turn a pipe filled with oil into a gigantic flamethrower then, as Donnie McGrain knew only too well, you could kiss the rig and everyone on it goodbye.

Herschel Van Dijk had spent no more than three minutes in the main control room before he worked out what the matter was with the platform's CCTV system: someone had hacked it. The feed to the control room had been cut off, but he'd bet his last buck someone out there was watching what was going on. He looked up at the terrorist who was glaring at him with a look of deep suspicion and mistrust right across his face and cradling his AK-47 in a way that suggested he wouldn't need much of an excuse to use it. *Wasn't your lot, was it, you bloodthirsty bastard? Too busy killing my brus. So who was it then, eh?*

There were no more than three or four men on board who had anything approaching the skills required to do a job like this. Van Dijk was one of them and the others were currently stuck in the canteen waiting their turn to die. That meant it was someone on the outside, and the very obvious reason why they'd done it was to help them get on the rig and move about it unobserved. So help was coming and now his continued existence on the planet depended on his ability to string his captors along for long enough that the guys in the white hats had time to get aboard and save the day.

He spent another couple of minutes scrolling rams of code across his screen, opening different files and generally trying to look like a man getting to the very depths of the problem. Somewhere off in the direction of the canteen he heard a burst of gunfire: that was another one of his workmates killed. Van Dijk kept the charade going for a little bit longer and then looked at the terrorist. "*Você fala português?*" he asked.

The man looked at him blankly.

Well, if you can't make out a word of Portuguese, you're not from Angola, Van Dijk thought. *So what the bloody hell are you doing on a rig in Angolan waters?*

He was pretty certain he'd heard the terrs' leader using French words, which meant that these men could come from any number of French-speaking African nations, from Morocco to Madagascar. So the next statement he made was in Swahili, the Bantu language that is the closest thing to a common tongue across a great swathe of Africa: "*Mimi haja ya kuzungumza na bosi wako—hivi sasa!*" or "I want to speak to your boss—now!"

293

"*Kwa nini?*" the terrorist replied: "Why?"

So now Van Dijk knew one thing about the men who'd attacked the rig: they came from a part of Africa where both French and Swahili were spoken, and that could only be the eastern half of the DRC. So they weren't Angolan, they were Congolese, and so, once again: what the hell were they doing here?

Staying in Swahili, Van Dijk said, "Tell him the reason the cameras aren't working is that the computer that controls them has crashed. Do you understand that, boy?"

The terrorist's liquid brown eyes narrowed. "Yes, I know what a computer is, *musungu.*"

Van Dijk grinned. When the first white explorers had arrived in East Africa, the local tribes saw these strange men walking across their lands, not knowing where they were going, and called them "*mzungu,*" which means "aimless wanderer." Since then the term had come to mean "white man' and was used, with regional variations, by tens of millions of Swahili speakers.

"Glad we understand each other, then," he said.

The terrorist was about to reach for his phone, but then he realized he had a problem: he couldn't make a call and point a gun at the same time. He frowned, trying to work out how to solve the problem. Van Dijk had to turn back to the computer so that he didn't laugh in the man's face. He'd provoked him enough already; any more and there could be trouble. He started tapping away at the keyboard, looking as if he was doing something to fix the system, while actually typing complete gibberish.

Van Dijk heard a noise behind him, no louder than a knock on the door.

A second later the terrorist's head and shoulders slammed down on the edge of the U-shaped desk at which Van Dijk was sitting, and lay there, gazing up at him through sightless, wide-open eyes. There was a small red hole at the back of his head.

Van Dijk spun around on his chair. A tall, broad-shouldered

man in a black drysuit was standing there. He had a scar over one eye and a nose that was either born crooked, or made that way by someone else's fist. In his right hand he was holding a stainless-steel pistol with a weirdly long barrel, while his left index finger was raised to his lips: "Ssshhh . . ."

Imbiss had told Cross to expect one hostile and one member of the rig's crew in the control room and that's exactly what he'd found. Better yet, the oilman had reacted with admirable cool to seeing a corpse hit the desk about two feet from where he was sitting. Keeping his voice low, Cross glanced at the dead terrorist and asked, "Any more of them around?"

"Not here," Van Dijk replied.

Cross nodded an acknowledgement and then got on the comms to Imbiss. "Control room cleared, one hostile down. Thanks for the steer, Dave. What's the score so far, over?"

"One hostile at the helipad. Paddy's waiting for the go-signal. Two by the wellhead, McGrain says they're laying a charge. Signal's intermittent but I think there are two more in the driller's room, and I count another pair in the galley. There's one more standing guard outside the canteen, seven inside. Add the one you've just taken out, I make that sixteen, which is all of them."

"Right, I'll take my lads up to the canteen. We'll deal with the sentry. Then we'll await your go-signal. Keep me updated with any developments. Over."

Cross turned his attention back to the man at the control desk. "It's about to kick off," he said. "So stay here and keep your head down."

"Wait," said Van Dijk. "What are you: white Zims? Kenyan? I hear Africa in your voice."

Cross didn't have time for expatriate chit-chat. "I was born in Kenya. What of it?" he asked impatiently.

"Because you'll get what I'm about to say. My Bantu friend here didn't understand a word of Portuguese, but he spoke

Swahili. And his boss kept breaking into French. See what I'm getting at?"

It took a second for Cross to focus on something other than the next stage in the anti-terrorist operation and follow what the man was saying. "So they're not Angolan or Cabindan . . ."

"*Ja* . . . and . . . ?"

"They're Congolese. French and Swahili, they have to be."

"Correct. And what are a bunch of pekkies from the Congo doing on this rig, eh? That's what I want to know."

Good question, thought Cross. He grunted once more, then said, "Thanks," as he turned for the door. There would be a time when that piece of information and the question it provoked might come in very handy. But now was not that time. Now it did not matter where the terrorists came from, only that they were taken out. The other three men in his squad had been checking out the offices and meeting rooms in the vicinity of the control center. None of them had found any hostiles, but they reported several bodies of dead crew members. Cross could see the discoveries had only made his men more angry than they already were. "Stay cool," he said. "Keep your emotions under control. Right, now we deal with the canteen."

Nastiya was leading a four-person squad, tasked with securing the galley area adjacent to the canteen. Imbiss had warned her to expect at least two hostiles. Her men comprised Lee Donovan, an ex-Para who was one of the two non-specialists McGrain had reckoned was ready for the swim, and two SBS veterans: Halsey and Moran. They were making their way down the passageway that led to the galley, with Donovan on point, Nastiya behind him and the two SBS men bringing up the rear. Halsey had pulled the canister on the swim to the rig. Now he had its contents on his back, two metal cylinders that made him look like a scuba diver. He had been positioned third in line, the safest place to be, but not because anyone cared particularly about him: it was the cylinders that mattered.

Suddenly they heard the sound of gunfire and screaming from up ahead. Nastiya picked up speed and ran down the passage and past the swing doors to the galley, coming to a halt with her back against the bulkhead on the far side of the door. Donovan took up a similar station on the other side of the door. Halsey held back, waiting a few meters down the passageway, with Moran standing guard over him and his precious load.

By the doors, Donovan pulled a stun grenade from a pouch. The whole operation had been conducted as silently as possible, but the cacophony inside the galley had rendered that an unnecessary irrelevance. Nastiya counted down with her fingers: three . . . two . . . one. On zero, she pointed at the doors. Donovan stepped up, kicked one door open and threw in the grenade, leaping back out of the way as a burst of firing came from the galley. Half a second later the grenade detonated in an explosion of dazzling light and ear-splitting noise. Nastiya and Donovan barged their shoulders through the swing doors and with both hands gripping their Rugers raised their arms so that they were already in the firing position as they entered the galley.

The move was just a precaution. The flash-bang should have left anyone in the vicinity of the galley entrance dazed and incapable of defending themselves.

But the grenade had rolled up against one side of the open door to one of the four walk-in refrigeration units that ran in a line down the left-hand side of the galley.

Two of the hostiles were on the far side of the fridge door, sheltered from the blast. One of them came out from behind it brandishing his AK-47 and fired a three-round burst that hit Donovan in a diagonal pattern across his chest, hitting his heart and lungs and killing him at once.

Nastiya fired back, but the hostile had darted back behind the fridge door. She aimed two more shots straight at the door.

297

The door was sturdily built with two layers of steel separated by tightly packed insulating material and the lightweight around failed to penetrate it. But Nastiya had anticipated that before she pulled the trigger. She just wanted to keep her enemies' heads down.

Now they had a stalemate. She and the hostiles were less than ten feet apart. If the men came out from behind the fridge, she would kill them. If she exposed herself to their fire, they would kill her.

Nastiya heard a moan coming from inside the walk-in fridge. It was silenced by two gunshots. She glanced around the galley. In front of her stood a cook's station with a steel work surface next to a six-burner hob that was positioned at right angles to the line of fridges. One of the cooks must have been about to prep a tuna when the attack began because the fish was lying on a chopping board, with a cleaver and filleting knife beside it. Nastiya noted the precise position of the two knives, fired another burst of bullets to keep her enemies' heads down, then slung her gun over her shoulder and, as silently as a cat on a fur rug, sprang forward, placing her hands on the work surface and vaulting over it. As she did, her right hand gripped the handle of the cleaver, so that when she hit the floor and turned toward the open fridge she was already lifting her arm and then bringing it down in a throwing motion that sent the cleaver through the air, end over end, right into the throat of one of the hostiles.

His comrade had his back turned to Nastiya and his gun hanging loose by his side as he faced into the fridge. When he saw his comrade go down he turned, and as he did Nastiya sprang forward, picking up the filleting knife in her left hand, transferring it into her right and twisting her body to mirror his turn, so when she reached him she was already behind him and her left hand was over his mouth, pulling his head back so that her newfound knife could fillet his throat.

As the man fell at her feet, Nastiya saw that he had been

holding a smartphone in his hand. The bastard had been filming what he and his pal had been up to. Nastiya muttered a string of contemptuous Russian expletives as she picked the phone up and tucked it away in a pouch, then she cast her eyes over the interior of the walk-in fridge. There were five bodies—all south-east Asian—lying between the shelves filled with provisions, like so many joints of meat. All had been shot multiple times at close range. She checked all the bodies for signs of life, but found none.

Five kitchen staff: that surely wasn't enough to provide three hot meals a day, each with multiple food options, to 120 hungry workers. Nastiya went back out into the galley and opened the next fridge door, ducking as someone hurled a large can of tomatoes at her.

"Stop!" she shouted. "I'm a friend!"

It was not so much her words as the female pitch of her voice and the fact that she was speaking English that registered with the eight cold, shivering, fearful catering staff who emerged from their hiding places behind, and in some cases lying on, the shelves.

"Are there any more of you?" Nastiya asked as they followed her out of the fridge.

"No," one of them said. "Just our friends"—he nodded at the other open door—"in there."

"If you want to be safe you must leave here," she said, leading them back out of the galley and into the passage. She pointed at Moran: "This man will look after you. Stay here and don't move unless he tells you to."

Nastiya waited a moment to make sure that she had been both understood and obeyed, then her voice took on a very different, impersonal tone as she told Imbiss, "Galley secured. Two hostiles killed. One man down, Donovan, killed. Multiple crew fatalities. Eight further crew secured alive and well. Am proceeding as planned. Over."

She heard Imbiss reply, "Message received and understood. Good luck. Out."

Nastiya looked at Halsey and said: "OK, let's go."

She returned to the galley with the SBS man just behind her, passing the carnage by the fridges, and heading into another area filled with bakers' ovens and wheeled metal shelf units stacked with loaves of bread. She stopped in the middle of the floor and looked up at the ceiling, where a steel mesh grill had been inset between two strips of neon light, reached inside the waterproof pouch attached to her drysuit and pulled out a gas mask.

"I'm going to need a leg-up," she said, before pulling the mask over her head.

Halsey stood beneath the grill with his two hands cupped. Nastiya placed her right leg on his hands and was lifted up into the air. She reached up as far as she could and pushed the grill up and out of the way, then gripped one side of the grill with both hands and pulled herself up into the open vent. Halsey helped her on her way, grunting with effort as he raised his hands above his head until Nastiya's shoulders were through the hole, then her hips and finally her entire body had disappeared up into the darkness.

Nastiya had been chosen for this part of the mission because she was the smallest, lightest and most nimble member of the team. But even she had precious little room to move inside the air-conditioning duct, and the gas mask not only impaired the already limited visibility but added to the claustrophobia that came from being in a cramped metal tube. With some difficulty, she manoeuvred herself until she was peering like a goggle-eyed monster from the vent through which she'd just climbed. She lay down on her side and stretched an arm down toward Halsey as he swung one of the cylinders off his back and held it up for her to grab.

There was a handle at the top of the cylinder. Nastiya

wrapped her fingers around it and pulled with all her might. As long as Halsey was giving her a hand from below the task of dragging the cylinder up into the duct was not too tough, but then it was beyond his reach and she was taking the entire weight. "Mother of God, this is heavy!" Nastiya muttered into her gas mask as she hauled the cylinder, inch by inch, up and over the lip of the vent until it landed beside her with a clang of metal upon metal that seemed to echo and reverberate off into the distance.

Nastiya froze. If any of the terrorists, less than twenty meters away in the canteen, had heard that crash and took it into their heads to check out what had caused it the whole mission was done for. She waited, her heart thumping and the sweat of tension and fear prickling her armpits. But the moment passed, there was no sound of any reaction from the canteen and very slowly, doing her utmost to drag the cylinder as quietly as possible, she crawled and slithered into the black embrace of the air-conditioning duct.

There were two vents up ahead, marked by the columns of light that rose from them and acted like beacons to Nastiya. She crawled around the first and went to the furthest one, where she placed the cylinder on its side. It had a short length of hose protruding from its top and Nastiya positioned this right above the vent, with its tip pointing down.

Next she went all the way back to the opening above the galley, where Halsey was still waiting, and repeated the whole painful, nerve-racking procedure, but this time leaving the cylinder by the first of the two vents she had earlier passed. Next to the hose, on the top of the cylinder, there was a flat around tap. Nastiya turned it, scuttled a little further into the depth of the air-conditioning duct and whispered: "Gas on."

"I hear you," Imbiss replied.

Then she crawled on down the duct to the furthest vent and turned the second gas tank on as well.

Then she slumped back against the side of the vent and took a series of slow deep breaths through her gas mask. She was calming her mind, gathering her strength. Not long to go now.

Té-Bo looked at his timer and saw that five minutes were nearly up. Time for another execution and another body to add to the blood-drenched pile that was building up in one corner of the room. A couple of the victims had soiled themselves in fear and the stench of their excrement was adding to the general smell of sweaty bodies crammed into a confined space. Not that Té-Bo was bothered. The slums he had grown up in had stunk far worse and it wouldn't be long now before they'd be on their way. Once the bomb was set beneath the derrick, he would order his men to fire at will into the hostages, killing them all, and then it would just be a matter of getting on to the helicopters and heading back to base.

"*Alors*, it is time!" he called out and then ordered two of his men to seize another victim from the crowd.

By now any thought of resistance seemed to have left the hostages. Té-Bo could see that they were all thinking of nothing other than saving their own skins, somehow staying alive long enough for someone to come to their rescue: *But that someone will never come.*

His men grabbed a white man with very pale skin and thinning red hair. He put up a feeble struggle as he tried to wriggle free of their grasp, but a gun-butt to his kidneys soon knocked the fight out of him. They were dragging the man back to the execution site, where Té-Bo was checking that his gun was still in perfect working order, when a man's voice rang out from the back of the room.

"Take me!" he said. "I know that man: he has a wife and children. I don't. I've got no one depending on me. Take me!"

Té-Bo laughed. "You are in luck, *m'sieur*," he said to the redheaded man, who had just been shoved down on to his

302

knees and was moaning, "I don't want to die, I don't want to die . . ." again and again.

"Take him away," Té-Bo commanded and the man was pulled back on to his feet. Again he resisted, unaware that his life was being saved until he saw the other man walking at a calm, steady pace through the crowd toward their captors. Now the condemned man realized that this newcomer was taking his place and he cried out, "Thank you, thank you! God bless you," before he was shoved back into the crowd.

Come on, Cross, get your bloody arse in gear! Sharman thought as he walked through the disbelieving crowd of hostages to the terrorists waiting to kill him. Their leader had a big grin on his face, clearly loving the idea that anyone would be so stupid as to volunteer for their own execution. His mates were poking each other with their elbows, grinning all over their faces, enjoying the show—all except for one, who was filming the whole episode, adding extra entertainment to the live snuff movie being uploaded for the whole world to see.

But dying was not part of Sharman's plan. He had positioned himself beneath one of the air-conditioning vents and heard the noise of someone moving in the duct above him, followed by the faint hissing of gas and the sweet smell that Imbiss had warned him to expect. He'd also found himself feeling a little lightheaded, even spacey. But his mind was still working clearly enough to know what he was doing. He was taking his time as he approached the small group of armed men, looking around him, spotting the first yawn here, a woman shaking her head as if trying to clear it over there. But there was no sign of anything happening to the terrorists just yet. They still looked full of beans. No . . . wait. One of them had just rubbed a hand across his face and another was blinking with slow, heavy eyelids. But the hands that now took hold of him were full of energy and strength and the terrorist leader with his big Beats headphones was bright-eyed as he shouted at the camera: "Are you watching, *Monsieur le Président*? Do you doubt the will of the Cabindan people? Do you think we are cowards or old women who collapse at the sight of blood? No, we are not! We are men and we will kill and kill again. The five minutes have passed and so another . . ." He gave a stifled yawn. ". . . another one must die."

Sharman saw his own killer come toward him with a gun in his hand. He saw the gun being raised. He prayed that he had actually seen a tremor of the barrel as it was raised to his head . . . And then his world went black and he was plunged into absolute nothingness.

Go! Go! Go!" Imbiss shouted into the comms system.

On the ladder just below the lip of the helideck O'Quinn and Thompson unholstered and loaded their Rugers. Then O'Quinn mouthed a single word: "Now!"

The two men sprang up on to the deck and started blazing away at the crew inside the glazed cockpit of the Hind that was sitting there, its rotors idling.

The Hind was armed with a devastating 12.7-mm Yakushev Borzov Gatling gun, with a 1,470-round magazine capable of destroying entire units of infantry. But the magazine was empty, for the very Air Force officers who had accepted bribes to let the two helicopters be taken for the night had refused to sanction the loading of any ammo or rockets, for fear that they might be double-crossed and find the Hinds' weapons being turned on them. So now the crew had no means of firing back.

This need not have mattered. The helicopter's armor was famously tough and well able to withstand small-arms fire. But the windows around the cockpit were made of toughened glass and it takes strong nerves for men to remain calm and immobile while bullets are cracking against windows right by their heads. The pilot did what Cross and O'Quinn had expected he would and powered up his rotors for the speediest possible take-off. He heaved the Hind up into the air, not noticing that his enemy had actually ceased firing, and turned the helicopter away from the platform and out to sea. The pilot of the second Hind, still circling above, saw what his comrade was doing, assumed—with considerable relief—that they were abandoning their passengers to their fate and followed his leader.

They'd cleared the platform by no more than 100 meters when O'Quinn said, "Patrol boat one, fire at will," into his mike.

Two missiles burst out of the darkness beyond the platform where the patrol boats were lurking, screamed across the sky and hit the Hinds beside their exhaust outlets. The helicopters exploded and burning wreckage fell through the rain to the foaming waters of the Atlantic.

O'Quinn spoke again: "Both birds down. The hostiles are now trapped on the platform. I say again, the hostiles are trapped." Then he turned to Thompson and said, "Right, let's see if Cross needs a helping hand."

McGrain had sent two of his men up toward the drillers' room. Any hostiles looking through its glass-fronted façade would have a clear line of sight, and thus of fire, down on to the area beneath the derrick where the hostiles had almost finished arming their bomb. So they had to be dealt with.

The second they heard the go-signal the men kicked in the door of the drillers' room and threw in a flash-bang, praying that its blast would be contained within the room's steel walls. Then they charged in, found two dazed, disoriented hostiles and killed them the old-fashioned way, with wire garrottes that sliced through their windpipes and the carotid arteries and left them bleeding and suffocating to death.

McGrain had intended to do the same to the men by the

turntable, but they saw him and Flowers coming, picked their rifles off the floor beside them and turned to shoot. McGrain had no option but to open fire himself: a few well-aimed rounds from a .22 pistol had far less potential to cause fire or explosion than two magazine-loads of automatic fire from an AK-47 sprayed at a moving target.

The two hostiles went down. Flowers had run straight to the IED. "So, can you disable it?" McGrain asked.

Flowers grinned. "Piece of piss, mate. Absolute piece of piss."

Nastiya turned off the tap on one tank of the sevoflurane anaesthetic that Dr. Rob Noble had supplied to Cross before the team left London and then scrambled along the duct to turn the other one off too. She rolled it away from the vent, kicked the vent open and dropped through it on to one of the canteen dining tables. As she landed, she saw Halsey and Moran burst through the door to the galley, race through the area behind the serving counter and enter the canteen itself.

Then she looked around through her mask and there, at the far end of the room was Cross.

There are times when stun grenades simply won't do the job. They work very well on a few closely grouped people in a confined space, but are much less effective against multiple targets spread around a wider area, such as a large works canteen. One alternative is knockout gas, but that has a less-than-noble history as a means of rescuing hostages. In October 2002, the Russians used the ventilation of the Dubrovka Theater in Moscow to distribute a chemical agent—its identity a secret ever since—that incapacitated around forty armed Chechen rebels and the 850 audience members that they had taken hostage. All the rebels were killed, but 130 hostages also died from adverse reactions to the gas. The Russians had never seen any need to apologize for their actions: better that than have all the hostages killed by the grenades, mines and improvised explosives hanging from their captors' bodies.

Cross accepted that logic, but if he ever used gas, as he feared he might have to on either the platform or the FPSO, he did not want to have to explain why his actions had killed any innocent people at all, let alone a hundred or more.

He'd put his requirements to Rob Noble: "I need a gas and a means of delivering it that will make the bad guys unable to fight without actually taking out any of their victims."

"You do realize that one requirement virtually cancels out the other, don't you?" Noble had replied. "I mean, if you really want to put someone out cold, the thing I'd choose is M99, otherwise known as etorphine. It's an opiate vets use to incapacitate large animals. Where humans are concerned it's a Class A drug, largely because it doesn't just knock people out, it's liable to kill them too. There is an antidote, but it has to be injected, and if you've ever got tens, or even hundreds, of people to worry about, that's a non-starter."

"So what do you suggest?" Cross had asked.

"Sevoflurane. It's an effective anaesthetic, frequently used in surgery, and it's perfectly safe if properly administered. Now, you're hardly going to have a platoon of trained anaesthetists caring for all the people you want to knock out, but you should be all right if you deliver it in modest concentrations and get it out of the air as fast as possible afterward."

"That's a bit tricky. Most ship's portholes and oil-platform windows are sealed shut."

"Well, blow the buggers open, then," said Noble. "I've never known you to be shy of a good, big bang."

So now Cross was charging into the canteen, which looked like the aftermath of a drunken, drugged-up night of debauchery as people sprawled across chairs and tables, or staggered around in slow, befuddled confusion. Ahead of him Cross saw the terrorists' leader, the one he'd labelled Beats Boy, trying to point his gun at Sharman's head. But the weapon seemed to be getting heavier and heavier in the young terrorist's hand and when Sharman slumped to the floor, it was the gas not a bullet that was responsible.

Cross hit Beats Boy with a double-tap. Looking around he saw other hostiles going down, dying in slow motion as the Cross Bow team took them out with cold, practiced precision. He picked up an AK-47 dropped by one of the terrorists and aimed it at a window. This was a far more powerful firearm than his lightweight pistol and it was time to let some air in.

The men who had stormed the rig had all been dealt with. Now the main priority was getting all the hostages out of the canteen before they suffered any side-effects from the sevoflurane, other than feeling very, very sleepy. Cross had gratefully peeled the gas mask from his face and was just telling Paddy O'Quinn to organize a body count of the hostages, rescuers and terrorists when Dave Imbiss came over the comms. "I've got some people here would really like to express their thanks for what you all just did, so I'm putting this out to everyone: go ahead, sir . . ."

"Hi, Hector, this is John Bigelow, I just want to say on behalf of everyone here at Bannock Oil and, I'm sure, of all the loved ones of the folks you and your people rescued today: you did a great job. I always had faith that you would rise to the challenges of working in this offshore environment, but I never dreamed that you would be called upon so soon, to face such a terrible situation."

"Thank you, John, that means a lot to all of us . . ." Cross replied, thinking, *Really? You didn't dream? Not even when I told you, in plain English, exactly what might happen?*

"We're just sorry we couldn't save everyone," Cross added. "But we did all we could and we certainly made sure that the people who attacked this rig paid a very heavy price for their crime."

"We're very glad you did," Bigelow replied. "It sends out a message to anyone who's thinking of assaulting an oil installation that they can expect immediate retribution. Now I'd just like to hand over to someone else who'd like to say a few words."

"This is Vice Admiral Scholz from the Fleet Forces Command of the U.S. Navy. We spoke earlier, if you recall, Mr. Cross."

"Yes, sir, you gave us a very clear picture of our situation," Cross replied.

Scholz laughed uncomfortably. "Which wasn't too good, as I recall."

"No, sir."

"Well, that only underlines the scale of your achievement. What you and your people achieved tonight, recapturing an offshore rig in the most testing weather conditions, with virtually no time to plan your mission . . . I'd say that constitutes a military miracle. If you were a U.S. serviceman, they'd be pinning quite a medal on your chest, and on all the personnel who supported you so valiantly."

"Thank you, sir. We were just doing our jobs to the best of our ability."

"And you should all be very proud of yourselves."

The line from the U.S. went dead, to be replaced by the sound of a dozen ex-soldiers making sarcastic remarks about the sudden stench of corporate and military horse manure.

"I could use some fresh air myself," said Cross and headed out on to the main deck to get it.

Hey, Johnny," said Chico Torres on the bridge of the *Mother Goose*, "you wanna do a countdown? Cause our baby's about to blow—just a few minutes to go now."

Congo laughed. "Yeah, let's be Mission Control, take it right on down to blast-off. So, which way do I look to see the big show?"

"Dead astern. Tell you what, why don't we go down to the bar, fix ourselves a good drink, you know, raise a glass to a job well done."

"Hell, we don't know it was well done," Congo objected.

"Believe me, Johnny. I was there, and it was done just fine. So, like I say, we get a drink, we go out on to the aft deck . . . you don't mind a bit of wind and rain, right? That's where we'll get the best view."

"I gotta tell you, Chico, I don't hold with getting wet, as a rule. But on this particular occasion, I might just make an exception. C'mon, let's go see what they got behind that bar."

The storm had abated and there was only a gentle drizzle falling over the Magna Grande field. Cross and O'Quinn were standing on the main deck of the rig, leaning on a guardrail and looking out over the ocean, straight toward the *Bannock A*, a mile away across the water.

"So, Donovan was the only man we lost," Cross said.

"Yeah, no one else was even wounded."

"He was a good man. Had a wife and a young kid, didn't he? Make sure they're looked after . . . Still, one man in fourteen: I'd have taken those odds an hour ago. How about rig crew?"

"Twenty-nine dead, more than forty wounded, but most of those are no more than bumps and bruises. There are also about a dozen missing, but it looks like a lot of people found places to hide, so it could be a while before they all come out of the woodwork."

"How about the ones with serious injuries?"

"There's seven of them and we're working out the best way of getting them treatment, either on the *Glenallen* or the *Bannock A*. There's a sick bay here, of course, but the medic was one of the hostages who got shot. He was number five."

Cross sighed and shook his head. "We lost too many crew, but I can't think of any way we could have got here sooner, or done a cleaner job."

"Don't even go there, Heck. You heard that admiral fella, you pulled off a military miracle."

"No, if it had been a miracle, I'd have walked on the water to get here."

O'Quinn laughed, but then said, "Seriously, he's right . . . We had no help from anyone, no air support, no proper training on the rig . . ."

"I'll bloody well have words with Bigelow about that. He can count his lucky stars his precious platform didn't go up in smoke."

"Exactly . . . Look, we saved three-quarters of all the people on this rig, and you were the man in charge. Suppose someone had saved three-quarters of all the people in the Twin Towers. Would you bollock him for not getting the other quarter out?"

"Of course not . . ." Cross grimaced. "But you know as well as I do, Paddy, that it only takes one smart-arse journalist or ambulance-chasing lawyer to say we could have done better and suddenly everyone's saying it was a disaster."

"Ach, screw them, what the hell do they know?"

"About the things we have to do?" Cross asked. "Nothing. They couldn't even imagine. And you're right, we did a good job tonight, a bloody good job."

On the *Mother Goose*, Torres and Congo were looking to the east, swigging from bottles of Bud and Cristal respectively. Torres was keeping an eye on the timer displayed on his mobile phone. "OK, baby, here we go," he said. "Ten . . ."

Congo joined in as they both intoned, "Nine . . . eight . . . seven . . . six . . ."

The submersible sled that Torres had towed behind the mini-subs was anchored to a spot directly beneath the stationary hull of the *Bannock A*. On it were approximately 4000 pounds of high explosive, with a sealed, waterproof detonator linked to a timer that was itself co-ordinated precisely with the one on Chico Torres's phone.

And so, at the very second that Torres and Congo counted,

"One . . . blast-off!" the gigantic bomb went off. The force of the shock waves pushing the water away from the epicenter of the blast created a giant air bubble directly under the *Bannock A*. This meant that the 300,000 tons of ship, refinery and oil that had been supported by the water in which it was floating suddenly had nothing beneath it. So the entire weight was suddenly bearing down on a keel that was effectively suspended in mid-air.

And the keel snapped.

From where they were standing, Cross and O'Quinn saw, but could not really comprehend, a series of events that took place in an astonishingly fast sequence.

The *Bannock A*, like the oil platform, was lit up at night like an industrial Las Vegas, topped by the flaming gas coming out of its towering chimney pipe.

Suddenly the lights seemed to rise up into the air.

Then they heard the muffled sound of the underwater explosion.

The dazzling display of lights now plummeted back down as the bubble that had pushed the *Bannock A* skywards collapsed in upon itself, dropping the entire vessel back down into the sea.

There was a second, far greater explosion as the *Bannock A* blew itself apart, a volcanic eruption of flame and smoke, followed immediately by a supersonic shock wave that hit Cross and Quinn and threw them to the steel deck, then the deafening sound of the detonation, and finally a wave as big as the one that had almost drowned Cross hurling itself at the oil platform in a fury of water and spray.

Their ears ringing so that neither could hear what the other was shouting, Cross and O'Quinn picked themselves up and staggered back to the railing. They looked out across the water through scorched retinas and saw nothing but darkness. There were no lights, no flames, nothing.

The *Bannock A* and every living soul upon it had been utterly obliterated.

Cross was stunned, his senses still befuddled by the sheer force of the explosion. He screwed up his eyes and stared as hard as he could, but still there was nothing to be seen except that now he could detect flames dancing on the water, as if the ocean itself was on fire. It took him a few seconds to work out that they were patches of burning oil, floating on the surface.

Cross thought about the people who had been on the ship. Cy Stamford, a colleague who had become a good friend, for whom this was never meant to be anything other than a last, very straightforward command before many well-deserved years of retirement. There was one of his own Cross Bow men on board too and to Cross's shame he could not for the moment recall his name, any more than he knew the names of any of the crew, more than 200 of them, who had gone down with their ship. But then his grief was forgotten as another, even more shocking realization struck him. The attack on the rig that had seemed like such a major event was in fact just a distraction, a feint to lure Cross and his men away from the real attack.

He had been lured to the rig like a River Tay salmon enticed by the fly on his line, and just like the fly, which was in fact a creation of feathers and thread, so he had been fooled by a fake. And he'd fallen for it hook, line and sinker.

The bomb that ripped the *Bannock A* apart set off a firestorm on land as well. Environmentalists were up in arms about the huge amount of oil discharged into the Atlantic when the FPSO went down. Meanwhile, Bannock Oil found itself under concerted attack from a horde of financial speculators, led by Aram Bendick. He made no secret of the money he was making from a crash he had loudly prophesied and was available to any reporter who wanted a quote. "People call me a prophet. Prophet, my ass!" he told one group of reporters outside his

313

Manhattan offices. "John Bigelow and his board were schmucks. They lost their shirts in Alaska, then they doubled-down in Africa and lost their pants as well. I warned them again and again that they were taking grossly irresponsible risks with stockholders' money. After the sinking of the *Noatak* drilling barge off the coast of Alaska, they should have retrenched, cut costs and concentrated on maximizing revenues from their Abu Zara fields. Instead they added to their debts, took a crazy gamble on an unproven field in one of the most dangerous, unstable regions of the world, and this is the result. Bannock is doomed. Its stockholders are going to lose every cent of their investments. This is malfeasance on a criminal scale and I cannot believe that, once the dust has settled, there won't be criminal charges against Bigelow and his senior executives, specifically Hector Cross, the security chief. This happened on his watch, under his nose. He should be held accountable."

Media coverage soon became fixated on the supposed failings of Cross and his team. The recapture of the rig was not reported as the daring rescue of almost 100 crew, but the bungled loss of more than thirty, for two of the seriously injured had died from their wounds. Then a reporter looking on the Bannock Oil website noticed that the two patrol boats were equipped with sonar, and so the question was asked: Why had Cross not ordered an underwater sweep of the area around and beneath the platform and the *Bannock A*? There was an obvious answer: no oil installation of any kind had ever been attacked by submarine before, so why would anyone be worried about that possibility when faced with the reality of terrorists occupying a rig and killing its crew? But that quibble was swiftly brushed aside by a host of self-proclaimed experts, all armed with perfect hindsight and keen to assure their audiences that they would certainly have anticipated an attack by water as well as air and deployed their sonar devices accordingly.

If Cross had hoped to receive some support from his superiors

314

and the military authorities, he was swiftly disappointed. Vice Admiral Scholz, who had been so swift to praise Cross, was suddenly engaged on other matters and too busy to comment.

John Bigelow, meanwhile, appeared before news cameras outside the entrance to Bannock Oil's headquarters, with his Corporate Communications man Tom Nocerino at his side and assured them that, "We fully accept that mistakes were made at the Magna Grande field. As I'm sure you'll appreciate, there's little that anyone here in Houston can do to influence a security operation taking place almost eight thousand miles away, on the other side of the world. So we placed our trust in our people on the ground and I guess they tried their best, but clearly that was not good enough. We will be conducting our own investigation into what went wrong and will of course co-operate with any official inquiry."

Hector Cross was thrown into a battle on completely alien territory. He was a soldier. Faced with a living, breathing enemy, armed with the weapons of war, he knew precisely what to do. But now he had to contend with superiors lying to save their own skins and reporters who had no interest in, let alone understanding of, the actual circumstances. To that was added the threat of ambulance-chasing lawyers wanting to sue him on behalf of those who had died on the rig or the sunken ship, and even district attorneys assembling criminal cases against him. For just as Bendick had suggested, there was no shortage of ambitious prosecutors, with eyes on a political career, who wanted to bring the villain of the Magna Grande disaster to justice.

"My people risked their lives to save the hostages on the oil platform and any Special Forces unit, anywhere in the world, would have been proud to recapture a rig like that with as few casualties," Cross protested when Ronnie Bunter called to discuss his legal situation.

"I know that, Heck, and so does anyone who looks at this with a fair, objective eye. But this is America. People can't accept that sometimes bad things just happen. There has to be a scapegoat and there has to be money on the table."

"Well, then I'd better go to America and state my case, because I'm damned if I'm going to be made a scapegoat by anyone."

"No, you mustn't do that," the veteran lawyer warned him. "In fact, my strong advice to you is to stay out of the country. The moment you set foot on U.S. soil there'll be someone wanting to slap you with a writ or an arrest warrant. Stay in London and get the best lawyer you can find because you're going to need someone to fight the extradition warrant when it comes. The U.K. government signed a crazy deal that allows the U.S. to take any British citizen who's accused of any crime, irrespective of the strength of the case against them, without any of the protection that we demanded and got for our citizens that the Brits want."

"But what crime did I commit, for Chrissakes? I was faced with a situation and I dealt with it. How was I to know that I should have been looking somewhere else? And which part of any of it is criminal?"

"Well, let's see now, give me a moment . . ." Cross sat on his end of the line, waiting while Bunter tapped away at his PC. Then he heard the old man say, "OK, here we go . . . Section 6.03 of the Texas criminal code, dealing with definitions of culpable mental states, deems that a person is criminally negligent when he ought to be aware of a substantial risk, and I quote: 'of such a nature and degree that its disregard constitutes a gross deviation from the standard of care that an ordinary person would exercise under all the circumstances as viewed from the actor's standpoint.'"

"Are you seriously telling me that an ordinary person would watch terrorists landing helicopters on a rig and think: Hmm, I should start looking for submarines?"

"No, Heck, I'm not, but a prosecutor might, and he might find twelve jurors dumb enough to believe him. And it might not be a Texan prosecutor, either. There are plenty of other

316

states with much broader definitions of liability, and I don't know how many states the folks who died came from, but I'm guessing it's quite a few. Any of them could make a case against you on behalf of their people."

Dave Imbiss wanted to go on the media offensive. "Listen, Heck," he said at one of an endless string of meetings in Cross's office. "You don't have to go to the States. We can win the argument from here. I've got the whole thing on tape: every bit of CCTV footage, every communication between me and you guys, and—which is the killer—every single word said between you, John Bigelow and Vice Admiral Scholz, before and after you went on to the rig. Just let me put together a package and release it to the media, or just put it out on social media and we can blow all the accusations away. An American admiral thought you were doing the right thing and wanted to pin a medal on you. No one's going to claim you were reckless or irresponsible when they see that."

But the idea was immediately squashed by Jolyon Capel, a British solicitor Cross had hired on Bunter's personal recommendation: "The man's got the sharpest legal mind I've ever come across, and don't be fooled by his appearance, he's as deadly as a great white shark." Capel certainly did not seem shark-like. He was a small, bespectacled, gray-haired solicitor with the quiet manner, furrowed brow and precise diction of a professor at an ancient Oxford college. And his first advice was not to go storming on to the counter-attack, as Imbiss had suggested, but to do nothing at all.

"I'm very sorry, Mr. Cross, I know this must be very frustrating for you, but you're going to have to hold your fire," Capel said. "The thing you have to bear in mind is that this case will first be fought in a British court and our approach to publicity is very different to the American one, where legal battles are fought as much in the court of public opinon as the court of law. In this country, however, judges are likely to take a very dim view of anything that might constitute an attempt to pervert the course of justice, and media publicity comes high on that list."

"But we aren't in court yet," Cross argued, "so there's no judge to worry about."

"Not yet, no," Capel conceded. "But we have to anticipate the moment when there is. The other issue to bear in mind is that anything you say before a case is a hostage to fortune once the case begins. It gives the other side a target to aim at, so to speak. They know what your argument is going to be and precisely how you are going to support it. If you were fighting a military battle, you wouldn't tell your enemy precisely what forces you had and how you were going to deploy them. Well, the same applies in a legal conflict: you need to retain some element of surprise."

Just to add to Cross's frustrations, Mateus da Cunha was busy denying that he had anything to do with the events at Magna Grande. "It is absolutely correct that the waters in which this appalling tragedy took place will belong to Cabinda when she is a free nation, taking her rightful place in the world. It is also true that I am leading the fight for a free Cabinda. But as I have said, time and time again, I am fighting a political and moral battle; I am not engaged in acts of violence or terrorism. And in this case, I can prove that this was not an action by Cabindan fighters. As the whole world knows, the leader of the attack spoke French. As any French person could tell, his accent was African, probably Congolese. He was certainly not from Cabinda, for there the people speak Portuguese. His so-called political demands were just a fig-leaf for his crime. This was a robbery, a stick-up, not the act of true freedom fighters. I deny absolutely any connection with this event and I express my deepest sympathy for all those who died and all who have been bereaved."

"You lying bastard," Cross muttered as he watched da Cunha's press conference on the BBC *News at Ten*. "You had plenty to do with what happened, you and Johnny Congo, and you bloody well know it."

"Come to bed, you angry old man," said Zhenia, gently teasing him as she stroked his furrowed brow. "Why would you want to watch bad people telling lies on TV when you could be making love to me?"

"Good question," said Cross, looking with something close to wonderment at the beautiful girl who had come so magically into his life. For all the negativity in his life, Zhenia Voronova had retained her faith in him. "Nastiya told me that you were a hero, and I believe her, so I do not care what anyone else thinks," she had told him with simple, almost childlike directness. "Also, I know you, Hector, the way that only a woman who loves a man can know him. You are a good, brave, honest man. That is why I love you." Then she had paused, giggled, given him a look of pure, lusty wickedness, run a fingertip down his chest and purred, "Well, one of the reasons, anyway . . ."

Minute by minute, hour by hour, Jo Stanley saw the life draining out of Bannock Oil. For all the Bunter and Theobald veterans, the various Bannock accounts relating to family members and the trust had been a central part of their professional lives from the moment they joined the firm. Now they were following Bannock Oil's stock price diving downward on their computer screens. There would be audible gasps as one barrier after another was broken and the decline went past 10 . . . 20 . . . 50 . . . even 80 percent.

The whispered conversations behind office doors became ever more desperate. People's bonuses, their salaries, their jobs, even, were dependent on Bannock Oil's continued prosperity, but now its very existence was in doubt.

Tension grew as the original Weiss, Mendoza and Burnett staff, right up to partner level, began to realize that this catastrophe could wreak havoc with their lives too. The three senior partners had gone out on a very long financial limb to raise the very high price—far too high, in the view of many legal bloggers and media pundits—that they'd paid for Bunter and Theobald. Now the only justification for that price was blowing up before their eyes.

Only one man in the whole set-up seemed unperturbed by the corporate and financial implosion taking place before everyone's eyes. Oh, Shelby Weiss did his best to hide it. He maintained a look of anxious concern, suitably overlaid by a somewhat desperate attempt to sustain the morale of junior staff that befitted a partner with his name on the door. But Jo Stanley had taken Ronnie Bunter's orders seriously. She had been watching Weiss with forensic attention to detail for the best part of two months now and, like a poker player mastering an opponent, she had learned to read his tells.

His doodles, for example, tended to be around and even swirly when he was relaxed, but tightened into jagged straight lines when he was anxious or tense. Now here they were, sitting in a partners' meeting, with the chief financial officer describing in painful detail what the effects on annual revenue would be if the Bannock accounts dried up—how many staff would have to be laid off; how they would have to cut costs, not least by moving to cheaper offices in a far less prestigious location—and across the table from where Jo sat, Shelby Weiss was covering one corner of his legal pad with doodles that were positively rococo in their profusion of curves and curlicues.

For a moment she thought there might be an innocent explanation. Weiss interrupted the litany of disaster to say, "Look on the bright side, people. If Bannock Oil goes under, then there are going to be some real pissed beneficiaries of the trust wanting to know who turned the money tap off. And they'll be suing anyone they can find to see if they can somehow get it back on again. We'll be generating more billable hours than ever, just you wait and see."

But his defiant show of optimism was almost immediately countered by his fellow partner Tina Burnett: "Nice try, Shelby, but that dog won't hunt. Right now, there are only two family members who could possibly take action. One of them's Carl Bannock, and no one's heard from him in months and even years. The other is Catherine Cayla Cross. She's just a baby and her daddy, Hector Cross, was the guy who was responsible for the safety of the Magna Grande oil platform that was attacked by terrorists, and the ship that got blown to the bottom of the Atlantic. If anyone takes legal action, Cross is going to the first guy they aim at. But is his little girl, who for all I know can't even walk or talk, gonna hire us to take her daddy for every cent he's got? I think not. And since Hector Cross's money comes from his deceased wife Hazel Bannock Cross, which means it's Bannock money, which is right now like saying no money at all, well, he ain't gonna be worth suing anyhow, now is he?"

It was a devastating takedown, which would have been enough to deflate any man. But Shelby Weiss merely kept on doodling all the same circles and swirls, which meant that he still felt just dandy. And as Jo watched him through the rest of the day, she realized that there was a real spring in his step and a secret smile he was having to fight to keep off his face. Shelby Weiss's firm was falling apart and it wasn't bothering him at all because something else was happening—something linked to the Bannock crisis—that was making him far more than he was losing. But what?

Jo Stanley made it her business to find out.

First she called Ronnie Bunter and asked him to send her an email that she could pass on to Weiss. "It can be anything," she said, "like, you're worried about the welfare of your former staff at this time of crisis and you want to know what plans he has to deal with that."

"Well, that's true enough. I'll get it to you right away."

Once armed with the email, which she printed up, Jo waited till she saw Weiss walking to the john. Then she picked the message and headed toward Weiss's office. His assistant, Dianne, was outside. Having started out doing secretarial work herself, Jo had always made a point of being polite and friendly to all the assistants, so she said hello to Dianne, exchanged a few quick words of chit-chat and said, "Is Shelby in? I've got a message from Ronnie Bunter that I hoped I could talk over with him."

"He's, uh . . ." Dianne gave her a conspiratorial smirk, and put her hand up by her mouth, as if to stop anyone else listening in. "He's in the little boy's room."

"Do you think he'd mind if I left it on his desk?"

"Of course not! You go right on in, hon. You can wait for him if you like. I'm sure he won't be long."

Jo did not quite know what she expected to find in Weiss's office, or what she would say to him to make him reveal what was going on. So it was pure chance that she saw his phone on his desk. Jo looked around. The office door was open, but Dianne couldn't see her here. Treading as softly as she could, with her heart pumping and her nerves on edge, she stepped around behind the desk and looked down. There were two alerts on the screen, one saying that Aram Bendick had called and the other that he had left a voicemail message.

But why would Bendick be calling Shelby Weiss, and, it was clear, calling him regularly enough to be in his contacts list? The obvious connection was Bannock, but why would a financier in New York be talking to an attorney in Houston about that? Had Weiss been feeding Bendick inside information? No, that wasn't possible. Even now, after the purchase of Bunter and Theobald, Weiss had no direct access to the inner sanctums of Bannock Oil. Unless . . .

"Miss Stanley, what can I do for you?"

The sound of Weiss's voice hit Jo like a slap in the face. He was standing in the doorway, staring at her with narrowed, suspicious eyes. She could not control the guilt that flashed across her face, nor the tremor in her voice as she said, "I was just leaving something for you, sir." She held up the email

322

printout. "It's a message from Mr. Bunter. He's concerned about his former staff at this time of . . . of . . ." Her mind had gone blank, unable to find a word to end the sentence.

"At this time of temporary uncertainty?" Weiss suggested, walking toward his desk and glaring at her as though she were a hostile witness about to undergo a savage cross-examination.

"Er . . . yes, sir . . . I guess," Jo blathered, getting out of his way as he sat down, feeling furious with herself for not responding better under pressure: *Pull yourself together, woman!*

"And why couldn't he just ask me this question himself?"

"I don't know, sir. I guess you'd have to ask him that. We were already in communication; maybe it was just easier for him to pass the message through me. Anyway, here it is."

She held out the piece of paper and Weiss snatched it from her. He cast an eye over the printed text and then glanced up at her.

"Well, since you and Mr. Bunter are already 'in communication,' as you put it, you can tell him that I've read his letter and I'll take it under advisement. As you can see, the situation's very fluid at the moment. No one really knows what's happening. When we do, Mr. Bunter will be the first to know."

"Yes, sir."

"You can go now."

"Yes, sir."

Jo returned to her desk and started joining the dots, putting all the facts she knew and the connections between them into the most coherent logical order. When she'd finished she sat in silence, trying to come to terms with what she'd concluded. It was crazy, unbelievable, and yet it made more sense that any other possible explanation. She had to tell Ronnie Bunter what was going on and discuss it all with him, but a phone call was out of the question. It had to be in person. Meanwhile, there was one other person who needed to know and in this case, it had to be done in writing. Jo opened up her personal Gmail account and began to type.

In his office, Shelby Weiss was talking to Aram Bendick. "We've got a situation. There's a woman here, Jo Stanley, works for Bunter—"

"The old guy you bought out, the one who was best buddies with Henry Bannock?" Bendick asked.

"Yeah, him."

"So what's the problem with this Stanley chick?"

"I found her in my office just now. I think she saw that you'd called."

"So? People call each other all the time."

"So she knows about, ah, our mutual acquaintance. He's mentioned her to me by name. My point is, she can figure it out. So what are we going to do?"

"We?" said Aram Bendick. "There ain't no 'we' in this. I am in New York City, on the other side of the country, and I've never heard of this woman before in my life. You, on the other hand, are just across the hallway from her. So you're the one that's gonna do what it takes to deal with the situation."

Weiss couldn't argue with that. So his next call was to D'Shonn Brown. "You and me need to talk. In private. I saw what you did for a friend of mine and I need you to do something for me."

"Yeah? And why exactly should I do that?"

"Because you never, ever want me to be in a district attorney's office, making a plea bargain, using whatever I can get to save my ass."

"Hmm . . . I see. Where do you wanna meet?"

When Hector Cross saw an email from Jo Stanley in his inbox, headed "Please read this: Urgent," he didn't bother to open it. He had more important things to think about than the pleadings of an ex-girlfriend who'd not had the guts to stick it out with him. His entire waking life had essentially become a salvage operation. It was obvious that Bannock in its present form was doomed. The most likely scenario was that its assets and operations would be sliced, diced and sold off in little pieces to the financial vultures waiting to pick the flesh off the bones of a once great company.

Meanwhile, the legal vultures were circling around him. Ronnie Bunter kept him informed on an almost daily basis as attorneys and prosecutors across the U.S. competed to be the ones who would lead the class-action civil suits on behalf of the victims and their families, and the potential criminal case for negligence.

"If you want my advice, you should make yourself as poor as possible," Bunter said during one of their calls.

Cross gave a bitter laugh. "I think the world is already doing that for me."

"Well, yes, everything you or your daughter have tied up in Bannock is probably worthless. But you've still got a couple of valuable properties, and then there are all the private assets Hazel left you—her jewels and antiques alone have got to be worth enough to keep you and your descendants very comfortable for the rest of your lives. Just make sure that everything is in Catherine's name, or in a trust—anywhere that a lawyer like me can't get at it."

"I've already got Sotheby's and Christie's both pitching for the right to auction the pictures," Cross said. "It's not just for Catherine. I want to make sure that all my people are properly looked after. They shouldn't have to lose out because people in Houston put short-term greed above the need for proper planning and training. And they certainly shouldn't be hurt because some legal bloodsucker wants to take me to the cleaners. I'll take my lumps, but not at their expense."

"That's very noble of you, Heck."

"Ah, not really . . . To tell you the truth, Ronnie, so long as I've got a roof over my head, some food in my belly and a good woman at my side, I couldn't give a damn about money. Just look at the Bannock family. How much good did all Henry's money really do them? Sure, they all lived lives of unbelievable luxury. From the day Hazel and I became an item, I never once flew on a scheduled flight, or caught a train, or did my own shopping, or ate at a normal pizza joint. Take those pictures. Every single one that was hung on any wall in any house or yacht or God knows what that Hazel owned was a copy. All the real ones were in bank vaults. So Henry Bannock had bought a bunch of masterpieces that no one could ever see. That's just crazy."

"There's a reason people say that the rich are different," said Bunter with a gentle chuckle.

"It's worse than that, Ronnie. I lost Hazel because that money attracted evil like the brown stuff draws flies. They're all dead— the whole Bannock clan, except for Catherine, and believe me, she's going to be brought up to be a plain, simple, bog-standard Cross."

"Technically, Carl Bannock isn't dead."

"Ha!" Cross exclaimed. "I'm in enough trouble already, so I won't contradict you. But let me put it to you this way. Johnny Congo has been rampaging around the world causing trouble for the past few months and in all that time there's not been the faintest sign, or hint, or sniff of the one human being in the whole world that Congo actually cares about. That should tell you something."

"Not if I don't want it to," said Bunter.

Since that conversation, Cross had stepped up the process of asset-stripping his own life before anyone else could do it. Dave Imbiss, speaking for all Cross's staff, had assured him that he had no obligation to beggar himself on their behalf. "We're all very, very good at our jobs," Imbiss told him. "That's why you hired us."

"It could be the other way around," Cross said, only half in jest. "It could be that I hired and trained you. That's why you're so good at your jobs."

"Either way, there's no shortage of work in this world for people like us. Not that we're looking for work, any of us. We're all be-hind you, Heck. You've never let us down. We won't do it to you."

But Jo Stanley had let him down—or so Cross, whose view of loyalty was very much black or white, my way or the highway, had persuaded himself. Even so, she had always been an intelligent, level-headed individual. If she thought something was urgent, maybe it was. So, eventually, he opened the email. It read:

Dear Hector,

One day I would love to talk to you about what went wrong between us, and how very sorry I am about how things worked out and how I behaved—how I panicked, I guess. But this isn't the time and that's not why I'm writing.

I think I've found something out about the whole Bannock Oil disaster that explains a lot about why it happened. Maybe it can help you defend yourself against all the terrible things people are saying about you. I really feel so bad for you. Anyway . . .

Shelby Weiss was Johnny Congo's lawyer, just before he escaped.

Then he got his firm to buy Bunter and Theobald—to get his hands on all the money from the Bannock Trust, if you ask me.

So now that Bannock's collapsed, everyone at the firm is feeling terrible and frightened for their future.

Except Shelby Weiss. He's as happy as a pig in you-know-what. And I wondered why that was. So I did a little snooping and I found that he'd been in touch with Aram Bendick, that hedge-fund guy who's been boasting about all the money he made betting that Bannock would go under.

So now I'm thinking, what if Bendick knew that Bannock would be in trouble because he knew that things were going to go wrong at Magna Grande?

And what if he knew that because Shelby Weiss had told him, because Weiss is still Congo's attorney?

I don't know, I don't think I've figured it all out yet, but I just hope there's something there that you can use, because you don't deserve to be attacked the way folks here are attacking you.

I know you, Hector. I know you are a good, brave man and

327

you would never do anything unless you truly believed it was the right thing. So if I can help you, maybe you'll think I'm not such a bad person, after all.

Please let me know if this has been any use to you,

Love,

Jo x

"You clever girl," Cross whispered to himself. "You clever, clever girl." It was as if Jo Stanley had completed a circuit in his mind. The last wire was put in place and suddenly the lights went on. Now Cross could see the whole conspiracy in its entirety, and Congo was right at the heart of it.

Congo had given da Cunha enough money to buy his way into the struggle for Cabinda, but that was just a front for his real purpose, which was to attack Bannock . . . *and attack me,* Cross thought.

That explained why the so-called Cabindan rebels on the platform spoke French, not Portuguese. French was the language of the Congo, the tongue spoken by the coltan traders Carl and Johnny had done business with in Kazundu.

Somehow Congo had made the connection with Aram Bendick. Was it through Weiss? Or had Congo just seen Bendick's name in the media and made the introduction himself? One thing was for sure: if Weiss had made money by getting in on Bendick's bets against Bannock Oil, Congo must have made even more.

Bendick was the key to it. He knew exactly what had gone down. And if that knowledge was ever made public, if the full extent of the conspiracy was known, then no one would blame Hector Cross or any of his people for what had happened at Magna Grande, because the true perpetrators of that evil would be known, caught, convicted and punished as they deserved to be.

Cross called Dave Imbiss. "Get the team together," he said. "I've got a job that needs doing, and if we get it right, there will be justice for all the people who died that night. And I want you to run it, Dave. It's time you got to show what you can really do."

"I thought you'd never ask," Imbiss said with a laugh. And then, in a much quieter, more somber tone, he added, "It's good to hear you talk like that, Heck. Makes me feel we've got our boss back again."

Hector felt his spirits rise. He was back in the game again and this time he knew he could win. When the phone rang and he saw Ronnie Bunter's name on the screen, he answered with a cheerful, "Ronnie! Good to hear from you. How's life in the great state of Texas?"

A silence descended on the line and then Bunter spoke in a voice that was cracking with emotion, "I don't know how to tell you this, Hector, but . . . something terrible has happened."

Jo Stanley left the office of Weiss, Mendoza, Burnett and Bunter at twenty past seven. This was much earlier than usual, but she'd seldom felt this dejected and lonely, as if everything had turned rotten and ugly and there wasn't a single person in her world that she could turn to for comfort or solace.

She locked her safe and put on her old mink and the brightly colored scarf that Hector had bought her in Marrakesh on that wonderful weekend which now seemed like fifty years ago. As she studied her face in the mirror of her compact she thought about him again. She had tried to put Hector Cross out of her mind, but it was five days since she'd sent him the email. He had not replied.

I just hope nothing bad's happened to him . . . as if the whole world falling in on him and Catherine Cayla isn't enough. Poor little darling—I miss her as much as Hector.

Jo stared at the reflection of her own face in the tiny mirror. *When did I get old? It seems like only yesterday I was young and carefree, but now I'm old and gray . . . and so damn lonely!*

She saw the tears welling up in her own eyes and she closed

the lid of the compact with a snap. *No! I refuse to weep for him. I wrote that bastard a grovelling letter and he didn't even have the decency to reply.* She drew a deep breath and squared her shoulders. *He is a hard, cruel man . . . and it's finished. I don't love him any more.*

But she knew it was a lie.

Jo pulled on her soft knitted cap and tucked the loose strands of her hair under the brim, then she turned for the door. She heard Bradley Bunter in his own room at the end of the corridor but she didn't want to talk to anybody, especially not Bradley. She closed the door to her own office softly and slipped off her shoes so that her stockinged feet would make no noise. When she reached the elevator she replaced her shoes, and rode down to the underground garage where her old blue Chevy was parked. As she drove up the ramp into the street she noticed another car coming up the ramp behind her, but she thought nothing of it. It was going-home time and there was a flow of vehicles in the street outside the rear of the building, so she had to wait a little before she was able to slip into the stream.

She remembered that her refrigerator at the apartment was almost empty so she took a right at the traffic lights on Maverick Street, and headed for the parking lot at the back of the Central Market.

Lobster! She decided. *And a half-bottle of Napa Valley Chenin Blanc. That'll cheer me up. And to hell with all men, they're not worth the tears and suffering.* She turned into the parking lot and cruised slowly down the row, found an open slot near the end of the row and reversed the Chevy into it. Then she climbed out and locked the doors and set off toward the market, without looking back.

The Nissan that had been following her since she left the offices of Bunter and Theobald was painted a color that had once had a fancy name like Mocha Pearl, but had long since faded to a nondescript shade of dust and dried manure. It drove slowly past Jo's

Chevy and parked near the end of the row of vehicles. The door on the passenger side opened and a Hispanic type in a dark-colored windcheater and baseball cap climbed out and sauntered back down the row of parked vehicles. When he reached the Chevy he took a large bunch of keys from the pocket of his windcheater. Working quickly he tried the keys in the passenger side lock one after another until the doors clicked open. He grunted in satisfaction and glanced around casually making certain he was unobserved. Then he slipped behind the rear seat and disappeared from view as he sank down as low as he could get between the seats and the floor. His companion remained hunched behind the wheel of the Nissan parked at the end of the row.

For a little less than ten minutes neither of them moved. Then Jo Stanley reappeared through the revolving doors of the market and hurried back toward her Chevy. She was toting a small plastic carrier bag. As she passed the parked Nissan the driver opened the door and casually trailed after her. While Jo placed the bag between her feet and busied herself with unlocking the driver's door—*Jeez, it's time I got a car with central locking!*—he walked on by without so much as glancing at her.

Jo got the door open and slipped behind the steering wheel. She reached across and placed her carrier bag on the empty passenger seat beside her, not noticing that the lock was still up on the passenger's door, slammed the driver's door closed, and leaned forward to insert the key in the ignition.

While her whole attention was fixed on getting the car started, the man crouched on the floor behind her rose up and slipped his right arm around her throat from behind. Holding her in a neck lock he leaned back with all his weight, pinning her to the seat and smothering the frantic cries she was trying to utter as her hands clawed ineffectually at his arms.

The second man who had walked on past the Chevy doubled back swiftly and yanked open the passenger door. As he slid into the seat beside Jo he reached into the front of his jacket

331

and brought out a ten-inch butcher's knife. With his free hand he ripped open the front of Jo's mink jacket and laid his open hand on the bottom of her ribcage which was arched backward by the neck lock of the first assassin. With the skill born of long practice he placed the point of the blade on Jo's skin, as precisely as a surgeon's scalpel and with a single hard thrust drove the steel full length upward into Jo's heart.

Both men froze, holding her from struggling, choking off any noise she might make. At the end she shuddered and her whole body slumped in death.

Neither of the men spoke a word throughout the entire procedure, but once she was dead the knife man used a small hand towel he brought out from his pocket to staunch the residual bleeding while he withdrew the blade from Jo's chest.

The man who had pinioned Jo ransacked her handbag quickly and found her wallet. He removed a small roll of ten- and twenty-dollar bills but left her driver's license. Then between them they pushed her corpse down on to the floor where she would not be obvious to a casual passer-by.

Then they slipped out of the Chevy unhurriedly, locked the doors and—still unhurriedly—walked back to their own vehicle and drove away.

Jo's dead," said Ronnie Bunter over the telephone.

"No, that can't be right." Hector Cross spoke quite calmly, certain that there must be some mistake. "I just read an email she sent me."

"I'm sorry, Hector, but it's true. She was mugged right outside the Central Market, on Westheimer. She'd just gone in to get some deli for her dinner and they were waiting for her when she went back to her car." Ronnie Bunter had a calm, punctilious, old-school lawyer's mind, but his distress had overwhelmed him. He was having difficulty forcing the words out past the sobs that Cross could hear gathering in his throat. "I can't believe I'm saying

332

this," Bunter went on. "I mean, it's a good neighborhood and she had a real nice apartment on Post Oak Boulevard . . . This is a safe area, Heck, I recommended it to her myself, but . . . but . . . I guess some guys, druggies or something, they were waiting for her in her car. They stabbed her, and took her purse . . . she died for a purse, Heck. What is this world coming to?"

"She didn't die for a purse," Cross said. "She died because she got too close to the Beast." He drew a deep breath. "I am to blame for this. But I promise you one thing. I will avenge her. You can count on that."

The following morning, Dave Imbiss informed Cross that he had devised a plan for dealing with Aram Bendick that would, at the same time, bring Jo Stanley's killers to justice. The O'Quinns were immediately summoned to a meeting at which the scheme would be discussed, analyzed and pored over for any possible weaknesses before a final decision to put it into effect was made.

"Please, Dave, don't tell me that your idea begins with me getting that disgusting man into bed," Nastiya joked as they helped themselves to freshly brewed coffee.

"Don't be daft, woman," said Paddy. "If I know Dave, he'll be after raiding Bendick's house and killing him before he can reach his getaway car. That's the kinda plan that always works perfectly, in my experience!"

"That's enough!" snapped Hector, bringing the meeting to order. "This is about getting justice for Jo and for all the poor beggars who died at Magna Grande. Let's not forget that, OK?"

The other three flashed glances at one another, like classmates who'd just discovered their teacher was in a bad mood, and sat down around the table without another word being said.

"Right then," Cross went on, "what have you got for us, Dave?"

"Well, as a matter of fact, I did consider the possibility of a honeytrap, as a means of blackmailing Bendick and forcing him to talk. And I looked at the likelihood of pulling off a forcible seizure, given that Bendick never has fewer that six bodyguards around him, both male and female, all trained by Mossad. But I rejected them both. Here's the thing, boss. Like it or not, Aram Bendick is kind of a public hero right now. The media's portraying him as a financial genius who called the odds and brought down an entire corporation, single-handed. It's like David killing Goliath and then walking away with several billion dollars. Plus, he's a blue-collar kid from the Bronx who made it all the way to the top. To us, sitting here, he's a sleazeball who made his money over the dead bodies of innocent people. To the American people, he's a hero. And you . . ."

Cross grimaced. "OK, I get it, I'm the Limey who screwed up and got everyone killed."

"I'm afraid so, Heck. My point is, you can't afford to be seen anywhere near the take-down. Nor can any of us because we're all toxic. It wouldn't matter what we made Bendick admit, he'd always be able to get out of it, just by saying we forced him, and the whole world would think we were trying to shift the blame for our mistakes. And that's if the operation went right. If we messed it up and didn't get to Bendick, or more people got hurt, well, if you think you've got legal problems now . . . man, they'd be a thousand times worse."

"You told me you had a plan," said Cross. "So far all I've heard is options that won't work. Give me one that will."

"It's real simple. You get the law to do the work for you."

"How do you mean?"

"Well, has there actually been a writ or a warrant issued against you yet?" Imbiss asked.

"Not so far as I know."

"And if I recall, didn't you have a contact at the Texas Rangers—Hernandez, or something?"

Cross nodded. "That's right. Lieutenant Consuela Hernandez was her name. She sounded to me like a damn good cop."

"Well, as I recall, the Rangers took the same sort of crap

from the media and the politicians when Congo escaped as you're doing now over Magna Grande. What I'm getting at is, if you go through Hernandez to her boss and you say you've got a way to solve the murder of Jo Stanley, and nail the man who helped Congo escape, and name the men who were really responsible for the sinking of the *Bannock A*, well, my guess is he'd be real interested in that proposition. He gets his career back on track, you get out from under the heap of crap that's been dumped on you and a bunch of guilty men get what's coming to them."

"That certainly sounds appealing," Cross agreed. "But exactly how do you propose to work this magic trick?"

"Before I tell you, I need to ask one last question: would Ronald Bunter risk putting himself in danger in order to help you out?"

"What kind of risk?"

"Making bad people very angry if things went wrong."

Cross thought about it for a moment. "If it was just me, yes, he probably would, though he'd really be doing it in Hazel's memory. If it's also to help avenge Jo, absolutely, he'd do anything."

"Then here's what we're going to do . . ."

An hour later, just as Cross was bringing the meeting to an end, Paddy O'Quinn said, "There is something that has been preying on my mind ever since it all happened. The thing is, whoever was behind the attack seemed to know a helluva lot about our whole set-up. I mean, those lads on the Angolan helicopters found their way around that rig like they were carrying maps. And the fella that put the mine under the *Bannock A* knew precisely where to find her."

"Are you suggesting someone betrayed us?"

"I don't know, it just seems odd to me . . ."

A vision flashed through Cross's mind, a memory of the terrorist leader, standing on the helideck, guiding his men to their targets around the oil platform. *He knew exactly what he was doing . . . he knew!*

"Suppose that's true," Cross said, "who was the mole? The only people who knew the whole picture and who had access to detailed plans are sitting in this room. I refuse to believe it was one of us. There isn't anyone here whose conduct wasn't exemplary . . . Are you saying I was the mole, Paddy . . . or Dave . . . or your own wife?"

"No, of course not!" O'Quinn protested. "I don't believe that for a moment. That's why I haven't said anything until now. It's just that the thought won't leave my head, that's all."

"Maybe there's an innocent explanation," said Imbiss. "You can get a pretty good picture of any rig in the world, just by going online. And it was no secret that Bannock Oil was opening up the Magna Grande field. Anyone who knew that wouldn't have a hard time locating a damn great floating refinery."

"I suppose . . ."

"And don't forget, Carl Bannock isn't officially dead," Imbiss continued. "So he was probably being sent corporate data, which means Congo would have seen it."

Cross sighed and then grimaced in frustration. "Of course he would . . . why was I so stupid?" He saw the puzzled expression on the other three faces at the table and explained, "Bigelow's spin doctor, Nocerino, called me . . . it was the night the *Noatak* went down. Anyway, he said he was putting together an investors' letter about the Magna Grande field. You know, a puff piece saying what a great success it was going to be. He wanted me to say something about the security we were putting in place. I didn't give away any big secrets, but the letter had a lot of information. Not enough to give Congo everything he needed to know, but enough to steer him in the right direction."

Paddy nodded. "Ah, well then, that explains it . . . John bloody Bigelow and his merry men gave our enemies the information they needed to destroy us, then prevented us from doing the training we needed to do our jobs properly. They didn't just shoot themselves in the foot. They slit their own throats as well, and probably stuck a stake in their hearts, just for good measure. Arseholes!"

The matter was settled. But that evening, just as Zhenia was leaving the O'Quinns' house in Barnes, en route for a night with Cross, Nastiya stopped her sister by the door and said, "Have you been working for da Cunha?"

Zhenia stopped dead in her tracks and stammered, "Wha . . . what do you mean? Why would I . . . how would I work for da Cunha?"

"I don't know. I just remember how sexy you thought he was. You sounded like a schoolgirl with a crush. Did you think he was sexy enough to make you betray Hector Cross?"

Zhenia looked appalled. "Betray Hector? But I love Hector. He's the best thing that has ever, ever happened to me. I would rather die than hurt him."

Nastiya looked at her, saying nothing, then nodded and said, "Good, I'm glad you said that. Because if I ever thought that someone I knew had betrayed Hector, even if it was someone I loved very much, with my own blood in their veins, I would kill that person without a second's hesitation. So, anyway . . . off you go! Spend the night with Hector Cross and show him how much you really love him."

Zhenia dashed down the front garden path to the taxi waiting for her by the curb. Nastiya closed the front door, paused for another second's thought and then walked toward the kitchen, cursing to herself as she realized it was her turn to make supper.

Three days after Dave Imbiss had set out his plan, an elderly gentleman in an old-fashioned, bespoke suit that was beautifully cut but just a little bit shiny at the elbows strolled up to the reception desk at the newly enlarged firm of Weiss, Mendoza, Burnett and Bunter. He smiled at the pretty young blonde in a headset behind the great slab of polished black granite that served as a reception desk and said, "Excuse me, my dear, but could you tell me where I might find the partners' boardroom?"

Her delicate little brows creased in puzzlement. "I'm sorry, sir, but that's only for the partners."

"Yes, I imagine that's how it got its name," he said in a kindly manner. "Luckily, I am a partner. My name is Ronald Bunter. It's right there on the wall behind you."

Despite the fact that she spent every working day seated in front of the four names etched on to a twelve-foot-wide glass panel, the receptionist could not help but glance behind her to check. "But that's a different Mr. Bunter, sir," she said.

"You mean Mr. Bradley Bunter?"

"Yes, sir."

"Well, he's my son and it's a matter of opinion as to which of us is the Bunter referred to on that sign. Nevertheless, I am a partner, I believe that a partners' meeting is scheduled for eleven o'clock this morning, which is to say, five minutes from now, and I aim to attend that meeting, as is my right. So please, would you be so good as to direct me to it?"

"I . . . I . . ." Faced with the possibility that she might either be allowing a random geezer onto the premises, or barring the way to an actual partner who could have her fired, the receptionist had no idea what to do. So she made the smart move and pushed the decision up the line.

"One moment, sir," she said with a brittle half-smile as she tapped on her keyboard. "Hi, this is Brandi. There's a gentleman in reception who says his name is Bunter and that he's our Mr. Bunter's father. He wants to attend a partners' meeting. Should I let him in?" She listened to the response, ended the call and then told Bunter, "Someone will be out to see you momentarily."

That someone turned out to be Bradley himself.

His presence alarmed the receptionist. "I'm sorry, sir, I didn't mean to disturb you. I just . . ." she twittered.

Bunter Jr. gave her a smile that managed to be both pred-atory and ingratiating as he said, "Don't you worry, Brandi sweetheart, you did great."

As she glowed in the warmth of his approval, Bradley turned to his father, "Gee, Dad, what brings you here today? I mean, it's great to see you, but this is kind of unexpected."

"I dare say it is, but here I am. Now, shall we go into the meeting?"

The other partners were no less surprised or more happy than Bradley Bunter at the arrival of the man who had been, until then, a very silent partner. And so Ronnie stayed all the way through the various items that the partners had tabled for discussion, almost all of which centered on the disastrous effect of the collapse of Bannock Oil, and by extension the Henry Bannock Family Trust, on the firm's finances. It took quite an effort of will, since Ronnie, who had written the terms of the trust himself, and then administered it for decades without the slightest blemish—other than the obligation to pay huge sums to the odious Carl Bannock—was now seeing his life's work fall apart before his eyes. Nevertheless, his lips were sealed.

Only when the partnership secretary asked if there was any other business did he raise his hand and say, "Yes, there are two matters, both linked to one another, that I would like to bring to my fellow partners' attention. May I have the floor?"

The other partners could not deny him his say, and so Ronnie Bunter began: "The first matter I would like to raise, though I had hoped and expected that it would have been considered by now, without the need for me to say anything, is the tragic death of Jo Stanley."

There was a low murmur of embarrassment around the table. Even lawyers could understand that there was something shameful about discussing their corporate and personal finances for almost an hour but ignoring the passing of a colleague.

"Jo worked for me for many years and I considered her a

close friend, almost a daughter in some ways, I guess. I appreciate that she was much less familiar to those of you who have only just become her colleagues, but I know that many of the men and women who worked alongside her at Bunter and Theobald will have been hit very hard by her loss. I don't know what plans have been made for her funeral, but I hope this firm will pay tribute to her in some way, and I absolutely insist that anyone who wishes to attend her funeral should be allowed to do so within working hours."

There were nods around the table and the matter seemed settled until Shelby Weiss piped up, "With all due respect, Ronnie, we're fighting for survival here. Every cent counts. Sure, it would be nice to commemorate Jo's passing, but if folks are going to go to her funeral, they'd better do it on their time, not ours. I mean, what if there's a wake and they end up getting blasted and dancing jigs when they should be back at work, racking up billable hours?"

Ronald Bunter was not a flamboyant litigator. He did not show off in front of a jury. He seldom even raised his voice. But he had a quiet, steely way of nailing a hostile witness or a lying defendant that was just as effective as any amount of showmanship. And it was that persona to which he reverted now.

"On a point of information, Mr. Weiss, Jo Stanley was not, to my knowledge, an Irish-American and so the question of a wake does not apply. I only met her parents once or twice and they struck me as delightful people: modest, understated and God-fearing. They loved their daughter very much indeed and I am quite certain that they will mark her passing in a way that reflects their personalities and their values. So I insist: the former staff of Bunter and Theobald, at the very least, must be allowed to attend her funeral without being penalized in any way for doing so. I trust we will not require a vote."

Even Weiss did not dare force the issue, and so Ronnie continued: "The other matter I wished to discuss also concerns

Jo Stanley inasmuch as it relates to the manner of her passing and the reasons behind the assault that was made upon her."

"What reasons?" Weiss snapped, with a vehemence that drew one or two puzzled looks from around the table. "She was mugged. Case closed. It's unfortunate, and I wouldn't wish it on my worst enemy, but, hey, shit happens."

"Thank you, Mr. Weiss," said Bunter, not feeling any need at all to match the volume or intensity with which Weiss had interrupted him. "You're making life much easier for me. You see, I had been a little nervous about making the allegations that I am now going to lay before my fellow partners. But all your words and actions only serve to persuade me of its strength. So let me state my case—"

"You can't just come in here and hijack this meeting!" Weiss shouted.

"Keep digging, Mr. Weiss, you're just making the hole you're in that much deeper."

"I'm sorry," Tina Burnett interjected, "but what the hell is this all about? Ronnie, what are you trying to tell us?"

Ronald Bunter paused. His brow furrowed. For a moment it might have seemed to the other occupants of the boardroom that he was just an old man who'd lost his train of thought. In fact, he was an old litigator who knew exactly how to put an audience on the edge of its seats. Finally, a fraction of a second before someone else said something, he replied, "I'm telling you, Ms. Burnett, that your partner Shelby Weiss was almost certainly responsible for the death of Jo Stanley, which I contend was no random mugging but instead a targeted assassination. I furthermore assert that the reason for the assassination was that Ms. Stanley had established a link between Mr. Weiss and the financier Aram Bendick, the same Mr. Bendick who, as you cannot help but have noticed, has been bragging about the vast fortune he made by betting against Bannock Oil. And I believe that further investigation will show that the reason

341

why this discovery of Ms. Stanley's was so dangerous to both Mr. Weiss and Mr. Bendick was that they were engaged in an international conspiracy to use an attack on the Bannock field at Magna Grande, off the coast of Angola, as the means to precipitate the collapse of Bannock Oil. And finally, I am certain, though I cannot as yet prove it, that the prime mover in this conspiracy was Mr. Weiss's client John Kikuu Tembo, better known to most of you by his alias Johnny Congo."

"That's a damn lie!" Weiss shouted as the partners' meeting descended into uproar. It took more than a minute before Jesús Mendoza, the oldest and most authoritative of the Weiss, Mendoza and Burnett trio, was able to restore order and say, "These are some serious accusations you're making, Ronnie. Do you have the evidence to back them up?"

"To the standard of criminal proof? No, Jesús, I don't. But do I have the kind of case you would have grabbed with both hands when you were the brightest young DA in East Texas? Hell yes."

"Then you'd better lay it out for us."

So Ronnie told the story, right from the moment Jo Stanley forced Hector Cross not to throw Johnny Congo out of the back of a plane, but to give him up to the authorities; to Congo's mysterious involvement in Cabinda; to Jo's observations of Weiss's strangely unconcerned, even upbeat mood in recent weeks; her discovery of Bendick's name on Weiss's phone (which, Bendick pointed out, Weiss had almost certainly observed, or at the very least suspected); her email to Cross and her sudden death.

He concluded, "I can't produce a smoking gun, or not yet, anyway. But if I were a young, ambitious DA, I would right now be getting subpoenas to seize all Mr. Weiss's telephone and email records, not to mention his bank accounts, though my guess is the dirty ones are all overseas. I think you're an evil bastard, Weiss, but you're not a dumb one. I'd also be calling the FBI, the Feds, the Securities and Exchange Commission and the U.S. Attorney for the Southern District of New York—I'm sure

I don't have to tell you that's the court that has jurisdiction over the financial centers of New York City—to put Aram Bendick under the microscope, too. I'd be looking into the trades Mr. Bendick made, and his movements, both inside the United States and beyond in the days immediately preceding the start of financial hostilities against Bannock Oil, and I'd call the State Department, because they'll want to start lobbying the Swiss and the Cayman Islanders and possibly the Panamanians to open up their banks to our investigation."

Weiss was sitting, white-faced and silent, as the recitation went on. He'd spent years reading juries, so he knew, just by looking at the other lawyers in the room, that they were buying Bunter's story, whether he had the smoking gun or not. Now he had to fight back.

"You've got nothing, Bunter," he snarled. "No evidence, no witnesses, no documentation—nothing but the crazy theories of a woman who was clearly desperate to appease the lover she'd walked out on, and to make up for feeling bad about keeping Johnny Congo alive. If you people want to listen to more of this garbage, fine. Me, I have had enough. I've got work to do. Maybe if you had some work, Bunter, you wouldn't be wasting time on garbage like this."

Weiss got to his feet, knocking over his chair as he did so, and stalked out of the room.

"Thank you, Ms. Burnett, gentlemen, for letting me say my piece. I thought it went very well, didn't you?"

Oh yeah," said Major Bobby Malinga of the Texas Rangers, who was sitting in a van across the road from the Weiss, Mendoza, Burnett and Bunter offices listening to the feed from the wire that he had attached to Bunter's chest a couple of hours earlier.

"Come on, Weiss, call your daddy . . ." Hector Cross muttered.

A second later Weiss dialled a 646 area code, indicating a Manhattan-based cellphone number. The number started ringing. "Pick it up . . . pick it up," Hernandez muttered. Then she pumped her fist and mouthed, "Yesss!" as the unmistakable voice of Aram Bendick answered, "What do you want?"

"We've been made," Weiss replied, sounding on the verge of panic.

"Whoa! Take a chill pill. Calm down. What happened?"

"You remember that chick I told you about, Jo Stanley, the one you said I should deal with?"

"No." Bendick's voice was flat, emotionless, crunching in the bluntness of the denial.

"Sure you do. You told me she was none of your business; I had to fix it. Well, I did."

"I don't know what you're talking about."

Now Weiss became angry and that helped calm his nerves. "Listen, smart-ass. I'm talking to you as a lawyer and I am telling you that Stanley figured out what we were doing. And she told her old lover, Cross, the guy who screwed up the Magna Grande situation."

"Ouch." Cross winced in the stuffy darkness of the van.

"And Cross told Stanley's old boss Bunter, who showed up at my office an hour ago and laid it all out, the whole thing, right in front of my partners. That's four attorneys, all of them officers of the law, who now know about a conspiracy to destroy Bannock Oil and defraud its stockholders. In case you hadn't noticed, we're guilty of that conspiracy. And that's not even the worst part. See, Bunter also suggested that the Magna Grande disaster was masterminded by my client and your investor Johnny Congo, specifically with the aim of lowering the price of Bannock stock, from which we both profited. And that puts us this close to a conspiracy to cause the deaths of more than two hundred people, more than half of them U.S. citizens. Do you hear me, Bendick?"

"Sure, I heard what you said, but you'll notice I didn't say anything because I honestly don't have a goddamn clue what you're talking about. I have a long record of backing my judgement on positions some folks think are crazy. Some I lose. More often I win. This was one of those cases, and I'd like to see anyone try and prove otherwise. See you around, Mr. Weiss."

"Damn!" Hernandez threw her headphones down on to the workbench in front of her. "That bastard's right, he didn't say a thing we can use."

"Did you seriously think he would?" Hector Cross asked. "The point is, we have a confession from Weiss and I'm sure that your colleagues in the Harris County DA's office can use that as leverage to get him to make a statement implicating Bendick, with evidence to back up his claims. I'm guessing that if he was acting for Congo in the commission of a crime then he can forget about attorney–client privilege. You heard what Ronnie Bunter said: Get on to every federal agency that has anything to do with money, terrorism or good old-fashioned crime and put them on the case. Forget how cool Bendick was on the phone, it's squeaky-bum time now. I bet he's got all his munchkins deleting emails, dumping files in the trash, shifting dirty money to offshore accounts. It'll all be kicking off."

"I don't know why you're sounding so goddamn cheerful," Hernandez said. "If he's doing all those things he's destroying the only evidence that could ever get him convicted."

"That's what you think." Cross dialled a number on his phone and pressed the "speaker" button. They could all hear the number ringing and then an American voice saying, "Hi, boss, what can I do for you?"

"Very simple, Dave, just let them know what you've been doing over the past few hours and days."

"Cut a long story short, I've been hanging out with some old buddies from the U.S. Army Intelligence and Security Command at Fort Belvoir, Virginia. They were real happy to help me track down the people responsible for the deaths of so many of their fellow citizens, some of them military veterans. So we got out our laptops, put our heads together, started writing code

345

just like the good old days and, what do you know? We hacked right into Aram Bendick's corporate computer system, so we already have all the evidence he's trying to hide, and can see what he's doing right now, as he does it. That means we can track all the money he's trying to hide, which so far amounts to a little over two point five billion dollars . . . no, sorry, make that two point seven billion . . . Man, he really made a lot of money out of killing all those folks!"

"That's great work, Dave. Tell all the guys who helped you thank you very much from me. And a massive pat on the back for you, too. I think you may just be an actual, living genius."

Imbiss laughed. "You're the boss, Heck, so I won't contradict you!"

Cross ended the call and turned his attention back to Malinga. "Here's what we just established today. Shelby Weiss had Jo Stanley killed. Question: Who would he go to if he wanted a hit? Answer: Whoever it was that organized Congo's escape, because don't tell me Weiss doesn't know who that was."

"Oh, don't worry, he knew," Malinga replied. "And he's not the only one. The guy in question is a businessman, claims he's legit, name of D'Shonn Brown."

"Any relation to Aleutian Brown?" Cross asked.

"Brother, why do you ask?"

"Oh, I bumped into Aleutian a while back."

"Did you, ah, bump hard?"

"Hard enough, but don't worry, it was a long way from your jurisdiction."

Malinga gave a wry smile of approval. "Well, then, I appreciate your efforts to keep the streets safe for law-abiding folks to go about their business. Hernandez, time we put a call in to the DA's office. We're going to need warrants for Weiss's office, home, phones: you name it. And as soon as you find any connection to D'Shonn Brown—one conversation'll do it—we go for warrants on him too."

"You make sure you get them," Hector Cross said to Malinga as Hernandez started barking into a phone. "Jo Stanley was a good woman, and she believed in the rule of law above all else. The least she deserves is for her killer to be caught, tried, found guilty and punished."

"Saves you having to do it, huh?" said Malinga.

"She's the only person I wouldn't avenge personally. I thought about it—I'd be lying if I said that I didn't. But she wouldn't have wanted it."

"Good, because I'd hate to be coming after you as well as Weiss and Brown."

"And Bendick, don't forget about him."

"Oh, I haven't, you can count on that. And I will make those calls you were talking about. Not to mention the U.S. Customs, Federal Aviation Authority and New York Port Authority. If Aram Bendick took a plane or a boat or any other means of transport to get out of the country in the weeks leading up to Magna Grande, I'm going to find out about it."

"Then what?"

"Then I'm going to hand the whole damn thing over to the Feds and watch them take the credit. I'm just a good ol' boy from Texas, Mr. Cross. So far as I understand, which is not too far, Aram Bendick was involved in an international conspiracy to commit acts of terrorism as a means of rigging the markets."

"Sounds about right," Hector agreed.

"You're going to let the Feds do their job, though, right? Not tempted to take any shortcuts?"

Cross laughed. "On occasion I am quite capable of obeying the law. Besides, I want the pleasure of following this story as it unfolds. I want to see Weiss and Bendick do the perp walk. I want to see the look on their greedy, lying faces as their lawyers deny all the charges. I want to watch all the evidence emerge . . . And one day, maybe, I want to see them locked away for a very, very long time." "Well, then I guess I'd better start making those calls," said Malinga as he cocked his white Stetson over his right eye at a jaunty angle.

There were only twenty-three of them gathered on the top floor of Seascape Mansions, Cross's safe house in Abu Zara. The Magna Grande disaster had left Bannock Oil in almost total disarray. John Bigelow had been forced to resign as the company's President and CEO as had the remainder of the board of directors. Bannock Oil had been placed in administration and the assets of the company sequestrated. The remainder of the company's drilling concessions in the Atlantic and the Indian Oceans had been sold off at fire-sale prices in a desperate bid to meet the company debts. The only properties that remained in the company's possession when the dust finally settled were the Zara oilfields, which had an estimated life of a mere fifteen years. All in all, the net market value of Bannock Oil Ltd had been reduced by a staggering 80 percent.

It was an abysmal low point for a company that had once been so illustrious. Nevertheless Bannock Oil still required protection and Cross had come through the disaster with his reputation almost untarnished. He had taken advantage of the Bannock asset sales to buy back Cross Bow Security for a fraction of what he had once been paid to sell it.

At least Shelby Weiss and Aram Bendick were no longer a threat. They had been found guilty by the Supreme Court of Texas of conspiring to cause the destruction of the Magna Grande drilling operation for their own gain, and causing the deaths of more than two hundred people aboard the Bannock A, many of them U.S. citizens. The judge has sentenced them in court to jail terms of fifty years and seventy-five years respectively. They would almost certainly die in prison before they even came up for parole. In a desperate bid to mitigate his sentence, Weiss had told investigators everything he knew that linked D'Shonn Brown to the operation that had sprung Johnny Congo on his execution

348

day, and it was only a matter of time before Brown was wearing an orange jumpsuit and eating prison food too.

Cross and his team, however, still had a job to do, protecting what remained of the Bannock Oil Company. So now he held up both hands for silence, and laid out the scale of the task. "We haven't seen the last of our enemies. The most virulent and dangerous of them are still out there, lurking in the undergrowth, keeping a low profile, waiting till the world is looking the other way. Mateus da Cunha and Johnny Congo, alias Juan Tumbo, alias King John Kikuu Tembo won't be appeased until they've wrested the Magna Grande oilfield from the control of the Angolan government. They intend to do this by completing the job that the Magna Grande disaster started. That's to say: creating unrest and anarchy, destabilising Cabinda to the point where da Cunha can step in, present himself as the nation's savior and declare independence from Angola. And if thousands more innocent victims are slaughtered and mass destruction is perpetrated once again, they won't care. It's all just part of their plan."

The atmosphere in the room had changed from lighthearted banter to serious, professional concentration. "They have time on their side and massive funds at their disposal," Cross went on. "For da Cunha, this is all just a matter of naked greed. He lusts after the mineral riches of Cabinda. Congo's different. He wants revenge for the death of Carl Bannock, for wrecking his personal empire in Kazundu, for sticking him on death row, for forcing him out of Venezuela. So he's got a vendetta against me personally. He wants me dead. And the feeling is entirely mutual. I want him dead too."

Cross paused for a moment to let his words sink in. Then he went on.

"So . . . we've been making plans. Most of you don't know this, but Nastiya O'Quinn, helped by her half-sister Zhenia, has been able to infiltrate the enemy camp and win da Cunha's trust. That gives her a lead to Congo too. Neither of them are aware that Nastiya and Zhenia are connected in any way to Cross Bow Security. They believe that Nastiya is a Russian financier who heads up a company that specializes in raising funds in her country of origin to invest in activities which can deliver maximum rewards, regardless of legality. Let's face it, the average Russian oligarch wouldn't be worth a rouble if he'd ever worried about the law."

There were knowing smiles on the faces of many of the audience, but a few of the others looked dubious. Then one of the Cross Bow men raised a hand.

"Do you have a question, Pete?" asked Cross, somewhat reluctantly.

"Yeah boss, it's about Nastiya. She was with us on the Kazundu job. What if Congo saw her then. No disrespect, Nastiya, but you're not the kind of woman that a man forgets."

That got a quiet laugh from the audience and a smile from the woman herself. Cross, however, looked thoughtful. "That's a good point. What's your reply, Nastiya?"

"Yes, of course I was on the expedition to Kazundu. But I was with Paddy, my husband, leading the attack on the airport. We never went near the castle where your team captured Congo."

"What about the return flight?" Cross insisted. "Are you sure he never had sight of you then?"

"Certain," Nastiya assured him. "You had Congo shot full of drugs, knocked out cold and wrapped up in a cargo net in the rear cargo cabin for the whole return flight. I was in the front passenger cabin. Congo never got so much as a peep at me."

Cross glanced across at Paddy O'Quinn. "That's how I remember it too. What do you reckon, Paddy? Has Congo ever seen your wife?"

"My wife is always right, Heck. You know that. And I'd kill the man who calls her a liar . . . if Nastiya hadn't got to him first."

There were a few guffaws from those who had reason to remember Nastiya's mercurial temper.

"OK, so we're all agreed that Nastiya is clean." Cross accepted the evidence. "Johnny Congo has never laid eyes on her and Mateus da Cunha is enchanted by her beauty and brains just like any other natural-born man. So far as da Cunha's concerned her name is Maria Denisova and she has even found four genuine oligarchs to invest in his plot to cut Cabinda out of Angola and turn it into his personal fiefdom."

"I am sorry to have to correct you, Hector," Nastiya cut in. "It is my father who has found the four oligarchs for da Cunha. And I must be losing my looks. When da Cunha laid eyes on Zhenia for the first time he made it very obvious that he had switched his romantic interest from me to her."

Nastiya looked wryly at Zhenia, who sat in the seat beside her, grinning at her triumph over her big sister.

"When did he ever see her?" Cross demanded, making no effort to hide his personal interest in the subject. "Is there something going on here that I should know about?"

"Nastiya is teasing you, Hector," Zhenia hastened to reassure him. "When she Skypes da Cunha I sit beside her and keep quiet, but I pretend to take notes just like a good secretary. Nastiya has even chosen a new name for me. I am called Polina Salko. This makes me sound like a polony sausage I think."

"No one could ever confuse you with a sausage," Cross assured her, trying to keep from smiling as his audience burst out with wolf whistles and ribald comments. He waited for them to quieten again before he continued, "So, the reason I've summoned you all today is that last night we got a lucky break. Da Cunha informed Nastiya that he's chartered an ocean-going yacht which he intends to use as a mobile base during his struggle to seize control of Cabinda."

Cross allowed himself a momentary half-smile of satisfaction as he added, "Apparently he made a point of boasting about the shell companies he had used to carry out the deal, so that no one would ever know he was the actual customer."

There was a murmur of excitement from his audience but Cross ignored it and went on speaking quietly. "Up until now Johnny Congo had disappeared completely from our radar. We're almost certain that he led the attack on the FPSO *Bannock A*, but we have no idea where he has holed up subsequently. However, I think it's reasonable to assume that both Congo and da Cunha are going to be aboard this yacht and that they'll use it as a bolt hole if their operations in Cabinda backfire upon them. In the meantime, however, da Cunha has invited both Miss Denisova and her secretary . . . "

"Señorita Sausage!" a wag piped up from the back row.

Cross glared at him, trying, not entirely successfully to suppress a smile.

". . . has invited both women to accompany him on his expedition. We don't know where or when he is planning to pick Nastiya and Zhenia up. All we know is that it will be within the next two weeks or so, but it won't be in Cabinda. My guess is that he'll be travelling around the world seeking financial, diplomatic and even military support for what he will present as a noble struggle for Cabinda's freedom."

Cross fell silent for a moment to let the tension build up, then resumed: "This could be our main chance, and possibly our only chance to catch both da Cunha and Congo in the same deadfall. So we need to start planning now. Dave . . . ?"

Dave Imbiss came up beside Cross and launched straight into his presentation. "Da Cunha told Nastiya that the yacht is a brand new seventy-meter Lürssen called *Faucon d'Or*, or Golden Falcon, for those of you who don't *parler français*. I've managed to get hold of a copy of the blueprints of the *Faucon d'Or*'s sister ship. Both vessels were built by the workshops at Lürssen's headquarters in Bremen-Vegesack. So listen up, people. Here's what you need to know . . . "

Imbiss spoke for almost thirty minutes, and he passed around photographs and blueprints of a magnificent modern motor

352

yacht. He ended by recapping the most valuable information he had regarding the ship's specifications. "So there you have it, ladies and gentlemen: seventy meters of luxury with accommodation for ten passengers in five staterooms. Her cruising speed is around twenty-two knots but she has a top speed of forty knots. There is not much afloat that is capable of running her down in a stern chase, I am afraid."

Cross wrapped up the meeting with a few final words. "That's all for now. We all have to be patient and wait until Mateus da Cunha gives Nastiya the rendezvous details for their next meeting. We have no way of anticipating where or when that will be; or if Johnny Congo will be aboard the *Faucon d'Or*. But Dave will work on building up the contents of his box of tricks, and Paddy and I will try to formulate some sort of plan to ambush the *Faucon d'Or* once we have an inkling of its whereabouts." He looked at the row of faces that confronted him and he shrugged. "OK, so as a plan of action it sucks like a newborn baby. But you know what they say—things can only get better. We'll meet again tomorrow to brainstorm the situation; ten a.m. on the rooftop terrace. I'll provide a good barbeque and a couple of cases of beer. I expect you lot to provide the good ideas."

By noon the following day they had downed a few dozen cans of beer and eaten several pounds of steak and chops off the coals. Catherine Cayla had stripped off her bathing suit and with shrieks of laughter soaked everybody who came within range of her miniature portable swimming pool. But she was the only one present who was patently enjoying herself.

"We simply can't cover all four oceans and the seven seas with a single boat," Cross continued lugubriously.

"Bot!" Catherine sang out, repeating his last word. Cross ignored her and went on:

"To do the job we'd need several hundred boats."

"Bots!" Catherine increased her volume to get his attention.

353

"For a pipsqueak your size you have a voice like a foghorn." Cross told her with paternal pride. "I definitely need another beer." He set off toward the self-service bar under the umbrella at the far end of the terrace.

Immediately Catherine emitted a banshee wail of "Daddy going!" and she launched herself out of the inflatable swimming pool and fastened herself on to Cross's right leg like a limpet.

Cross stooped, picked her up and tossed her high in the air. He caught her again as she dropped. "Sorry, baby!" he told her. "Daddy is not going. Daddy is staying with you."

"Daddy staying!" she rejoiced, and hugged him around the neck. Cross found himself another beer and the two of them came back and dropped into the canvas chair beside Dave Imbiss.

"I hope you don't mind if I interrupt your father-daughter bonding session, Heck," Dave asked. "We need to figure out a way of tracking Nastiya and Zhenia when they go aboard the Faucon."

"What do you suggest?"

"Well, a smartphone is about as good a GPS tracking device as you can get these days. Nastiya's already got a Maria Denisova phone, loaded with contacts, photos, notes and apps that support the legend for her cover. If we give Zhenia something similar then as long as they're near the phones, we can just track them on Find My Phone and we'll know where they are."

Cross considered the suggestion for a moment, then replied, "Only as long as da Cunha doesn't take the phones, remove the batteries and prevent then sending a signal."

"Well, an iPhone is a sealed unit, so he can't take the batteries. And I don't think he can take the phones, either, not as long as the Voronovas' cover holds. I mean, so far as da Cunha's concerned, Maria Denisova's the link to his biggest investors, so he's not going to insult her by taking her phone. These days if you take someone's phone, that's like taking one of their limbs."

"Okay, point taken. But da Cunha can ask her politely to disable Find My Phone and then what do we do?"

"Have another app in there that does the same thing, disguised as a shopppng app, or a game or whatever. So he thinks he's solved the problem, but he hasn't."

"How is she going to get a signal in the middle of the ocean?"

"Not an issue. The kind of people who charter yachts like the *Faucon*'s demand total connectivity, anywhere on earth. It'll have satellite comms, phone signals, Wi-Fi, you name it."

Cross nodded, accepting the argument and was about to say as much when he was interrupted by the high-pitched squeal of an attention-seeking toddler.

"Bot!" Catherine declared, attempting to stuff a chubby little hand in her father's mouth to silence him, so that she could be the center of the conversation once again.

Cross ducked his daughter's fist and went on airing his thoughts. "So where are da Cunha and Congo going to be? Logically, they've got to be somewhere in easy reach of Cabinda, which means the Atlantic, off the coast of West Africa. But that still leaves a helluva large patch of water. Even if we know the *Faucon d'Or*'s location, we've still got to get on board and the speed that yacht can cruise at, we'll have a hell of a hard time catching up."

Catherine seized a handful of her father's hair and twisted his head around until he was facing out toward the Arabian Gulf. "Bot!" she squeaked. "There bot!"

For the first time Cross looked in the direction that his head had been pointed for him. "Good God!" he said in tones of wonderment, looking at the fastest, meanest, blackest, sharpest-looking craft he'd ever seen in his life racing across the dazzling expanse of water. "You know, she is right. There is a boat out there. What a clever girl!" He looked back at Dave. "Do you have any idea what that is . . . and where we could get one??"

355

"Whoa!" Dave gasped, oblivious to Cross's question. "You don't see one of those babies too often."

Cross looked at his deputy quizzically. "And . . . ?"

"That's an Interceptor. Made by an outfit from Southampton. The concept was a forty-eight-foot powerboat with teeth, something that could chase down any pirate or drug smuggler on the water, or land a dozen Special Forces troops so fast it would be in and out before the enemy even knew it was there. They claimed that thing could do 100 miles-an-hour, even gave one to the Top Gear guys to play with. Without the guns, obviously."

"Thank God for that. But speaking of guns . . . what does it have?"

"In full military spec? Oh, man . . ." Imbiss grinned contentedly. "Up at the bow you're talking about a Browning M2 .50-caliber heavy machine gun, mounted on a retractable Kongsberg Sea Protector weapons platform and firing control system, complete with smoke-grenade launchers. Aft of the cockpit, say hello to a Thales Lightweight Multi-Role Missile launcher, that's got surface-to-air and surface-to-surface capability, so it can take out aircraft and ships."

"Handy," said Cross. "Where can we get one?"

"Well, normally I'd say we can't because the makers went out of business."

"Really? From what you say it sounds like a fantastic bit of kit."

"I don't know, maybe the Interceptor was just too fantastic for its own good. You know what bean-counters are like, Heck. They don't trust anything that looks like that much fun. But a few of 'em were built, just as unarmed speedboats and they come up for sale from time to time. And seeing as how that one's got the royal crest of Abu Zara flying from the stern . . ."

"By God, so it has," Cross said, screwing up his eyes against the glare.

". . . I think I know who got his hands on one of them."

"No, don't tell me. Let me guess!"

356

"Right first time." Dave laughed as the boat slowed, made a nimble, ninety-degree turn to port and headed toward the shoreline, coming straight toward them. "That's one of His Royal Highness Emir Abdul's latest toys."

"I'd love to see it running at its top speed." Cross went to the railing of the terrace, still carrying Catherine, and he looked down at the outlandish craft as it loafed along just offshore. Suddenly one of the panels of black armored glass which enclosed the bridge slid open and a helmeted head appeared in the opening. The helmet was removed to reveal a familiar face, accompanied by a cavalier wave.

"His Royal Highness is at the controls. Perfect!" Cross grinned. He returned the cavalier royal wave and then handed Catherine to Nastiya in order to free his hands. He waved his iPhone above his head and pantomined receiving a call from HRH.

Even though he had a special relationship with the Prince Cross was not privy to his personal number. The Prince understood his message immediately. He ducked back into the cabin and emerged again holding his phone to his ear. After a short pause Cross's phone rang.

"Good afternoon, Major Cross." The Prince spoke into his ear.

"She's a beauty, Your Royal Highness! Would you let me see you give her the full gun?"

"Of course, Major. It will be nothing but a pleasure." The Emir waved again. His head disappeared and the armored glass panel slid closed behind him.

Suddenly the air was filled with a high-pitched whine like a Boeing jet engine starting up. Then the sound rose swiftly to a pitch that threatened to pierce Cross's skull and bore into his teeth. The bows of the sleek ship rose out of the water for half its length. Then she stood on her tail and started to run. Cross thought she'd been moving fast the first time he saw her. Now he realized that had been a mere amble compared to the speed she could reach when she really tried. The wake was hurled high into the air like a shower of glittering white salt, shot through with rainbow colors. Seemingly within seconds the long elegant black hull was a distant speck on the horizon.

"I don't believe it!" Cross shook his head and Catherine shook hers every bit as vehemently as her father had done.

"Naughty!" she scolded Prince Abdul. "Naughty man!"

With a determined expression Cross turned back to Dave Imbiss. "You'll never guess what I am thinking," he challenged him.

"It's written all over your face in capital letters, boss."

"His Royal Highness owes me one."

"More than one," Imbiss nodded, "the number of times you've saved his precious oilfields from rebels and terrorists over the years."

"I'll take Nastiya and Zhenia with me when I go to call upon him. You know what Abdul's like. He can seldom deny anything to a pretty girl, let alone two pretty girls."

Cross, O'Quinn and Imbiss were in full dress uniform with decorations. The two Voronova sisters wore long skirts and veils to cover their hair, so as not to give offense to His Royal Highness, but still made these traditional Islamic outfits seem sensual and exotic. They arrived at the palace in a pair of Land Cruisers, to be met at the main gates by a squadron of the Emir's camel corps, much to Zhenia's delight. The only time she'd ever seen camels at close range before had been at the Moscow circus.

The visitors were escorted up through the lush green gardens to where His Royal Highness waited to receive them at the main doors of the palace. This personal greeting was an exceptional honor, normally granted only to fellow royals, but the two of them were old companions. A few years previously Cross had hosted him on a lavish hunting safari to East Africa which turned out to be an unqualified success. Prince Abdul was an avid shikari and, having paid a fortune in permits as if he were tipping a waiter, he bagged a mighty bull elephant whose tusks tipped the scales at a little over 200 pounds the pair. Even more importantly the prince harbored wonderful memories of Cross's deceased wife Hazel Bannock. As head of the Bannock Oil Company, she had made the fateful decision to reopen the Abu Zara oilfield when every man in the oil industry thought it had run dry. She proved them all wrong, and earned vast fortunes both for Bannock Oil and Prince Abdul.

He and Cross embraced and bussed each other on both cheeks. Then HRH did the same to the ladies, but he lingered longer and more attentively in the process. Finally he shook hands with Paddy and Dave before he took Cross's arm and escorted him through to one of the splendid pavilions in the inner gardens. The others trailed along behind them. In the pavilion they were ushered to embossed leather armchairs arranged in a circle, and as soon as they were seated a file of white-clad footmen served them with sweetmeats and iced fruit juices.

They conversed in Arabic, which Cross spoke fluently, another reason why HRH held him in such high regard. The others tried to look intelligent and from time to time nodded and smiled as though they also understood what was being said.

The two men chatted for almost an hour before Cross felt that he had approached the real object of his visit sufficiently obliquely not to make himself seem callow and give his host reason to be offended. Even then, he made his speech courtly, almost flowery to disguise any suggestion that this was a mere business meeting.

"I must tell you, Prince Abdul, that I was amazed and envious of the racing machine in which I saw you yesterday. I hesitate to call it a speedboat for that would give entirely the wrong description of such an extraordinary craft."

HRH's eyes twinkled but he kept his expression nonchalant as he waved his hand dismissively. "I imagine you are speaking of the Interceptor? It is kind of you to remark on such a trivial acquisition, hardly worth mentioning, of course. But I thought it might be an amusing toy for my elder sons to play with when they return from Oxford University at the end of term. I had to buy four of them so as to prevent the boys squabbling over them."

"A wise decision, I am sure. I would fight to the death over such a beautiful machine if I were given the chance."

HRH smiled at Cross's confession, and then went on to extol the virtues of the craft in loving detail. "The hull, you know, is composed of Kevlar and carbon-fiber, making it immensely strong, yet also very light. The diesel engines produce around sixteen hundred horsepower, which is almost twice as much as the current generation of Formula One cars, although they are little more than battery-powered toys these days." He paused and chuckled contentedly. "But please forgive me, my revered friend, I do not wish to bore you with such a trivial subject."

"You are certainly not boring me, Prince Abdul. On the contrary I am utterly fascinated."

"Then perhaps after we have eaten the midday snack that my chefs have prepared for us, you will allow me to take you for a short trip around the bay?" the Prince suggested eagerly.

"I can think of nothing that would give me greater pleasure, Your Royal Highness."

All of them hurried through the luncheon, paying scant respect to the magnificent banquet that was served to them by more uniformed staff and chefs in high hats. Then they were conducted down to the private dock by the Emir in person, where moored against the jetty with its engines idling was one of the midnight-black machines. Sinister. Forbidding, and absolutely thrilling in its coat of non-reflective paint, it seemed poised to charge into action.

The Emir ushered his guests into the marina building where they changed into lifejackets and crash helmets, and were given a safety briefing. Then they were on board the Interceptor. The Emir dismissed the ship's captain from the controls and took his place in the throne-like driver's seat. Cross buckled himself into the co-pilot's seat alongside him. Zhenia's laughter and light chatter slowly faded into an anxious silence as they were led to their seats. She seized her big sister's hand and clung to it as they were strapped in.

"Will we be in danger?" she whispered anxiously, and Nastiya made calming sounds and shook her head.

Finally a worker on the jetty cast off the mooring lines. Prince Abdul eased open the throttles. The engines murmured and the Interceptor moved sedately out through the entrance to the yacht basin and into the open water of the Gulf.

As the engines produced more power the Interceptor rose higher out of the water, and the sandy golden beaches began to flow past them sedately at first, but gathering speed swiftly.

"Brace yourselves!" the Prince sang out, and suddenly the boat seemed to have wings. Nastiya retained her calm expression, but she clung on to her seat with both hands, while Zhenia screamed like a teenager on her first ride on the roller coaster at Coney Island Fair, and flung both her arms around her big sister's neck.

The shoreline flew past the windows, blurring with the speed of their passage. The other craft they passed seemed to be frozen in the water. Nearing her top speed the Interceptor leaped from the tops of the waves, taking flight like a gull to cover prodigious distances with a single bound, passing over the three or four intervening crests without touching them, then crashing down on top of the subsequent wave and raising a glittering tower of spume. Every person aboard was thrown forward violently against their safety harness, but almost immediately the mighty engines drove the hull on once more and they were thrown back against their heavily padded seat. Every head nodded vigorously in unison.

"One hundred miles an hour!" Prince Abdul sang out in English at the top of his voice. Cross let out a cowboy yell, and Zhenia cried almost as loudly in Russian:

"Please God! I know I have been a bad girl. Just let me live and I swear I will never do it again."

"Include me in that, O Lord!" Nastiya muttered grimly. "Whatever it was my baby sister did."

An hour later the Interceptor returned to the private dock and the minute she touched the quay and HRH cut the engines Zhenia threw off her safety harness and leaped from the seat. With both hands covering her mouth she raced for the toilet at the back of the cabin. She made it just in time, but the sounds of her distress carried clearly through the flimsy door to an interested audience.

When Zhenia re-emerged she curtseyed to the Prince and asked to be excused from the rest of the visit to the palace, so Cross sent both sisters back to Seascape Mansions with Paddy and Dave Imbiss to take care of them. He felt sorry for Zhenia, but the opportunity to be alone with the Prince was too good to pass up.

As soon as they had left HRH invited Cross up to his gun-room, ostensibly to show him the matching pair of Holland & Holland 12-bore Royal Deluxe Sidelock shotguns that had been delivered to him by the makers the previous week. The true reason became apparent, however, as soon as they were alone and the Prince had locked the gunroom door.

"Now I am sure that a nice glass of iced tea would refresh us both?" he said, and without waiting for a reply from Cross he keyed open one of the steel gun safes and reverently brought forth a bottle of fifty-year-old Glenfiddich Scotch whisky and two crystal tumblers. He half filled the tumblers and as he carried one of them to Cross he dropped his voice: "Glenfiddich only releases fifty bottles a year!"

"Say no more!" Cross followed his example and whispered back. They clinked glasses and drank. After a long, companionable silence Prince Abdul sighed with pleasure and set his glass aside.

"Now, my old friend, you can tell me what really happened to the Bannock Oil Company that reduced it from one of the giants of the industry to a pygmy struggling for its very existence. This is of pressing concern to both of us. You must have suffered as cruelly as my family and I have done."

Cross blinked at the idea of his financial status being compared to that of the Oil Sheik of Abu Zara, but he recovered swiftly and nodded.

"Indeed, Your Highness, the past few years have been the most tragic period of my life. First Hazel's murder, and then the ruin of her company . . ." He paused, drew a deep breath and went on: "Forget what they're saying in the media. The men who've been jailed aren't the real perpetrators here."

"I know that Congo was one of the men who murdered Hazel," Prince Abdul said, and Cross nodded again.

"Yes, him and Carl Bannock," Cross answered him. "Her own son-in-law."

"Ah, yes! I remember now!" HRH said. "Of course I remember how you captured Congo and handed him over to the U.S. marshals here in Abu Zara. But I don't know what happened to Carl Bannock. He seems to have disappeared . . . ?" HRH made it sound like a question.

"Carl Bannock is dead, but his corpse will never be found," Cross answered. "But Congo's still alive. He put together the Magna Grande attack with a self-proclaimed African freedom fighter called Mateus da Cunha . . ."

"The name sounds familiar . . ."

"I'm sure it does. He's not shy of publicity, when it suits him. If you want to know why Bannock Oil is now virtually worthless, don't look any further than them."

"Tell me what happened," said Prince Abdul. "Not the media story, but the truth."

The Prince remained silent but his expression was intense as Cross recounted what had happened. "What chance do Congo and da Cunha have of taking control of Cabinda?" he asked, when the story was done.

363

"Well, the Feds seized all of Bendick's funds when he was in-
dicted, so Congo lost all the money he was hoping to make by
short-selling Bannock Oil. But the fact remains, they got to the
rig and the *Bannock A* and that's put the wind up all the other
oil companies in the region, and it's made Cabinda even more
vulnerable. My guess is that a lot of people were thrilled by the
sight of Africans humbling a mighty U.S. oil company. It won't
take much to get them on the streets, demanding independence."

"I can believe that," the Prince agreed. "But aren't Congo and
da Cunha worried that they might be betrayed? Weiss was Congo's attorney, Bendick knew him by his Juan Tumbo alias. Surely
it would be in their interest to co-operate with the authorities."

Cross shook his head. "They've been pleading the fifth for
months and frankly I don't blame them. Congo can reach into
the U.S. prison system like a kid reaching into a sweetie jar.
They'd be dead the moment they opened their mouths."

"So now they want to get their hands on Cabinda. Well, in a
way I do not blame them. I of all people understand the value
of oil. But a plan like theirs, to create a war of independence,
costs money. A great deal of money. Where are Congo and
Mateus getting theirs?"

"Those two young ladies you took for a ride on your Interceptor this afternoon have found Russian investors willing to
finance the seizure of Cabinda."

"I take it your people cannot be assisting this plot . . . ?"

"Congo and da Cunha think they are, which is what matters
to me," Cross explained. "But don't worry. I've not gone rogue."

"I'm very glad to hear it, old friend. So, do you know where
the two conspirators are now?"

"Yes and no. Their precise location is currently unknown. But
da Cunha has a large and very comfortable yacht, the *Faucon
d'Or*, at his disposal, and wherever it is, I'm betting he's on it,
and Congo with him. I believe that they'll use the ship as a
command post for their operations inside Cabinda. Da Cunha's

invited the Voronova sisters to join him, officially so that they can report back to his Russian investors. Unofficially, I'm sure he has other ideas."

"Quite," said the Prince, understanding precisely the reason powerful men invite beautiful women onto very large, expensive yachts.

Cross got back to business. "We'll be tracking the women via their smartphones. Once they're on board *Faucon d'Or* they can guide us to where it is cruising."

"Then you will arrest them and hand them over to the U.S. authorities, yes?"

Cross looked right into the Prince's eyes, his jaw set, his expression unflinching. "In my experience, arresting Johnny Congo is a total waste of time. Next time I am going to save everybody a great deal of trouble, simply by killing him out of hand."

The Prince frowned, gave his head a short, vigorous shake and then put a fnger in one ear as if to clear it. "You know, it is the strangest thing, but sometimes I am a little hard of hearing. Perhaps I go shooting too often. They say that loud gunfire can damage one's eardrums." He paused for a moment, and then nodded. "So, we understand one another . . . Now, tell me, how are you planning to effect the capture of da Cunha's yacht while it is at large upon the ocean?"

"We're going to go hunting, with the *Faucon* as our prey. We should have no trouble catching up with it, seeing that we will be travelling at almost a hundred mph."

Prince Abdul stared at him in blank incomprehension for a few moments and then what Cross had said sank in and his voice rose. "You don't really expect me to give you the use of one of my beautiful new XSMG Interceptor attack boats, do you?"

"Why ever not?" Cross asked with wide-eyed innocence, and the Emir threw his head back and guffawed with laughter.

Through his mirth he grunted, "I have always said that the

English are the most arrogant people in the world. You are the living testimony to the truth of that statement."

Ihe good news is that HRH has given us the unrestricted use of one of his Interceptors," Cross announced to a meeting of the top brass of Cross Bow Security a few hours later. Dave Imbiss pumped his fist with a shout of, "Yes!" as Paddy O'Quinn slapped him on the back, Nastiya said, "Oh, well done, Hector," and Zhenia blew him a discreet little kiss.

"The bad news, however, is that we don't know precisely where we should deploy it." The excitement in the room suddenly abated as they all came back down to earth. "Also, the Prince bought his boats for pleasure, not warfare, so they are entirely unarmed. And the Interceptor has a range of two hundred and fifty miles at a steady cruise, but the miles per gallon go way, way down once you put the pedal to the metal."

Now his team were looking positively glum. "Don't despair, children," Cross chided them. "All is not lost. We have a pretty good idea of da Cunha and Congo's likely whereabouts, so if we aim for the waters off Cabinda—which we all know far too well—we won't be far off. And it really doesn't matter if there aren't any machineguns or missiles on board because we can hardly strafe the ship let alone sink it if we have two of our people aboard. And thanks to there being no weapons, the Interceptor weighs next to nothing—barely ten tons, in fact—which makes it light enough and small enough to fit in the belly of a C-130 transport. And you all know what that means."

"Hello again, Bernie and Nella," Paddy piped up.

"You've got it," said Cross. "Mr. and Mrs. Vosloo are back on the payroll."

The couple were part of a small group of pilots for hire who specialized in flying people and cargoes in and out of dangerous places across the African continent, frequently under fire. They operated a battered old Lockheed C-130 Hercules that looked as though it was only held together by the power of prayer. But they'd got Cross and his team in and out of more tight spots than he could count and the plane, its pilots and their passengers were all still more-or-less in one piece.

"That's all well and good, Heck," said Paddy, more seriously now, "but that Interceptor's not built to be at sea for extended periods. It's going to need refuelling and servicing. I don't see us pitching up in a yacht basin, even assuming there is such a thing in that part of the world. That boat would attract more attention than a Ferrari in a supermarket car park."

"I agree," nodded Cross. "But we don't need a marina. Our old friend the *Glenallen* has been sitting in a dock in Luanda, Angola, waiting for someone to buy her as part of the Bannock Oil everything-must-go sale. The current dismal state of the oil industry, particularly offshore, means that there aren't many takers. So the broker is happy to charter her out to us at a very reasonable rate. She'll be crewed, fuelled and ready to go in a matter of days."

"Go where, though?" Imbiss asked.

"Libreville, Gabon. It's just up the coast from Cabinda and Gabon is as peaceful and democratic as one can expect in that part of the world, as well as being one of the richest countries in sub-Saharan Africa, which means that people are a lot more reasonable. Being naturally concerned that his precious boat doesn't fall into the wrong hands—an over-attentive customs man, for example—Prince Abdul has agreed to declare it official diplomatic cargo, bound for his consul in Libreville."

"Does he have a consul in Libreville?"

"He will by the time we get there. So Dave, I need you to stay here with a couple of guys—I need two with naval experience—to supervise the loading and transport of the Interceptor and then to crew it at the far end."

"What about a mechanic?"

"It comes with its own engineer, like a horse with its groom.

HRH insists. I need that boat in the air within the next forty-eight hours at the absolute maximum. Thirty-six would be better. Twenty-four would be best."

"Got it."

"Meanwhile, Paddy, you and I are going to go ahead to Libreville. I'm envisaging an assault on the *Faucon d'Or* with two teams of three men. That's you and me, with two men each."

"Will that be enough?"

"I reckon so. There won't be many hostiles on board the yacht. Those things are only built to take a maximum twelve passengers, plus crew. Any more than that and they count as commercial passenger vessels and all sorts of additional rules and reg's apply."

"I can't see Johnny Congo worrying too much about health and safety," Paddy observed.

"True, but I can see Master Mateus caring very much about his own comfort and about putting on a show for the ladies. He won't want armed men crammed into every nook and cranny. Besides, Paddy, there's something very, very wrong with the world when six well-armed, highly experienced men with Special Forces training can't take down a floating gin-palace like the *Faucon*."

"Good point, boss."

"Then it's agreed. We'll take a spare man for each team, just in case, and we'll fly commercial from Dubai to Libreville. There's an Air Ethiopia flight via Addis Ababa that gets us there in under ten hours, and a Turkish one that's a lot longer. If we stagger our arrivals over three flights and book every ticket individually, none seated together, that should avoid setting off any alarm bells anywhere. Dave, can you be responsible for bringing all our gear in the Herky-bird? If it goes with you we can get it covered by diplomatic privilege, along with the boat. Everybody clear so far?"

There were nods of assent all around.

"Good," said Cross. "With a fair wind and a bit of luck we

should be able to get everyone in place by the time Nastiya and Zhenia are taken aboard the *Faucon d'Or*. It's an absolute priority, so far as I'm concerned, that you two women spend as little time as humanly possible onboard. You're going to be in very grave danger, and if your cover's blown, then God help you. So you two matter more than anything. It's far more important to me to see you both alive than to see Congo dead."

"To see both would be best," said Nastiya.

"Quite so. But you don't have to go through with this."

"Don't worry about me, I've been in much worse situations, you know that. But Zhenia, you have not been trained as I have. You don't have my experience."

"She's right," Hector said gently, looking at Zhenia. "Nastiya can do this alone if she has to. She can say that you're ill or make some other excuse. No one will think any the worse of you."

Zhenia did not hesitate for a second. "I am going," she said. "It is time that I stopped being a spoiled little girl and became a woman who is worthy to stand alongside all of you. I know all about nasty, violent, abusive men. My father is one of them. Believe me, I can look after myself. And if I can't, well, I have my big sister to protect me."

Cross was sorely tempted to pull rank and take Zhenia off the job. He hated the idea of sending the woman who meant more to him with every day and night they spent together into danger. But if he did that, he would show her up in front of the others and brand her as more special to him than them, thereby infuriating her and upsetting the balance of the team. So he went against every one of his protective, alpha-male instincts and said, "Well done. That's just the attitude we expect at Cross Bow Security." He saw Zhenia stand just that little bit more proudly and a fractional nod of Nastiya's head told him that she approved, too.

"You and Nastiya stay here till you get the call from da Cunha. Then wherever he is, fly via Moscow. He probably knows about my connection to Abu Zara by now and Congo certainly does, so any flight from the Gulf will attract suspicion. Once you're on the move, keep us informed where you are for as long as you can. Once you go silent, we'll keep tracking your phones. Dave, talk them through the procedure."

Imbiss explained how there would be a separate tracker app in case da Cunha was smart enough to insist on them disabling Find My Phone. "So, I need to hide it within an app that you would normally have on your phone. You guys got any preferences?"

"Net-a-Porter?" suggested Zhenia.

"That's my little sister for you, always shopping!" laughed Nastiya.

"I do other things too . . . isn't that right, Hector?" replied Zhenia, smiling sweetly at him.

Cross rolled his eyes as the others all laughed. He was tempted to call a halt to proceedings. They were supposed to be conducing serious business. People's lives were at risk. Then he stopped himself. *Yes, that's right. Any one of these people could be dead before the week is out. So let them laugh. There'll be time enough to be serious before this operation is through.*

A day had passed, filled with planning, listing, trying to think of everything, fitting into hours what in an ideal world would take weeks. "It's like packing for the holidays," Paddy O'Quinn had blithely remarked. "But with guns."

Now a new day had dawned and Cross was on his way. Before he got into the cab that would take him to the airport for the flight to Libreville Cross stopped for one last look back up at his apartment. Right now, he knew, Catherine Cayla's nanny Bonnie would be holding her up to one of the windows that looked down from the penthouse floors of Seascape Mansions. He waved up at the tower, smiling broadly, trying to look jaunty, as if nothing could possibly happen and Daddy would always come back.

For now, though, there was hard, dangerous, bloody work to be done, and Cross set his mind to think of that and nothing else. By the time the cab was pulling away from the curb he was already dialing the Vosloos' number: again. Normally it was never hard to get hold of them, even if one did have to make oneself heard over the sound of straining engines and passing bursts of anti-aircraft fire. But not this time. His first call had been put straight through to voicemail. So had his second, six hours later. This was his fourth attempt, and once again the only answer he got was a recorded message. "Come on!" he muttered to himself, "Pick up the bloody phone!"

He had to have that Hercules. Without it the mission would be over before it had even begun.

Two hundred feet above her father, Catherine Cayla had recognized him and shrieked with excitement until he disappeared into the cab. Then she cried out, "Daddy going!" and dissolved into bitter tears and a wailing lament of half-formed words that might as well have been Tibetan chants or the hunting songs of an obscure Amazonian tribe for all that anyone other than Bonnie could understand them.

"Daddy coming back soon," she consoled her charge and took her through to the kitchen to watch her favorite Peppa Pig DVD and eat her dinner. Zhenia, who had been feeling a little tearful herself when Cross had finally extricated himself from her farewell hug, given her one last kiss and gone off to war, came into the kitchen too, to make herself a consoling cup of coffee.

She sat herself down at the table, next to Catherine's high chair.

"I know how you feel, little one," she said, smiling sympathetically at the sad little child, who was snuffling in bitter and inconsolable misery.

Zhenia was fascinated by Catherine. She knew that if her relationship with Hector was to have any hope of surviving in the long term, he had to know that his woman and his daughter were friends. So sheer self-interest necessitated Zhenia making an effort to be nice. But more than that, having thought of herself as a daughter and a little sister for so long it fascinated her now to find herself as the big one: not a sister and not yet a stepmother—she was not yet ready even to imagine herself as that—but an adult with a responsibility to care about a child, if not to care for her.

For her part, Catherine was of course still far too young to understand that Zhenia was her father's girlfriend. But instinct told her that this lady was important to her daddy, and she was fascinated by Zhenia's big eyes and her soft lips that smiled so nicely. The little girl liked being the object of the young woman's attention and the woman felt a warm, calming pleasure when she was close to the child. They basked in one another's company quite happily for a few minutes while Bonnie made Catherine's porridge and smiled to herself at the relationship being built on the table beside her. Then she placed the bowl on the tray of Catherine Cayla's high chair and advised Zhenia, "I'd stand back if I were you, dear."

"I'm sorry . . . ?" said Zhenia, looking up at the nurse with a puzzled expression on her face.

A second later, all was explained. Catherine had made an instant, heroic recovery and was merrily attacking her porridge with all her father's energy and determination, as if determined to coat herself and everybody else within splashing distance.

"Oh!" cried Zhenia, scrambling to her feet as a large dollop of porridge sailed through the air and straight into her coffee cup, sending an eruption of espresso and skimmed-milk foam across the table.

"I tried to warn you!" laughed Bonnie as Zhenia too collapsed in a fit of the giggles.

The noise attracted Nastiya to the room. "Enough of this nonsense!" she declared, working hard to maintain a suitably severe look on her face. "Come, Zhenia, we have work too!"

"Did you hear that?" Zhenia said to Catherine, who had stopped eating for a moment, distracted by the new arrival in the room. "That is my mean big sister. Isn't she mean and cruel?"

Nastiya folded her arms, but said nothing. Zhenia looked at her, realized that further resistance was futile and, like a good little sister, followed her back to work.

The Voronova sisters were nothing if not industrious. They arranged accommodation and transport for the men arriving in Libreville, along with a truck to carry the Interceptor from the airport to the water. They liaised between the Abu Zara Foreign Ministry and the authorities in Gabon to ensure the unimpeded passage of the Interceptor and everything about it when it arrived in that country. They cajoled, sweet-talked and begged the shipbroker who was chartering out the *Glenallen* to get her to sea even more quickly than he had promised. They worked on installing a complete identity, suitable for a top businesswoman's personal assistant on the smartphone Imbiss had given her. But in the end there came a time when all the calls and emails and texts dealt with, they'd installed everything that was needed on the phone and all they could do was wait for the one call that mattered most of all: the one from Mateus da Cunha.

Hector was on the ground at Addis Ababa airport when he finally got the call from Nella Vosloo. "How's it going, Heck, you old rogue?" she asked.

"I'm fine, thank you, Nella," Cross replied. "You have no idea how glad I am to hear your voice."

"Ach, don't try to woo me with flattery, Heck. Just tell me: how soon do you want us? How far do you want us to go? And how much are you going to pay?"

Cross chuckled at Nella's unmatched ability to cut straight to the chase. "I want you yesterday. I need you to fly a boat . . . "

"I fly planes, Hector. For boats you need a sailor."

He tried again: "All right, then, I need you to stick a boat in your plane and fly that, plus Dave Imbiss, a couple of his men and the boat's engineer from Abu Zara to Libreville, Gabon. And I'll pay you less than you want but more than I think you deserve, same as usual."

"You always were a miser, Heck," she said, though they both knew that he paid in full, on the nail every time.

"So, where are you right now? And why couldn't I get through to you?"

"Jordan. We were getting a family of Syrian Christians out of the country, one step ahead of those Islamic State bastards. It got a little hairy."

"Is the plane in one piece?"

Nella burst out laughing. "You know you're supposed to ask how your friends are before you inquire about their belongings, right?"

"I know you're all right just by listening to you," Cross pointed out. "I know Bernie must be all right because you wouldn't be talking this way if he wasn't. What I don't know is how the Hercules is doing."

"Oh don't you worry about that. You know what those militia men are like, couldn't hit an elephant's arse at ten paces. Pray and spray, that's how they shoot."

"So you can do the job?"

"Give us a night's sleep and we'll be on our way in the morning."

"And the money?"

"Don't you worry about that, Heck. We'll send you an invoice when the job's done."

The hours dragged by painfully slowly for the Voronova sisters. They played with Catherine Cayla and chatted to Bonnie and when this palled they played fiercely competitive chess, and accused each other of cheating. Then they described to each other in detail the lives they had lived while they had been separated, and agreed that they were infinitely happier now that

374

they had found each other. Nastiya was struck by how many lovers Zhenia claimed to have sampled in so short a space of time, and she accused her little sister of exaggerating, which was the subject of more argument and detailed discussion. They had a lot of lost time to catch up on. Without their menfolk to intervene and distract them they discovered that they actually liked each other more than they had expected to. But mostly they just waited, and waited, and then they waited some more.

Da Cunha had Maria Denisova's number. He'd said he would get in touch to set up the voyage on his yacht. But no call came.

"I am too old to be sitting by the phone, waiting helplessly for a man to ring," snapped Nastiya. But she waited nonetheless.

Another day went by. The Vosloo's Hercules arrived in Abu Zara and the work of loading the Interceptor began. Dave Imbiss called a couple of times, just to let off steam about the frustrations of dealing with Hassan, Prince Abdul's engineer, who was evidently so terrified of his master's wrath, should there be even the faintest scratch on the ship's paintwork, that he was making it almost impossible to get the job done. Imbiss had picked Darko McGrain to be one of the men responsible for helping him transport the Interceptor to Libreville and then crew it once they were on the water. It said a lot for Hassan's obsessive concern for his boat's well-being that not even McGrain's fearsome temper could make him more co-operative.

There was another hold-up with three of Cross's men who had taken the Turkish Airlines flight to Libreville, which went the scenic route, via Istanbul and Kinshasa in the Democratic Republic of Congo. Evidently there was strike action by Turkish air-traffic controllers and they were stuck in Istanbul, even further from their destination than they had been in Abu Zara.

But these seemed like minor inconveniences and no reason to worry. So Nastiya turned to Zhenia, said, "Don't you hate waiting for a man to call?" and texted da Cunha: "So, when are we going to meet? Maria x."

He replied within the hour: "Where are you?"

"Moscow."

"How soon can you leave?"

Well, I have to get to Moscow first, she thought, then replied: "One day. Have work to finish here first."

"OK. Fly to Accra, Ghana. Give me your flight details. You'll be met at airport with onward tickets."

"OK. Cool x"

"Just as long as we don't end up with Ebola," Nastiya said, pulling a long face at Zhenia as she sat down at her laptop and started looking at schedules. There was an Aeroflot flight the next morning from Moscow to Accra via Amsterdam. "Thank God! The plane is operated by KLM," sighed Nastiya who considered herself a patriot, but not when it came to air travel.

They flew overnight to Moscow, they waited for three hours at Sheremetyevo airport in Moscow then made the surprisingly short, six-and-a-half hour flight to Kotoka International in Accra.

At the arrivals barrier there was a Ghanaian taxi driver, who spoke only pidgin English holding up a board with Nastiya's name ingeniously misspelled upon it. He drove them to the Tulip Inn in central Accra. There they found that a reasonably comfortable suite had been pre-booked for them. They fell into bed exhausted by the journey and slept until late the following morning. When they went down to the dining room for lunch there was a message from Mateus da Cunha at the reception alerting them to the fact that the next leg of their journey had been arranged to commence the following day at 9 a.m. But in the meantime they both had appointments booked at the hotel beauty parlor for the afternoon and for the dining room in the evening.

The bill for dinner had been pre-paid and included a bottle of Pol Roger. Zhenia remarked as she sipped the champagne, "Mateus da Cunha may be a crook but he has good taste; you and genuine French champagne."

"Don't tell my husband," Nastiya pleaded.

While they were dining the receptionist came through from the lobby with another message: "A car will pick you up tomorrow morning at eight o'clock."

"Should we send a message to Cross to tell him what is going on?" Zhenia asked.

Nastiya thought aloud. "Can da Cunha monitor our phones? No. Not until we're on the boat. He's not the CIA."

She texted Cross: "In Accra. Pick up at 08:00. Destination unknown."

A few minutes later came a reply. "In Libreville. *Glenallen* fine, but no Interceptor and men still stuck in Istanbul. Be careful."

"What did Hector say?" Zhenia asked as Nastiya read the message.

"Oh, nothing much. He's in Libreville. He says we have to be careful."

"The Voronova sisters . . . careful?" Zhenia laughed. "Does he know us at all?"

After dinner, a three-piece band was playing loud jazz in the bar lounge. Nastiya took a table as close to it as possible, and under cover of the music she quietly took Zhenia through their cover story, and the details of the fictitious oligarchs who were reputedly eager to invest in the Cabinda project.

"Oh, we've been through this so many times, I'm bored with it. I know the story. You're my boss. I'm your PA. If anyone asks me a difficult question, I'll just play the dumb secretary and say, 'How should I know?' Now, please, can we have some more champagne. Mateus can afford it."

"No," said Nastiya, firmly. "I want you looking sharp and beautiful tomorrow. We must be ready to dodge any surprises that get thrown at us. Now it's bedtime for you, and eight hours' sleep."

Cross went to bed at midnight and was woken an hour later by Dave Imbiss calling from Abu Zara, which was three hours ahead. "We've got a problem, boss. The Herky-bird's here, and being refuelled now. Bernie and Nella are grabbing some shuteye, but they're basically all systems go. Trouble is we're not going anywhere because I cannot get this sonovabitch engineer to understand that our mission is (a) time-sensitive, and (b) more important than scratching or denting his damn speedboat."

Cross could hear children screaming, a woman shouting and a man pleading with all of them to quieten down. "Where the hell are you?" he asked.

"At home with the Hassans. I guess they aren't happy I woke them all up. Can you have a word with him, make him see the light? Here, I'll put him onto you . . . "

"Peace be upon you, Hassan," Cross said, and was greeted by a torrent of furious Arabic, which even he, who spoke the language, had a hard time following. But the gist was unmistakable: Hassan was not happy about having his beauty sleep disturbed and was now even more determined to be as uncooperative as possible.

Funny how a jobsworth sounds the same in any language, Cross thought to himself. But he had dealt with the type before and had long since realized that there was no point arguing, or not on their terms, at least. So he waited until Hurricane Hassan had blown itself out and then said, "I am going to tell you two things: what is going to happen, and why it is going to happen. And while I am speaking, you will listen to me, as I have listened to you. Do you understand?"

Cross took the resentful grunt that was Hassan's only response as a form of assent.

"Then understand this, too. His Royal Highness, the Emir Abdul, peace and blessings be upon him, has honored me with the inestimable privilege of his friendship, unworthy though I am. As a token of his esteem he has, with infinite generosity, seen fit to bestow upon me the use of his magnificent boat. Thus, what is going to happen is that you are going to assist

378

my associate Mr. Imbiss and his men to load that boat upon the airplane that is going to carry it to me."

There was a brief verbal flurry from Hassan, though the tone had turned from furious indignation to a feeble, plaintive whine. He was, it was clear, terrified of the repercussions to him and his family if the boat entrusted to him should suffer any damage in his care.

"I hear your concerns, Hassan," Cross said, a little more emolliently. "So now I will tell you why you will do as I say, and why it will be to your benefit to do so. You will agree, I am sure, that His Royal Highness places his honor as a prince, a man and a friend above mere trifles such as money and possessions."

Hassan did indeed accept the truth of this proposition.

"To you and I, this boat may be a magnificent machine, but to His Royal Highness it is a mere trifle. Now, the reason why he has bestowed the boat upon me now is that I am engaged upon a mission, one that will lead to the death of a wicked man, who is my enemy, and thus His Royal Highness's enemy too. As part of this mission, two very brave women have been called upon to risk their lives, so that this evil man may be defeated. I treasure the lives of these woman, and thus His Royal Highness treasures them too."

"Of course, of course," said Hassan, with something close to eagerness.

"Thus, any man who helps with this mission and contributes to its success will gain great glory and receive my thanks, and that of His Royal Highness. He can be assured of rewards and blessings. But . . . " Cross let the word hang in the air, "Should any man hinder the mission, and should it fail because of his unwillingness to be of assistance, he can be sure of His Royal Highness's wrath, for he will have dishonored his Emir as well as himself, and betrayed his Emir's friend and then he will have made two enemies who can make his life a very short, and miserable, and uncomfortable existence, so that he is crushed,

379

like a scorpion beneath a boot, and ground into the dirt like a scrap of camel dung, and his family must live forever with the shame of his disgrace."

There was total silence on the other end of the line. Then Cross heard the distant sound of a string of plaintive, heartfelt apologies, then profound assurances of immediate assistance.

Imbiss came on the line. "Great work, Heck," he said. "It's going to take a while to put this baby onto a pallet and get it in the hold. Then we've got to stow all the other kit. So I can't promise to be in the air much before seven-hundred hours, our time. But the Vosloos have promised to put the pedal to the metal. Call it ten hours flying time, maybe a shade more. That makes our ETA between fourteen and fifteen hundred your time, with the boat in the water an hour after that."

"Damn, that's cutting it fine," Cross said. He could hear a door slamming then footsteps: Imbiss and Hassan must be on their way. "The girls are being picked up from their hotel at eight this morning. From that point on, we have to assume that they're in the hands of the enemy."

A thought suddenly struck Cross: something so obvious he could not imagine how he'd missed it before: "Will you be able to track them while you're in the air?"

"I think so, sure. Seems like Bernie and Nella have been doing all right for themselves lately. They've given the plane a total overhaul. You wouldn't recognize it, Heck. I mean it actually looks like it might fly."

"That's a change!

"Totally. Hang on a second . . ." A car door opened, there was a brief pause, then a car engine starting, then Imbiss again: "What was I saying? Oh yeah, the Vosloos have dragged the communications systems into the twenty-first century. They've got satellite connectivity for phone and internet. Should be fine. Nastiya and Zhenia are in Accra, Ghana now, right?"

"Yes, which means the *Faucon d'Or* has to be in the Gulf

380

of Guinea. That makes our lives a lot easier trying to find it. Da Cunha and Congo can't sail north or east because they'll run into Africa. They won't go west unless they've suddenly decided to cross the Atlantic. And Cabinda's to the south. So pound-to-a-penny, that's the course they'll take."

"Which'll lead them straight toward Libreville," Imbiss said.

"Exactly. I've told the skipper of the *Glenallen* not to stop here but keep heading north, to close the distance as much as possible between him and the *Faucon*. We can catch up with him in the Interceptor."

"Still, there's got to be seven hundred miles of ocean between Accra and Libreville. Hell of a distance."

"Don't remind me. But we'll find the *Faucon d'Or* and we'll get to it in time."

"Damn right we will!" Imbiss replied.

They both spoke in tones of absolute certainty. But as Cross ended the call, and laid back in his bed he knew that for all their shows of confidence, the odds were still against them.

After breakfast the next morning the Voronovas' taxi driver was again waiting for them downstairs in the hotel lobby. "Where are you taking us today?" Zhenia demanded of him.

He laughed delightedly and answered, "Yes! *Da! Jawohl!* Today. Me taking us." This turned out to be the limit of his vocabulary, and the end of the conversation.

"I guess we'll know when we get there," Nastiya consoled her little sister.

The taxi crept at a walking pace through the incredibly crowded streets of the city. Their driver began sounding his horn as soon as he engaged the clutch and did not lift his hand from the button until they reached their destination, almost an hour later.

This turned out to be a small creek on the outskirts of the city. It was surrounded by a grove of coconut palms, under which native fishing boats were drawn up on the beach, with their nets spread out to dry. The taxi drove down to the edge of the water and parked alongside a floating jetty against which were moored three floatplanes, one of them an amphibious Twin Otter.

The taxi driver climbed out and yelled something in the local language and after a while a head appeared behind the windscreen of the Otter. The pilot had obviously been asleep in the cockpit. He opened the door and climbed down on to the jetty.

"Are you the passengers for the *Faucon d'Or*?" he shouted in a South African accent. Once assured that they were, he and the taxi driver carried the girls' luggage down the jetty and loaded it into the plane. The pilot paid the driver and they took their seats in the back of the floatplane, which taxied out through the mouth of the creek and lined up into the breeze and the chop of the water.

As soon as the pilot had taken off and settled into flight Nastiya leaned over the back of his seat and asked him, "What are you doing in such a godforsaken part of the world?"

He grinned. "I work for a company who services the oil-exploration ships. Mostly we fly pretty girls and other goodies out to them."

"I am sure my husband would love to hear you describe me as a goodie," she told him primly.

"Sorry," he apologized. "You look much too happy to be married."

Nastiya kept a straight face and they flew on in silence across the blue waters of the Gulf of Guinea. Zhenia was slumped in her seat, fast asleep. *Good, she needs her rest,* thought Nastiya, and then, *My God, I'm turning into her mother!*

It was almost midday now and the pilot was flying into the sun, so they were heading south, toward Libreville. Toward *Hector and Paddy!* But how far had they come? Trying to sound as casual as possible, Nastiya asked, "How fast have we been flying?"

"Ach, just the regular cruise speed. Call it two-eighty kph, about a hundred and seventy miles an hour. Our journey's roughly five hundred miles."

"Will you fly straight back to Accra?"

"Not unless I want to run out of fuel and die! No, I'm heading on to Port Harcourt, Nigeria. Got some other clients waiting for me there."

An hour in the air stretched into two, then three. Finally the pilot pointed ahead through the windscreen.

"There she is: the *Faucon d'Or*. Nice little dinghy, isn't she?" He began to bleed off altitude and banked steeply over the yacht, which lay at anchor a few hundred meters off a narrow beach with dense jungle further inland. "That's Nigeria you can see beyond her."

Peering down at the yacht Nastiya was astonished by the size and pristine condition of the vessel. Zhenia had woken and was looking down at it too. "That looks good enough for Roman Abramovich," she said.

"No way!" the pilot laughs. "That's just a dinghy next to one of his!"

There was barely any wind and the plane landed on the flat calm water with barely a bump. As the pilot taxied toward the ship a motor launch detached itself from the bottom of the gangway and came to meet them. Nastiya and Zhenia climbed down on to one of the floats and hopped across to the launch. As soon as the crew had transferred the girls' luggage into the launch it headed back toward the yacht. Behind them the pilot of the Twin Otter took off and headed back for the Ghanaian shore.

As the launch approached the *Faucon d'Or* a tall and elegant figure appeared on the aft deck and looked down at them.

"Who is that?" Zhenia demanded with sudden interest.

"That is Mateus da Cunha," Nastiya told her.

"If you are sure you don't want him, then I don't mind taking him off your hands as a favor, my darling sister."

"I thought you were in love with Hector Cross?"

"I am, but it's not an exclusive relationship." Zhenia kept a straight face but when she winked at Nastiya they both burst out laughing.

"Now I know beyond any shadow of doubt who your father is," Nastiya told her.

Nastiya climbed the gangway to the deck of the *Faucon d'Or* ahead of her sister as befitted her status. A bodyguard, dressed in a charcoal gray suit, white shirt and dark blue tie, as if completely indifferent to the fact that he was on a yacht off West Africa, rather than a street in New York or Paris, helped her aboard. He looked her up and down, examining every inch of her, mentally undressing her. Nastiya knew that the guard's interest was anything but sexual. He was deciding whether she was carrying a concealed weapom. Evidently satisfied that the perfect cut of Nastiya's white, knee length dress left no room for an excess ounce of flesh, let alone a knife or gun, the guard gave a little nod of the head. Then da Cunha stepped forward to greet her and kissed the back of the hand that she offered him.

"Welcome on board the *Faucon d'Or*, Mademoiselle Denisova. I hope your journey from Moscow was not too onerous?" he asked solicitously. "I must apologize for not meeting you personally at Accra, but I'm sure you appreciate that these are critical times and I am concerned to keep you out of general view until our objects have been achieved."

"We Russians are accustomed to hardships. I am certain our journey will be very much worthwhile in the end, and this small inconvenience will soon be forgotten."

"Let us hope that is the case," Mateus observed, and then turned to greet Zhenia as she stepped off the gangway. Watching him without seeming to do so, Nastiya saw the pupils of his eyes dilate slightly, and his expression soften as he realized how lovely she was, with the bloom of youth still fresh upon her. She felt a stab of concern as she wondered if she might have led her younger sister into a dangerous situation. She was just too beautiful for her own good, and their hosts were ruthless killers and criminals. A stab of anxiety struck her. *I just hope Hector gets here soon. That text last night was really worrying.*

Nastiya forced any negative thoughts from her mind and smiled easily at Mateus.

"This is my assistant, Polina Salko. She graduated from Moscow University with a first class honors degree and she has been employed by me for three full years. I can vouch for her discretion and her acuity."

"You are both more than welcome." Mateus lingered over the slim white hand just a little longer than was necessary. Then he stood back. "There are suites prepared for both of you, which I hope will live up to your expectations. The stewards will take you to them. Your luggage will follow momentarily. Take as long as you need to freshen yourselves. Then when you are ready, please ring for your cabin steward who will escort you to the salon. I will then take the opportunity to introduce you to our other important guest, His Majesty King John Kikuu Tembo."

Nastiya felt a quick frisson of excitement to hear him use Congo's alias. The huntress in her sensed that they were nearing the climax of the chase. The quarry was gathered on the killing ground. All that remained was for the hunters to assemble.

"There is one minor matter with which I must trouble you. I'm sure you appreciate that His Majesty's personal security is of paramount importance. So if I could ask you to disable the location finder on your phones that would be very much appreciated."

"Of course," Nastiya said. She and Zhenia went through the procedure while da Cunha looked on.

"Thank you so much," he said when they were done and Nastiya was suddenly struck by the strange artificiality of the situation. A woman with a false identity complying with the security requirements of a freedom fighter who was really a thief on a giant scale, and a king who was a convicted murderer.

Their situation was as absurd as a farce, and yet as deadly as the bloodiest tragedy.

The stewards ushered the two women to the lift in the entrance lobby and they descended to the lower passenger deck. The suites which awaited them were luxurious but compact in accordance with the limited space available in the vessel. They were situated at opposite ends of the central passageway that ran fore and aft, but Nastiya thought this fact was of little significance.

Before she and Zhenia parted she said, "I will be ready in half an hour, Polina. Come to my room then and be sure to have your iPad with you. I'm sure we'll be taking notes."

As soon as Nastiya reached her own suite she closed and locked the door, then while she brushed her hair she scanned the deck above her and the hull and bulkhead surrounding her for any indication of a CCTV camera hidden in them. She was suddenly aware of the sound of engines and a gentle vibration through the hull. They were getting underway. At the end of the agreed thirty minutes, there was a tap on the door.

"Thank you, Polina," said Nastiya. "And now, I think, it is time to greet His Majesty."

As they entered Mateus stood up from his easy chair, but his companion remained seated and fixed the two girls with dark and brooding eyes. Nastiya paused on the threshold and returned his scrutiny with an equally noncommittal expression, but inwardly she felt deeply disturbed.

She knew who this was. She had seen photographs and video images of him. She had even seen him in the flesh as he was carried on board the aircraft at the Kazundu airfield after his capture by Hector and Paddy. But then he had been unconscious from the massive doses of sedatives that they had injected into him, and trussed up in a rope cargo net that would have immobilized a silverback gorilla.

She had never seen Congo as he was now: fully conscious and

focused, a massive, menacing figure. He seemed twice the size of a normal man. He was dressed in black linen trousers and a black silk shirt, with most of its buttons open to reveal a heavy gold necklace on his chest. The aura of restless, menacing evil that emanated from him was so intense that it took a massive effort of will for her to remain still and hold her ground, rather than to recoil from him.

"Your Majesty, may I present Mademoiselle Maria Denisova?" da Cunha introduced her. Nastiya held her breath while Johnny Congo examined her; but he showed no sign of recognition. His only reaction was to incline his head slightly to acknowledge her existence, but in return Nastiya swept him a deep curtsey. When she rose to her full height once more she moved aside to give Zhenia space to step up beside her, but she addressed Johnny Congo:

"Your Majesty, may I present my assistant Miss Polina Salko."

Zhenia was clearly as overawed as her elder sister had been, but she did not hide it as effectively. She attempted what was probably the first curtsey of her life. It was not a success and Nastiya recognized it as a nervous reaction to fear. *It's not a problem. She's meant to be a secretary. Of course she's over-awed in the presence of royalty.*

Da Cunha indicated that they should take the couch opposite the King and he returned to his easy chair; while Congo listened da Cunha immediately plunged into the business in hand, asking Nastiya to give him details of the men who were prepared to risk their wealth on backing his venture to wrest Cabinda from greater Angola, and then questioning her shrewdly. In doing so da Cunha displayed his crisp intelligence and full command of his subject, but Nastiya had prepared for this with Hector and Paddy so she was able to keep pace with him, occasionally referring queries to Polina to be followed up after the meeting was concluded.

Congo sat with his hands thrust deeply into his pockets and

his knees slightly apart. He said little, and when he did speak his accent was American and his speech patterns were hardly those of an African monarch. Even so, Nastiya could not help but notice that his observations were sharp and his questions cut straight to the point. He seemed particularly interested in the money that was being invested, the terms on which it was being given and the precise means by which the procceds, when they came, would be divided.

"Your Majesty has a remarkable grasp of finance," she said, and the compliment was one of the few completely sincere things she'd said since she'd boarded the yacht. "Might I ask where you acquired it?"

"The street, the yard and the school of hard knocks," he said, flatly. When he looked at Nastiya his pupils were speckled like agate and cruel as those of a predator; but the whites of his eyes were bloodshot and smoky.

"Well," said Mateus da Cunha, "shall we have lunch? We eat under an awning on the rear deck. The breeze is very cooling there and the chef has prepared a superb buffet for us." He spoke as if they were all decent people, engaged in reputable business in the finest possible surroundings. But the pretence of civility was like a fragile paper screen, behind which a monstrous danger lurked, pacing up and down in the darkness, gathering its strength, waiting to be unleashed.

Libreville airport was just a stone's throw from a long expanse of golden beach, but the Interceptor had to be fuelled and that meant taking it a few kilometers down the highway to Port Mole. A massive construction operation was underway there, transforming an industrial dock into a massive complex involving a marina, hotels and beaches for tourists, and tens of thousands of affordable homes for the locals.

"Damn, that's impressive," said Imbiss as they sped past the vast building sites.

"Welcome to the new Africa," Cross replied. "People in the West still think of starving kids with swollen bellies, holding out begging bowls, but Africans aren't like that any more. They don't need our charity, however much some people want to give it to them, just to feel better about themselves. What they need is our business."

"Speaking of business . . ." said Paddy.

"I hadn't forgotten," Cross said. "Not for a second."

"So, the latest readings I have from the trackers show the *Faucon d'Or* cruising southeast at about twenty knots, past the Nigerian oilfields. Their next landfall is the island of Malabo, off the coast of Equatorial Guinea. They've got a volcanic nature reserve on the southern end of the island: incredible landscape, rainforest, black sand beaches. If I were da Cunha and I wanted to impress an investor who looked like Nastiya that's where I'd moor up for the night, maybe have breakfast on the beach in the morning."

"And if I were Johnny Congo, I wouldn't wait that long to make my move on one or both of the women," said Cross. "If we aren't on the *Faucon* a lot sooner than breakfast we'll be too late."

"Amen to that," Paddy sighed.

"So," Cross continued, "this is how we play it. And it won't take long to describe because I'm keeping it simple. First we get to the *Glenallen*. I want a fast crusing speed. We'll still be able to catch up without any problem and there's no need to risk blowing the engines by going flat-out until we absolutely have to. We winch the Interceptor aboard the tug. Hassan gives it the once-over, while we check our kit. Any questions so far?"

He looked around the white Mercedes minibus that was taking them to the dock. There were a couple of shakes of the head, but no one felt any need to speak.

"Right. We launch no more than five miles from the *Faucon d'Or* then keep the Interceptor in the lee of the *Glenallen* as we close on the target. If anybody's looking at the radar, I want them to see a single vessel."

Now Imbiss said. "They're still going to see a ship closing on them. What do we say if they ask who we are and what the hell we're doing?"

"Simple. We give them the name of the *Glenallen*, tell them it's an oilrig support vessel—if they check they'll find both those statements are true—and say we've chartered it to use working the rigs up in the Nigerian oilfields."

Imbiss nodded, satisfied by that.

"Okay," Cross continued. "We keep the Interceptor hidden behind the *Glenallen* for as long as possible and try to stay downwind of the *Faucon*, so that the sound of its engines is blown away from the target. I don't want them to hear us coming a mile off.

"Then, when we're no more than eight hundred meters from the target, we hit the gas and go like stink. Chances are, they won't have a full-time radar operator, but even if they do, he's not going to believe his eyes. We'll be closing on him like a torpedo, not a ship. So he'll ask someone, and they'll come and look, and before they've decide what the hell to do, it'll be too late.

"The lowest part of the *Faucon* is the stern, so that's what we aim for. I don't want to hang about gentlemen. Three of us get over the stern rails while the second group of three keep us covered and suppress any enemy fire, then they come on over the rail, too. Paddy, you come with me and one other man in the first group. Dave, I want you to lead the second group."

"At last! Action!" Imbiss exulted.

"Listen, we want to detain and if necessary terminate Congo and da Cunha. But more than anything else, we have to make sure Nastiya and Zhenia, are safe. We'll start at the top of the ship, with the outside decks and reception tooms, then move down to the cabins below. This isn't subtle. It's not complicated. But it does require everyone to be focused, disciplined and ruthless in the execution of their duties."

And we have to get there on time, Cross added to himself. *Above all else, we have to get there on time.*

But it was almost four in the afternoon now, and they still weren't in the water.

The women had lunch and tried to combine polite conversation with some pretence of doing business as the *Faucon d'Or* motored southeast, past a steel forest of rigs and platforms.

"Did you know that the gas and oil from those installations is worth more than one hundred billion dollars a year to the Nigerian economy, in export revenues alone?" da Cunha said. "One day, Cabinda will be that rich."

"And so will we," Nastiya said raising her glass in a toast.

"To black gold!" da Cunha exclaimed.

He was a charming, attentive host, as befitted a man of his privileged background. Congo, however, was a sullen, brooding presence. He had gone into his shell and his silent presence loomed over the table like a massive thundercloud on the horizon, coming ever closer, bringing with it a mighty storm.

In the afternoon, the Voronovas changed into their swimming costumes and sunbathed between dips in the yacht's outdoor whirlpool tub. They chatted to one another and to da Cunha, too, though Congo still barely said a word. Nastiya kept a discreet eye on the suited figures of the bodyguards, counting three of them, though it was possible that more might be below deck, resting before the night shift. She thought about alerting Cross to their presence. *No, the risk is too great. If the message is intercepted, we're dead.*

Soon the afternoon had drifted by and it was time to change for drinks and then supper: a lobster bisque, followed by a *supreme de volaille* (the chicken meltingly tender within its crisp brown skin) served with rice and miraculously fresh green vegetables, with a perfect *crème caramel.* The meal was simple, yet cooked to a three-star Michelin standard that raised it to something close to high art. The wines, notoriously difficult to maintain in good condition at sea, especially in the tropics, were as well chosen and delicious as the food. It was a meal to raise the lowest spirits, good enough to allow the sisters to forget, at least while they were seated at the table with the canvas awning pulled back to reveal the infinite majesty of the cloud night sky, that they were in mortal danger.

Somewhere to the south, aboard the *Glenallen*, three men were doing their best to restrain their own instinct for violence.

"For God's sake, boss, forget the bloody radar signal and just let the Interceptor rip," Paddy O'Quinn pleaded. "My wife's aboard that bloody yacht."

"And my woman too."

"Yes, I know, I'm sorry . . . But Jesus wept! So what if they see us coming. There's no way they're carrying anything that can hurt us."

"They don't have to hurt us, do they? They hurt the women. Look I get it. If we go too slowly, anything could happen to them. If we go too soon, anything could happen to them. We have to time this exactly perfectly, or . . . "

Cross didn't finish the sentence. He didn't have to. Every man there was thinking about Nastiya and Zhenia. They knew exactly how the rest of the sentence went.

Dinner had been concluded. There had been more talk, more drinking, more silence from Congo. Finally Nastiya had said she was going to bed, pleading exhaustion after two nights and days of travel.

"Of course, I quite understand," said da Cunha. "We shall be stopping for the night soon, so that you will be able to sleep more peacefully and then, in the morning you will wake and—voilà!— paradise. It is called Malabo. I think you will like it very much."

"I'm sure I will," said Nastiya, for the way da Cunha had

392

enunciated "Malabo" in his French accent did indeed make it sound irresistible. "I think you should go to bed, too, Pola," she said to Zhenia. "I'm sure there will be work to do in the morning . . . Once we have visted paradise."

The two sisters went down to Nastiya's cabin. As the door closed behind them, Zhenia snuggled into her sister's arms.

"I am so glad I found you," she whispered. "I was so lonely without you."

"I am glad also," Nastiya agreed, "but it's well after midnight now. We both have to get some sleep. And I'm supposed to be your boss, who only cares about your ability to do your job. Time to get back to your cabin."

"Oh very well, then." Zhenia pouted. "But I shall miss you."

"Don't forget to lock your door," Nastiya added, speaking to her sister's back. *Did she hear me? Should I go after her?* she wondered. *Oh, stop worrying! She's a grown woman. She can look after herself.*

What kind of shit was that you made me eat tonight?" snarled Johnny Congo.

"That," replied Mateus da Cunha, who was regretting his involvement with Congo more with every second that passed, "was French cuisine, the finest food in the world."

"Yeah? French faggot food was what it tasted like to me. Just gimme a plate of home-cooked fried chicken, or nice fat ribs, barbecued Texan-style till the meat falls off the bone. Now that's what I'm talkin' about."

He brooded a little longer, a crystal tumbler filled with neat Scotch clutched, barely visible within a giant fist, the fury inside him now almost tangible. "Gohn' play me some music," he growled. "Listen to my man Jay-Z." He fiddled with his phone, found what he was looking for and linked in to the ship's sound system. "This is about a brother tellin' a dumb white cop, 'You can't touch me, fool.'"

A second later the entire room seemed to explode with the ear-splitting volume of "99 Problems. It sounded to Mateus da Cunha like a physical assault on his ears. Congo listened to the rapper chanting over the pounding heavy metal riff then walked across to da Cunha. He had to shout to make himself heard. "I got business to attend to. Touch the music, I'm-a rip your damn face off."

Da Cunha stayed in the room. Congo's behavior was the last thing he needed. In a few days, the first of the apparently spontaneous riots that would start the process of insurrection was due to hit Cabinda City. He should be planning, concentrating, thinking of every eventuality, but couldn't hear himself think over the music. Then again, no one could hear him shouting at the door Congo had just walked out of, either, screaming how much he hated him.

The captain of the *Faucon d'Or* had supervised their mooring off the coast of Malabo. He left one of his men on the bridge, just in case the clients changed their mind and decided to sail off again in the middle of the night. People who could afford to rent this sort of boat never stopped to wonder whether their demands were reasonable or practical. They simply expected them to be obeyed, at once, without question. So there had to be someone ready to do that.

That issue dealt with, the Captain settled down for the night. He grimaced at the racket coming from the main lounge, but he was well used to late night parties and kept a stock of the very best noise-reducing earplugs for precisely this eventuality. Once they were in, the only thing he could hear was the sound of his own breathing.

Up on the bridge, the First Officer had checked the radar, established that the only ship in their vicinity was a tug sailing north to Port Harcourt, then settled down to play Call of Duty on his tablet, mixing the clients' music, which he didn't mind at all, with the sound of gunfire from his game. He nodded contentedly, thinking the two went pretty well together, all things considered.

The three bodyguards were down in the crew's quarters, with the fourth member of their team, whose turn it was to take the nightwatch and who had, as a consequence, been asleep all afternoon. Two of them were Serbians, one Frenchman and a Belgian, all employed by a Paris-based contractor. Their boss was a former mercenary, who'd seen countless African coups come and go and he smelled another one the moment he heard from da Cunha's people. So he'd not sent any of his best men, ones that he'd miss if they were rotting away in an African jail. Instead, da Cunha got four hard, tough fighting men, all of whom had criminal records and none of whom gave a damn for anyone but themselves.

Right now they were sharing a bottle of brandy, playing poker and making a desultory attempt to chat up the two French girls who served the meals, fixed drinks at the outdoor bar and generally made client's voyages as pleasant as possible. In theory, someone was supposed to be topside, as a lookout. But the team leader, Babic, who was one of the Serbs who had been up to the bridge, talked to the First Officer and ascertained that there was only one other ship remotely near and that was sailing north up to Nigeria. So there was no need to worry. The Belgian, Erasmus, was meant to be handling the night watch. Babic would send him topsides in a while, just to check that all was well. In the meantime, he was happy for them all to sit with the booze, the cards and the stewardesses.

Then Babic heard something. "What's that sound?" he said.

Erasmus, who was dealing, stopped flicking cards across the table. He frowned in concentration, "It's just the shit music from the lounge."

Babic shook his head. "No, it's coming from outside. Check it out."

"Can I finish dealing?"

"No."

Erasmus sighed, picked up his handgun, stuck it in the back of his trousers and walked away, his shirt outside his trousers, not bothering to put on his suit jacket.

He's out of shape, thought Babic, catching a flash of Erasmus's bulging gut beneath the loose shirt. *Time I did something about that.*

On the Interceptor, Cross and his men were readying themselves to go into battle. He and Paddy were taking Frank Sharman as the third member of their team. He'd earned the right after his exceptional conduct on the rig. Imbiss was leading Carl Schrager and Tommy Jones in what he and Schrager liked to call Team USA, Much to Jones's disgust. The yacht was a far less dangerous environment than the oil installations at Magna Grande had been, with little risk of a stray bullet sending the whole vessel up in flames. So they were armed with Canadian Colt C8 assault rifles in a Close Quarter Carbine configuration. In recent years the C8 had become the standard individual weapon for U.K. Special Forces, which was all the recommendation that an ex-SAS man like Cross needed. The men were all dressed in a Special Forces style: black jumpsuits and balaclavas, goggles, and black body armor over their chests. They were linked by a short range communications system.

The rules of engagement were simple. Anyone who was unarmed, female or looked remotely like a non-combatant was off limits. Congo, da Cunha and anyone fighting on their behalf was to be engaged with maximum force and minimum scruple.

They were now so close to the *Faucon d'Or* that it seemed to fill the windscreen of the Interceptor's control room. "Bloody 'ell, she's lit up like the Blackpool illuminations," muttered Sharman.

"Cut the engines," Cross said. The Interceptor had enough momentum to cover the last hundred meters without the need for power. It seemed as though they'd got this close without being spotted. That was close to a miracle, but he wasn't going to push his luck any further. From now on they would close on their prey in silence.

Nastiya had difficulty falling asleep. Even when she succeeded it was fitful and she kept starting awake with her heart racing and dark fantasies lurking at the back of her mind, unable to shake off the unease of feeling defenseless in the stronghold of her enemies. She had no idea when Hector and Paddy would arrive. It might just be a few hours, or it might be days.

Nastiya dreamed of angry, insistent rhythms, men shouting, a woman screaming, calling to her. She tried to ignore it, but it became more urgent until she shot upright in her bed, fully alert and awake. She listened, expecting that the voice would fade away as the other sounds had done. But it didn't happen. Instead the voice grew more insistent, until suddenly she recognized it.

"Zhenia!" she screamed and leaped from the bed. She ran to the door and fumbled with the lock but her fingers were clumsy and numbed with sleep. At last she got the door open and ran out into the passageway in her short nightdress. Zhenia's cries were louder now and more frantic: jumbled shrieks for help, fighting against the blare of music, interrupted by squeals of agony and appeals for mercy. Nastiya raced down the passageway and reached the door to her sister's cabin. From within she heard the sound of heavy blows, and an instantly recognisable man's voice.

"Did you jus' bite me bitch? Gonna knock your teeth out for that."

Congo! Nastiya turned the door handle and tugged at it with all her strength but nothing gave. It was locked from the inside. She backed away until she reached the bulkhead behind her. Then she ran at the door, leading with her right shoulder. The impact was brutal, but the sturdy oak panel was resilient as steel and stopped her dead in her tracks.

Again she backed away and gathered herself. At that moment the sounds of distress from behind the door rose to a crescendo that pierced Nastiya's very heart. She clenched her fists at the level of her belly, hunched her shoulders and screamed the three words of power that unlocked the innermost recesses of her strength. Then once again she launched herself at the door. This time she hardly felt the impact, but the woodwork exploded in a cloud of splinters around her as she ran into the cabin and turned to the double bed at its center.

Johnny Congo reared up from a jumble of bedclothes. He was so tall that his head almost touched the deck above him. His shoulders seemed as wide as the bed itself. His body was stark naked, every inch of it polished as anthracite, fresh cut from the coalface. His belly was heavy and protuberant. From below it his penis reached out as thick as his wrist, pulsing and kicking to the impulse of his blood and his lust.

He still held Zhenia by one arm. She was struggling weakly and her face was swollen and bruised and splashed with blood where he had beaten her. When he recognized Nastiya he gave a bellow of laughter and threw Zhenia carelessly aside. She struck the bulkhead and slid down it to sit on the cabin floor. Congo drew back his right leg and delivered a full-blooded kick into her lower belly. Her cry of pain was cut short as the air was driven from her body and she doubled over.

Congo took no further notice of her, but he moved quickly to cut Nastiya off from her escape route to the doorway.

"Well look who's here," he leered, "you been high and mighty all day. Let's see how you act when I got you on your back, beggin' at me to stop."

Before he finished speaking Nastiya launched herself at him feet first. His chin was still raised and his throat was open, guffaws of laughter spilling out of it. She went for it, aiming her rock-hard heels at his bulging Adam's apple. The force of it would have broken his neck. But with the quickness of a great jungle cat he lowered his chin and took her heels in the center of his forehead. Even so it drove him back three paces into the bulkhead behind him. But this caught him and kept him on his feet.

Congo's reflexes were unimpaired, still so finely tuned that as Nastiya dropped back toward the floor, he reached down with both hands and grabbed one of her ankles in each great fist. He swung her around, head first and she smashed into the bulkhead. The blow left her barely conscious, robbed of any ability to fight, completely at Congo's mercy.

Up on deck, Erasmus couldn't hear a thing, except for the rap. He walked up to the bows and looked into the darkness. There wasn't much of a moon that night and clouds were scudding across the sky, obscuring its faint light. He was damned if he could see, or hear anything out there. Muttering curses at Babic for sending him on a fool's errand, he walked along the port side of the yacht, which was facing toward the island they were supposed to be visiting in the morning.

Erasmus reached the stern of the *Faucon d'Or*. He leaned against the rail, thinking how much he'd like to light up a Gauloise right now, rueing the fact that smoking was banned for all staff aboard ship. Then he saw something, out of the corner of an eye, something moving out on the water. He looked again and saw it, something low and black, as sharp and pointed as a dart, gliding across the water at extraordinary speed, coming straight at him.

"*Merde!*" Erasmus muttered, and reached behind him for his gun.

Dave Imbiss was leading the second group to board the yacht. That meant he had to cover the first. So he was standing on the bow of the Interceptor, roughly at the point where the for'ard weapons system would be mounted, with his C8 held across his body.

He'd been watching the man at the stern rail, uncertain whether he was a combatant or not and, waiting for him to make a move. Then he saw him look directly at the Interceptor, and their eyes met, like lovers across a crowded room, except that there wasn't the slightest shred of love in this first sighting.

Imbiss saw the man reach behind him, he raised the C8 to his shoulder, and took aim.

He saw the hand emerge with something clutched in it.

He waited a fraction of a second to make certain what that something was.

Then he fired.

The bullet hit Erasmus in the throat and killed him instantly. Now the *Faucon d'Or* had no one to defend it against the men coming in from the sea.

Zhenia was curled on the floor, still doubled up with agony, both her arms nursing her lower abdomen where Congo had kicked her. Already she was bleeding from between her legs, she heaved herself upright, her face grimacing at the effort and staggered over to protect her sister.

Congo shouted with wild glee, "Yeah! Come get your head beaten in, you dumb bitch." He swung Nastiya's body like a club and Zhenia was unable to dodge the blow. She was hurled back against the bulkhead once more. Her fingernails scrabbled against the woodwork as she tried to keep her balance and prevent herself from falling. Blood was streaming from one corner of her mouth and dribbling down her naked chest on to the deck. Her knees buckled under her and she slid down the bulkhead and collapsed on to the floor, only half conscious, sobbing weakly with pain.

"I ain't done with you yet," Congo told her, "gonna take care of this other one first. But you're gettin' every inch of what you need."

He swung Nastiya once more and this time when she hit the

bulkhead her right arm, which was wrapped around her head to protect herself, caught the full force of the impact. The bone in her elbow shattered with a sharp crack, and she screamed.

Johnny Congo dropped her on the bed, and stood over her breathing heavily. "Open up, sugar," he grunted. "Papa's comin' in."

Even in her agony Nastiya tried to sit up, but with his left hand he shoved her back on to the mattress and forced his knee between her thighs. "Shit!" he muttered, looking down at his crotch. "Damn dick's gone soft on me." He took it in his right fist and with a few quick strokes restored its stony rigidity.

Now he was ready to do his thing.

The men from the Interceptor swarmed over the stern rail, stepped across Erasmus's corpse and fanned out across the rear of the *Faucon d'Or*.

There was no one else on the outside decks. Cross, O'Quinn and Sharman slipped like black wraiths past the whirlpool tub, across the deck where da Cunha, Congo and the Voronova sisters had taken lunch and into the main lounge.

They found da Cunha pacing up and down, talking to himself, completely oblivious to their arrival until Cross was standing in front of him with a gun-barrel pointed right at his heart. It took seconds to immobilise his hands behind his back with cable ties and cover his mouth with duck tape so that he could not alert anyone else.

Cross waited the few seconds it took for Imbiss and his men to arrive. "Jones, you watch this sorry bastard. Dave, Schrager, secure the bridge and take command of the vessel. Paddy, Sharman, we're going below."

Sharman went aft toward the crew quarters. The first two doors he knocked open revealed sleeping men in bunks. White crew uniforms were hanging from hooks on the wall beside them. Sharman put a finger to his mouth to silence one of the men, who woke, propped himself up and peered, bleary-eyed at the intruder.

Then Sharman came to the door to the crew's mess. He could hear voices inside, men's and women's. From the way the men were talking, they did not know the women well. So they weren't crewmates.

Sharman kicked open the door. Three men were sitting at a table. The women, two of them, were standing a few feet away, clutching mugs, not wanting to get any closer to the men.

That made Sharman's life a whole lot easier. So did the Sig Sauer pistol lying on the table, the one that one of the men was reaching for.

Sharman hit all three before any of them had got a bead on him. He stopped, looked, noticed one of the men stirring and hit him again. The echo of the shots reverberated around the cramped space. None of the men moved.

"Excuse me, ladies," Sharman said. "Best be on my way."

Cross and O'Quinn were heading toward the passengers' staterooms, Cross leading the way. He came to a room with a partially open door, stepped up to the side of the door frame and indicated to O'Quinn to carry on to the next room.

Cross counted three, silently in his head, then kicked the door fully open with the C8 at his shoulder, seeing everything through the gun sight as he looked left, then right and saw nothing. The room was empty.

Congo's attention was so completely concentrated on the woman between his legs that he did not see the black-clad figure that appeared silently as a ghost in the doorway that Nastiya had smashed open. He did not see him raise the slender long-barreled pistol to his masked face—but he sensed him. And he reacted.

* * *

O'Quinn had Congo in his sights. All he had to do was fire. But then he saw Nastiya on the bed beneath his target. Beneath all his banter and blarney, O'Quinn was a true professional soldier. He was disciplined, calm, well used to fighting and killing men up close and personal. But this was too personal. The sight of his wife distracted him, made him hesitate. Only for a second, but that was enough.

Congo rolled himself from the bed with feline speed for such a gigantic body, fired by an animal instinct that had saved him fifty times before; a prescience beyond normal human reasoning; an intuition forged in battle and mortal danger.

He landed on all fours beside the bed and then sprang forward, straight at O'Quinn, his legs pumping, driving him across the cabin floor like an Olympic sprinter, bursting from the starting blocks.

Congo had no idea who the man behind the black balaclava was and he didn't care. He hit O'Quinn like an avalanche, knocking him off his feet. He got down on his knees, straddling the fallen body, and pulverised the faceless head with four sledgehammer blows to his temples, two on either side.

O'Quinn's C8 was trapped between him and Congo. The punches to his head left him dazed and concussed. His grip on the weapon loosened and Congo ripped it from his hands.

Nastiya was in a world of pain and confusion, unable to make sense of what was happening. Zhenia was still curled up against the cabin wall.

Congo got to his feet, the C8 in his hands. He pointed the rifle down at O'Quinn and fired three times at point-blank rage: head shots, blowing his head to pieces.

Then Congo ran for the cabin door and went through it . . .

. . . just as Cross was coming out of Nastiya's cabin. He saw Congo's naked form emerge from the other cabin, saw the C8 in his hand, realized he must have taken it from Paddy O'Quinn and then hurled himself back into the cabin as Congo raised the C8 and fired a second quick, three shot burst.

Congo saw the second intruder disappear behind the cabin door. He didn't stop to find out if he'd hit him too. He reached the companionway within three long strides and went up it, taking the stair treads four at a time. When he got to the top he glanced through the glass doors into the lounge. Da Cunha was on the floor, dead or merely disabled, Congo wasn't sure. Another one of the masked men—by now Congo was figuring this must be some kind of Delta Force attack—was there. The man spotted Congo. This time he fired first and the glass shattered as the bullets hit them.

Congo ran out onto the deck, heard a voice shout, "I have a visual on Congo!, heard a gun firing and threw his own away as he ran to the side of the deck, vaulted the rail and plunged down into the black Atlantic waters.

Cross ran to the door of the other cabin and saw that O'Quinn was dead. For now that only registered as a fact: man down. The mourning and grief would come later.

The two women looked like they were in bad shape. But they were alive and they were no longer in harm's way. Not unless Congo survived long enough to attack them again.

By the time he was on deck Cross knew that Congo was in the water. He spoke into his mike: "Man down below decks. Paddy's dead. Someone go and look after the girls. I'm taking the Interceptor, going after Congo."

When Cross reached the boat, Darko McGrain was at the helm as he had been since they'd left Libreville. "Stand aside," Cross ordered him. "I'm taking the helm."

One look at Cross's face and McGrain knew that there

was no point in debating the issue. "She's all yours, boss," he said.

The water covered Congo's head for a few brief seconds. Then he shot to the surface and struck out for the distant shore.

The moon had emerged from behind the clouds and there was enough light in the sky to show the black outline of the jungle-covered hills of Malabo. That was where he was heading. His great bulk gave him buoyancy and he was a natural-born athlete and a tireless swimmer. He sliced through the water with powerful strokes of both arms and legs, keeping his head low and not breaking his stroke until he saw that the shoreline was already perceptibly closer.

Congo rolled over onto his back for a moment to look back the way he had come. The *Faucon d'Or* was still brightly lit but the vessel was so far off that he could see only its superstructure. He felt a lift of relief that there was as yet no sign of pursuit. He rolled over in the water, put his head down and swam on with no diminution of effort or of speed. After another couple of minutes he paused again to draw breath, to tread water and to listen. He found that now he was short of air and there was a pounding in his ears. His chest was laboring. Age and good living had taken their toll. He desperately wanted another few minutes of rest.

Then he heard something unusual. It was the sound of an engine running at high revolutions, almost the sound of an aero engine at take-off power. He turned in the water and looked back the way he had come and saw the beam of a searchlight suddenly leap out and begin sweeping the surface of the sea, lighting the crests of the wave tops like day but leaving the troughs in darkness.

He realized that the beam of light emanated from the low and streamlined superstructure of a strange craft, which was dancing toward him across the surface of the darkling sea. His spirits quailed and he was possessed by a deep and sudden dread.

He turned and pitted all his strength and determination against the promise of death that he knew was contained in that beam of dancing light.

Now his thrashing legs kicked up a froth of luminous spray, and the beam of light fastened upon it. Congo glanced back over his shoulder and the light struck him like a physical blow, dazzling and blinding him. He turned away from it and swam on toward the land. Behind him he heard the engine beat of the pursuit craft rise to a shriek, like the hunting cry of the Black Angel of Death.

Cross turned the wheel half a revolution to starboard, lining up the bows with the patch of broken water, and smoothly eased the throttles open.

"It's Congo, no doubt about it. I'm going to take him out."

"Hit him hard, boss," said McGrain.

"Count on it," Cross assured him, and turned the helm fractionally to port, lining up the bows with Congo's head.

At the last fraction of a second before impact Congo duck-dived under the bows. He threw his massive legs high in the air and the weight of them pushed his head down swiftly below the surface. The Interceptor roared over the spot where he had disappeared just seconds previously.

"Damn it to hell, I missed him," Cross muttered. But as he spoke they all felt a sharp rap on the hull under their feet.

McGrain gave a shout of joy. "No you didn't, you tagged him."

Cross throttled back and circled the disturbed patch of water in which Congo had disappeared. The beam of the searchlight caught patches of bright crimson where blood was rising to the surface. Suddenly Congo's head appeared above the water.

* * *

406

The propellor had sliced off Congo's left foot like a meatcleaver. His face was contorted in pain, but that only intensified the hatred with which he glared at the Interceptor. His agony and defiance came together in a single, wordless bellow, then he fell silent again, waiting like a wounded bull before the matador for the *coup de grace*.

Cross circled back and then looked beyond Congo. "What's that?" he asked, but there was no need for an answer as the searchlight picked out a dark triangular shape knifing across the water toward Congo's bobbing head.

Cross scowled. "Sharks! I'm not going to let those greedy bastards kill him before I do."

He opened the throttles of the Interceptor and the boat surged forward once again. Congo could barely keep his head above water now, let alone take evasive action. The boat smashed straight into him, driving him deep below the surface. Cross circled back and cut the engines. They drifted over the blood-stained wake until slowly Johnny's corpse floated to the surface upon its back, and stared up at the dawn sky through empty sockets.

The sharp bows of the Interceptor had parted his skull down the center to the level of his chin. Both of his eyes were dangling loosely from their sockets; popped out of his ruined skull by the impact.

"D'you want me to haul him out, boss?" McGrain asked.

"No, I've finished my business here. The sharks are welcome to him now."

It seemed like only seconds before the first gray reef shark came scrounging down the trail of fresh human blood. It drifted down below the floating corpse and came up beneath it to sink its multiple rows of triangular teeth into Johnny's buttocks and worry off a mouthful of his flesh.

Soon the water was boiling with the long sleek bodies and

black-tipped fins and tails. They fed until the last scraps of Congo's body were devoured and then they gradually dispersed.

Cross felt no sense of triumph. He had done all this for Hazel. But it struck him now that Congo's death had stripped away the last traces of her existence from his heart, for she had somehow been kept alive, in spirit at least, by Cross's desire to avenge her.

"He's gone," Cross murmured to himself.

"Aye," said McGrain. "And he's no' coming back again, either."

They took Paddy's body back to Libreville aboard the Glenallen, stored in one of the ship's walk-in freezers: better that than have him rot in the tropical heat.

Early the following morning, Cross arranged for a doctor to be flown up from Cape Town in a private jet to look after Nastiya and Zhenia once they reached dry land. He spent the rest of the day by the sisters' bedsides. With the passage of time, Cross's grief at Paddy's death deepened along with his guilt. He had planned and led the assault on the *Faucon d'Or*. Therefore the death of one of his men was his responsibility, and the fact that Nastiya, battered and bereaved as she was, insisted that it was not his fault only made Cross feel all the more culpable.

Paddy had been his brother in arms and his dearest friend. And so, through a long night on the water, Cross sat around a table with Imbiss, and the other Cross Bow team members. One bottle after another was added to the clutter on the table in front of them as the men let their emotions pour out. They veered from one extreme to another at bewildering speed, from wild laughter as they competed to tell the most outrageous stories of Paddy's madcap exploits, to bitter tears as the reality of his passing hit home. Cross was the last man to weep. But when the dam burst and the tears finally came, he was inconsolable.

When they arrived in Libreville, the two women were examined in hospital. The doctor assured Cross that neither had suffered any lasting injury: with time and rest both would make a full and relatively speedy recovery.

Cross still had work to do. The *Faucon d'Or* had yielded a treasure trove of evidence—phones, laptops, a mass of printed material—which he handed over to the Gabon authorities, who immediately prepared for da Cunha's extradition to Angola.

Cross took his leave of da Cunha at the quayside. The would-be President of an independent Cabinda was a sorry sight: unwashed, unshaven, still dressed in the clothes he'd been wearing when they'd captured him. The cable ties had been removed from his wrists, but only so that they could be replaced by handcuffs.

"Farewell, dear Mateus," Cross saluted him. "An Angolan jail isn't the kind of accommodation you're accustomed to, I'm afraid. They say most prisoners would rather die than spend the rest of their lives rotting in that particular hell. So . . ." Cross paused to savor the moment: "I wish you a long, long life."

Da Cunha's facial expression was a strange mixture of fury and despair, but before he could reply one of his captors thrust his baton into da Cunha's kidneys and he fell to his knees, gasping with the pain.

For a second, Cross almost felt sorry for him.

It was another three days before the women were allowed to travel. "I'm going back to London with Nastiya," Zhenia said, once the doctor had delivered his verdicts. "She needs help organising Paddy's funeral."

"I'll come with you," Cross said. "I can help, too."

"No, we'll be fine. Go back to Abu Zara. See Catherine Cayla. It will do you good to be around life, instead of death. And she needs her daddy to be with her."

"You're right, I should have thought of that. But we'll be in London, both of us, in plenty of time for the funeral."

"And I'll be waiting for you . . ."

* * *

Cross emerged from customs and entered the arrivals terminal at Abu Zara International Airport. Suddenly Cross heard a high pitched shriek of excitement as Catherine Cayla spotted them, broke free of Bonnie's grip and raced to meet her father.

Cross laughed as he tossed Catherine high in the air before catching her and kissing her. As he put her back down on the ground he looked in wonder at this gorgeous little girl whom he loved and who loved him in return. He thought of the woman waiting for him in London. He had spent the past week immersed in death, but now he knew that life had to go on and that this girl and this woman represented life and hope and joy to him. Together they had the chance to be a family, to build a home, to find a shelter from the storm that had surrounded him for so long.

He was in the car on the way back to Seascape Mansions when his phone pinged. He had a text message. It came in three parts. The first said, "I feel much better. But . . ." The second was a selfie of Zhenia flashing him a wicked, ravishingly sexy smile. The third said, "I need my man . . . beside me, on top of me, in me . . . Now!! xxxx"

A broad grin spread across Hector Cross's face.

"Happy daddy!" said Catherine Cayla.

Cross looked down at his daughter and then, sounding slightly surprised, as if he'd just been told something that he had never realized before he said, "Yes, quite right. I am a happy daddy."